D0193036

# SIGN HERE

# SIGN HERE

## Claudia Lux

BERKLEY

New York

BERKLEY
An imprint of Penguin Random House LLC

Copyright © 2022 by Claudia Lux
Penguin Random House supports copyright. Copyright fuels creativity, encourages diverse
voices, promotes free speech, and creates a vibrant culture. Thank you for buying an authorized
edition of this book and for complying with copyright laws by not reproducing, scanning,
or distributing any part of it in any form without permission. You are supporting writers
and allowing Penguin Random House to continue to publish books for every reader.

BERKLEY and the BERKLEY & B colophon are registered trademarks of
Penguin Random House LLC.

ISBN 9780593545768

Printed in the United States of America

Book design by Daniel Brount

This is a work of fiction. Names, characters, places, and incidents either are the product
of the author's imagination or are used fictitiously, and any resemblance to actual persons, living or
dead, business establishments, events, or locales is entirely coincidental.

*For my father, Thomas Lux, whom I miss*

And in the lowest deep a lower deep
Still threat'ning to devour me opens wide,
To which the Hell I suffer seems a Heav'n.

—JOHN MILTON

What makes bitter things sweet? Hunger.

—ALCUIN, ADVISOR TO CHARLEMAGNE

# SIGN HERE

# BEFORE

# PEYOTE

**YOU ALREADY HAVE A** lot of ideas about Hell. It's amazing what Dante and thousands of years of folklore can do to a place's reputation. I mean, I'm not going to lie to you: it is Hell. It's not fantastic. But let's see if this is relatable: You're late to your aunt's boyfriend's birthday brunch because your alarm was on mute even though you know you turned it up the night before. You barrel onto the subway, managing to squeeze yourself between the woman blasting a Techno for the Lonely playlist and the man who farts every time he sneezes, and, just when the lights of the station are out of view, the train lurches to a stop with a death rattle and goes dark. The woman elbows you in the gut as she hits Replay, and the man's snot tickles as it sprays your cheek, and you think about how you don't even like your aunt's boyfriend or even your aunt and you hate brunch, and what do you say? I'll tell you; I've heard it a million times. You say, "This is Hell."

Well, you're right. That's Hell. At least the top floors of it. Your priests and grandmas have good intentions—the ones who don't wind up here—but their job is to keep you decent above ground, and if they said Hell was a never-ending brunch, you would be out there stealing and raping constantly.

Up here it's not the fire-and-brimstone thing you think it might be. It's music that's too loud, food that's too rubbery, and kissing with too much tongue. Doesn't sound that bad, right? But don't forget: it's forever. I mean for-all-time forever. Not a lifetime. That's a pebble compared to what I'm talking about. Hell is agitation for eternity. You can't possibly fathom eternity; your little mortal brain would explode. A century feels like an hour, less with each millennium. With endless time and no peace, everyone breaks eventually.

I was about to break too. But then I got a promotion.

# PART I

# PEYOTE

"PEY, TEAM MEETING IN five," KQ said, rapping on my desk. I jerked up from my screen. It was already ten o'clock.

"Right, I'll be there. Thanks!" I replied, but she was knocking halfway down the row, her knuckles creating a muffled echo. I grabbed my notebook and my pen case, freed a mangled Cup O' Noodles from the back of my drawer, and went to the kitchen.

"Heya, Pey, how's it hanging?" Trey asked as he stood in front of the microwave, watching his frozen meal dissolve and recongeal.

"Just fine, thanks," I said, peeling back the top to my lunch.

"The hot water is out."

I looked at the coffee machine: OUT OF ORDER. I rolled my eyes. I filled the Cup O' Noodles with the hottest water the sink allowed and got in line behind Trey.

"Who do you have nowadays? Anyone interesting?" he asked, opening the microwave before it beeped. The steam from his lunch hit my face. It smelled like warm broccoli.

"No one too good," I answered. But for the first time in ages,

I wasn't worried. I did have something. Something big. I just wasn't going to tell Trey.

He stayed in front of the microwave as he stirred his food, his smile almost as thick.

"Too bad, buddy, too bad. Did you hear I landed Spence Norwood? Wrapped that set up like a present."

"Yeah, Trey, I heard. That's great," I said as I edged past him. I punched the thirty-seconds button and fished a plastic spoon from a drawer.

"Don't worry, buddy. It'll happen for you too. You've only been here, what, a minute?"

"Just about."

The microwave beeped. I pulled the handle to find my cup drooped to one side, soup dribbling out. I pushed the sloppy Styrofoam back up, but it wouldn't stick.

"Come on, dipshits!" KQ yelled, her hand on the conference room door.

"Coming!" I responded, trying to rip off a paper towel square and getting only a quarter piece.


"OKAY, EVERYONE, LET'S GET down to business. First things first: we have a couple of new faces here today. We didn't ask for them and we don't need them, but here they are anyway. So this means everyone is going to have to work even harder to prove their worth around here, assuming none of you is itching for the days of cleaning out the meat grinders Downstairs."

The woman next to me slumped down in her chair, as if hoping to melt onto the floor and get out unnoticed. I reached for a bottle of water and offered her one, but she shook her head.

"Second: congratulations are in order!" KQ went on. "Trey, well done with the Norwoods! You've been chasing that white whale for a while, slick! Your fifth Complete Set!" KQ put her hand on his shoulder and gave it a rough shake.

Trey beamed. "Thanks, boss."

Broth spilled out of the sunken lip of my Cup O' Noodles and pooled on the laminate tabletop.

My lunch looked like a mouth in a nursing home.

"Pey? Where are your numbers?"

I startled and pushed my notebook into the puddle.

"Well, it's been a bit of a slow—" I started, my notebook creating a trail of soup like the foot mucus of a gastropod.

"What is it we say in this office, Peyote?"

Trey shot his hand into the air.

"Which saying are we talking about, exactly?"

"Ooh!" Trey shouted. "I know!"

"Mr. Trip?" KQ prodded.

"No excuses," I said, my cheeks hot.

"I knew that," Trey said.

I pulled four pens from my pen case and clicked the back of the fifth.

It wouldn't write.

"Now that we all know that excuses are not an option, what else do we have to say for ourselves? Our numbers are decreasing. With the Internet, people are turning to different solutions for their problems. Trey? Tell the newbs which pitch you went with to land Norwood," KQ said as she kicked her heels up on the table. I could see where her stilettos had sunk into the dirt on her walk over. I could see little scraps of grass. They reminded me of the beard hairs I used to find under my fingernails after scraping off faces with sandpaper.

"Well," Trey said, leaning forward and rubbing his hands together, thinking. He always made a big deal out of thinking. It seemed to require a great amount of concentration. "I've been watching this guy for a while, so when his firm's Tokyo deal fell through, I knew I had him. You know his wife just bought that fifth horse, right? And his daughter was about to get married, in *Nantucket.*"

Everyone snickered.

"So I went with a standard SnowFlake, with some slight adjustments, of course."

KQ pulled off one shoe and kneaded her foot.

"Does everyone know what a SnowFlake is? Because you'd better."

The woman next to me put her hand up and then pulled it right back down.

"Newbie wants a turn!"

"Oh, no, I just thought—"

"What's your name, little mouse?"

"Oh, I—"

"If you don't have a name yet, I can give you one. How about Churchy? Or Squeaks?"

"I—"

"Disease-Carrying Vermin?"

"I'm Cal," she said, before clearing her throat and sitting up straight. "Calamity Ganon. Like in the video game? But everyone calls me Cal."

"Cal? Meh. I think I'll stick with Squeaks," KQ said. "So, go ahead, Squeaks. What's a SnowFlake?"

Cal put her hand on her orientation binder but didn't open it.

"It's when the sales associate uses flattery and validation to—"

"It's ego fellatio," Trey interrupted. "Tell them they are special, that you've been waiting for them. That they have some kind of bigger purpose. Humans love that shit."

"Did you tell him who you are? What he was trading?" Cal

asked, her high and apologetic voice all but confirming the permanence of her new nickname.

Trey scoffed. "I handed him the tablet, if that's what you mean."

"Nowadays we do everything digitally," I said. "The mark still signs a contract, but now all they have to do is click 'I agree to the above terms' before they sign. It's up to them if they read the fine print." I spoke mostly to my puddle of lunch, only looking over at her once.

"Which he didn't," Trey said. "Because I got him really fucking drunk. Ego sucking and whiskey, hombres. It works every time."

Everyone clapped, and I felt Cal redden next to me. All that blood in her face made my shoulder warmer.

"Hey, sorry. KQ can be a bit of a hard-ass," I said when the meeting ended, my notebook blank and dripping. "Cal, right?"

I put out my hand, and she looked at it like she thought it might bite her. Anything is possible here.

"You're not going to go with 'Squeaks'?" she asked, eyeing me.

I laughed. "My name is Peyote Trip," I said. "I'm not exactly one to judge. I'll call you whatever you want."

" 'Cal' is great," she said, and she took my hand.

"How are you liking our beloved Deals Department so far?" I asked. I was being sarcastic, but her face lit up.

"Oh, I love it. I'm so happy to be here. I was on Third before."

I caught my surprise in a whistle. "Yikes."

Deals was on the Fifth Floor, second highest. For Hell, it was the dream job. But, just like on Earth, it's easy to forget to feel lucky here.

"Well, you must be doing something right to get sent up here."

She blushed again. Once you've seen the insides of so many bodies, it's hard to think of blushing as anything other than the presence of blood. Her face looked bloody to me. But still, I didn't hate it.

"Why do you have so many pens?" she asked, looking at the bulging zipper on my case.

"They didn't tell you? You need at least fifteen here. Did you not down there?"

"We didn't use pens."

I forgot that pens were an upper-level treat.

"Right," I said. "It's been a while since I was on the bottom floors. Well, the first five pens you try won't work, but, you know, you've gotta try them anyway."

"Wow," Cal said, throwing her pen in the trash. "Thanks for the tip!"

I stood up and paused, unsure if I should walk away or wait for her. As she started gathering her things, I lingered, pushing my chair in farther than it needed to go. I would stay and help out the newb. Courtesy was stark in Hell.

She tried to pick up her binder, but it toppled from her arms and landed on the floor.

"I'll carry it for you," I said, picking it up and tucking it under my arm.

"Oh . . . okay, thanks. Thank you."

"So, got this bad boy memorized yet?" I asked.

"We have to memorize it?"

I laughed. "Not exactly, but you might lose the nickname if you can answer KQ's questions quicker."

"It's a lot, isn't it? All of the rules, the goals, the terminology . . . it's very different from the Third Floor."

"The main thing to remember is the Specs. You can spend your whole time here going after Ones and Twos, but you don't make the big numbers until you start focusing on Fives."

Cal sighed.

"Yeah, okay, Fives take the most work. For sure. But if you want to make a splash around here, I would recommend tracking a couple, just in case."

"Maybe I'll just give up now, change my name to 'Disease-Carrying Vermin,' and be done with it," she said. I racked my brain for encouragement, but then I saw that she was smiling. It was a good smile. Small, but good.

"It's not the worst name I've heard KQ call someone," I said. "It's kind of cute, actually."

There went her blood again, all over.

"Thanks, Peyote." She stopped in front of her cubicle and took her binder from under my arm.

"Call me Pey."

"Thanks, Pey," she said, and smiled once more before ducking behind her divider.

**THE FIRST THING I** did when I sat down at my desk was check on the Harrisons. I had four generations of Harrisons under my belt. All I needed was one more, my Spencer Norwood, and I would have a Complete Set. One more direct-descendant-Harrison deal, and everything I had done—everything done to me—would be worth it.

I turned on my monitor, and the white house with the black shutters appeared in front of me, late-afternoon light lapping at the weathered clapboard like the tide on a boat. It was empty now, but they would be there soon, and I liked the way it looked when it was empty. Like it was waiting for them.

Evan built that house with his dad, after he dropped out of school to join the family business. Evan was my fourth Harrison, but I have to admit I didn't think it would be him. I was tracking his debt-heavy sister right up until the day Evan called, palms down on the dining room table, a second cup of tea across from his. I liked Evan; he knew exactly what he wanted. His son, Silas, and his daughter-in-law, Lily, proved harder. That happens sometimes with generations. One person makes a deal: *I'll sell my soul if my family never wants for anything.* And then their family gets well and accustomed to never wanting for anything, and they don't need to make any deals. But you know what always happens the generation after that? They make the biggest deals of all. They are so used to wanting for nothing, they take to wanting with an appetite.

I had a good feeling about the older grandchild, Sean. He was into some sick shit on the Internet. Never underestimate teenage hormones high on dungeon porn.

The younger one, Mickey, was different. She wasn't exactly clean; she had her own sticky parts. But she was quieter in her head than Sean, which made her more intriguing. She felt like her grandpa. Of course, I celebrated the night I signed Evan; he was my fourth Harrison. But it didn't feel like I thought it would. Somehow, I walked away feeling like it was me who got played. Mickey made me feel the same way, and I liked it. Sean was my safety school; Mickey was my reach.

But then there was Ruth.

None of us were prepared for Ruth.

# LILY

"**YOU'LL ONLY BE A** few hours away," Gavin said, tracing the line of Lily's underwear where it hit that tattoo she got on her eighteenth birthday. The one she pretended she regretted, but that she still secretly loved as much as the day she got it.

"It might as well be a world away," Lily answered, pulling her shirt over her head. Gavin's hand fell back to the bedspread. Lily freed her blond hair from her collar, feeling the weight of it on her shoulders. Gavin loved her hair. They all did.

"I could come up there, come see you."

Lily inhaled to button her jeans. She could feel the cold, dirty thing slither into her gut.

"No, you can't."

Gavin didn't respond.

"Gav, you know you can't."

She turned and looked at him. He was working his belt buckle into the third loop, sitting on the edge of the bed. She watched his hands, the way they gripped the leather.

"It'll be six weeks," she said. "And I'll see you before I go. At least once, I promise." Gavin let go of his belt and grabbed her wrist, pulling her whole structure down.

"I could meet you somewhere nearby," he whispered into her hair. "There have to be places like this in New Hampshire."

"Sex hotels?" Lily asked. Her voice was strict, but the rest of her wasn't.

"No, not a sex hotel. Something classy. I promise," he said as he kissed her neck. "It'll be classy."

"It's the family vacation," she said.

Gavin took a deep breath and fell back against the pillow.

"And tonight is a Tuesday," he said. "What's the difference?"

Instead of answering, Lily kissed him with her full mouth, even though she tasted like sex and dehydration.

"Just six weeks," she said, gathering her coat from beside the bed. "Then I'll be back, and it'll be like I never left."

"It's never like you never left."

As she turned the key in her car, Lily clicked on her cell phone. No missed calls. She checked her reflection in the rearview mirror: she had that sex-stung look, but it was nothing she couldn't cover with lip gloss and enthusiasm. She could say she went on a walk after work. She could say she witnessed an accident. She pulled the car out of the motel's parking lot. It would only be six weeks, she thought, turning up the radio to block out every thought that followed.

"I'm home!" she said as she hung her keys on the ring next to Silas's. "Babe?"

"Back here!"

Lily dropped her bag and coat in the front hall and walked through the house to the kitchen. Silas was bent over the stove, a knife in hand.

"Welcome home!" he said, not looking back. He was carving meat, being cautious around the bones.

"Are they home?"

"Sean is in his room. He said he was doing his homework, but I'm pretty sure he snuck the PlayStation in there again. I haven't been able to bust him yet; you know how careful you have to be with lamb," Silas answered, throwing a dish towel over his shoulder. Lily leaned against the island in their kitchen.

The air smelled like rosemary and long-simmered wine. Lily smelled like Gavin. The two scents mixed as she spoke.

"Mickey still at camp?"

"She should be back any minute."

She thought about going up to Silas and sticking out her finger for a taste of his sauce, the way she used to. Pushing her face under his arm until he lifted it and made room for her.

"Any word on the house sitter?" she asked instead.

"Amanda can do it," Silas answered. He shook a spice jar over the saucepan.

"The whole time? Six weeks is a long time for a teenager."

"Lil, she's just going to water the plants and get the mail. I think she can handle it." He put down the jar and grabbed another one.

Lily looked around the kitchen. "We need to clean this place before we go."

"We still have two weeks," Silas said. "We'll get it done."

The New Hampshire Harrison home. Silas had grown up spending his summers there, and, ever since she was sixteen, Lily had spent hers there too. It was old and made lonely sounds at night, but it was beautiful. The kids loved it.

"Dinner will be ready in thirty. Wanna go ground your son while you're waiting?" Silas asked. Lily looked up the stairs toward Sean's room and shook her head.

"I'm going to take a quick shower first; I worked out after work."

Silas turned to face her, and it caught her off guard. Sometimes, in movement, Silas looked exactly like the boy she fell in love with. When he was still, she noticed the way the skin around his eyes had begun to pucker, as if already starting the slow migration into the ground. But when he was in motion, she noticed only his eyes: kindergartners' sky blue, so fiercely blue that the marker bleeds right through the page. Those hadn't changed since high school. In fact, they looked even brighter behind his slightly graying hair.

Lily thought about Gavin's hands on her that afternoon. The way he grabbed for her, reached for her. Like she was the surface and he was drowning.

"What kind of workout did you do?"

Lily's heart kicked up a notch, but only a notch. Sometimes she wondered which would be worse: to get caught, or not to.

"Treadmill," she answered.

"You look good."

He didn't come near her, but he looked like maybe he wanted to.

"Well, someone's gotta fix what those monsters of ours did to me," Lily said, her palm slick on the banister.

"Twenty-five minutes," Silas said before turning back to the stove.

Lily stopped in front of Sean's door, listening to the hacks and slashes of the PlayStation. He would hear from her later, she thought. Just as soon as she washed the spit from her thighs.

# PEYOTE

**MY MONITOR BEEPED, AND** I clicked out of the Harrisons' to check my inbox. It was a Spec Three, my personal favorite. I hadn't been at this job for too long, but it was long enough to know which people were my favorites. For Hell, I mean. Not for socializing.

I clicked on the message, and the video came up.

"Please," a girl said, her hands pressed together on the top of a mailbox. The rest of the scene filled in around her: a tree-lined street, dappled sunlight glinting off the windows of big houses. "Please, please let me get in. My mom will kill me if I don't get in. Please, please, God, or whoever is listening: I'll do whatever you want if you just let me get in."

I grabbed my tablet and clicked Confirm.

It was go time.

**BEFORE I GO ON,** I suppose it's important to know how time works down here.

Surveys say that this is a complicated concept for your spit glob of a brain, so we have designed a metaphor for your consumption. Imagine the entirety of existence is inside a post office. Earth as you know it is a wall of PO boxes, and Hell is everything outside of that. For you, inside your PO boxes, time passes. But for us, on the outside, time doesn't exist. There's no aging, no ticking pressure of mortality. No pressure to survive or procreate. Some Fifth Floor employees find it easier to hold on to the loose framework established on the surface, using words like "millennia" to describe the passage of time. This can help some people keep the insanity at bay, but ultimately it doesn't matter. We are here, doing this, forever. But there is no second death, so we don't have a choice!

You are all inside time, and we are outside. Got it?

When we get a request on our tablet, the place and time of the request will flash on the screen. When we accept, it is like opening a particular PO box. We are able to go into that time, secure the deal, and then return to our side of the wall. It doesn't matter what the time is; I rarely pay attention anymore. But it allows for making deals across centuries, granting full and unlimited access to humanity's gaping pit of need. The only time period we can't access is the time we were alive. That's so that we can't go back and inform ourselves about our inevitable fate, which would cut down on the Hell workforce significantly. But I don't notice this because I can't remember when I was alive, and neither can the rest of us. Probably for the best.

So, this girl was upset about maybe not getting into college at some point in time, during which I, as a human, apparently never existed. After about a trillion of these deals, you stop caring about the rest of the details. There are a couple of other points they put in our orientation binder that you should probably know if you want to keep up. I'll summarize them for you, but just this once.

Deals Department employees are allotted only a certain amount of time per deal. Whenever we select a new deal, the timer will reset, but if we spend too long in one place without signing a deal, our heartbeats (manufactured by the travel device for display only) will slow until the timer stops, and our unconscious sacks will be shipped back down to Hell, where we will be reassigned to the Downstairs immediately. That's why I watch for symptoms such as weakness, inability to freeze time consistently, and physical pain. If I were to pass out, I'd know it was too late.

While on the surface, we have the (limited) ability to freeze time. This provides the chance to pause and check notes whenever a deal gets stuck, or when the performance of minor parlor tricks is necessary to make humans find us impressive and therefore trust us.

Some tablets can be customized to allow for multiple team members' arrivals and departures. Meaning, if given a position of authority by KQ, I could hold on to a subordinate or subordinates when traveling, or ship coworkers back down to Hell if they were no longer contributing to a deal.

That's enough education. If you don't get it by now, you won't make it on the Fifth Floor, and I'm wasting my breath.


I HAD TO SIT on the curb for a second before I could stand. It was a hard transition, going from Hell to Earth. But it was even harder on the way back. The air on Earth is so delicious. I can't understand why you people insist on ruining it. It's like you've been given the best feast in the world, and you let nine billion people use the table as a toilet. But then you freak out if your neighbor's dog poops on your lawn.

"Can I help you?" I asked as I approached the girl. KQ made us practice our Trustworthy poses during every Thursday meeting, but the girl startled anyway. They always do.

"Who are you?"

"I'm the answer to your prayers," I said. It wasn't a total lie. I was *an* answer.

"What—how—?"

"You said you wanted good news, right?"

"Yes," she said, the mailbox between us.

"Well, I'm here to help."

"I—I can't—" she said, looking at her front door.

"Don't worry, they can't see me. I've paused everything." I reached my hand out just over her ear. She flinched, but I didn't touch her. Instead, I plucked a butterfly from the air, frozen in flight. I placed the butterfly on the girl's index finger and flicked my wrist. It fluttered into movement. I flicked my wrist again, and it dropped back to her finger. Her eyes went wide.

Humans always turn to putty around butterflies.

"So," I asked, "how can I help you?"

"If I don't get into Stanford, my mother will kill me," the girl said, wide eyes welling. "I mean literally *kill me.* Like, I won't be allowed to do *anything.*"

This is why I love Spec Threes: they have the softest expectations of what it means to die.

"I don't know what to do," she went on. "The letter should be in here, but I'm too scared to open the mailbox."

"Don't worry . . . ," I said, pausing in the way that makes a person tell you their name.

"Katherine," she answered.

"Don't worry, Katherine. I'm here to help." I tried a new smile I had been practicing: bored pity. I had gotten feedback during our last evaluation that I could be a little overeager, especially with teenagers, which was a big target demographic. *Get 'em while they're young,* KQ always says.

The new smile seemed to work, because I could feel Katherine move from fear to thirst.

"What can you do?" she asked.

"Well, let me see what we have here."

I put my hands on the mailbox and closed my eyes. I could go a few ways with this one, but given her palpable insecurity, I figured I wouldn't have to work too hard with the Lil' Nibbler, and it was too nice a day out to work hard. I often lingered during my deals, another one of the points off during my evaluation.

"Oh wow," I said, frowning. "You're lucky I showed up."

Her hand flew to her mouth, spiking the frozen butterfly down to the lawn.

"Oh God, it's bad, isn't it?"

"Aren't there plenty of community colleges in this area? I bet your mom would love the opportunity to keep you home another couple of years. Think of all the bonding time during the commute!"

Katherine winced. She had freckles across her nose like someone blew all the punctuation off the page of a book.

"Listen," I said, softening my boredom into pity. "If it's what you really want, I can get you into Stanford."

"Are you serious? How?"

"Actually, it's pretty simple. You just need to sign something," I said, pulling out my tablet.

"What is it?" she asked, but the stylus was already in her hand.

"Oh, nothing, just a basic agreement. I'll hold up my end of the bargain right now, and then eventually, way, way down the line, when you're old and have accomplished everything you and your mother have ever wanted for you, I'll come find you and ask you for a tiny little favor."

The favor, of course, was not a favor; it was a demand. And it wasn't tiny; it was an eternity. She would know that if she read the terms and conditions. When people say dealing with legal contracts is a great introduction to Hell, they don't know how right they are.

"And you promise I'll get into Stanford?"

"And so much more. What do you want to be when you grow up?"

"I want to be a veterinarian."

"Done," I said.

"What? Just like that?"

"Well, you'll have to try a little bit in school so it's not suspicious, but yes, just like that."

It was true. She would go to Stanford, and then the best vet school in the country, and she would be very successful. Here, at least.

She dragged the stylus along the document, skimming.

"If you want to run it by your mom first, I can wait. I know there are a lot of big words in there."

She looked from the tablet to her house and back again.

I had her.

After she signed, I slipped the tablet back in its case and put both my hands on the mailbox once more. I closed my eyes and started slowly shaking until I reached a fervor a notch too dramatic, even for me.

"You will have everything you've ever wanted," I said as I stepped back and snapped my fingers. The air around us flickered back to life.

"I got in?"

Katherine pulled out the mail, flipping through it madly. She landed on one envelope and tore it open.

"Oh my God, I got in!"

I heard a screen door slam, and out came a woman who looked like Katherine after children and too many skin treatments.

"I got in! Mom, I got in!"

Her mom ran down the walkway and grabbed the envelope. Then they were both screaming and hugging, and I knew my work here was done, even if I wasn't quite ready to leave that sweet, sweet atmosphere.

"Thank you!" I heard right before I pushed the button. I looked at Katherine as she twisted around, no longer able to see me. "Thank you!" she said again.

"You're welcome," I said while the air turned the kind of foggy it does right before you go back to Hell.

The truth is I didn't actually do anything to the mailbox. The rest of her life, sure. Vet school, good paychecks, nice feeling of purpose—I took care of that. But I didn't touch the envelope.

People should really open their mail before they call on us.

THAT EVENING, I WAS filing the paperwork for Katherine when I heard my computer ding with a different sound. Something lighter, more jovial.

It was a message.

CALAMITY GANON: Burning that midnight oil, huh?

I peered down the hall and saw the glow of a desk light.

PEYOTE TRIP: Paperwork is 75% of the gig.

All of the lights between us were out. It was quitting time. I thought about my apartment. I hadn't done dishes in so long, I was eating food off other surfaces: magazines, old books I got from the dump. That's right; we have a large collection of hardcover books in the dump here. Don't act like that's a huge surprise.

I typed.

**PEYOTE TRIP:** Are you about to head out? Want to grab a drink?

I waited. I signed the last of the paperwork and stood up to bring it to KQ's desk. She would be pleased, but not pleased enough to mention it at the morning meeting. Typical.

My computer beeped again.

**CALAMITY GANON:** Actually, that would be great. Meet you at the elevator up front in 5?

We went to Jack's. It's my favorite because it's the quiet option on the Fifth Floor. The Sixth has two bars *and* a Mexican restaurant, according to the rumors, but at Jack's, there is a secret draw. You see, bars in Hell serve only Jägermeister. Even if you like Jägermeister, if it's the only option day after day of cleaning up human pulp, you will hate it in a year, tops. Jack saw the market and started a little bootleg operation a while back. He charges an arm and a leg (not literally, although that joke would kill down on Second) and might not give you anything, even if you pay up, if he doesn't like your face. But it's worth it for anything that doesn't taste like Lord Licorice nutting all over a Christmas tree.

"So, have you gotten used to the puddles yet?" I asked, eyeing the lower half of her pants, soaked to the knee.

Cal reddened as she shrugged off her coat.

"Yeah, I don't know what happened. Guess I misjudged how deep it was?"

I grinned. "Nope, not you. They're set on random here. The depths change constantly. One time, when I first got to the Fifth Floor, I stepped off the curb and wound up soaked to my elbows. It took three people to pull me out."

Jack glanced our way, and I put my hand up in a brief wave.

"Heya, Pey," Jack said, sliding a bowl of peanuts toward us.

"Jack, this is Calamity, our newest recruit."

Jack put out his meaty hand, and Cal looked at it the same way she had looked at mine. But then she glanced at me, smiled, and shook it.

"So, in a few centuries, do you think you'll be as haughty as this motherfucker?" Jack asked, nodding his head toward me.

I harrumphed.

"That big fancy office, it'll go to your head, princess. Be careful."

"I'm . . . I'm brand-new," Cal stammered. She had the perpetual air of someone who just made a very loud noise in a museum.

"You know the deal, Pey," Jack said, putting his hand on the bar, palm up. I pulled my wallet from my pocket and gave him all the cash I had. I took it out earlier that week, knowing I would need a visit to Jack's before the weekend. Cal reached for her wallet, but I put my hand on her arm.

"My treat," I said.

"I can't—"

"Consider it a welcome present."

"I'll see what we've got," Jack said, and turned down the basement stairs.

Cal stared at the bar.

"Peanuts?" I asked, tilting the bowl. She shook her head. I looked at the TV. It was the Hell welcome video, again.

"I don't mean to be square, but I don't . . . I don't do drugs."

I looked at her and saw she was genuinely scared. The blood that went so easily to her cheeks earlier was nowhere to be found.

"What?" I asked.

"Whatever it is you're getting here, I won't judge you, but I just can't . . . I don't want any."

Newbs always held on to their morals, as if morality were still worthwhile currency.

"You're lucky I still got some," Jack said, coming back up the stairs. He positioned himself against the bar, blocking the booths from view, and opened his flannel to flash the bottles: amber and glistening.

"Miller Lite, and don't you dare bitch about it."

"I would never," I said, holding three fingers to my heart because I saw some kid do it during a deal once and it made him look extra sincere.

Jack nodded and poured the beer into frosted pint glasses, splashing a bit onto the cocktail napkins placed beneath them.

"Enjoy." He winked at Cal and walked off down the bar.

"It's beer," she said. I caught the smile in her voice before I saw it.

"Infused with heroin, of course," I answered, swirling my glass and savoring the droplets of condensation against my fingertips. Have you ever touched a drop of water so gently that you can still feel the edge of it? I love that feeling.

I miss the edges of things. Without time, it's hard to find edges.

"I'm kidding," I said. "Management is way too cheap to put heroin in the beer."

Cal laughed. I liked it.

"Well, I feel like a doofus," she said, pulling her beer toward her and admiring the color. "Horror, I've missed beer."

"I think you might be the first person to ever say 'doofus' in this establishment."

We were both quiet for our first deep sips. I used to think crap beer tasted like Velcro, but this tasted like honey. The only constant is change.

"If you don't mind my asking," I said, "how long have you been down here?"

Cal wiped her mouth.

"You don't have to tell me if you don't—"

"No, no. I can. I've been here for . . . what is it now? Four millennia. I spent the beginning—only the first millennium, really—Downstairs. Then I worked up to the Third Floor, and last week they transferred me up to Deals."

I had heard people mention the Downstairs like that—like it was any other floor—but I wasn't expecting it from her. A millennium Downstairs was a rough way to start, even if it was a relatively short stay. I looked at her as she sipped her beer, eyes closed. I could feel her knee next to mine, bouncing slightly beneath the bar. She looked small and timid. Gun-shy. I wondered if she had always been that way, or if the Downstairs had done it.

"A millennium Downstairs, huh? I started on Second. I spent a lot of time Downstairs, what with working the factory line and all, so I know it. I know it very well. But obviously . . . well, it's a different experience. Are you—how did you—"

"I'll tell you; I prefer it up here!" Cal said, and she pushed her glass against mine so it clinked, a hopeful sound.

I took the hint.

"So, what do you think of our fine department so far?" I picked through the bowl of peanuts, looking for anything but empty shells. I thought about waving Jack down and asking for more, but decided against it. It's important to stay on your bartender's good side.

"It's . . . well, can I tell you the truth?"

I grabbed a peanut shell and put it in my mouth, just to taste the salt. Or Hell's version of salt, rather, which is more like skin two days after the beach.

"Of course," I said. "I'm very trustworthy."

Cal laughed. "Didn't the whole team have a How to Be Trustworthy training session not too long ago?"

"You'll be so convincing, you'll start to trust yourself!" I said, mimicking the poster.

"Honestly, I'm still reeling. I'm so grateful to be here—I mean, I'm so grateful. But I can't help thinking they made some kind of mistake. There's no way I can keep up with you all. I mean, just look at Trey! He is so impressive . . . I could never sell like him."

"Trey?" I exhaled out my nose, quick but obvious. "You could definitely outsell Trey."

"But in our meeting today, he got a Complete Set! And I know the last time he got a Complete Set, he was awarded with memory clearance, right? Isn't that basically unheard of—getting so many Complete Sets you are allowed to investigate people's memories?"

I cracked my neck. "Yeah, he did get memory clearance. I was there when KQ gave him the honors. She did a whole ceremony after his fourth Complete Set. But it's really not that rare. Not at all. It hasn't happened in a while, sure, but it happens plenty."

"He just seems like a really hard worker."

"Trey wouldn't know hard work if it killed him. He's a bar snake."

"A what?"

"A bar snake. He hangs out at bars and gets deals from the drunks at two in the morning. If that's hard work, sign me up."

"Well, as long as we're being honest, he does seem a little . . ."

"Asshat-ish?" I finished. Cal laughed, more loudly than we had been talking, a burst of a laugh that made me think of a dry river-bed after it rains. Of water moving freely, the way it should.

We finished our beers, chatting in between sips but not really saying anything. It had been a while since I'd shared a beer with someone; I tried not to make friends in Hell. But it was nice, sitting there with her.

"Wow, it got late!" she said when we stepped outside. I could tell from that alone that Cal had had a good time. The sky doesn't change in Hell the way it does for you. Our sky is caught forever in gray scale, hazy enough to make you feel like an intruder upon a sleeping world but bright enough to leave everyone squinting. The ending of one day or the beginning of another, just the same. So when she said it had gotten late, she didn't mean we were so captivated that the world around us had gone on turning and we hadn't even noticed. Rather, she meant the time we had spent together had passed quickly. They might sound like the same thing, but there's a difference between finding something so entrancing that you are able to forget, for even just a minute, the ticking pressure of mortality, and feeling pleasantly surprised that the contents of your daily slop-bucket of time are less rotten than usual. You would've eaten the rot just fine, but this was . . . better.

That's the highest compliment anyone can get here.

"Hey, listen, I want to say thank you for tonight. It's been a weird transition, and it's nice to know I have a—well, it's nice to see a friendly face."

"My friendly face is here for your enjoyment whenever you need it!" I said. I could feel the beer toasting me from the inside, and her words and my warmth combined to make me want to do something crazy. I wanted to hug her. I almost did it too. I really almost hugged her. But she started walking before I remembered how it worked: putting your arms around another person. Where would my hands go? What if her hair got in my mouth? In the end, urge lost to etiquette, and I watched her walk away.

Did humans hug in their caves? I went back into Jack's and thought about it the rest of the night. Who was the first person to seek comfort in another? Did it work?

And if not, who was brave enough to try again?

# MICKEY

**MICKEY HARRISON HATED SOCCER.** But she hated it less than piano or ballet, and her parents had nothing else to do with her in the afternoons. Even though she hated it, Mickey was good at soccer. She had the right kind of body: one long line, knees and elbows that looked like cartoon dog bones. No cleavage, nothing to get in the way. And she could run without getting winded. She could run for miles.

"Harrison, be aggressive!" the coach yelled, and Mickey snapped into action. She saw the ball coming toward her, and she squinted, imagining the swift kick it would take to knock the ball out from between the other girl's feet, to send it the way Mickey wanted it to go. She darted forward, but the girl saw her coming and pivoted at the last second. Mickey kicked anyway, and her cleat connected with the other girl's shin. She went down faster than the girls Mickey read about on the bathroom walls.

"What's your problem?" the girl squealed.

The coach blew his whistle.

"Bench," he said, pointing.

"You said to be aggressive."

"Bench, Harrison," he repeated. Mickey shrugged and kicked the ball square in the middle, sending it flying directly into the goal.

"That doesn't count!" the goalie yelled. "We were on time-out!"

"I know," Mickey snapped back, rolling her eyes. She fucking hated soccer.

The girl was fine, but she sat out the rest of the game anyway. It was obviously because the boys played on the next field over and she wanted to watch them—or, rather, be watched by them. Mickey picked at the seam of her uniform as she watched the other girl lean back, her training-wheel breasts lifted toward the sky as if it were the most comfortable thing in the world. Mickey leaned back briefly, just to see. It was not.

When the game ended, the girls lingered around the benches, gathering their things and making weekend plans. Mickey ignored them, searching the bin the coach made them put their cell phones in before practice.

"How did you get hurt?" a boy asked, sliding onto their bench. Mickey found her phone in the bin and unstrapped her shin guards.

"That psycho," the girl answered, jerking her head at Mickey. "She basically attacked me."

Mickey felt her face get hot, but she didn't look up. She didn't even unfasten her shin guards faster.

"Yo, what's your damage?" the boy asked. Mickey laid one shin guard on top of the other in the grass. Her legs were tingling and slick with sweat. She hadn't started shaving yet; Lily said she had to wait until high school. Three months to go.

"Are you deaf?"

Mickey recognized him from school. His name was Eliot Marks. She had no doubt he didn't know her name.

"Not deaf, just not interested," Mickey said. A chuckle passed along the bench.

"*You're* not interested?" the boy said, incredulous. Mickey had learned that word—"incredulous"—from her father. She thought it when she looked at Eliot, older than she and taller, but not taller than Sean. If she needed to, she could go for his knees.

"Are you even supposed to be on the girls' team? You don't look like a girl." One of the boys whooped, and the girls giggled in unison, like there was a button for it.

Mickey shrugged.

"Oh, what? You're confused? It's not that hard to figure out, you know. Just check your pants."

*Did you learn that from watching your mom?* It was a decent—albeit unimaginative—comeback, but she couldn't get it out. She flushed with anger, her eyes on the grass as she picked up her soccer ball and balanced it under her arm. Eliot took a step toward her, high on the other girls' laughter, and threw out his elbow, knocking the ball from her grasp. Mickey looked back at the coach, but he was on the field with the ref, not paying any attention to them. The day was over; he was off the clock.

"Move," Mickey said.

"Apologize for hurting—" Eliot stopped and looked back at the bench, holding out his hand to the girl with the training-wheel tits.

"Steph," she said.

"Apologize to Steph."

"Sorry," Mickey mumbled, even though she hated herself for saying it. She didn't mean it, and Mickey wasn't a liar. Her grandpa taught her not to be.

"Check the bathroom on your way out," Eliot said. "See if you're playing for the right team." Laughter followed Mickey off the field and out of earshot. Yet she could still hear it well after the group had moved on to other things, had forgotten all about her.

# PEYOTE

**"PEY, GET YOUR ASS** in gear. Morning meeting," KQ said, slamming her hand against my cubicle so hard, I spilled coffee down my shirt. "And clean yourself up; you look like the poor fucks in the blender aisle."

To be clear, Hell is not a department store. When she says "blender aisle," she means the aisle in the Downstairs in which people are put through blenders.

"Good morning, shitstuffers," KQ said as we all took our seats. "I'm looking at our numbers, and they are a pile of crap."

Even though I knew she wouldn't, I still felt a drop of disappointment that she didn't remark on my deal yesterday.

"Not a pile—they are an anthill of crap. A teaspoon. So, seeing as whatever it is you're doing on your own isn't working, I'm going to try something new." KQ kicked her feet onto the table. "Look to your left, and then to your right. Who do you see?"

I didn't bother looking to my left; I knew Trey was there. I could smell his cologne and coffee-tinged breath mints. I looked to my right and caught Cal's eye.

"These people will be your partners this week. Work together and wow me!" KQ said as she squeezed something out of one big toenail and flicked it on the carpet.

"Um, ma'am?" Cal said.

I winced. That wasn't smart.

"What did you just call me?"

"I'm sorry, I was just trying to be—"

"Insulting? Obnoxious?"

"I'm sorry, it won't happen again."

"What is wrong with you people? I'm probably younger than you."

She definitely wasn't.

"It's just that," Cal pressed on, "if we all look both ways, we can't split up."

She had a point. KQ flashed red and rolled her eyes. "Must I do everything for you plebs? Fine, count to three, like infants. Go on, Trey—start us off."

"One," Trey said, as if it weren't an insult at all.

"Two," I said, half-relieved I wouldn't be in the same group as Trey and half-disappointed I couldn't hang out with Cal during work.

The rest of the table finished, counting the way children do with sheep at bedtime.

"Great. So, now, the first three: you're a group. The next three: you're a group, and so on. If you can't figure that out, you can go down a floor." KQ stood up and shoved her feet into her heels. "Now, go on and make Hell proud."

Trey spun around in his chair to face us.

"So, brainstorming dinner tonight?"

I couldn't think of an excuse fast enough, so I nodded. Cal nodded right after me, almost like she was waiting to see what I said.

"I know a great place," Trey said, writing down an address, followed by his beeper number. If you were wondering where beepers went, Hell is the answer. They all went to Hell, and now we have to use them. "It's on Fourth. Beep me if you have any problems getting in; the line can be long. But don't worry, the bouncers know me." Trey winked and pushed out of his seat.

"This is going to be horrible, isn't it?" Cal asked as soon as he was gone.

"Nothing short of horrible," I answered. Cal shoved her pens into their case, which wouldn't close all the way. She tugged on the zipper. I reached into my pouch for a rubber band.

"It will never close," I said, handing it over.

# MICKEY

"SO, WHAT'S THE VERDICT?" Eliot asked the following day, when Mickey reached the bench and grabbed her water bottle. The other girls were ready, all giddy stares. They must have talked about it. What they didn't know was that Mickey was ready too. She wouldn't get stuck this time.

"Are you switching to our team? Or are you going to grow some tits?"

Water caught in her throat.

No boy had commented on her body before. Her voice, the way she ate, the way she scrunched her eyebrows when she read, the way she breathed at night—all of that was fair game with her brother. But never her body. She turned red, which made her angry, which made her turn redder. She opened her mouth, but her mind drew a blank. All of her comebacks fled.

"Congratulations, it's a boy!" Eliot shouted, clapping. "At least now you can stop wearing that bra." He jammed his fingers under the strap on her shoulder, pulled back, and released it onto her sunburned skin. "You don't need a bra for bee stings, just Neosporin."

Lily had bought the bra for Mickey earlier that month. She talked about "breast buds" with the department store clerk as Mickey shimmied and squeezed into one after another, and she shrugged absently when her mom suggested this one. But secretly, Mickey loved it. It was gray with pink straps, the delicate kind. She should've refused the bra, she thought furiously. She should burn it. She wanted to scream at her mother for doing this to her. She decided she would as soon as she got home.

But then she heard a new voice from over her shoulder. "Her boobs will grow, which is more than we can say for your dick, Marks."

And then there was a shriek loud enough that the coach had to work not to hear it. Mickey looked up and saw Eliot bent at the waist, his shorts in a pile around his legs, his thighs so much whiter than the rest of him—so white they looked translucent in the setting sun. He pulled frantically at the elastic band of his shorts, but they were tangled in the Velcro of his shin guards. The group's laughter turned on him beautifully, like a school of fish. Eliot burned red and squatted down, covering himself with his hands. Mickey could see his small pink ball sack peeping below his fingers. The way it hung there reminded her of the crust her dog used to get in the corners of his eyes.

"Catch ya later, dipshit."

And then an arm landed across her shoulders, and they were walking. Mickey looked at the girl pressed against her, warm and smelling like baby powder deodorant. She knew her; everyone knew her. She was in the grade above Mickey; she transferred into their school in seventh. Her arrival caused quite the stir, with her long hair the color of honey on toast and her hips already taking the shape of something powerful and dangerous under her jeans. As far as Mickey knew, this girl had no idea who Mickey was, but she walked with her like they had been friends for years. Like she regularly pantsed boys on Mickey's behalf. Mickey looked back at Eliot struggling to stand up, and she couldn't help it: she let out a squeal of laughter. The kind of laugh Sean ridiculed. The kind of laugh she tried to change except for when she truly couldn't.

That was how she met Ruth Caroway.

# PEYOTE

"**WELCOME TO THE HONEY** Pot!" Trey said as he gripped my arm and led me through the red curtain, perfume and smoke as thick as the velvet. The loud music and the warm flashing lights provided aggressively synthetic comfort. Everything was sticky and sickly sweet.

"I got forty dollars in ones," Trey said, handing me a stack of crumpled money. It was damp.

"How about you just keep it?"

"No, no, no. We're at the Honey Pot!" he said, shoving it into my chest. "You can pay me back tomorrow."

"Where is Cal?" I asked.

"Late," he answered. "Come on, let's get our party on!" He snapped his fingers in the air, and a waitress came over. "Three Jäger shots, please," he said, clapping me on the back.

I grimaced.

"It's the house specialty!"

I felt a buzz in my pocket and, without knowing anything about the message, was grateful for it.

"Trey, I gotta answer this; it might be Cal," I said, holding up my beeper.

"Hurry back," he said. "Or I might need to drink your shot!"

When I got through the crowd and out the front door, the air almost tasted fresh. Not quite, but almost. You know that feeling when you're in a theater or the subway and you really have to cough, but you're doing everything you can to keep it in? That's how the air feels in Hell, all of the time. Even so, when I got out that door, I looked up, some ancient part of me still hoping to see stars.

"Pey!"

I checked the line, which had grown since I arrived. Cal was there, smashed between a crowd of men with thick rings on even thicker fingers. I pulled her forward.

"She's with me," I said.

The bouncer looked me up and down and, after an excruciatingly long time, gave the smallest of nods. I pulled Cal past him and through the front doors, the smoke and fog of the club hitting me as hard as waking up in the bathtub.

"They wouldn't let me in without a man," she said, smoothing her work shirt.

"I didn't choose this place."

"Oh, hey there, wet blanket! Way to finally join the party!" Trey shouted at Cal when we arrived. I helped her take off her coat and put it on top of mine. Trey handed us both shots. Cal looked at her glass and back at Trey, miserable. I smiled brightly and clinked my shot glass with his, then tossed the liquid over my shoulder before bringing the glass to my lips.

"Pey!" Cal shrieked. I turned and saw a dark brown stain running down her shirt, as if made by a giant slug.

"I'm sorry," I said, grabbing napkins.

"Party foul, Trip! I'll get another round, but you're buying," Trey said, snapping his fingers again.

"It was a nice try," Cal whispered into my ear as I dabbed at her shirt with napkins. I took the next shot in one gulp and gave the waitress my credit card.

"The first thing you two can learn about sales is how to make yourselves approachable. That's why I brought you here." His eyes were already at half-mast, but that's another thing about Hell: you have no idea what alcohol will do to you. You could drink all night and not feel a thing, or have a few and get completely hammered. It depends on your intention. If you want to stay responsible, you will get wasted. You'd think we'd have figured out a system by now, but we haven't. Regardless, you always wake up with a hangover. Never debilitating, but very unpleasant.

That's our comfort zone.

"I don't think you're supposed to be teaching us anything," I said. "Plus, I'm just about to complete my own—"

"So, what I want you to do is sell one of these strippers on buying us a round of drinks," Trey finished, ignoring me. And then he leaned back, proud of himself.

"They work here. Why would they buy us drinks?" Cal asked. I could hear the edge of panic in her voice.

"That's the point. If you can sell a stripper at a strip club on the deal of paying for booze for her customers, then you'll be ready for the real thing," Trey said.

"I actually really am close to—"

"No one cares, Pey," Trey said, pushing my cheek with his hand, a slap in slow motion. "Go! Go, grasshoppers! Go!"

I stood up just so he wouldn't touch me anymore. Cal stood too. We walked over to the stage and looked up at the dancers, moving like eels in a tank. I swallowed.

"Look, I can take care of this, okay? Don't worry," I said.

"I don't think this is a team activity."

"I won't tell if you don't."

Cal looked at the stage and then back at me, her eyes shaking a little. I smiled the best I could.

"Are you sure?"

"Yeah, I've got this. You get some air."

"Thank you, Pey," she said, putting her hand on my arm. It had been a long time since someone touched me. Someone I hadn't just swindled into eternal damnation, I mean.

The way I saw it, there were two ways to get strippers to buy me drinks. One: I play the sympathy card. I tell them I'm getting bumped Downstairs, and I cry everywhere until they buy me a drink to get my sadness off them. Two: I pay them. Option number two seemed like the lesser amount of work; I didn't have any tears built up. So I leaned over the stage in front of me.

I wasn't watching Cal. I didn't even think to.

That was my mistake.

First of many.

After an hour of deliberation, I got three women to buy us all drinks if I paid them double. It was a fair-enough deal, all things considered. If this helped Cal and me get out of this nightmare, it was worth it. I paid them up front to secure their secrecy. When we got back to our table, it was already crowded with slick skin and bikini strings and empty shot glasses. A few men orbited nearby, panting. I pushed forward, looking for Trey.

"Hey, I got three ladies here who would like to—" But I stopped when I saw Cal.

On our table, a woman lay splayed out on her back, naked save a lime in her mouth and a full shot glass balancing over her belly button. Cal knelt between her split thighs and took the shot glass in her teeth. She gave a little twitch as the booze went down, and then she pulled herself up the length of the other woman's body to the lime, pausing over her bottom lip long enough to get a "Sweet Jesus" out of Trey. Then she flipped the lime into her mouth and bit down, juice running down her neck.

The woman rose on towering heels and sent an empty glass to the floor, where it shattered, all sparkle against the liquor-soaked laminate.

"I'll get a broom," the next in line said, but Cal shook her head.

"Don't bother." And to the crowd's delight, she sank back to her knees. Then she looked up at me. Her cheeks were red, but a different kind of red than I had seen before. This looked less like blood and more like fire. The girls I'd paid fidgeted behind me, embarrassed to be on my team.

"Welcome back, Pey," she said, balancing a new shot on the next stripper's stomach. "I honestly thought you would pussy out."

Trey laughed.

"Good one, Cal! Pey *is* a pussy!"

She ignored him, holding my gaze.

"Nobody eats limes with Jäger shots," I said, shock rendering me dumb.

"This is Hell, Pey."

Cal stood up and turned away from the table, from the woman on the table, from Trey. She turned away from everyone but me. Then she bent over and dragged one finger along the club's floor, glistening with glass and booze and blood.

"We can do whatever the fuck we want."

She put her finger in her mouth, and the crowd went wild.

# SILAS

**"HOW WAS SOCCER?" SILAS** asked when Mickey came through the front door. He stood over the stove, stirring paella. Recently, Lily had been working late most nights at the gallery, even though it was left to her when her parents died and was run seamlessly by the primary curator, to whom she had nothing to prove. Silas guest taught at the local college's business school, but the semester was over and he had given the final tests to his TA to grade, so he was officially on summer vacation, waiting for everyone to catch up. He heard Mickey kick off her sneakers and drop her bag on the staircase before she walked back to the kitchen.

"Hi, Dad," she said, stepping up to the stove and putting her head under his elbow. He opened his arm and pulled her against his chest, keeping the spoon in the pot. Sometimes his daughter reminded him so much of Lily, he would forget, just for a second, who was who. Mickey looked more and more like her mother every day. She was getting closer to the age Lily and Silas were when they met—closer than he felt comfortable with. He kissed the top of her head, which was a different color from her mother's, but not by much.

"What am I missing?" he asked, holding out the steaming spoon. Mickey touched her lips to the wood and scrunched her nose. She looked the most like Lily when she concentrated, Silas thought.

"Cayenne," Mickey said.

"God, you're good," Silas answered, and nodded toward the cabinet. Mickey hitched herself up on the counter and pulled down the spice. She stayed there, her knees squared with his hips, golden hairs on her long legs. *Legs like her mother's*, he thought. He searched her face, looking for something of his. He could hear himself in her voice sometimes, but he was hard to find in anything physical.

"How was soccer?" he asked again.

"Good."

"Oh yeah?" Usually, she would only shrug or beg him to let her quit. "Good" was a whole new ball game.

"I think I made a friend," Mickey said, dipping her finger into the pot and sticking it in her mouth. She nodded. "That's better."

"A friend, huh? No one as cool as your old man, though, right?"

He handed her the cayenne, and she twisted around to put it back on the shelf.

"She helped me out at practice."

"With your footwork?"

"With some asshole."

Silas raised his eyebrows at his daughter. "What asshole? Also, don't say 'asshole.'"

"Some kid was being an ass—was being a jerk," Mickey said, swinging her legs a little, just enough to make a hollow sound on the cabinets below. "She stood up for me."

"Do you need me to break some kneecaps?" Silas said.

Mickey smiled. "No, thanks. She pantsed him."

Silas laughed, despite himself. He hadn't heard that word in a long time. He wanted to tell Lily, see if she had the same memory of that away game senior year.

"Who is this girl?"

"You have to keep stirring, Dad."

Silas went back to stirring.

"Her name is Ruth."

"Is she your age?" Silas asked, keeping the spoon moving. The broth in the pot steamed.

"Going into tenth grade," Mickey answered. "She's super cool. Really pretty too."

"Well, look at you, Miss Thang," Silas said. Mickey rolled her eyes.

"No one says 'Miss Thang' anymore."

"One person does," Silas answered, pointing to his chest.

"Where is Mom?" Mickey asked, pushing herself off the counter and opening the fridge.

"Work. She'll be home soon."

Mickey grabbed a can of seltzer and closed the fridge door. Silas thought she looked disappointed, but he couldn't tell if the disappointment was because of Lily's absence or her inevitable return. Lily and Mickey's dynamic had shifted recently. Silas and Lily's friends said it was normal teenage behavior: daughter taking out her anger on mom. Silas always secretly hoped his kids were above all of that typical development stuff, but it was becoming clear that they weren't.

"Shower before dinner?" he asked.

"How long do I have?"

"Long enough—you're gross," he said, patting her head and making a big deal of wiping sweat on his pants.

"I wouldn't be gross if you didn't make me join this stupid team," Mickey said. "I would be clean all day long."

"But you wouldn't have met your cool, pretty new friend," Silas said, and Mickey smiled. It surprised him, how happy she looked.

*Ruth*, he thought. He'd have to check the school website and see what he could find out. There couldn't be too many Ruths in Mickey and Sean's school. It wasn't a name he heard often.

"She seriously pantsed him, Dad, like, in front of everyone."

Mickey was beaming now, with a dreamy look. That was the word that came to mind when he considered her, leaning against the fridge: "dreamy."

"That sounds pretty mean."

"Trust me, he deserved it," Mickey answered, and Silas did. Trust her.

"Dinner in twenty," he said when she leaned in and put her head on his chest for a second, a hug without arms. "Tell your brother."

"I'm not knocking on his door."

"Just yell it in the hallway."

He stirred the pot, added more salt and pepper. He wanted to put on a new record, but he couldn't abandon the food. He wished he had asked Mickey to do it before she left, but he heard the water in the pipes upstairs and knew he had missed his chance.

Silas had been in charge of dinner since he married Lily seventeen years ago. Lily didn't cook; she would've lived on Pringles and wine if he let her. She would go a full day without eating like it was nothing. Silas couldn't do that. He loved dinner in particular. He centered his day around it: what he would cook, what he would need to make it perfect. He thought about it at work; he thought about it on Sundays when he made sauce and packed extra Tupperware for the kids to bring to the neighbors. He took a swig of his beer, and let the bitter aftertaste linger on his tongue.

Silas was the kind of man who took pleasure in the little things. His father had been the same way. His brother, Philip, was the serious one. Silas watched Sean sometimes and saw Philip in him. It made him both proud and nervous, seeing his older brother's face in his son. He saw him most in some of Sean's sideways glances, the way he watched more than he spoke.

Soon the whole family would be going to New Hampshire. Silas had been going to his New Hampshire house since he was born. He saw Lily naked for the first time in the third-floor guest room when they were sixteen, touched her until she bit his shoulder hard enough to draw blood. He reminded her of that every summer, lingering in the doorway, thinking maybe the memory would raise something in her. It used to. Silas thought about it as he stirred the pot. When he felt himself getting hard, he took another sip of beer and willed the thought away. He didn't know when he started to associate desire with shame, but somewhere along the way, they had become deep, disgusted bedfellows. He never felt one without feeling the other.

Lily would be home soon. They would eat dinner, and he would tell her about Mickey's new friend, the one who pantsed a boy on her behalf, if Mickey didn't tell her herself. He thought Lily would like that story, but he wasn't sure. Silas felt like he was getting to know his wife less with time. He didn't know how that was possible, but it was. When they were kids, he always knew what she liked, how to make her smile or laugh or storm off. He knew all of her buttons and how to push them just right. Now he wasn't as sure.

He brought the spoon to his mouth.

"Perfect," he said to the empty kitchen.

# PEYOTE

**IT HAD BEEN A** long time since I had an opinion about going into work, but after storming out of the Honey Pot, I didn't want to go. This sudden change—the dread in my gut—did not feel good. I swallowed it down with some Alka-Seltzer and told myself it was a hangover. I've had a lot of practice lying to myself. I could pretend that's a Hell thing, but it's universal.

I made it to my cubicle without seeing anyone. I hung my jacket over the back of my chair and sat down, which was when I saw the bottle.

One beer.

Coors.

I snatched it and pulled it in to my chest before I realized how ridiculous I looked. How pathetic. But I didn't put it down. There was a folded piece of paper underneath.

*Don't be mad.*
—C.

She knew where to get beer. The whole time at Jack's: the wide-eyed look, the hushed tones, the I-don't-do-drugs-but-you-can-do-what-you-want moment—all of it was an act. She lied the whole time.

I shoved the beer into my briefcase. If it had been anything else, I would've put it on her desk. But I wanted that beer, and I wasn't going to suffer on principle. Down here, principles are worthless. I had forgotten that for a second, but not forever. If nothing else, Hell gave us plenty of time.

"Hey, buddy." Cal knocked on my cubicle divider, fidgeting with the seam of an oversized sweater. "Did you get my present?"

I nodded. "Regret showing Trey your true colors yet?"

I was being sarcastic, but she pitched forward instantly.

"He's batshit, huh?"

I looked at her with my eyebrows raised until she backed up. "You should drink some water," I said, nodding toward the kitchen. "They keep bottles in the fridge."

She pulled harder on her sweater as she shook her head.

"Listen, you seem like a good guy, so I'm going to level with you. I was trying to go for a long game; I really was. I wanted to work the sweet-sad-girl angle for as long as possible, but I think I showed my cards too early last night. We didn't have booze on Third; I guess I'm a bit of a lightweight now. Trey won't shut the fuck up about it; he beeped me all night. If he tells KQ, I'll be back to square one. I'll have to go with a whole new character, and that's just not how I planned it. I know I'm not your favorite person right now, but do you have any interest in making Trey sound like a moron?"

"What makes you think I'm a good guy?"

"If you counteract whatever stories Trey tells about last night, I'll owe you." She inched back into my space just enough for her knee to touch my elbow. "And think about how much fun it would be!"

I rubbed my eyes with my palms.

"Think about it: if we can put a chink in that Trey-is-perfect armor of his, maybe KQ will finally stop tea-bagging him long enough for the rest of us to get some recognition. You'd like that, wouldn't you?"

I would. I would like that very much. But at least I knew what to expect from Trey. Cal was a wild card.

"Fine," I said eventually.

Cal clapped her hands and grabbed my face, kissing both cheeks.

"We're going to be great friends," she said. "For real this time."

She tugged her sweater down over her hips, a lifeless sack from her shoulders to her thighs. She was going for nondescript, and she was nailing it. She mimed clapping again, her eyes bright, and disappeared behind my cubicle wall.

"HOW DID OUR LITTLE learning experiment go yesterday, fucknuts?" KQ asked when she sat down. She leaned back in her chair, legs splayed. She was wearing a skirt. I kept my eyes on my granola bar, the only thing that didn't get stuck in the vending machine.

"Turns out we have ourselves a real firecracker over here, everyone!" Trey said, throwing his arm around Cal and shaking her. She stayed limp under his attention. "This crazy bitch *tore up* the strip club last night."

Everyone looked skeptical.

Cal blushed, red flooding her neck and cheeks. Even her blood knew how to lie.

"What does a night at the strip club have to do with sales?"

KQ asked. "Not that I can't appreciate a good time," she added, smiling at Trey. Her knees were strangers at a party.

"I thought to myself, Trey, where would be the hardest place to sell something? How about somewhere where *other* people are selling things? And then I thought, let's make it even harder. Let's sell the thing that they are selling *back to them*." He paused after this emphasis, letting the brilliance sink in. "Do you follow?"

"I'm following," KQ said, her voice the polyester cousin of intrigue.

"So I asked my little grasshoppers here to get the strippers to buy *us* a round of drinks."

When I walked in the door, I had been fifty-fifty about whether to help Cal. But Trey could go fuck himself. I was nobody's grasshopper.

"How creative!" KQ exclaimed. "How did you all do?"

"Like I was saying, we might need to keep this one locked up, boss. I volunteer for the first watch!" Trey grabbed Cal's wrists and pinned them to the table with one hand. With the other, he did an elaborate mime of locking her down, swallowing the key, and rubbing his belly.

Cal just sat there, wide-eyed and red-cheeked, drowning in a grandma's sweater.

"Hey, Trey, maybe we should touch base as a group before we present anything," I said, loudly enough for everyone to hear but quietly enough to make them think they shouldn't have.

"You snooze, you lose, Pey. Shouldn't have gone home early."

"Pey didn't—" Cal started. She gulped audibly before pressing on. "Pey didn't go home early, Trey." Then she whispered like I had. "I think we should check in, just to make sure your memory is on track."

"What are you talking about?" Trey asked, not tempering his voice a bit.

"Let's just talk after the meeting, and then we'll present. Is that all right, KQ?" I asked. She eyed me.

"No," she said. "Talk now."

"Swoosh!" Trey yelled. "Anyway, it was fucking awesome. She had the finest honeys the Honey Pot has to offer lined up for body shots before Pey even got back from the bar! Top twenty nights at the Honey Pot, hands down." He slapped the table. "I think I really have a knack for this training thing, boss."

Cal and I looked at each other like we had rehearsed it.

"Trey, I think you might be misremembering things. You did have a few drinks," I said.

"What are you two implying?" KQ asked, picking up on our heavy hands.

"Ma'am—I mean, I'm sorry, I mean KQ—I don't want to speak out of turn, but—"

"Oh, for Darkness' sake. Just talk, you little rodent."

"Trey spent most of the night passed out in the booth," I interrupted. "Cal and I had to put him in a taxi before we could even try to sell anything." I shrugged. "I'm sorry, Trey, I just can't lie for you. Not this time."

Trey opened and closed his mouth like a fish.

"Pey actually made the sales, and got five of the strip—five of the ladies—to give up names of folks on Earth who might want to make a deal," Cal said. "It was actually . . . It was really impressive. I'm grateful I got to see him work." She smiled at me in that sweet way she had smiled the day we first met, and I was relieved by the comfort of feeling nothing.

"It was no big deal."

"That's bullshit," Trey said, shaking his head. "That's not at all what happened. I was *there*. This dipshit went home early, and Cal and I tore the place up all night! I watched her fingerbang two strippers, y'all. It was the bomb."

KQ looked at Cal and then back at Trey. I could see the wheels in her brain turning as she tried to imagine this little church mouse knuckles-deep.

"Trey, remember the Christmas party?" I asked gently. I watched as everybody in the room recalled Trey vomiting into a lampshade and then wearing it around his neck "because the doctor said I can't chew on my own junk anymore!" I watched as the women in the room remembered his liquor-soaked breath as he leaned in and said, "I can still chew on your junk, though."

There was a collective sigh.

"Trey, you know you can't get that kind of hammered on work time," KQ said, putting her feet back on the floor.

"I didn't—I don't—"

"He was harmless, truly. Just peacefully asleep," Cal said. I had to bite my tongue to keep from laughing. It was the perfect addition. Trey would rather be the office drunk than harmless.

"Okay, well, that's about all I need to know about that. Trey, dock your time. We can't be paying you for getting drunk. Pey, good work. Follow those leads and see what we get. Squeaks—well, I'm glad you got to see some good salesmanship. Maybe you can learn something, if your brain isn't as dense as your sweater."

I didn't look at Cal, but I wanted to. Maybe we really could be friends after all. Whatever that meant here.

"Okay," KQ said. "Who's next?"

# MICKEY

RUTH LAY ON MICKEY'S bed, swiping through her phone. It had been two weeks since that soccer practice, and the smell of Ruth's hair had become a part of Mickey's pillows. Candy apples and baby powder. It was everywhere. Mickey begged her mom to find the shampoo Ruth used, but none of the ones she bought came close.

"Why do you have to leave me?" Ruth whined, throwing her phone onto the pillow next to her and rolling onto her stomach, her chin in her hands.

"I don't want to," Mickey answered, pulling shorts from her drawer.

"Not those," Ruth said, wrinkling her nose.

"Why not?" Mickey asked. Ruth snorted.

"Come on, Mick," she said.

Mickey threw them back into the drawer.

"What am I supposed to do for the next six weeks?" Ruth asked, picking at Mickey's quilt.

"Hang out with your cooler friends."

"You know they're all out of town."

It had been only two weeks, but Mickey's whole life was different. She had a best friend. She'd never had a best friend before. Mickey opened her drawer of shirts and began rifling through them, throwing options into her open suitcase. She was positive she would wake up one morning and everything she'd gained would be lost, just like that.

"Oh, come on, Mick. You know you're my favorite. Other girls are so fake. They're boring."

"I wish I didn't have to go," Mickey said. She loved going to her family's New Hampshire house. She looked forward to it all year. But here she was, saying she wished she could stay home and meaning it.

Silas walked past her door and caught her eye.

"Your mom is going to be so happy to see you're packing," he said, pausing in the doorway. He had a beer in his hand.

"Go away, Dad."

"Don't be rude, Mick," Ruth said. "Hi, Mr. Harrison!"

He had told her to call him Silas from the beginning, but she never did.

"What are you up to this summer, Ruth? In the market for new parents? We might be looking to adopt," Silas said, smirking. He leaned against the doorframe and took a sip.

Ruth shrugged. "I'm not doing anything. It's so cool that you can go back to your childhood home every year! Mickey says it's beautiful. I'd love to see it sometime."

"Your family doesn't go anywhere?"

Mickey blushed. Ruth's mom didn't have a second home like the Harrisons, or the families of most of the kids from their school. Mickey wanted to interrupt him; she wanted to do a dance to distract them both. She was embarrassed because she thought Ruth might be. Embarrassment can be contagious like that. But Ruth wasn't. She just shrugged.

"We don't have anywhere to go," she said. Ruth had a way of doing that: saying the truth. Mickey's family wasn't used to it. The blunt truth, Mickey noticed, raised the Harrisons' collective heartbeat. Mickey loved it.

Silas swirled his beer.

"You should come with us! What do you say, Mick? Want to bring a friend this year?"

Mickey's heart surged with a mix of excitement, terror, and jealousy. She had noticed that happening lately: all of her feelings had at least two other feelings right on top of them. It was, unsurprisingly, confusing. Mickey looked at her father, and then at Ruth.

"That would be great!" Mickey said, mostly telling the truth.

"Are you sure?" Ruth asked her, not looking at Silas. The way Ruth did that, asked Mickey like she alone was the authority, made Mickey want her to come something vicious. She nodded.

"I would love to, Mr. Harrison!" Ruth said. She hopped off Mickey's bed and threw her arms around Silas's neck, so fast it spilled a bit of his beer. She let go, and he stepped back, flushed.

"Well, you ask your parents, and we'll go from there," he said, smiling and close to breathless.

"It's just my mom," Ruth said. "She'll be fine with it."

"Okay, well, just ask to be sure. Then Lily and I will give her a call."

"Okay," Ruth answered. Silas caught Mickey's eye, and she smiled wide, letting him know it was all right. In fact, it was great. Mickey Harrison had a best friend, and they were going to spend the summer together.

When Silas left the doorway, Ruth squealed and ran to Mickey, wrapping her arms around her shoulders.

"Vacation twins!" she said, before pulling back and looking at her. "Are you sure it's okay that I come?"

"Absolutely!" Mickey said. "Will your mom really let you?"

Ruth rolled her eyes and fell back on Mickey's bed. "Do me a favor," she said. "Give your folks my cell to call, okay? My mom uses it too . . . It's like a communal cell phone."

Mickey nodded. It wasn't until later that week that she remembered she had called Ruth on her home number before, that she even had one. But by then, her parents had already talked to Mrs. Caroway and were satisfied enough with her responses to bring Ruth along.

"Okay, now, let's go through these clothes for real," Ruth said, throwing open Mickey's closet door. "We are summering!"

# LILY

"**WE DON'T EVEN KNOW** her!" Lily said. She hovered between her closet and the bedroom, blindly working the clasp of her necklace.

"Of course we do. She's been here every day for weeks. Plus, what is there to know? She's Mickey's friend," Silas said, pulling back the covers.

"This is a *family* vacation, Si," she said, reclasping the necklace once it was freed and hanging it on her closet door. Mickey used to play with her necklaces, pretend they were hers and she was a princess somewhere far away. She loved the chunky colorful ones, the heavy ones made of clay.

"We used to bring friends all the time. You didn't start out as family either, you know," Silas said, leaning into the pillows. Lily stepped behind the closet door to undress. She did it casually, but intentionally. It had been a long time since she undressed in the full view of her husband.

"It's good she's made a friend. Let's let her enjoy it."

"We have to talk to this girl's mother," Lily said through the door.

"I already left her a message."

"I just can't believe you made this decision without me."

"I don't see what the big deal is. We have plenty of room."

Lily walked to the bathroom. Her heart was pounding. They never brought another person to the lake house. Not since the summer before Silas and Lily got married. She breathed against the mirror, her palms on the sink.

"Sean is going to want to bring a friend now, you know."

"Sean would rather die than introduce us to any of his friends."

It was true. Lily caught glimpses of kids around Sean when she would go pick him up after school, but if he had any real friends, he hadn't brought them home.

"Well, now we have to ask, thanks to you," Lily said, pulling a bathrobe around her shoulders. Silas shrugged.

"Do what you want."

"I don't *want* to do any of this."

"Say it once more, Lil, for the seats in the back." Silas put his book down on his lap and looked at her.

"You know what I mean."

"Sure," he said, and went back to reading.

Lily paused in front of her son's room. She couldn't hear anything through the door, but she hadn't been able to in years. Not since Sean started listening to everything through his gigantic black headphones. One time Silas called them his "Princess Leia look," and Sean didn't speak to him for a week.

Lily thought about stopping by Mickey's room first, to talk about this Ruth girl and see if Mickey really wanted to bring a friend to New Hampshire. But she told Silas she had to talk to Sean, and she did, if she wanted to make her point. She wondered if other moms were this nervous before talking to their teenage sons or if she was the worst one there ever was, and then she knocked.

"Sean?" she said, opening the door a crack after hearing some kind of grunt.

"What?"

Lily opened the door all the way and stepped inside. The room felt smaller than it had when they first bought the house. Sean had covered the walls in pictures of bands Lily didn't know: men with sour faces and haunted eyes. She would've preferred *Sports Illustrated* Swimsuit Issue pullouts, which was saying something.

"Did your father talk to you about New Hampshire?"

She knew full well that he hadn't, but she threw Silas under the bus anyway. Habit.

"I'm packing, Mom. Fuck. Relax."

"Hey!" Lily said. "Language. And that's not what I'm talking about."

Sean shrugged. He didn't ask her what she was talking about; he just looked back at his screen. He seemed to be doing five things at once.

"Is any of that homework?" she asked from over his shoulder. Sean clicked a couple of buttons, and the screen went black.

"What do you need, Mom?" he asked, looking up at her.

"Your sister is bringing a friend to New Hampshire this year. Your father okayed it without talking to me, so apparently that's what's happening now. I'm here to see if you want to bring a friend too."

Sean cocked his head, and for a second, he looked like he did when he was eight and couldn't understand how the shark got into the aquarium. But he looked away before Lily could get deep enough into the memory to siphon out any of its flavor.

"Who is she bringing?"

"Ruth Caroway," Lily said. "Have you met her?" Lily watched as her son caught his own surprise, turned over his own feelings.

He thought he was so guarded, but he was the most open person she knew. All she had to do was watch, not listen.

"For the whole summer?"

"The whole time we're there," Lily answered. She thought he would be mad, maybe mad enough to make a whole thing out of it and prevent it from happening. But he wasn't.

"That's cool," he said. And then, "Everyone I know is busy this summer."

"Do you know this girl? Ruth?" Lily asked, leaning against Sean's desk. She eyed his walls. She could barely see the paint behind the posters. It was light green. She and Silas painted it together, thinking they were elevated for not picking blue.

"Everyone knows her."

"What does that mean? Is she not . . . is she not a good girl?"

"She's not a dog, Mom," Sean said, his eyes back on his screen.

"What?"

"*Good girl!*" Sean repeated, panting.

"Har har," Lily said.

"I need to finish my homework."

Lily could see Silas in his face, particularly in his eyes. She could see parts of herself in him, too, but they weren't as visible. When Sean was a child, he had blond hair like hers, but not anymore. With each day, she faded from him. Or he from her.

"Are you sure you're okay with this? You don't want to bring anyone yourself?"

"I'm set," Sean said. Lily didn't know what that meant exactly, except that it seemed like an ending.

"You'll tell me if you change your mind?"

"I won't."

Lily stood over him. She saw where the hairs on the back of his neck matted to his skin under his sweatshirt. She could tell he hadn't showered, but she didn't want to push it. She wanted to tuck him in, to find his pajamas with the trucks and the feet, and squeeze him until he was small enough to fit back in them. Even if it hurt him, even if it damn near killed him. She wanted to make him small again.

"Okay, sweetheart. Go to bed soon, all right?"

Sean mumbled and nodded. Lily paused, and then, like a refugee seeking a border, she swooped down and kissed his head. She left before he could react, making sure to close the door behind her.

**LILY STOPPED IN THE** hallway. Her head was spinning, maybe from the wine at dinner, or from the body spray that seemed to have replaced oxygen in her son's room. She didn't want to go back to her bedroom, back to Silas. She wanted to call Gavin. She reached into her bathrobe pocket and pulled out her phone.

"Do you have the delivery schedule?" she texted, and then she walked downstairs. The kitchen still smelled like spices and seafood. Lily turned on the faucet and rinsed dishes, putting them in the dishwasher. The kitchen gleamed in the darkness, stainless steel and ceramic tile. She felt a buzz in her pocket and grabbed for her phone. It was Gavin. She exhaled and slunk out the front door onto the porch.

"What's up?" he asked as soon as she answered. He was worried. She had never used their code before.

"I'm sorry, I know it's late and we're not supposed to—"

"It's okay. Melanie is with her mom. Are you okay?"

Lily sat down on the long-abandoned play set's swing, startled by the way the chains groaned. She looked up and didn't see any movement in the windows. She could always say she snuck out for one of her five cigarettes a year. She reached behind the plastic tunnel and grabbed her hidden pack, just in case.

"I don't know. I'm kind of freaking out about this trip, Gav," she said. She pulled out a cigarette and the lighter before she remembered she was pretending.

"I know," he said. She could hear him sit down. She imagined he was in his living room. She imagined what it might look like, what colors made up his life away from her.

"I just found out that Silas invited a friend of Mickey's to come with us, for the whole time."

"Seriously? Who?"

"What do you mean, who? What does it matter? A teenage girl, that's who," Lily answered. "And he's acting like I'm the crazy one."

Gavin sighed.

"What am I doing," Lily asked, but it wasn't a question.

"You're taking care of your children," Gavin said. Lily nodded and inhaled from the cigarette she didn't mean to light.

"I don't know if I can do it this year, honestly. I mean, what is he thinking? Inviting a stranger? A girl? He has to know what that will bring up."

"Since when has that mattered?" Gavin asked. It was the truth. Lily took another deep inhale and felt the combination of nicotine and Gavin's voice flood her veins and slow her down.

"I miss you," she said.

"I miss you too."

There was nothing for a minute but night song: a violin bow against the wings of countless crickets, the quiet sizzle of her cigarette's tip.

"What if I can't do it? What if I just can't do it?"

"You always do it," Gavin said. "You always do it."

Lily took another drag of her cigarette and held it as long as she could, until her vision swam with blacks and grays. She didn't want to say good night. She didn't want to take any steps forward, not even one breath.

Until eventually, as always, she didn't have a choice.

# PEYOTE

**"I CAN'T BELIEVE YOU** made such a big deal out of the beer at Jack's," I said, cracking open another Miller Lite and tossing the cap onto the kitchenette counter. Cal smirked and shrugged, going so far as to hold her palms up. I laughed. I couldn't help it. Also, I had already had three whole beers, which was more than I had had in a row in centuries. I was euphoric.

"I hope you can forgive me."

"I'm going to drink all of this," I said, pointing to the fridge with a full six-pack still inside. "You owe me that much."

"Fair enough," Cal said. "You really were a work of art in there."

I smiled and fell back against Cal's couch. I hadn't been in another person's Fifth-Floor apartment in a long time, but it was exactly the same as mine.

"It was a pleasure," I said, and I meant it. Watching Trey's face fall—I took so much pleasure in it, there was no denying I belonged here.

"Can we talk about KQ and her fucking feet?" Cal asked, sitting down next to me.

I snorted. "She's a nightmare."

"And with the skirt today? Did her vagina take a power-pose workshop or something?"

I laughed again, so hard I almost slapped my knee. Almost. I took a sip of beer.

Cal stood up suddenly and reached her hands up until the tips of her fingers pressed against the popcorn ceiling. Her T-shirt rode up with her hands, and I could see her stomach, her belly button. I hadn't seen another person's belly button since I'd worked on Second. I'm not proud of it, but I stared. If you go too long without seeing parts of yourself in others, you start to think you're made wrong.

"What do you want from this life, Pey?" Cal asked, holding her arms out to her whole apartment, the whole of the Fifth Floor, the whole of everything.

"This isn't life," I said. "This is what comes after."

"Quit dodging the question," she said, waltzing to the stereo and clicking up the volume. The music in the living room got louder. We have only a couple of stations in Hell, but unlike our booze, our music is personalized against our tastes. For example, in my apartment, my only musical choices are Jock Jams and K-pop. Yours would be your own worst cacophony. Cal's was deep and throaty.

"Dave Matthews?" I asked.

"Creed," she answered. "I think they might be growing on me."

I smiled, remembering the words to some Korean song I'd memorized but couldn't understand.

"I want to keep going exactly like I have been," I said. "Except I would like less Trey."

That was, of course, a lie. Not the Trey part, but the rest of it. I had big plans, bigger than she could imagine. But they were all mine.

"Well, that's horribly boring," Cal said, spinning to the music and falling back on the couch.

"What do you want, Squeaks?"

"I want a lot of things," she answered. "And I think if we work together, we can make a pretty little life for ourselves here."

"There is no 'working together' with people like you," I said. "You don't know what loyalty is."

Cal gave me a smile, but it caught on something first. I could see it in her eyes.

"We can call it a temporary alliance."

"Look, if we're fucking with Trey, I'm in. If it's anything bigger, thanks but no, thanks. I'm not trying to make waves."

I couldn't say any more without telling her why, and I could feel the beer in my veins, eager for friends. I couldn't risk it. I went to the minifridge and picked up the six-pack.

"Goodbye, Calamity," I said, tipping a nonexistent hat. "Thank you for the hospitality."

"What? You're not going to drink them with me?"

"See you at work," I said as I walked to the door.

"Listen," she said, and it might've been just the beer, but I swear she sounded disappointed. "I know you don't trust me, and you shouldn't. But you helped me out in a tight spot, and that's not something I'll forget. So if you do come up with a bigger plan for your life"—she looked at me as if every thought I'd ever had were written on my forehead, as if keeping secrets from her were the most pathetic thing she'd ever seen—"and you need my help, I'm here. No questions asked. As long as it doesn't interfere with my plan, of course."

"What if it does?" I asked, reaching for the doorknob.

"Well, then I'd have to kill you," she said.

This time, I was the one to put my hands up. "Too late," I said.

# MICKEY

**"GET UNDER THERE WITH** her, Mick!" Silas yelled, digital camera in hand. Mickey ducked under the WELCOME TO NEW HAMPSHIRE sign and gave a lopsided smile.

"Oh, come on, you can do better than that!"

"Let's jump on the count of three!" Ruth said, grabbing Mickey's hand and pulling her down to a crouch. On three, Mickey jumped and flailed, limbs everywhere, with Ruth's hand tightly in hers.

"Just like gazelles," Silas said.

"One more!" Ruth pleaded. "This time, let's be sexy." Ruth extended her arm and, a tiger with a pout, scratched at Silas as he held the camera back to his eye. Mickey froze, looking from her dad to Ruth, unsure if she should act like she'd never heard the word "sexy" in her life or if she should jump right in and copy her friend. And if she went with the second, she had no idea how to make her eyes look dangerous like that. Like those of a predator with soft fur.

"Come on, Mick!" Ruth cajoled, elbowing her. "Work that fine ass!" She slapped Mickey on the butt. Mickey rolled her eyes, frustrated by her father's stupid grin behind the camera. She cocked her hip and butted Ruth back.

"Yeah, just like that!" Ruth pushed Mickey forward so her hands landed on her knees, and swiveled her own body as if climbing onto Mickey, one hand on her waist and the other in the air, claws outstretched. The light caught the chipped red tips of her fingers, glistening like blood.

**"HOW CAN WE GET** these, Mr. Harrison?" Ruth asked when they were back in the car. "I want to post them! You're such a good photographer."

"I did minor in photography in college," Silas said.

"Jesus, Dad."

"Seriously, Mr. Harrison. These are so much better than the ones we take ourselves! You should think about doing it again. You know, professionally. I bet you'd be really good at it."

Mickey cringed, burning with embarrassment that her brother now knew she took selfies. He had his headphones on, but she couldn't hear the usual beat coming from them, high and fast like the heart of a small animal.

"Thank you, Ruth. You are quickly becoming my favorite child," Silas said, pointing into the rearview mirror to Mickey and wagging his finger.

The roads got thinner as the woods got thicker. The trees were long and lean and clustered so closely, Mickey thought of brush bristles. Their green was shared among them, a blur of growth and shadow. Mickey rolled down the window and pulled the pine scent into her. Ruth leaned over her lap.

"God, it smells like a real-life air freshener," she said, her eyes closed.

Silas laughed. "Fresh air will do that!"

"Just wait till you see the lake," Mickey said. "There are these little islands we can take the canoe out to; they are so cool."

"Is the water really cold?" Ruth asked.

"Not if you just jump right in," Silas answered.

"Do you like swimming, Ruth?" Lily asked. She had rolled down her window too. The air was working its magic on all of them.

"I love it, Mrs. Harrison. I was a lifeguard at the Y for a few summers, but I've never been in a lake. I can't wait!"

"Maybe we'll even get Mom in the water this year," Mickey said, laughing. Ruth leaned forward from the middle seat.

"You don't swim, Mrs. Harrison?"

"Mom wouldn't swim in that lake if I were drowning in it."

"Of course I would," Lily snapped.

"You've never gone in deeper than your knees!" Mickey retorted.

"Well, you've never been drowning."

"Pssh," Sean said, and Mickey jumped, remembering him. "I had to save her that one summer."

Mickey had forgotten about that.

Sean snuck into the canoe during Marco Polo. He glided past Mickey's blind, outstretched hands over and over, each of his "Polos" and hoots of laughter coming from an opposite direction. Mickey swam until her arms went rubbery, and then she kept swimming. She resisted the urge to cheat and open her eyes. If he was able to swim that fast, so could she.

But she couldn't.

When she finally opened her eyes, the shock of her distance from shore took the last of her energy straight out of her, as if her body decided to quit before it had to fail. She slipped under the water with zero dramatics, barely any splashing. She could hardly remember it now, except that her bathing suit had a ruffle, a mangy tutu that billowed out around her, like a tutu is supposed to. It had flowers on it, that bathing suit. She remembered that.

"You saved Mickey from drowning?" Ruth asked Sean, turning in her seat to look at him. "That's incredible!"

Sean shrugged, his color deepening.

"It was his fault in the first place."

She had been nine at the time. She remembered his arm around her chest, the way he kicked straight and hard for the shore. She remembered the way he held her up for air, even when doing so pushed him down.

"You must be a really strong swimmer," Ruth said. Then she did something so crazy, Silas almost swerved off the road. She threw one arm around Sean's neck and pulled his upper half into her, his sweatshirt fabric gripped in one hand and one of his headphones smooshed against her cheek.

"Mick might be ungrateful that you saved her, but I'm not!"

Ruth let go after one tight squeeze, and Mickey could feel her parents hold their breath, watching him. Mickey watched him too. As far as Mickey knew, no one had touched Sean like that in years. Certainly, none of the family. When they used to try, he made it clear they never should again.

"It was—I mean, whatever," he said, shrugging again and collapsing back against the car door, adjusting the neck of his sweatshirt. "She's my sister."

Mickey wanted to hug him then too. She couldn't remember the last time she wanted to hug her brother, but suddenly her arms ached with it. She wanted to bulldoze his walls the way Ruth did. Walls Mickey watched him build, brick by brick, until she couldn't see him at all. Walls that Ruth couldn't see, or didn't believe were real. Mickey had no idea that was an option, to simply not believe in them. She watched Lily put her hand on Silas's, and watched Silas pull her fingers in between his.

Maybe Ruth really was exactly what they needed that summer. Not just Mickey, but all of them.

# PEYOTE

**THE CALL CAME IN** before lunch. I'd spent the better half of the morning watching a father of four in Wales uncover his wife's affair. He'd gone through her phone for photos of the kids, but instead he found photos of her boss, tonsil-deep. The husband had just drunkenly hurled his wedding ring off a bridge when KQ opened her office door with a bang.

"Pey!" she barked. "Get in here!"

The man stumbled as the water, white rapids like bared teeth, swallowed his faith.

"Boss, I've got a Four on the line right now—he's just about to call; I know it."

"Give it to someone else. This is more important."

I gave my computer a longing glance before crossing into KQ's office and closing the door. But when I scanned her screen, I forgot all about my lonely Welshman.

Domestic hostage situation in Illinois. A man with an AK had forced his way into his girlfriend's apartment and was threatening to kill her, her two children, and himself. The police were already outside, the street blocked off with yellow tape. They were waiting for their negotiator, and from a distance they looked almost nonchalant, bored. Among them was the kids' father, who had gotten a frantic call from his daughter when the boyfriend unloaded a clip into their front door, but he hadn't been able to reach her since. Down the street lived the gunman's mother. As of now she was oblivious. But not for long.

KQ laughed and slapped the table.

"Ladies and gentlemen," she said to no one but me, "the bases are loaded."

**EVEN THOUGH I ARGUED** against it—going so far as to suggest Trey instead—KQ demanded that Cal be our Grand Slam third. So a few seconds later the three of us landed at the neighborhood playground, a bona fide Scooby Gang. The sky was ablaze with sun and flickering red and blue lights, reflecting off the windows and the metal bits that held the slide together. KQ was in the grass, head thrown back.

"Fuck, I love this air!" she yelled through loud, sloppy breaths.

"I'm going for the guy with the gun," I said, looking down at my tablet. "Jake Sutherland. Twenty-five. He hasn't killed anyone yet, so we can still make a deal. Cal, you could take either Mark Vernon—the kids' father—or Veronica Sutherland, Jake's mom. Preference?" Cal looked toward the three-family home, outside of which Mark paced, his movements quick and fierce. I could taste it in my throat—terror, and terror's favorite companion. Rage.

It made me hungry.

"I want the dad," Cal said, smiling the kind of smile of those who throw themselves out of airplanes for fun.

"Boss?"

"I can take Jake's mom," KQ said as she pushed herself up, but

79

I could feel how badly she didn't want to. I could feel both of them, their itching anticipation, their collective high on the sweet atmosphere. They could feel me too.

"All right, team," she said. "Don't forget—we need to get the same deal at the same time. If the dad wants Jake dead and Jake wants to headline Warped Tour, we've got nothing. Needs to be *exactly* the same. Pey, you're taking the lead on this. What's our deal?"

Cal looked at me with something like deference and maybe, if I were arrogant enough to believe it, admiration.

"Let's keep it simple," I said. "Parents on both sides are certainly going to wish this never happened, and I bet I can get Jake to agree. How about a Rewind?"

"Okay. Hop to it! If we pull this off, we can get a beer before we have to go back." KQ clapped once and disappeared. Cal gave me a thumbs-up and took off toward the house. I rolled my shoulders and closed my eyes.

I could hear him, Mr. Jake Sutherland. Not out loud, of course. I could hear him on the inside, asking for me.

Asking for someone, at least.

When I opened my eyes, I was in the hallway.

I don't remember much about my life on Earth. But every once in a while the ancient part of my brain still sticky with human sap will catch a scent and send me flying backward. This was one of those moments. The hallway was long and cool and dark, especially compared with the bright sunshine outside, and it smelled of darkness. The stale air was circulated over wood floors and faded wallpaper only by the whir of fans, turned up all the way at night. It was a disappointing smell, but a safe one. The smell of coming inside to do chores instead of playing with friends. Hints of dinnertime and sunscreen and Lemon Pledge, the things well-loved kids complain about.

Up ahead there was a bang, the butt of a gun against wood. Jake was pounding on the bathroom door.

"Rebecca, just talk to me!"

"Hello there, son," I said as I approached, my hands out. Of course, bullets couldn't touch me. But I was going for Trustworthy.

"Who the fuck are you?" Jake yelled. He was tall and pale, sweating in his black hoodie. He still looked like a kid. Not in the way his young hostages did—the ABCs way, the I-know-you-are-but-what-am-I? way—but he held his gun sideways like in the movies and wasn't much older than Sean.

"You prayed, didn't you? You asked for help? Well, here I am."

I kept my hands out and did a slow spin.

"That's impossible," he said, but his voice wavered.

"How else do you think I got in here? Got past the police? Who are gathering, by the way."

I closed my eyes and felt through the wall into the white-tiled bathroom. I could see them clinging to one another in the old claw-foot bathtub, the cloudy-looking shower curtain pulled across them. The room smelled like urine, and I could see the boy's pants were wet.

"Fuck, fuck this—fuck!" Jake yelled, and he shoved the muzzle of his gun deep into the fleshy underside of his jaw, pale like the soft part of a turtle. If he offed himself before I got to him, we would lose the whole deal.

"Jake," I said, taking another step. "You don't have to do that. I can fix this for you. That's why I'm here."

Jake slammed his fist into the wall. I could feel Rebecca's pulse surge through the door as if I held her neon heart in my fist.

"If she hadn't been such a fucking *cunt*—"

"Rebecca," I said. "Your girlfriend. You were about to celebrate one year together."

"How did you know that?" Jake snapped, pointing his gun at me. I fought the urge to roll my eyes. We didn't have time for this.

"I told you—I am here to help you. I know everything, Jake."

"So you know she fucking *dumped* me when I said I wanted to marry her? When I said the realest thing I've ever said to anyone, when I tore my goddamn heart out for her—she fucking dumped me, because she wants to 'work it out' with her rich ex. *To be more stable for the kids*, she said. Fuck that. She's nothing but a gold-digging whore."

From behind the bathroom door, a whimper pierced the silence.

"I know, Jake. But you didn't want it to go like this, did you?" I took another step toward him. "Let me fix it."

"Fix it how?" he asked, studying me.

"I can undo all of it. I can rewind time, Jake. And then I can make Rebecca love you, marry you, whatever you want."

"That's impossible. You're a fucking cop."

"You met Rebecca when you were on your first landscaping job. She was working at the plant nursery. She helped you choose the right plants—the ones you'd picked out would've died in that soil. The first thing you noticed about her was how the freckles exploded across her nose when she stepped into the sun. You used to go for girls your mom would call 'cheap,' but Rebecca was different. Even your mom agreed Rebecca was different that night she cooked you both lasagna, right?"

Jake fell back against the wall and took a ragged breath.

"Are you God?" he whispered.

"I'm here to save you."

It wasn't a lie. I was saving him from something.

"I'm not a bad person," he said. He waved the pistol as he talked and it hit the sleeve of a little raincoat hanging on the hook next to him. The raincoat had ducks on it.

"Of course not," I said.

"She's the one who— She won't marry me because I'm not a fancy lawyer. Because I don't make as much money as her ex. *That's* fucked up."

I felt outside of myself for Cal in the parking lot. She was talking to the kids' father. His terror and rage had become one simple annihilating feeling: desperation. He was ready. I sent my mind out farther and caught KQ in Jake's mother's kitchen. As KQ explained away the fine print, Veronica's eyes were as wide and deep as wells, frozen on the news coverage on TV.

It was closing time.

"Listen, Jake. We can sit here and talk religion if you want, but the police are getting ready to storm this place, and they aren't going to hesitate. You're holding a woman and two children hostage at gunpoint. The media is here. Your mother is watching the news coverage as we speak. You're not getting out of this. So you have three options, which will happen whether or not you decide to kill anyone. One: the cops kill you. Or, if by some miracle they don't shoot you on sight, they arrest you and send you to prison, where, I've been told, folks do not take kindly to people who hurt kids. Two: take that gun you've got there and kill yourself right now. And I do mean *right now*, because, like I said, time is of the essence."

Jake slumped farther down, snot running into his meager mustache.

"Or, Jake, we've got option number three. You accept my deal, and I erase all of this. Send you back in time, give you a redo. I can make you forget all about Rebecca, or I can make her love you so much she never talks to her ex, or anyone else, ever again. Whatever you want. I just need you to sign this and poof, you get a second chance."

I was next to him now, holding out my tablet. I had already scrolled to the bottom; all he had to do was click and sign. I could feel Cal's and KQ's deals coming to a crescendo the way you can feel a wave swell while standing in the ocean. The energy between us pulled and tightened. Despite what I wanted to think, we worked well together.

Jake was silent until he let out one sob, rough and broken like wood after a storm.

"I'm not a bad person," he said again as he took the tablet.

There was the crackle of a megaphone; the negotiator had finally arrived. Then I snapped my fingers and the whole thing disappeared.

**"SAY WHAT YOU WANT** about humans, but they certainly got this right," KQ said, shoving another mozzarella stick into the marinara sauce. We'd found a dive in town with blistered red booths and a deal on pitchers. Cal chugged her second glass of water and gestured to the waitress for another.

"To Pey, for leading a successful Grand Slam!"

"We did good work," I said, smiling despite myself and clinking my beer with hers. Our greasy fingers left smudges on our glasses.

"Did the guy give you any trouble?" KQ asked, as she licked sauce from her thumb.

I shrugged. "Not nearly as much as he could have."

"He'll fit right in Downstairs," Cal said. "Whenever he gets there."

"Which should be in just about . . . forty-five minutes."

"Bus?" KQ asked.

"Failed brakes," I said. "He should've paid more attention to that warning light."

KQ laughed, an unadulterated cackle that startled the couple in the booth across from us.

Cal squinted at KQ and me. "What are you talking about?"

"They aren't supposed to read the fine print, Squeaks. But you are," KQ said, a mozzarella stick between her teeth.

"There's never any guarantee that Rewinds will go the way they did the first time around," I said. "No matter how bad a day might seem, you take a risk that you'll get something even worse."

"Like getting hit by a bus," KQ said.

"Or driving with faulty brakes," I answered.

The waitress dropped off another water at the table for Cal. I took a sip of beer, reveling in the combination of salt and fat and bubbles. Everything is flat in Hell. Cal finished the water in seconds.

"What's up with all the hydration?" I asked. "You know we have water in Hell, right?"

Cal wiped her mouth, looking embarrassed. "It's just better here."

"I've gotta pinch one out," KQ said, slamming down her empty glass. "Be ready to go when I get back."

"Can I ask you a question?" I asked Cal once KQ was gone. "Why pick the kids' dad over Jake's mom? That was the hardest one."

"Hard how?"

"Eternal damnation for wanting your kids not to be shot—it's just a tough gig, is all."

"If you think about it like that, sure," she said, but her eyebrows were higher than the Downstairs's electricity allowance.

"How do you think about it?"

Cal sighed. "You're talking like one of them," she said, and nodded toward the group across from us, who had kept their eyes down since KQ's descriptive announcement. "Like a human."

I opened my mouth, but she went on.

"You're thinking of it as a morality issue, but morality isn't our framework anymore. It's like when you learn a card game—let's say Go Fish. That's all you play until someone says, *Hey, you know what else you can do with those?* And they teach you a brand-new game. A faster, more fun game. Same tools, different rules. We've outgrown morality, Pey. I mean, technically, we failed it. But either way, we are onto the next game."

She was right. My skin burned with it, how right she was. I felt like the neighborhood kid who still used training wheels. I felt like a goddamn joke. I met her eyes for one second, and she saw it.

"Wait—" she said, cocking her head. "You didn't think you were . . . what? 'Doing the right thing'?"

KQ returned and rapped the table with her knuckles, knocking the patronizing look off Cal's face.

"What'd I miss?"

"Nothing," I said.

"Then let's blow this Popsicle stand!"

She flicked her wrist, freezing the scene around us, and lifted the man's wallet off the other table. She took out a twenty and slapped it down on the table. Then she swirled her finger through the dregs of the marinara sauce, popped it into her mouth, and waved her free hand to restart it all.

When I stood up to follow, Cal grabbed my arm.

"You're not human anymore," she said, her face so close I could smell her Chapstick. "These aren't your people. We are. The sooner you figure that out the better."

Then KQ tapped a button on her tablet and the world went blank.

# LILY

THE KIDS TOOK OFF as soon as Silas pulled to a stop in the gravel driveway. Mickey and Ruth sprinted to the dock, shrieking with laughter. Lily watched Sean hesitate, watching them, before shouldering his backpack and knocking his way through the screen door, which slammed with the specific sound a screen door makes. The slowness of summer hit Lily like a lead blanket.

It was going to be a long six weeks.

The house smelled the way it always smelled, as if the air from the past summer had caught between its walls, a perfect artifact. It smelled like mothballs and sunscreen and the faintest hint of rot from the spare room with the leak in the roof. Like evening sunshine, and gin and tonics, and woodsmoke. It smelled exactly the same as it did when they were sixteen and Silas brought her there for the very first time.

Lily swallowed and pushed the memory from her mind.

"So, what do you think of her?" Silas asked, dropping bags of groceries on the kitchen counter and crouching behind the fridge to plug it in.

"Of whom?" Lily asked, sorting fruit.

"Ruth."

Silas stood up and wiped his hands on his jeans. The old refrigerator coughed and sputtered into its usual hum.

Lily opened the cabinets, blew dust from the liners.

"I'm sure she's just fine."

"You know, Lil," Silas said, putting his hands around her waist, "she reminds me of someone."

Lily took the affection without giving any back.

"Who's that?"

"Headstrong, smart, energetic. Unafraid of new people, new places. Sassy."

He pulled her back against him, kissing her earlobe. Just a brush of his lips, more of an exhale against her skin than anything else. "I seem to remember bringing another girl like that here not too long ago."

Lily pushed out a laugh. "If you're talking about me, your timing is way off. And if you're talking about someone else, you should remember your audience."

Silas stepped back.

"Of course I was talking about you."

"Well then, you should check a calendar, because it's been a bit longer than not too long ago." Lily closed the fridge. "I'm going to make up the kids' rooms." She gave her husband a quick kiss and headed for the stairs.

The New Hampshire house looked large from the outside, but it was tight and narrow inside. The bedrooms were all connected to the main hallway, some with their own bathrooms, some with steps or doors that opened into other bedrooms, other, smaller staircases. It was a labyrinth of hand-stitched quilts and cool-toned walls, windows with frayed rope and painted sills that got sticky in humidity. The wood planks of the floor were three times the width of their linoleum counterparts at home, laid down back when nature was plump and ripe for the picking. The ceilings upstairs were low enough that Silas could touch them with his head if he stood on his toes. Lily had always found the old-world feel charming, but now it was suffocating. She opened the windows in Mickey's room and pushed apart the curtains, letting in the summer air, slow and lazy. She would need to put a fan in there if Mickey and Ruth were going to get any sleep. She made the bed, a double that would hopefully be big enough for the two girls. There were enough rooms in the house that Mickey and Ruth didn't have to share, but when Lily mentioned that, Mickey said that they *obviously* would anyway with such vehemence Lily didn't argue. The truth was, Lily didn't know what to expect. She didn't know what Mickey was like for that long around a friend. Mickey had always been a quiet kid, drawn inward. Silas and Lily never went hangdog to a parent-teacher conference on her behalf, the way they had many times for Sean. But Mickey had also never listened to someone the way she listened to Ruth. Like a believer.

Lily could hear splashes and laughter but couldn't see the girls out beyond the boathouse. The lawn between them was thick, green, and lovely, a demonstration of the word "alive." The grass under the bird feeders was already padded flat by the bunnies that nibbled there in the early mornings. Lily made a mental note to refill the feeders. She took her time with the girls' pillowcases and, lingering over the corners, pulling and tightening, smoothed down one of the quilts Silas's mother had made. Mickey wouldn't care; she wouldn't even notice. But Lily liked making things nice for her daughter. She liked the idea of her sleeping on a pillowcase Lily had touched.

Lily next stopped in front of Sean's door, which had once been

Silas's door. She could hear Sean on the other side, his phone making the sounds of some game he played constantly but refused to explain to her.

"Knock, knock."

"What?"

"I'm going to make the bed," she said as she moved Sean's backpack to the floor. "Don't bite my head off."

Sean rolled his eyes and put his headphones on. He had his phone in one hand and in the other his pocketknife, the one Silas had given him a few years before. It had belonged to Philip. Sean clicked it open and closed against his jeans over and over, and Lily was happy she'd made the "Only in New Hampshire" rule.

She snapped open the fitted sheet and lifted the mattress.

Despite everything that had happened, this was still her favorite room. The walls were dark blue, with faded patches where Silas used to keep posters of football players and a *Playboy* model in a schoolgirl costume with the words *Study Hard*. In a corner Silas's old TV set still hunkered, the bulky kind with the built-in VHS player, to the back of which he would tape twisted sandwich bags of pot. The first time Lily ever got high was in that bedroom, out of a bong Silas made from a honey bottle shaped like a bear. She remembered the way colors got brighter and the katydids got louder, singing in individual tones instead of their usual collective sound. She felt so connected to everything that night, including Silas. He taught her how to put her mouth on the bear and hold the smoke in even when it burned, and how to blow it out the window through a toilet paper roll capped with a dryer sheet. He was always teaching her things, back then. How to hold a tennis racket. How to understand Faulkner. Even how her own body worked, how touch could bring to the surface parts of her she hadn't known. At sixteen, he was the brightest person she had ever met. Not just smart, but white-hot bright. A star. The whole school knew Silas Harrison. The kid who could throw a football fast enough to blow off your hat the same day he aced a history test. The kid who called other kids' parents "Mr. and Mrs.," who remembered things about them and asked after them later. Lily's mother was over the moon when Silas called to ask her out. *Silas Harrison, Lillian! Lucky girl! Better skip dessert tonight, dear.*

If he hadn't been Silas Harrison, Lily wouldn't have been allowed to go that summer. Anyone else and her mother would've said, *Absolutely not, sixteen-year-old only daughter of mine. You cannot spend weeks on end with your boyfriend in his summerhouse.* But because it was Silas Harrison, Lily's mother practically packed her bag for her. She looked at Silas and saw Lily's future. But who could blame her? Lily did the same exact thing.

At sixteen, Silas Harrison had the kind of smile girls could build a future on.

# PEYOTE

**"AT THE RISK OF** sounding moony, I had fun today," Cal said as she lingered in my cubicle, her jacket over one arm.

I swallowed. "Ditto."

I wanted to celebrate. I wanted to go out and get a drink, have a few laughs. But as much as I wanted that, I knew I couldn't have it with her. Cal had flat out told me she came from the Downstairs, for Darkness' sake. You have to make some extremely poor choices above ground to get sent to the Downstairs right off the bat. And to work her way up to Fifth . . . there was no denying she was dangerous. Any other time, I would've been bored enough to welcome some danger. But not now. Not this close to my goal.

"I have to admit," Cal said, fingering the hem of her jacket, "we work well together."

I shrugged.

"Come on, Pey. You have to admit that."

"I don't have to do anything," I said as I clicked off my computer and began gathering my things. I hoped she would get the point, but instead, she slid into my cubicle and sat on my desk. I moved around her, straightening files, filling my pencil case.

"Come on, quit being such a pussy!"

She said it loudly enough that I heard a pause in the keyboard clacking of my neighbors. I grabbed her wrist and pulled her down below the divider.

"What do you want from me?" I hissed, my face close enough for me to see where her eyelashes clumped together in the corner of one eye, moving as one under my breath. "You're a nutjob, and I don't want to be friends with you. So whatever game you're playing, stop. We worked together today because KQ made us. It wasn't particularly good or bad, all right? It was a job. Get over it."

I let go of her wrist, but she kept her hand clasped over mine, holding it there.

"If you keep talking to me like that, I'm going to start to want you."

I huffed and yanked my arm free.

"Look, I admit it. The Honey Pot stunt was stupid. No one regrets that more than me. Just think of all of the things I could've gotten out of you if you still thought I was some lost little mouse? It was a poor decision on my part, and I think I might be the first person to ever do this, but I blame alcohol."

I laughed but covered it with my hand like a cough.

"Please don't make me hang out with anyone else in this shit-box tonight. I'm begging you."

Most of the smells in Hell are very unpleasant. People smell like old coffee and plaque, sweat covered in perfume. But Cal smelled like soap. Just soap. I'm sure it doesn't sound like much to you with your gorged senses, but to me it was perfect.

I shook my head.

"I'll see you tomorrow," I said, and I walked past her.

I'd like to think I was in love at some point on Earth. I must've been, right? I don't remember a thing about it. But I've seen people sign the craziest deals while high on that homemade drug. I had one kid who sold his soul so a girl in his tenth-grade class would ask him to a Sadie Hawkins dance. He could've asked for her to strip naked every time he came into the room. He could've asked for her to fall to her knees and beg him to let her carry his child, or whatever it is that humans in love want to hear most. But, nope. He just wanted her to ask him to a dance. When I go Downstairs, sometimes I think about that kid; if it was worth it. The romantic answer is yes, of course. *Anything for a single moment of her hand in mine.* But even after just one day Downstairs, no one answers like that. After just one hour, most people would serve their beloved on a silver platter, lobster forks and bibs for all. Love is all-powerful, until you learn firsthand what happens when a vegetable peeler meets the far-back surface of your tongue.

# MICKEY

**THE PAST COUPLE OF** years of Mickey's life, magic seemed to be going extinct. Games of make-believe, movies she could watch over and over without getting bored, all of the ways she used to explore outside her own little existence—they had all faded, cheapened, like turning the lights on in a movie theater. So as they drove down the familiar highways, she worried the New Hampshire house would also lose its magic. That it would feel different, less than. She worried about what Ruth would think. But then they arrived, and the weight of worry rose off her.

She knew it for sure when she saw Ruth's face as they took the bend in the gravel driveway and the house came into full view for the first time. The white wooden clapboards with black shutters, the long green lawn unfurling into the lake. The battered wood of the boathouse, a dark blue gone light gray. The way the water sloshed against the concrete of the dock. Ruth saw it all exactly as Mickey saw it, as Mickey had always seen it.

Regardless of whatever happened in the outside world, magic made its home here.

"How far does your property go?" Ruth asked after she and Mickey rushed from the freezing water to the sand, sunbaked and crispy on the top. She flipped her head over and wrapped one of their worn beach towels around her hair, twisting it. Mickey fell headlong into her own outstretched towel and rolled over onto her back, sun from the sky and the sand warming her all over.

"I can show you!" Mickey said, looking toward the woods between her house and the Watersons', where the lawn went from cropped green grass to underbrush. She didn't fully realize how much she had worried about Ruth's seal of approval until she received it. Now her heart thumped with pride.

Ruth dropped her towel back in the sand.

"Lead the way!"

The woods were as untamed as always, and Mickey regretted not putting on her flip-flops. The path was still there, but branches weaved under the fallen leaves in unknowable places, unpredictable patterns. She stepped quickly but with caution, picking her way down a hill. Ruth followed.

"Mick, this is seriously so beautiful."

Ruth had used the word many times since they arrived. She said it about the lake, and the view of the house from the wooden float off the dock. She said it about the sand and the grass and the way the tied-up canoe slapped the surface of the water.

"Come on," Mickey said, stepping over a fallen log.

The woods opened up to a small clearing. Instead of being all sand like the little man-made beach next to the boathouse, this clearing was mostly trampled grass and the mulch of old leaves. There were exposed roots and flat stones perfect for skipping. A small slope like a dirt tongue extended into the water, which made quiet sounds as it met and remet the earth.

"This is so cool!" Ruth said, spinning in a circle, her arms out and her eyes directed up at the treetops. In the middle of the clearing there was a firepit, sloppily made but resilient. Stones encircled a pile of wet pine needles and old ash like sediment.

"Did you and Sean make this?"

"My dad did," Mickey said. "With my uncle, when they were our age."

Ruth squatted over the firepit. She lifted up a curled strip of aluminum, a piece of a crushed beer can burned beyond brand recognition.

"Your dad is kind of a badass, isn't he?" Ruth asked, the aluminum glinting in the light of the low-hanging sun. "Or at least he was, in high school."

Mickey laughed. She ran her finger over a rock from the shore, examining it.

"He definitely was," Ruth went on. "He's a total babe."

"Gross!" Mickey shouted, kicking shallow water toward Ruth.

"I'm just saying, with those eyes and those arms, I bet he slayed."

"That's when he met my mom." Mickey threw the stone in Ruth's direction, missing on purpose. "High school."

"No way!" Ruth said.

"They started dating junior year. She came up here with him that summer, and every summer since."

"I would love to hear those stories! I bet they had some crazy parties down here."

"My dad would love to tell them. He's addicted to the glory days."

"God," Ruth said as she threw an arm over Mickey's shoulder. "Promise me our lives will get better than high school."

When she looked at Ruth, Mickey thought that for the first time in her life she understood why they called them "glory days." Why this time would be something to relish. Something she would never forget.

"Obviously," she lied.

Ruth turned around and looked at the firepit.

"Can we use this?"

Mickey shrugged, looking for another smooth rock.

"We've made s'mores down here a few times."

"That's adorable."

Mickey's face flushed, but she wasn't exactly sure why.

"Does your uncle use the house too?"

Mickey's lip went to her teeth. Her parents never told her not to talk about Uncle Phil, but somewhere along the way, she learned his name came with electricity. It made her parents jump—just a little jolt before they recovered, but it was enough to cause her to develop her own reaction. Eventually, it was enough to make her sidestep his name—the whole idea of him—entirely.

"No," Mickey answered.

"Why not?"

Mickey kicked at a pile of leaves and inspected its wet underbelly.

"He's dead," she said. "He died in prison."

It was the truth, and beyond the bare-boned facts of what happened that night all those years ago, it was about all she knew.

"Damn!" Ruth said, her eyes wide. "What'd he do? Did he kill someone?"

Mickey swallowed. "Yeah, actually. But my dad says it was by accident."

"No way." She took a step closer to Mickey and hit her on the arm. "Tell me everything!"

"It was in high school. Dad always said he was kind of a weird kid—like, a sensitive, artsy type. He had a motorcycle—it's still here, in the shed—and made my grandparents totally crazy. When he was a senior, there was some accident and a girl died. He didn't mean to kill her, but it was his fault, I guess."

Mickey had never told anyone about Uncle Phil, but she saw

Ruth's attention as if it were physical, a cord floating free around her, and she had never wanted to hold on to anything so badly in her life.

"That's crazy," Ruth said. "That's so crazy."

"Yeah, we don't talk about it."

Ruth nodded. But then she yawned, her eyes squeezed shut like a cat's.

"It happened here."

That Mickey knew she wasn't supposed to share. Her parents didn't even know she knew that, but Sean had told her. It was a few years ago, on one of the nights when they made s'mores around the firepit. After they had packed up the marshmallows and graham crackers, Mickey tripped over her flip-flop and stepped straight out of it. Sean picked it up, grinning. Then he leaned in close and whispered, *This is where Uncle Philip killed that girl,* and ran away with her shoe, moonlight reflecting off his basketball shorts. Mickey froze right in that spot. She couldn't move an inch. It was dark, and so much darker when she was alone. She stayed there, shaking and crying, until her dad noticed she wasn't with them and came back for her. But no matter how many times Silas asked her what Sean had said to make her so scared, she never told. She knew instinctively, even then, that seeing her dad's reaction would be so much worse than experiencing her own. He died before she was born, but she was nevertheless raised under Uncle Phil's weight, the space in which he should've lived occupied, instead, by her father's bone-dense grief.

"Here?" Ruth asked, and she wrapped her arms around herself, despite the thick heat of the New England summer.

Mickey nodded. She felt guilty, using her uncle like that. But Ruth's yawn had hurt like a slap. She needed Ruth's eyes back.

"That's crazy," Ruth said. But she didn't look like Mickey did when she learned it. Ruth was grinning.

# PEYOTE

**I THINK IT'S TIME** that I tell you what I'm actually working on.

This might not come as a huge surprise, but I wasn't born Peyote Trip. Same with Calamity and KQ and everyone else. When a newb arrives in Hell, that lucky winner gets a new identity, stupid name and all. The idea is to strip us of our humanity. We have no use for that here.

Everybody starts off remembering their real name. I don't know how it goes for the folks on the conveyor belts, but for the rest of us, repeating our real names becomes our version of prayer. Even so, with so much time and distance, we forget. Eventually, we all become whatever name we were given.

I would have done the same, if it hadn't been for Slippery Pete.

Slippery Pete was my bunkmate on the Second Floor. He was a veteran Second-Floor man, and proud of it. He must've been a butcher topside, or maybe a serial killer. He knew about pressure points and how to snap a joint unlike anyone else I've ever seen. He seemed to like the Second Floor, as much as anyone could. It was honest work by Hell standards, and he was good at it.

I got lucky with Slippery Pete. Other people's bunkmates would bring their work home with them. I heard stories on the factory line, and screams in the nearby bunks, followed by whimpers followed by the kind of muffled silence that is worse than all the rest. Slippery Pete looked like he could be that type: as big as a house, skin blistered from fire and callused. His fist was the size of my neck. But despite appearances, Slips was one of the good ones. He worked himself ragged on the job and had no torture left in him by quitting time.

It was a century or two into my stint on the Second Floor. I still remembered some details of my life above ground then, chanting, on the top bunk as Slips snored like an angry bull beneath me, the words I've long since lost. Slips never said his own memory prayers, never threw out his own cut anchors. He must've heard me, night after night, but he never said anything.

Not until the night he told me about the loophole.

That day had been a particularly tough one. We spent the whole afternoon practicing organ removal and consumption, à la father-on-a-porch-with-his-shotgun: *If you hurt a hair on her head, I'm going to pull out your heart and make you eat it.* Needless to say, we had to get our hands dirty. Slips worked deftly and silently, as he always did. His rhythmic breathing, a metronome under the screams, stilled my own. That was, until he suddenly stopped.

The Downstairser on the belt was a woman, no older than forty. Not to be a traitor to my sex, but we didn't see a lot of women come across our factory line. The Downstairs is a bit of a boys' club. So even before Slippery Pete's breathing caught in his throat she stood out, staying his never-before-stayed hand.

A pause on the factory line was unacceptable. We had a lot of people to torture. But Slippery Pete wouldn't budge. He just stared at her, the braided ship ropes of muscle in his arms tense under a rubber apron. I saw someone look up and down the line, which led to another glance, and then another. The overseer would be next. No one wanted his attention.

"Slips," I said, just loud enough to be heard over the wails and slosh.

Nothing.

The woman had the look we saw on any Downstairser who wasn't on his or her first tour, when fear and pain lose their sparkle. Happiness and the affiliated feelings are always the first to go. Then, after quite a while, anger. By the time a person loses fear and pain, they're nothing more than breathing meat. I remember her hair was long and black. It looked like she had once kept it very soft.

I looked back up at the overseer, who had noticed the holdup. Second-Floor workers had been sent Downstairs for less. He would be on Slips soon.

I did something then that I was sure I would regret, but it turned out to be the best decision I ever made as Peyote Trip. I left my post and pushed myself in front of Slips, who stepped backward without saying a word. I heard murmurs of confusion from the workers next to me and the unmistakable tap-tap-tap of the overseer's steel-toed boots. I hunched down in front of Slips's monumental weight, took the bread knife from his fist, and did what had to be done, before hitting the buzzer to send the woman down the belt to me.

"Snap out of it," I hissed as I sidestepped toward my position and readied my pliers. "Incoming."

Slippery Pete shook his head and stepped back up to his post. He didn't blink once before plunging the knife into the next in line.

That night, after they turned out the lights and we fell, bone-and-innards weary, onto our regulation mattresses, Slippery Pete spoke to me for the first time.

"Why did you do that?"

I was already almost asleep.

"You were going to get busted," I said.

"Yeah, but why did you do it? You could've gotten busted too for stepping off the line."

I sighed. I didn't know why I did it, honestly. Except that for some reason I couldn't not.

"I suppose I didn't want to roll the dice with a new bunkmate," I said.

Slips was quiet for long enough that I thought we were done. I closed my eyes again.

"She looked just like my daughter."

I exhaled. "Fuck."

I found myself jealous that he could still remember anyone's face. But on the other hand, it was proof that forgetting could be a blessing.

"So you remember her?" I asked. "Your daughter?"

Slips took his time answering, a habit I learned during our time together was not about disdain but rather about the sheer effort of thinking, a skill he had lost the use for long before.

"I remember enough," he said finally.

"How? I'm forgetting by the minute."

I heard Slips shifting on his mattress. He lowered his voice even though we were alone.

"I have a list of facts, memories. The really simple ones. And that list is the one thing I think about."

"I'm doing that too. But it's slipping anyway."

"I mean, it's the *only* thing I think about. The absolute only thing. When I'm on the line, when I'm eating, when I'm lying here. The list. That's it. Nothing else."

Even at that point in my time on the Second Floor, I'd heard the rumors about Slippery Pete. How he passed up transfers, promotions. He had been there longer than anyone, and had never said a word. To learn a new skill would require new thought. To move up would mean to move on.

He took his Hell, but he wouldn't give up his humanity.

"If you have to hold on to just one thing," he said, "remember your last name."

I rolled over, lowering my voice like his.

"Why? I'd much rather remember people—"

"You're not going to stay down here like me," he said. "You'll move up, sooner rather than later. And if you keep moving up, you'll get to the Fifth Floor."

I had heard about the Fifth Floor. Private studio apartments, multiple eateries. A salary of some kind. I caught the scent of stomach acid under my fingernails and thought the Fifth Floor sounded like Heaven. Or close enough.

"If you can remember your last name, you can get out of here."

"The Second Floor?"

"No," Slips said. The conversation was hard for him. I could hear it in his pauses. I wondered what details of his list he was sacrificing as he spoke to me. Whose scent he had just lost.

"Out of Hell."

I thought I'd misheard him. This was Hell. The lack of an exit was paramount to the brand.

"That's impossible."

"Just remember your last name," he said, before his heavy breathing gave way to heavier snores.

I rolled onto my back again and stared at the ceiling, unable to sleep. After endless kvetching, begging, and groveling on my knees, I had accepted my fate. I was in Hell, and there was nothing I could do about it. But now I saw a sliver of light through a pad-locked door. Once I saw it, I could never unsee it. I could never go back to acceptance.

Maybe there was a way out.

I closed my eyes and took a deep breath, pulling up the memories that faded like dreams with the morning news.

I clasped my hands together.

"Harrison," I whispered.

# PART II

# LILY

AT SEVENTEEN, LILY WAS a stranger to forgetting. She was too young
for it to creep in uninvited, and things were good enough that she
had yet to invite it. On the contrary, at that age, Lily wanted to
remember everything. She'd be at a sleepover with her friends or
on the school lawn with Silas as he kissed her neck, and she'd take
a mental snapshot, telling herself, *You'll want to remember this.* It
started with something her mother used to say as she leaned
against the doorframe of Lily's bedroom, watching her get ready
for bed. *You should enjoy this body of yours, Lillian. Before you know
it, it will all be gone.*

Of course, she didn't actually mean Lily should enjoy her
body—as in delight in all of the pain and pleasure from each slippery little inch. Rather, she meant Lily should take full advantage
of the power a young woman's body gave her, because when it was
gone, she would be nothing.

It wasn't until she got the news that Philip had killed himself in his cell while she was picking out wedding flowers that
seventeen-year-old Lily made her first conscious effort to forget.

Once she got that call, she took to forgetting like everything else she had set out to accomplish: utterly, and with teeth. In fact, she forgot so well over the years that when she first saw Gavin in the frozen-food section of Market Basket, she didn't recognize him.

## "LILY THOMPSON?"

Lily stopped her cart and swept her new bangs from her face—an ill attempt at keeping up with the trends that her hairdresser pushed on her, along with free wine and compliments.

"What?"

"Lily Thompson, Sweeney High?"

Lily crumpled her shopping list in her fist and smiled at him. He looked familiar, but only in the way the whole town looked familiar: white skin and whiter shirt collars.

"Yup, you got me," she said, checking the yogurt selection. Mickey was flirting with veganism after watching a documentary in health class, but Sean still loved the yogurt with the separate pouch for candy or crunch.

"You probably don't remember me," he said. "I didn't go to Sweeney, but my sister did. Sarah."

"Oh really?" Lily asked, flicking her eyes, briefly, to his face. "Sarah who?"

When she looked back, it was in that moment—the moment she actually took the necessary second to look at his face, her mind on nothing but how to keep the dairy products cold when she knew she still had bakery and produce to go—that the first of her ancient memory blockades formed its inaugural crack.

She could see his sister in his features. His long face, thick hair, something in the eyes that seemed to suggest she wasn't in on a joke. He was older now than she had been, of course. His life had allowed him that. Gray started at his temples and fanned out, an army with a plan.

She remembered him. Or, rather, even after so many years of trying to forget, she remembered her. Sarah.

"Gavin," she said, her hand back in her bangs. "Of course."

"How have you been?" he asked, his slate eyes holding hers. She was surprised to see no blame in them.

"Fine," she answered, glancing away. Not because she was distracted, but because, for the first time in a very long time, she wasn't. "Good. I mean, I have two beautiful children, and Silas is—" She froze.

"How old are your kids?" Gavin asked.

"Sean is almost seventeen, and Mickey is thirteen. What about you? Do you have kids?"

"I have a daughter," he said, "Melanie. She's four." He reached into his pocket and pulled out a worn leather wallet. Lily could make out a photograph of a young girl through a hazy plastic sleeve, and she smiled appropriately.

"She's beautiful."

"Thanks," Gavin said, snapping the wallet closed. "I like her. I only get her on the weekends nowadays, though."

"Oh," Lily said, and she surprised herself by putting her hand on his wrist, where it lay against the handle of the shopping cart. "I'm sorry to hear that."

"You're doing a lot of apologizing for a grocery store encounter with a stranger."

Lily laughed. "Sorry, I—"

Then they both laughed, and she fell the-first-few-percent in love with him. It felt so much like panic that she could barely tell the difference at the time, but when he asked her six months later when she first knew, that was it. The first time she touched his skin, the first time she watched him inhale, easily, when she made him laugh.

"Listen, I don't want to overstep, but I'm in this group at Eaglewood Presbyterian, for grief. And we're doing a kind of memorial next weekend, for the anniversary. We do it every year. I'd love to have you there, if you'd want to come."

Lily blinked, her eyeballs suddenly hot.

"Oh, I don't know if that would be—"

"I won't tell them who you are if you don't."

Lily had been beautiful her whole life, and therefore no one thought to care about the strength of her character. All they did was tell her to be grateful for the beauty, as if they already pitied her for who she would be—what she would have left—if she came to outlive it. So when Gavin asked for something else, she felt the starved rest of her rise, grateful for the challenge.

"Okay," she said. "I'll think about it."

Gavin reached into his pocket, furrowing his brow. Later, Lily would tease him for that concentration face of his. She would use two fingers to smooth the wrinkle between his eyebrows when he ordered room service or lost his way around construction. But in that moment, everything he did was new.

"Here's my card," he said, handing her a worn slip of paper. "It would mean a lot if you came."

Lily took it warily. It had been the better part of two decades since the media had pounded at their door, but she hadn't forgotten the feeling of being used for a story.

"Not because you're Silas Harrison's wife," Gavin said, as if she spoke it. "Just because you knew Sarah."

Lily couldn't help but notice how much his smile looked like hers.

"It was good to see you again," Gavin said, running a hand

through his hair. "Damn, *the* Lily Thompson. Tenth-grade me would be freaking out right now."

"Oh, stop; we're all grown up."

"Doesn't make you any less *the* Lily Thompson."

It wasn't until she'd loaded the groceries in the back seat and strapped herself into the front, her heart still pounding, that she realized she should've corrected him. She was Lily Harrison now. She hadn't been Lily Thompson in a long time.

# PEYOTE

**I WENT A WEEK** without talking to Cal, and things started to feel the way they had before I met her. Normal. Predictable. It felt good, having her out of my life. Like removing a splinter.

Then KQ called me into her office.

"Yo, Peyo!" she hollered when I knocked on her door, as if she hadn't just summoned me.

"What's up, boss?"

"Come in; sit down. I have a proposition for you."

I closed the door and pulled out the chair across from her. She was excavating her mouth with a toothpick, and some unknowable mass from between her teeth hit me on the cheek. I winced.

"I've noticed the work you've been putting in, Pey. Slow but steady wins the race, right?" She laughed, and I managed to laugh with her. "No, but seriously, you've got a great record here. A mostly great record. A passable record, Mr. Trip."

"Thanks, boss."

"It's time you take on more responsibility."

KQ widened her jaw, reaching for her back molars. Her tongue curled and pushed against her teeth, undulating with every flick of her wrist like a blind creature from the deepest part of the ocean. I looked away.

"That sounds good."

"Look, I know that we are not known for our teamwork here. But the truth is, our success is judged by our whole floor. If we don't succeed as a team, we don't succeed at all." She threw the toothpick at the garbage next to her desk. It landed on the floor.

"Sure," I said.

"So I want you to be a coach. And I don't mean Little League; I mean ice-skating. The ones who take sad little girls and starve and torture them into fucking magical ice ballerinas."

I stared at her. I even looked behind me, as if she were talking to someone else.

"You want me to . . . teach people?" I asked when I found the office door still closed and the two of us alone.

"Well, I would rather think of it as bullying people, but sure. Whatever gets results."

I had absolutely no interest in taking time out of my day to teach anyone how to do anything. I had one goal and one goal only: to get my fifth Harrison and complete the set. Everyone else could burn, for all I cared.

"I don't expect you to do this out of the goodness of your heart, Pey," KQ said, as if reading my mind. "I'm willing to make you an offer to sweeten the pot."

"What's that?"

"Access to the Sixth Floor."

That got my attention.

"You won't live there, obviously," KQ said as she swung her feet off the desk. "But I can give you a limited-access elevator pass, so you can use their amenities. And trust me, Pey. You want to use their amenities."

I swallowed. The Sixth Floor was the highest floor in all of Hell. It didn't get better than that without crossing into Earth's delicious atmosphere. Not only that, but the Sixth Floor had one thing even Earth didn't have, and my plan was impossible without it.

The Looking Glass.

"Okay," I said. "Yeah. I'll do it. Thank you." I smiled and reached across KQ's desk and took her hand, forgetting the toothpick and all of the repulsive things I'd seen her do with it.

"Fantastic. Here is your first target. Student. Whatever. I need you to be with them every second you can be. On your calls, at your meetings—take them into the bathroom if you do anything impressive in there. Teach them whatever you've got. Ride them as hard as you want; I won't do much monitoring. But if they don't start meeting the marks, your ass will be on the line."

She handed me a manila file. There was a paper clip on the front, which held a small card. The elevator pass. I grazed the smooth surface with my fingertip and had the urge to pull it to my lips. I fought it, instead slipping the card into my ID lanyard.

"Don't fuck it up."

As soon as I'd walked out of KQ's office, I opened the manila folder.

I should've seen it coming. I bet you did.

*Calamity Ganon.*

I turned around, about to bang on KQ's door again. About to point out that Cal wasn't bad; she was just new. About to say whatever I had to say to get her away from me. But then I remembered KQ's words. I could do whatever I wanted to get results. I would be the one in charge. I sat down at my cubicle and flipped open the folder again.

Plus, now I had her file.

# SILAS

**SILAS FELT HIS KNEES** crack when he crouched down to the liquor cabinet to brush the winter's dust off the gin bottle's neck. He would need to get more later that week. He stood back up, extending his leg a few times and listening for the pop. He had noticed his bones more lately, the way they sizzled and snagged on one another. He wasn't an old man yet, not nearly. But his body had more to say than it ever had before, and he didn't quite know how to listen. He poured heavy and pushed the bottle back onto the shelf. His fingers were sticky with lime juice, freshly squeezed. He used the bottled stuff at home, but not in New Hampshire. This house was about taking the time to do things right. He watched the tonic fizz over the ice and pulled open the screen door onto the porch, then took a seat on the deep lounger that overlooked the yard out to the lake.

He'd heard the girls out on the water earlier, but now the yard was silent. As silent as it ever got here, which was way less silent than their suburban neighborhood back home. This house had always been drenched in the sounds of life, wild in all its forms except for human. Right now, in the thick golden light, Silas could hear the sounds of the katydids rise and fall. If he closed his eyes, he could mistake their rhythm for his own breath, the way their noise overtook everything else until it was inside him. Silas sighed and took a sip of his drink.

This house was his favorite place on Earth. It was his home, in the truest sense. No matter what was happening in the Harrison family, they came here every summer. Silas could walk through the halls and point to each stain on the wallpaper, each dent in the screens, and tell its story. When his children were little and interested in him above all else, he would do exactly that. He could still remember the way they would ask for more, always more. It had been a while since either of his children had asked him for anything of his, other than his wallet. Of course, being back at the New Hampshire house was bittersweet. Every inch of that house held atoms of his brother, cells from his skin or his breath. Silas looked at the driveway, at the motorcycle he had wheeled out earlier from its tomb in the shed. Silas took out Philip's bike every summer, first thing. He loved the process of caring for it, washing away the winter of neglect with gentle coos like it was a missing pet that had just come home. In those moments, Silas could pretend he could wash the time back.

When his mother was still alive, she couldn't stand the bike. She couldn't stand seeing any of Philip's things, and it was the only fight they ever had. Silas hated how she changed Philip's room into an art studio just a few weeks after he died, as if his grunge posters and blackout shades had never existed. As if he had never slept there until well past noon, awaking only to Silas's persistent knocking, begging him to come outside and throw the ball or take him for a ride. His mother wouldn't talk about it, but Silas watched her face enough to know it wasn't just sadness that kept Philip's name, his memory, at bay.

She was enraged.

Whether with Philip himself or with the lifetime of choices and fate that put him there that night—the weather, the traffic, the high school she enrolled both her boys in that promised skills for a successful future—Silas didn't know. He had often wondered if the rage was meant for him, for throwing the party in the first place. If she couldn't look at Philip's things without hating her one surviving son. It wasn't until he found himself a parent of a teenage boy who favored few words and closed doors that he realized the truth. She was enraged with herself. But by then, she was gone, too, the death certificate saying ovarian cancer but Silas knowing it was the rage that killed her: she grew those tumors like teeth to eat herself alive.

The girls' voices shot out beyond the trees before their bodies did.

"That's not fair; you ran cross-country!"

"Nobody likes a sore loser, Mick!"

Silas stood up and walked to the edge of the porch.

He watched Ruth fall against the biggest oak tree in the yard, her outstretched hand making contact first and the rest of her body following, eager and panting. She wore a white bathing suit, the kind that ended in bows on each hip and had one in the middle of the chest. Her skin was lighter than his daughter's, pale like that of the good girls asleep in fairy tales. Her auburn hair was wet and darker for it, stuck against her neck as she caught her breath. She didn't have any shoes, and she kicked up one leg to inspect the sole of her foot, twisting her body effortlessly. Everything about her was spun long and lovely, and so very new.

"You should know, Ruth, we've never taught Mickey how to lose with grace. Parental oversight," Silas said. Mickey stumbled out of the tree line, her cheeks red.

"Shut up, Dad."

Ruth turned to the porch where Silas stood and, holding the tree with one palm, gave him a deep curtsy. "I'm honored to be the one to teach her this lesson, Mr. Harrison."

Silas chuckled and leaned his hips against the railing.

"Just don't hold her mother or me responsible if she bites off an appendage."

"Do you bite?" Ruth asked Mickey, laughing.

Mickey came to a stop in front of Ruth.

"Whatever," she said. "I'm going to get our towels."

Ruth put her hands on her hips and watched Mickey walk down toward the dock, huffing. She looked up at the porch, and Silas caught her eye. Ruth's face was flushed from running, and her eyes glittered from winning. Silas knew the feeling. Even when it was just a silly thing like that, winning never got old. She smiled, a big, wide grin, and Silas smiled back. Then she turned and chased after Mickey, threw her arms around her shoulders and hoisted herself up to wrap her legs around Mickey's waist. The girls fell together into the grass, their shrieking laughter echoing off the covered porch.

He watched them, lying there tangled together, until he went inside to pour himself another drink.

# PEYOTE

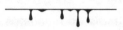

HUMAN'S RESOURCE FILE
Name: CALAMITY GANON
Current Location: FIFTH FLOOR

Calamity Ganon, human name redacted, got her taste for blood the first time one of her brothers beat another to death in front of her. To be fair, her brothers had all been given time to prepare. They trained for this. If one couldn't survive, he was meant to carry on the battle in the afterlife. And clearly, Cal thought as she yanked the warm soda tab from around the defeated boy's neck, this one was destined for that side of the fight.

It wasn't until she was older that she understood "brother" wasn't exactly the right word. The boys the General brought home and fed and trained alongside her weren't technically her brothers, despite what he called them. The Pigs showed her their "missing" posters—the ones who had people missing them, at least—in the station the day they stormed the barracks and carried her out, kicking and screaming, wrapped in a gray blanket meant to put out fires.

When the Pigs approached her, with their quiet words and new crayons, she did as her father taught her. She spat in their faces and said nothing. No matter what they told her about his record, about his *mental health issues* and *pattern of paranoia and violence*, she said nothing. When they pointed out her brothers and called them names she didn't recognize, names their first fathers gave them, she said nothing. When they asked after their bodies, where their families could at least find their bones: nothing.

"Brother" might have been the wrong word, but "father" was not.

No matter what the Pigs and the social workers and the foster parents said about him, she had a father. No matter how few people wanted her, how few people would even meet her after reading her file, at one point, she had belonged to someone.

And thanks to him, Cal was a fighter.

The first person Cal killed on her own was her fourth foster mother. She had an idea of how Cal could pay her own expenses, and it involved belts strapped to bedposts and a revolving door of houseguests. Over the days she was held there Cal worked one of the posts loose, twisting her wrist raw until she felt the wood give. When the woman came to collect her for her bathroom break, Cal pulled the wood free and cracked her straight across the face. She didn't even bother to bury her. She just took the sharpest kitchen knife that fit in her jacket pocket and all the cash the woman had and set out on her own.

She was twelve.

She spent her next three years on the road, looking for the Farm.

He told them stories about the Farm. About the fresh vegetables and meat grown and harvested right there, so that everything tasted like the wide-open Arkansas sky. About the schoolhouse with enough books for everyone and the bunks with real mattresses, one per person. The way everyone worked together to keep it safely hidden from the Pigs, an Eden for the worthy. Cal's favorite stories, besides those about what comes after the Almighty War, were the ones about the Farm's weapons caches, which the General said were wider and deeper than they could possibly imagine. Much bigger than their meager stockpile in the unplugged fridge at the barracks.

Cal knew her way around a knife, but nothing made her giddy quite like a gun.

The General said he was sent out to find an army, fighters strong and true enough to be deserving of such a place, and they would go there once he could march them home with pride. And in those rare moments when the General was feeling sentimental, he would make quiet promises just to Cal: if they ever got separated, he would wait for her there.

She was fifteen when she finally found the Farm, and it was just as beautiful as the General had promised. It was no sparkling fortress—it had been hard to find for a reason—but after years of gas station bathrooms and nameless cities' corner blocks, Cal had forgotten the earth could be clean until she saw it under that much sky.

At first, the leaders humored her, the wiry girl in the tattered camouflage jacket who slept with her knife so tight in her fist, her fingerprints took on the pattern of wood grain.

They gave her soup and a cot, even let her sit in the back of the classroom during the children's lessons on US history and the upcoming Almighty End. But after a couple of days, once she had slowed enough to chew her food, they decided to tell her the truth.

None of them had ever heard of her father. They had never been moved by the prophetic power in him, never sent him out to recruit their army. There was, as far as they knew, no special-ops mission handed down from Heaven itself. Not that they were willing to share with an outsider, at least.

Right up until then, Calamity Ganon's afterlife forecast was golden. The kind reserved for those who have already been through Hell once, without the fun of sinning. But when she threw the grenade into that little schoolhouse, she forfeited her right to call any future suffering unjust.

She didn't care, she thought as she squeezed through a gap in the Farm's chain-link fence, the grenade pin clinking against the soda tabs hanging from her neck. She was still a soldier, even if she had nothing left for which to fight.

A couple of times, she thought she found him. She would recognize the back of his head as he dipped around the corner past the local bar, or the loping gait of a passerby who limped the same way he did ever since one brother shot him in the leg. But it was never him. So she went on searching, killing as she searched. She would've gone on killing everyone until there was nobody but him left, but she didn't have the chance. The police shot her dead when she was twenty-six, and she went straight to the Downstairs.

# MICKEY

**"DO YOU EVER LOOK** at someone and think you'd love to rip your nails through their face?" Ruth asked, her foot aligned along the porch banister, hand hovering with the nail-polish brush.

"Of course," Sean answered. He held his book like he was reading it, but he hadn't turned a page in over ten minutes, preferring instead to click his pocketknife open and closed over and over, a metronome with an edge. He was faking. He was looking at Ruth without looking at all. It was pathetic, Mickey thought. She had never seen her big brother as pathetic before. Cruel, stupid, sure. But not pathetic.

"Really?" Mickey asked. "With your nails?" She reached out with her foot and pushed the couch swing under him, disrupting his false concentration.

"No, I mean, not with my nails," Sean said, setting his feet solidly onto the ground. "With my fists."

"Fists leave bruises," Ruth said as she leaned over her knee and blew on her toenails. "Bruises heal. Nails do real damage. They rip you open, leave tears. Haven't you ever really wanted to rip into someone? Not just punch them in the face—I mean really change their surface. Ruin them."

Mickey and Sean were silent.

"Come on, guys, don't act like you haven't thought about it."

Mickey hadn't. She honestly hadn't.

"Of course I have," Sean said, "but you make it sound sick."

Ruth blew on her nails again and spread her toes. Their nails were dark green. They matched the trees behind her.

"Wanna go for a swim, Mick?"

"You'll mess up your toenails."

"Worth it," Ruth said as she leapt off the porch railing into the grass.

Sean looked up. "I could go for a swim," he said, putting his book down.

"Too bad we didn't invite you!" Ruth yelled over her shoulder, already running toward the lake. She reached her hand back for Mickey, and Mickey caught it.

**THEY SWAM OUT TO** the float off the dock and pushed themselves up over the edge, gulping for air. Mickey lay on her back. Ruth lay next to her. It was a perfect New Hampshire day, just like every summer memory.

"Whose face do you want to rip off?" Mickey asked, squirming against the dry wood's heat.

"No one's in particular," Ruth answered. She lay perfectly still. She never fussed with her body, never writhed like she was a thing caught inside it. Mickey always felt that way.

"So why did you ask that?"

"I wanted to freak Sean out."

She laughed, and Mickey did too.

"He would do anything you said," Mickey said, "including rip someone's face off."

"Well, I better start making a list, huh?" Ruth asked, rolling onto her stomach. "Who has wronged me?"

"I brought you here," Mickey said, holding her hands up.

"Your face will stay intact."

Ruth stretched, and Mickey noticed the light blond hairs under her arms, hairs Mickey didn't have. She wanted to reach over and touch them, but she didn't.

"You'll get boobs soon."

Mickey laughed a too-hard laugh and sat up.

"I wasn't looking at your boobs."

"What were you looking at?"

Ruth kept her face up toward the sky, her eyes closed.

"You have to shave your armpits."

Ruth twitched but didn't put her arms down. If Ruth had said that to Mickey, Mickey would've died of humiliation. But Ruth didn't seem to care. She dared Mickey to challenge her insecurities. Mickey stood down.

"What does it feel like?" she asked finally.

"Which?"

It was the perfect question, and Mickey's truest answer would've been, *All of it.* What it felt like to be Ruth, to live in her skin. Mickey glanced down at her own body. Her two-piece bunched and sagged, a resolved grimace of an outfit.

"You can touch them if you want."

"What? Why would I?" Mickey asked, shoving her hands under her butt.

"You'll have them soon too; you might as well touch them. See what it's like."

Mickey couldn't breathe.

"Come on, Mick, don't be such a square." Ruth grabbed Mickey's wrist and put her hand on her bathing suit top. Mickey could feel the rise of her nipple through the slick fabric.

"Go ahead, squeeze it."

"Does it hurt?"

"Nope."

Mickey squeezed her fingers together, felt the meat of her.

"It feels . . . squishy."

"Way squishier than a dick, that's for sure."

"How do you know?"

It was the wrong question.

Ruth sat up and adjusted her bikini top. Then she shaded her eyes, looking out toward the horizon.

"Who's that?"

"Who?" Mickey asked, sitting up and following Ruth's gaze. A boat had just pulled into the residential shallows, motor cut in accordance with the buoys.

She recognized the Waterson boys immediately. The four of them had logged countless hours of tag and make-believe in the woods between their houses, but that had stopped as soon as Cody decided playing with girls—especially younger girls—was gross. But now, the way Josh held one palm on the steering wheel and one over his eyes made Mickey's heart skip like a knife through vegetable skin. Like a close call.

"The Watersons," Mickey said, putting up a hand in a small wave.

"Who are the Watersons?" Ruth asked, stretching her long legs out to the side.

"Our neighbors. Josh and Cody."

"Our age?"

"Josh is Sean's age; Cody is yours," Mickey said.

"Are they cute? They look like they could be cute."

Mickey's skipping heart nicked her throat. She was hesitant to tell Ruth, but she didn't know why. This was what girlfriends were for, after all.

"Josh is pretty cute, I guess."

Ruth slapped her on the shoulder. "Oh my God, Mick, do you have a summer crush? That is the best thing I've ever heard. Like a movie."

Mickey shrugged. "They're mostly Sean's friends," she answered, realizing it was no answer at all.

"Well, we are definitely making this happen," Ruth said as she threw her hand up in the air and whistled.

"Ruth!" Mickey hissed, all the heat in her sun-soaked body rushing to her cheeks. But the boat was already sliding up beside them.

"Heya, Josh," Mickey said. "Cody. This is Ruth, my friend from school."

"Best friend," Ruth added, and Mickey beamed.

"Mick, been a while," Cody said, but even through the glare of the sun on the water, she could tell his eyes were on Ruth. "Wanna go for a ride? We've got the boat for the afternoon, a cloud-free sky, and a six-pack we swiped from the house. What more could anyone want?"

Mickey glanced back at Ruth.

"Oh, come on," Cody said. "It's a lake; we can't go far. Bring your phones; it'll be fine. Your mom loves me."

"Actually, she prefers Josh," Mickey said.

"Can you blame her?" Josh said. His voice was deeper than she remembered, and Mickey noticed the way Ruth moved her body when he spoke, the littlest bit, only enough for the sun to hit her chest just right.

"What do you think, Mick? I've never been on a motorboat!"

"I'm sorry, did you just say you've never been on a motorboat?

Well then, it's settled; you're getting on this boat right now. It's time we pop that motorboating cherry." Cody grinned widely and reached for the nylon rope looped around the float.

"I don't know," Mickey said.

Ruth flicked her hair over her shoulder as she stood, wiping nothing from her skin and adjusting her bathing suit bottom before turning to Mickey.

"It'll be fine, Mick," Ruth said. "I promise." She held out her hand, and with the midday sky so bright blue behind her and the sun all in her hair, she looked like an angel. Like the kind of person put there to be followed.

# PEYOTE

**"THIS'LL BE FUN!" CAL** said through the last bite of her vending machine sandwich.

Even with my steel stomach, her file had been hard to read. I had to skim some of the details about the barracks in New Mexico, the only place she ever called home. About the General, her father, and what he did to build his army of God. Her childhood had nothing of the usual variety: no sleepovers, no team sports, no school. Every day was spent with a rotating cast of stolen or susceptible boys, training for combat, for survival, for the Almighty End. Her old man watched every fight from the sidelines, fingers steepled. He never moved, never grinned or grimaced. Never reached for her, in victory or the bloody otherwise.

As I watched her eat, I thought of the time she crawled on hands and knees to pluck her teeth from the dirt of the arena. She tossed the two front ones over the barrack's barbed-wire fence—their permanent replacements would grow in soon enough. But she kept the molar, burying it deep in the pocket of her coveralls. For the next week, she spent hours after lights out jamming that molar back into place, rolled-up slivers of grip tape refusing the wet socket of her jaw, until she gave up and began swallowing her stewed meat whole.

"I'm glad one of us is excited."

Cal crushed her plastic sandwich wrapper into a ball, trapping crumbs and stringy edges of sliced ham, and launched it into the trash.

"Pey, you need to get the fuck over yourself. This whole wound-licking routine is boring. We're going to be working to-gether; that much is clear. And I want to learn. So can we please just make the best of it?"

I sighed.

She was right. I was being pathetic, holding my hurt feelings like baby field mice, blind and velvet soft. If working with Cal could get me to the Sixth Floor, to the Looking Glass, it was worth it. I didn't have to like her, and I certainly didn't have to trust her, but I did have to get the fuck over myself. Calamity Ganon be-longed in Hell. That wasn't debatable. But at one time, she had her own feelings, her own field mice, exposed and thumbtack-small. And when she held them out, they were crushed in her palms.

"Yeah, okay. You're right. Let's do this. But we're just working together. No beers or hanging out or anything."

"You're such a prude."

"First lesson: don't talk shit to your teacher."

"Aye, aye, Captain."

Not to mention, now I had the upper hand. I had information on her. Even worse than that, I had pity.

That, I knew, would crush her.

"So, tell me about your marks. Who are you looking at?" I asked, pulling out my pencil case. She opened her notebook.

"After the incident in Illinois, I was thinking it would be good to track events like that, see if I could catch some Spec Ones. So

I set an alert for any kind of gun violence. But that was way too much; my computer almost crashed. So I scaled it back to mass shootings of ten or more, and added natural disasters. I got a few hits after a fire got out of control in California, but I haven't seen much else." She clicked through her pens as she spoke, putting the useless ones in a pile.

"You should expand that search to include anticipated natural disasters. After a disaster, a lot of people are too focused on meeting immediate needs to think of making a deal. Most folks will reach out right before the thing happens. Anxiety about the future is excellent for our line of work."

Cal clicked the sixth pen and started writing.

"That's great. You're already helping!"

"Have you tracked any Spec Threes? You would be good at Threes."

"Why's that?"

"You're good at telling people what they want to hear."

Cal flashed a bright smile. "Thanks, Pey! You're good at things too."

"The best place to get Threes is in big cities," I continued. "Look for high-powered jobs, or people with ridiculous amounts of money. Especially those who come from it. You want to find the people who confuse deserving a good life with being handed one."

Cal pulled a sheet of paper from her notebook.

"How about this guy? He's a politician somewhere in Asia—I've always been shit at geography. He was supposed to use the taxes he demanded on the schools and roads, but he funneled them into his own accounts. The people are starting to revolt, and he's out of options. He's almost ready to make the call."

I fingered the edge of the page as I glanced over it.

"Cal, think about it. Why would this guy be a waste of your time?"

She stuffed the sheet back in her notebook, her face flushing all the way to her ears.

I could get used to this teaching thing.

"Look at all the fucked-up things he's done," I said. "We don't make deals for souls that are already ours."

"But what about redemption?"

I laughed.

"Are you seriously telling me one wrong step and we're all fucked?"

"This guy is about six thousand wrong steps beyond one, Cal."

She pulled a strand of hair loose from her ponytail and threaded it through her fingers.

"I guess the romantic in me just wants to believe people can always turn it around, you know? If they want to."

I had gotten cocky in my understanding of Calamity Ganon. I looked at her now and couldn't find the seam in her sincerity. I couldn't prove it false, even though it must've been. There was nothing romantic about her.

"I guess he doesn't want to," I said finally. And then, because I simply couldn't help it:

"Did you?"

# MICKEY

**MICKEY GRIPPED THE HARD** lemonade between her knees until condensation mixed with sweat and trickled down her legs. Ruth was almost done with hers, but Mickey hadn't taken a sip.

"Ooh, turn this up!" Ruth yelled, standing next to the captain's seat and balancing in the space between the two windshields.

"DJ, take the wheel!" Cody said, reaching for the cell phone attached to the boat's speaker. Ruth squealed and fell over him, grasping the wheel with both hands and landing squarely in his lap.

Mickey eyed Josh on the other cushion up front. His hair was longer than she remembered, but it had been at least two years since they last saw each other. It looked good. She liked the way the wind pulled it forward and back and the way Josh didn't seem to mind at all. She imagined what it would be like to run her fingers through those deep brown curls, to have access to the parts of him she found herself wanting, so badly, to touch. When Cody cut the engine in a cove, the silence rushed in like something forgotten and hungry.

"We can swim here," he said, cracking another bottle open against the boat's gunwale "Or whatever we want."

Ruth ran her hand along the wooden dashboard of the boat, polished to a gleam.

"Do you have a lot of these?" she asked.

"Boats? We have a few," Cody answered. "My dad is a collector."

"Of boats?" Ruth asked, flabbergasted.

"Boats, antique hunting rifles, handsome offspring," Cody said with a wink. "Whatever he can get his hands on."

"Are you saying your dad puts his hands on you? You should tell a safe adult."

"Funny. Very funny."

Ruth stood up and stretched, and Cody watched, not even trying to be subtle. Mickey looked around to see Josh watching, too, and she pushed herself deeper into the cushions. And then Ruth did what she always did, the thing that made up for all the ways she made Mickey feel invisible just by breathing.

She turned to her.

"Come on, Mick, let's go swimming," she said, grabbing Mickey's hand. Mickey's drink splashed against her knees.

"It doesn't work if you don't actually drink it," Ruth said, pushing the end of the bottle up until gravity made the liquid pound on Mickey's lips.

"That a girl!" Ruth shouted when Mickey finished the hard lemonade, coughing. "Come on."

She took off her tank top and shimmied her shorts onto the deck. She could've been the most exciting exhibit in the aquarium, the way all eyes were hers. Mickey fumbled with the collar of her shirt, which had gotten tangled with the tie of her only two-piece, which she had worn every day since they arrived. Her hands were sticky from the hard lemonade and feeling thicker with each second.

"Ready?" Ruth asked, spinning around.

"I can't—" Mickey said, tugging on the tag of her shirt.

Ruth squinted and looked at the boys.

"We don't need our tops, do we?"

Mickey froze. "Ruth, what the—"

"I want to go swimming. So come *on*," she said, pulling Mickey's shirt up. "I'll do it too. They won't look; they're perfect gentlemen. Aren't you, boys?"

Ruth lifted Mickey's shirt again, and Mickey grabbed the hem.

"No freaking way, Ruth," Mickey hissed, ripping the fabric back down to cover her belly button. Ruth stepped back.

"Fine," she said. "Suit yourself."

She hopped up onto the back seat of the boat, wavering just enough for Cody to offer his hand, but she shook her head. The lake lapped quietly against the boat's hull, the glitter of it reflected in her eyes. Or maybe the glitter in her eyes reflected in the lake.

Maybe Ruth was there first, and the rest of the world was built in answer.

Ruth reached with one hand to the middle of her back, grabbed the red string of her bikini top, and pulled. She did it slowly, so even Mickey hung on every stitch. Until, finally, the whole thing fell, limp and accomplished, to the deck. She hugged one arm across her bare chest and glanced back over her shoulder. The contrast of her tan against her nakedness upped the drama of it all: the pure engulfed, literally, in the grip of the exposed.

"You got another Mike's?" she asked Cody. "I have a feeling the water is going to be pretty cold."

Cody nodded and handed her his without taking his eyes off the length of her back, uninterrupted. She took a long swallow with the bottle straight overhead, her free arm silhouetted against the sun. Which was how Mickey first saw it. The delicate network of lines that crossed Ruth's arm's most tender flesh, the part closest to her heart. They were straight and clean, like a completed to-do list. Her body hadn't made them.

In an instant, Mickey forgot about Josh. She wanted to touch those raised white lines much more than she had ever wanted to touch anything else. But there was a splash and Ruth was gone.

# LILY

**THE WEEK AFTER SHE** met Gavin in the Market Basket, Lily went to group. Or, rather, she went to the Eaglewood Presbyterian parking lot. All week, she thought about his invitation—about him in his entirety. It was as if he had spread to her when she placed her hand on his wrist, creating a new, buzzing layer of skin. And every time she imagined seeing him again, she felt that animal satisfaction of an itch properly, gloriously scratched.

So when the day came, she got herself to the church—leaving a note for Silas, an appropriate lie followed by a line of $x$'s—but she couldn't get herself to go inside. She turned off the sedan in the parking lot and watched, sitting low, as people filtered in. She had put on a baseball cap, but it made her feel ridiculous. Like a teenager, or, worse, an unimaginative woman trying not to be recognized.

Twenty minutes after the meeting began, Lily, still in her car, turned the key in the ignition and told herself she was going home. She pulled out of her spot and drove the length of the church, thinking that if she got on Maple, she could stop by the dry cleaner's. But that's when she saw him through the large windows.

Gavin stood at the front of the room, behind a wooden podium. The audience, on plastic chairs in a semicircle, was small but rapt. Sunlight beamed through the old paned windows to fill the remaining space. His face was drawn, and after each of his sentences all the heads in the room nodded, so that together they created a rhythm. Even then, just her second time seeing him all grown up, his face hit like the sweetest of punches to her gut. She was caught off guard by the force with which she wanted to reach out and touch him, and she had to grip the steering wheel instead.

Lily pulled into a spot out of view and crossed the spit of manicured lawn to stand next to the open windows of the church. She leaned her back against the bricks warmed by the sun and closed her eyes.

"Almost two decades ago, my twin sister, Sarah, was murdered. I know that it's been so long because of the calendar on my phone, and because when I look in the mirror, I am not the teenage boy I was on that day. Not nearly."

The crowd chuckled kindly.

"But, to be honest, the most immediate part of me has no idea it's been so long since she died. The most immediate, accessible part of me—the me in my center, the fundamental me that hasn't been touched by time—every day, every minute, learns and relearns over and over that she is gone. That is why I am so grateful for this group. The people in this room come from all over—different hometowns, different families, different identities. But we all share one fact in common: here, we are free to release the constant need to make other people comfortable with our pain. We can stop pretending it gets better, because it doesn't. That doesn't mean time doesn't change things, not at all. It doesn't mean I haven't had a full life. But what it does mean is this: even though it's been so many years, I still lose my sister every single day."

To hear him talk about his loss in such an open, raw way was unlike anything Lily had ever known. Like it wasn't a sore to be hidden, something that made him wounded, weak, less than. Like loss didn't have to be lonely.

"Would I rather have her back instead? Of course. But I don't have that kind of power. The power I do have, however, is this. Standing here with you all, telling my story. Hoping that maybe just one of you will feel seen for the first time since you lost someone, that you will come back and sit with us. It's not much, but it's all I've got. And I find myself on this day, all these years after the worst day of my life, grateful for it."

The crowd clapped, and Lily stayed perfectly still, both sad and happy, and warm all over. She couldn't remember the last time she let herself feel the contentment in sadness. She never let her own sadness bloom enough to produce that particular fruit. For a few minutes, she stayed there, her back against the warm brick, her eyes closed, and let herself feel it.

Then the church door groaned, and her eyes snapped open. The chattering women walking out went silent when they saw her. Lily reached for her hat, grateful for what she had, just moments ago, felt embarrassed by. But it didn't matter; it was too late.

Theirs was a small town, and she was *the* Lily Thompson.

She didn't bother to smile at the women, the way she did when she was younger, so at least they couldn't say she was rude. By then, Lily knew they would say whatever they wanted. Instead, she pushed off the church wall and turned away from them, knowing she'd have to do a loop of the parking lot to get to her car but also knowing it was worth it. Still, she could hear them whisper.

"That's Lily Thompson, Silas Harrison's wife. What on earth is she doing here?" And then, as if they all didn't already know, "Her brother-in-law was Philip Harrison. The one who killed Sarah."

# PEYOTE

**"WELL, THAT WAS A** motherfucking rush," Cal said, wiping blood from her cheek. It was our third war zone of the day, and every inch of me was coated in a thin layer of sand.

"That was a good haul," I said, calculating our deals on my tablet. Four in total. Not bad at all.

"Want to see if we can beat those cadets at poker before we go?"

I shook my head. "Let's quit while we're ahead."

"Come on, we could make one hell of a bet!"

I knew that Cal's childhood was traumatic, to say the least. But there was no denying the sheer joy she got from war. It made me wonder if her father had, in fact, seen something in her, something he attempted to nourish and encourage the way some parents coach their kids' Little League teams. I couldn't tell, as I watched her eyes glitter in the lingering grenade smoke, if her love of the bloody came from nature or nurture, or some twisted combination. But it was clear that here, she thrived.

"Come on, Pey," she whined, pulling all of the syllables long and sharp. "I don't want to leave yet."

"We need to get back; we have a team meeting."

Cal kicked a rock, rousing dust from the desert's camouflage. Anything around us could have been the body of a snake. I was about to argue my point when my tablet gave its insistent beep. Cal pulled her army helmet straps and beamed.

"Okay," I said. "One more."

I don't know why the tablet picked up this one. It was in a different time and a different time zone, all the way across the world. Maybe it was a coincidence, luck of the draw. Or maybe someone was testing us, testing Cal. I accepted the request before I had time to think about it.

We came to in front of a house that wasn't quite abandoned but was too far gone to be called something cute like "rickety." The lawn was all rough edges and the ghostly heads of dandelions, bent and huddled as if gossiping in the late-afternoon light. Cal picked up the mailbox, which lay on its side with the red flag rusted permanently up.

" 'The Culvers,' " she read.

The house wasn't a trailer, in that it had a foundation that locked into the earth. But the shape was the same: a brick home without any brick. Paneling, meant to look like wood but warped and collapsed in places real wood never would be, wasn't organic enough to rot. A screen drooped in its window.

"What do you want?" a man said from the doorway. I took him in, unwashed, uncombed, and bloodshot. Just our kind of guy.

"Mr. Culver?"

"Who's asking?"

"Can we come inside? We got a message from you."

This guy would be thanking us soon enough, full-on snot-in-the-beard-crying kind of thanking us, just like the rest of them. But for now, we were the same as people selling knives or cookies or God. Useless at best.

He nodded and stood aside.

It took a second for my eyes to adjust to the darkness inside. It was that red kind of darkness—like when the sun is so bright you have to close your eyes, but you can still see the burn. The kind of darkness that comes not from a lack of light but rather in rebellion against it. But the light bled in anyway, rushing through the cracks between the window frames and the pieces of cardboard held there with duct tape, seeping into the piles that cluttered the tattered couch and around the circular table. It was the same light that I had relished so deeply many times before, but now it felt like a predator, claws and tongues curling under the door.

Cal elbowed me as I rubbed my eyes.

"I know I haven't memorized the whole book," she whispered. "But this has to be breaking some kind of rule."

I squinted in the gloom, my hand on my tablet. That's when I saw the piles of clutter weren't piles at all. They were people. The tiny living room was damn near bursting with men.

"All right, boys," Culver said. "Let's make ourselves a deal."

# SILAS

**SILAS COULDN'T REMEMBER THE** last time he saw Sean read anything besides the Internet, and certainly not for pleasure. But there he sat on the porch, watching the girls as they dashed for the water, an open book on his lap. Sean had always been a quiet kid, like Philip. But unlike a lot of the quiet ones, Sean was never much of a reader. He didn't like escaping into other people's prefabricated worlds, preferring to build his own. As a child, he spent countless hours sprawled on the floor of his bedroom, lining plastic soldiers along his bed frame, making war sounds with his mouth. One time, Silas opened Sean's door and was met with a downpour of green men from a pillowcase rigged above his head.

"Guerrilla warfare," Sean had said, grinning.

This was back in the days when Silas could freely open his son's door. Although, as Silas thought about it, he realized maybe Sean had always wanted privacy, but it was only recently that he learned the vocabulary. He seemed to walk around inside something invisible, everything just a few inches from his skin. Even his clothes were baggy enough that Silas rarely saw the shape of his son's body. That seemed to be the point.

Silas wiped off his hands the dirt from the vegetable garden, where he grew enough for a couple of highly celebrated salads each summer; then he shaded his eyes and walked up the hill.

"What are you reading?"

Sean tensed at his father's voice, as if he hadn't seen him coming the whole way across the lawn.

"Just something I found on the shelf."

"Is it good?"

Sean shrugged, his own language. Silas sat down next to his son and extended his legs, hoping if he looked comfortable, he might somehow become comfortable.

"So," he asked, "what do you think of Ruth?"

Sean had been willingly around his sister more in the past week than Silas had seen in years, and it wasn't about Mickey. Maybe having a crush would be a good thing for Sean, Silas thought. Get him out of his head.

"She's fine," Sean muttered.

"I think she seems pretty great," Silas said, smiling sidelong. "She's cute too."

"Gross, Dad."

"She is! Don't you think?"

Sean's face turned red, which made Silas smile more brightly. He sank back into the lounger.

"You totally think so."

"Whatever."

"You should talk to her," Silas went on. "Ask her questions. Girls like it when guys ask questions."

"Can we not talk about this?"

Silas jostled his son's shoulder. "The opposite of that."

Sean shifted on the polyester cushion. "I don't even understand why she's friends with Mickey. She's older, and she's popular. It's weird."

Silas put his hand on his son's neck and gave him a shake. His neck was wet with sweat, the collar of his T-shirt damp.

"Maybe the Harrisons are more hip than you thought."

Sean shrugged out from his grip.

"How about you go join them for a swim before dinner? I bet the water feels nice."

"I'm set," he said. He got up before Silas could say anything more, and the screen door slammed shut behind him.

"Good talk!" Silas yelled, his hands flat and wide on his knees.

When he opened the door to the darkened house, the inside air felt clean for its coolness. He went up the stairs, creaky and steep, and into the back room. He kept his clothes there, sacrificing the only closet in the master suite to Lily. He pretended he was being magnanimous, but the truth was, Silas liked having his own space. He pulled off his dirt-streaked T-shirt and jeans and tossed them in his suitcase with his other laundry. The early-evening sun was at its warmest and butter smooth, melting against the paned windows. He looked over the lawn again and caught the girls as they stumbled out of the water onto the patch of sand his father insisted on calling a beach. He smiled, thinking of Sean's blush. A girlfriend was exactly what Sean needed. Ruth might be a little out of his league, if Silas was being honest. But liking her was a start.

Silas pushed through his shirts on their hangers, wanting a button-down for dinner, even though it would be only the five of them. The sound of the girls' laughter floated around him like wind chimes. He loved hearing Mickey so happy.

Silas never felt awkward with Mickey. True, she was barely fourteen and therefore only just beginning, but Silas wasn't worried. He understood Mickey in a way Lily never had, in a way neither of them had ever understood Sean. Silas and Mickey were cut from the same cloth. Mickey was a naturally happy, bright little girl. But Silas could see the other part of her, the part he recognized only because he had spent so long looking for a name for it in himself. The moments when the happiness he trusted as normalcy would drain right out of him, leaving neither sadness nor anger in its absence, just nothing at all. In these moments, he honestly believed that he could stop whatever he was doing, turn on his heels, and walk straight out of his life without looking back. That he wasn't even human, that none of it had ever been real or his or anything at all. Leaving it all behind would be as easy as walking out of a movie theater, as putting down a novel without a hook.

"Can I use this shower instead of the one inside?"

Ruth's voice was directly below his open window, rich despite its youth and loud enough that he could've been right next to her. Silas sidestepped out of view on instinct, his chest bare.

"If you like spiders," Mickey answered.

"Challenge accepted!" Ruth yelled back, pulling the weathered shower door closed behind her. Silas recognized the creak so deeply he could almost feel the bricks beneath his feet, slick and uneven with years of water and soap scum. Evan built the outdoor shower, as he had most of the jerry-rigged add-ons to the house. Silas and Philip spent so much time running back and forth from the dock, Rose finally insisted he make something so the boys could at least rinse off before coming inside. She was tired of finding sand and flecks of lake grass between their sheets and under the dining room table, where their knees would bounce until they were excused to run to the dock once more.

Lily loved the outdoor shower. She said it made her feel *dangerous*. They used to make love against the grayed wood panels while the kids played on the beach, their happy voices the kind of soft-pedal soundtrack he never would've thought of as soothing before becoming a parent, but that became exactly that. Kids happy, safe, and otherwise occupied. That was before Lily had pulled away from him, back when he still knew what each shift of her shoulders meant and what had caused it. Silas hadn't used that shower in years.

"If you leave your bathing suit over the door like that, I might have to steal it."

"Don't you dare, Mick."

"I won't, but no promises about Sean. Who knows where that perv might be?"

"Shut up!"

The girls laughed, and Silas heard Mickey's footsteps come up the stairs onto the porch, the screen door to the house slapping open and then closed behind her.

Next came the screech of the showerhead. A high-pitched whine before the pressure kicked on and the bricks were pummeled, water ricocheting off and onto the lawn like the constant breaking of glass. Until Ruth stepped under it, and the water softened against her.

Silas closed his eyes.

There was a clink as Ruth reached for the soap. It was the same soap they always kept in the metal dish Evan had drilled into the wall. The soap smelled like what dryer sheets were manufactured to smell like. Fresh scent, they called it.

He could've pushed back from the window. He could've grabbed a shirt and turned his back to check the mirror. He could've walked downstairs and started chopping carrots for the beef bourguignon.

But he didn't.

Silas could recall each feeling Ruth experienced as she was

experiencing it. He knew the bite of the open air like electricity, how she would feel cold everywhere outside of the thrum of water. The way the soap would slip in her hand, thin and cracked in places like tree bark, palm-perfect and worn smooth. The feeling of being exposed, wild in a safe way. Naked but unseen.

Silas knew exactly how she felt. So much so that he was practically there with her, all steam and wet hair pulled long and slick.

So much so that there was no point in keeping his eyes closed anymore.

So he didn't.

# PEYOTE

"**LET'S JUST HOLD ON** a second," I said, taking in the room.

There must've been at least twelve of them. They all looked to be in their early twenties, except that they sat so still. They had varying skin tones and colors in their short-cropped hair, but somehow all of them looked the same—human bootlegs.

It was as if a Boy Scout troop had fallen into a communal coma a decade earlier and had just, communally, woken up.

"Here, I bet y'all are wanting these," the man said as he tossed Cal a bottle of water. She opened it immediately. I flicked my wrist when he threw me mine, and everything stopped but the three of us, the bottle stuck mid-arc.

"Mr. Culver," I said through a grin, "it's great that you have so much support. But we don't usually perform for an audience."

"It's Jason," he said as he circled the water bottle midair. "Damn, that's cool."

"Okay, Jason. How about you tell me why you called us here, and we'll go from there?"

I glanced over at Cal, who had moved toward the boys on the

couch. She bent down in front of one and swept the hair from his stilled eyes.

"I need you to bring me someone," Jason said. "He has something we need."

"With all due respect, Jason, there are taxi services that charge a Hell of a lot less than us."

Literally.

I heard Cal stand up and expected her to come to my side, but she moved around the room, fingers lingering over faces and in the dust on the shelves.

"And if I knew where he was, I would've called them. But he's been dark for years. He's not dead, though. I know it. We just can't find him."

"And who exactly is 'we'?" I asked, glancing around the living room.

"He stole from all of us," Jason said. "But from my understanding, you don't need a scrapbook; you just need a soul. Am I right?"

My Trustworthy face faltered, but only for a second. There was no point in sugarcoating it: if he had called us with all of the information, he had already come to terms with what he would lose. Whatever he wanted was worth it. At least he thought it was, on this side of the dirt.

"How do you know the target is alive?" Cal interrupted. "That he still has what you're looking for?"

"Just when we think he must've kicked it, he'll show up. A connection of mine saw him a few years back, said he was masquerading as a preacher. He's run since, but no doubt he's just set up shop somewhere else. And he always has it."

I felt Cal tense from across the room. I reached out my mind to hers like I had during our Grand Slam, but she blocked me with a shock.

Something was not right.

"Well, Jason," I said, "if you want him dead, we can do that right now from this living room. But—and I don't mean to be harsh—one soul is not enough to send us on a wild-goose chase."

I put my hand on the doorknob and nodded to Cal. She was kneeling in front of a frozen boy on a folding chair. She traced the neck of his T-shirt, rolling between her fingers a thin chain that hung there.

"Come on, let's go."

"Wait," Jason said, almost walking into the suspended beverage in his kitchen. "What if you get all of us? What if you get fifteen souls?"

I hesitated.

"We'll do it," Cal said, tablet ready.

We were gone before the bottle hit the wall.

# LILY

THAT AFTERNOON, LILY MEANDERED through the market's floral aisle, touching petals when no one was looking. She took the car into town, the grocery list not nearly long enough to require a trip tucked purposefully into her shirt pocket. She had spent sixteen summers in the same place Sarah died, there the very minute, second, year after year. Never once had she and Silas done anything to acknowledge the day, except maybe pour their evening drinks a little early, a little strong. She paid for a bouquet of poppies in cash. She drove the long way back, and parked between their property and the Watersons'. She didn't want to go to the clearing through the backyard. She needed to be alone for this.

THE DAY OF THE night Sarah died, Lily nursed her hangover on the float, diving off the edge whenever she needed to feel cold water. Madeline and the other girls joined her in the beginning, all rowing the canoe out so they could bring the stereo, but, as always, they abandoned their towels and tanning oil when they heard Phil's bike.

"Not into the hog?" Sarah asked as she pulled herself up the ladder. She twisted her hair and shook it out over her shoulders. Usually, it was the color of a sunset or the forest floor in the fall, but sometime that summer, she got highlights that, to Lily's delight, looked terrible.

Lily shrugged. "He's Silas's brother; I can ride it whenever I want. I'm surprised you're not up there, though."

Sarah stretched out next to her and threw her hair, damaged but still enviable in its volume, over the edge of the float into the lake. "I live dangerously enough on my own two feet."

Lily snorted. "Did you practice that line in the mirror?"

"How else would I have nailed it so flawlessly?"

That time, Lily laughed for real.

"So, Silas Harrison, huh? How's that going?"

Whatever fragile camaraderie there was between them was lost the minute Lily heard Sarah say his name. Like it was at home in her mouth.

"That's definitely none of your business."

"I think it's cute," she said. "You two make sense, you know? Like *Happy Days*. I'm sure it's really nice."

"It's a whole lot more than nice."

"I'm sure. You seem . . . wild." Sarah grinned and closed her eyes against the sun.

"What about you and Dan? Or was it Kevin? Or wait . . . no. I think it was the whole baseball team," Lily said as she sat up, using her perfect twenty-five-inch waist to block Sarah's sun.

"Basketball, actually."

"Why are you even here?"

"I was invited."

"By Phil? Don't get too big a head from his little crush; he would stick it in anyone who would have him. You're just his best bet."

"Well, aren't I lucky!" Sarah said, but Lily could hear a little crack in her witty armor, and it was enough.

"You didn't know he wants to fuck you? That's why he's here this weekend; usually he'd stay home. But he wants . . . whatever this is," Lily said, sliding one finger under the string tie of Sarah's bikini bottom and letting it snap, like she was emptying a rattrap.

"Phil and I are just friends."

"That's not what he tells the boys," Lily said, leaning back on her hands. "Apparently, you get real frisky with just a little tequila . . . Is that true?" She went sweet on the upward inflection, in that poison way teenage girls do.

Sarah's eyes fluttered, but she kept them closed. "Phil wouldn't say that."

"I guess we'll see when they get back from the liquor store."

Lily stood and stretched, showing the whole length of her body. She was long from start to finish, a ray of light straight from the sky.

"Later," she said, and she dove into the water with barely a splash.


**WHEN LILY REACHED THE** clearing that afternoon, she stood at the lake's edge and plucked the petals off all of the poppies but one, throwing each into the water. No matter how far she tried to throw them, they gathered back at her feet.

"I'm sorry, Sarah."

Gavin said he talked to Sarah out loud all the time. He said it helped. But to Lily, it felt showy and self-indulgent. What good was a conversation if the other person couldn't push back? The presumption that the dead are happy just to listen was a selfish, desperate side effect of loss.

"I don't have any excuses, and I'm sure you wouldn't even care. But for whatever it's worth, I'm sorry. If I had gotten up earlier, or if I had done something—"

Lily wished beyond anything else that she hadn't gotten up that night. She wished she hadn't stumbled out onto that lawn littered with plastic cups and moonlight, shuffling one foot in front of the other over roots and leaves down the path to the clearing, her head thrumming with heavy vodka Sprites. She wished she had just stayed in bed where Silas put her, next to a trash can and a glass of water. If she had just rolled over and gone back to sleep, everything could've been different. Not for Sarah—Lily couldn't do anything about that. But for her, and Silas. And, of course, for Philip.

Lily laid the last flower whole on the spit of shore, the bright red garish against the murky silt, as if showing off. Bragging about being alive.

As if it didn't yet know that it was not.

# PEYOTE

**"WHY WOULD YOU AGREE** to that? It doesn't matter how many souls he offers us; we can't go traipsing around the globe looking for—who are we even looking for?" I said when we landed back in the office.

"Not here," Cal hissed, unsnapping her tablet and putting it back in its cubby. "Meet me at my place after work."

I lifted my eyebrows.

"Just do it," she said before she turned down the hall between the cubicles, raising her hand to greet someone on the other side of the divide.

**CAL DIDN'T KNOW I** had her file. I held that card the way one holds an autograph, preciously and proudly. I can admit that I fantasized plenty about the moment I could tell her and wipe that smug we-can-pretend-you're-in-charge-but-we-all-know-I-am smile straight off her face. Not the way we used to Downstairs, of course, with Agent Orange and a scrap of steel wool. I knew I would have to catch her off guard. But it was becoming clear that Calamity

Ganon didn't get caught off guard. She'd never even tried it—loosening into the capable hands of another. Cal knew nothing but guard her whole life, both in the blip of regular and the forever of after.

So I made her wait. I walked around her neighborhood for hours before knocking. Not because I had any other plan, but because even with the trump card in my pocket, I still felt the need to take every opportunity to keep her in the dark. Until, finally, I could no longer stand the nonstop sound of a car alarm, so I went to her door.

"What took you so long?"

"Have you ever tried to find it?" I asked as I kicked sludge from my boots. I had misjudged a puddle around the corner, but luckily it was only up to the ankle. "That car alarm that's going off, I mean."

Cal shut the door behind me.

"I went looking my first week here, but the alarm moves from car to car in whatever direction you're headed." She shrugged. "I barely notice it anymore."

"Don't say that too loud. We had an ice-cream truck that was like that in my neighborhood, but then some idiot had blocked it out long enough to say, 'What ice-cream truck?' and the next morning we got a century of Hell Week pledges on those bike-and-drink trolleys. I started humming myself to sleep with 'The Entertainer,' I missed that damn truck so much."

"That's yours," she said, pointing to a beer on the counter. "It's not my fault if it got warm."

"So, care to tell me what's going on?" I asked before I took the whole thing down in a deep and greedy gulp.

"Okay," Cal said, exhaling. I could tell that's what she was doing—exhaling—which meant she did it slowly enough that it could've been manipulative. Or she was simply breathing. "So, when I was in the Retribution Management Department on Third, designing punishment plans for individuals on the belt, I was in charge of this one case."

"You know," I said, and paused for another sip. "I was the person who had to actually execute those plans. You could've been more considerate of the well-being of your colleagues working the belt."

I expected a sassy retort so completely, I didn't even look at her, but after a minute of nothing, I turned. Cal's eyes were trained on the mangy carpet.

"What?" I asked.

"It's just rich," she said. "Complaining to me about the conditions on the belt."

My face burned, and I realized it had been a while since I had felt shame from the natural wellspring within instead of what they pumped into the air here.

"Sorry," I said. "I forgot."

"Anyway, he was a con man who got his start coaching high school football. You know how folks get about football in Texas, and there were some real promising guys on that team, already being scouted by colleges, maybe even destined for the NFL. And it was Homecoming weekend, so all these people in the town, the alums and parents—you'd just never believe how high the bets get around this kind of stuff. Something about knowing the players personally—or enough for it to feel personal—that makes people double down."

"Does this story have a point, or are you just recapping a feel-good after-school special?" I asked. I felt warm and broad. I flexed my arms against the counter and reveled in my own strength. *This is why I drink*, I thought. Ninety-nine out of a hundred times it sucked, but that feeling right there was why I kept trying.

"This guy—my case—made his first real chunk of change during that Homecoming game. He pumped the team's watercoolers full of steroids, or maybe it was their thighs? But the week of the championship, he swapped out the steroids and placed his own bets heavy against them. The team completely fell apart on the field. A couple players even got seriously injured. But it didn't matter much; when they all tested positive, their careers were over either way."

"I'm still waiting for the point."

Cal rolled her eyes hard enough to hurt her neck. "Catch up, Trip! Those guys today were the team. I'm sure of it. The timing lines up, and I recognized things about them from my intel. Jason said their target stole something from all of them . . . What can be stolen that is big enough to warrant the consequences of a deal?"

I rubbed my chin. I couldn't remember the last time I did that, but I did it then, and I did it with class.

"Oh, for Darkness' sake, you're not a fucking gentleman detective," Cal said. "Sit down."

And just like that, she sucked the booze ego out of my blood with a straw.

"Fuck you," I mumbled as I sat.

"Their coach stole their futures, and now they want to give us the deal of a millennium. Fifteen souls at once? We'd be office legends. KQ would have to give you some pretty amazing perks if you were able to pull that off in the first couple of weeks of training me," she added, probing my leg with her toe.

"You can't use intel from Third on Fifth. Privacy policy. You could get in a lot of trouble if they find out."

"That's why they won't find out." Cal kicked off her shoes and turned to face me on the couch, cross-legged.

"Okay," I conceded. "But that still doesn't explain how we're going to find this guy. Or what it is he has that they could possibly want. Proof, maybe?" I took another beer from the minifridge and put my hand on my neck. "Maybe we could make a beacon shoot out of him, like a beam of fire?"

Cal shook her head. "I have a better idea."

"And that is . . . ?"

"Let's use the Looking Glass."

**I HAVEN'T TOLD YOU** much about the Looking Glass yet, have I? Of course, I know I haven't. I'm just being coy.

In short, the Looking Glass finds what's been lost. Be it a person, an object, or a moment in time, the Looking Glass has access to it all. If you have the right keywords, every single thing every single one of us has ever thought or seen or touched during our time on Earth can be rethought, reseen, retouched. It is Google for the entirety of human memory, and it is the only thing in Hell that is used with respect. Even the people who work on the Sixth Floor have limited access, if any. My elevator pass alone wouldn't get me in the door. It takes a special kind of case or a special kind of person to gain access.

I needed the Looking Glass, too, you may remember. Not for this deal, but for my whole grand plan: I needed what only it could find. I had been thinking for weeks about how to get myself in, now that I had an elevator pass. What story to feed KQ so she would sign over approval.

And then here was Cal, holding the door wide open.

She was right—KQ wouldn't be able to deny fifteen souls at once. As for how I would use that access for my own means, or what I would do when she realized I didn't search for the results she expected, I would figure that out later.

For now, I just needed Cal to think the whole thing was her idea.

"What's the Looking Glass?" I asked.

# MICKEY

**"DINNER SMELLS DELICIOUS, MR. HARRISON!"** Ruth said as she jumped the last two steps into the kitchen, Mickey close behind. Mickey wore one of Ruth's dresses, a gauzy blue sundress she had admired but would never ask to borrow, certain Ruth's clothes would somehow be embarrassed to be seen on her. But Ruth said she thought it would bring out her eyes. Mickey felt like a fairy as she ran her fingers over the fabric, so fragile it felt whimsical, as if stitched by songbirds. She loved the way it fluttered after her on her way down the stairs.

Silas threw a dish towel over his shoulder and turned to face the girls. When he saw Mickey, his hand went to his heart.

"What—where is my daughter? Who is this princess in my kitchen?"

He staggered like the mere sight of her ripped him apart.

"Shut up, Dad," Mickey said, punching him on the arm.

"Well, at least she still talks like my daughter."

He reached out and wrapped an arm around Mickey's shoulders, pulling her in. "You look beautiful, sweetheart," he said into her hair. Mickey rolled her eyes and pulled free, reaching for the wooden spoon.

"What about me?" Ruth asked, spinning. Her dress was yellow with red flowers and a delicate white belt. It highlighted her skin the way the sun already had. Ruth seemed to live bathed in light.

"You are both Oscars ready," Silas said, bowing his head. "We are not worthy!"

Ruth laughed and curtsied.

"You girls can set the table," Silas went on as he turned back to the oven. "Dinner will be ready in five."

SILAS SERVED THE BOURGUIGNON on trivets, and its steam mingled with the humid evening air enough to make everyone tug at their collars. Ruth took Mickey's plate and piled it high before reaching for Sean's.

"Thank you so much for this beautiful dinner, Mr. and Mrs. Harrison," she said as she took the next plate. "If I lived with you all the time, I'd be a whale!"

"Oh, I doubt that," Lily said. Mickey hadn't seen her mother that day; she had gone into town to run errands. She looked tired, more so than usual for New Hampshire. She looked more like Home Lily, not Vacation Lily.

"So, Mick told me you two first fell in love here at this house in high school! That's so romantic." Ruth held her own plate now, gesturing with the serving spoon.

"That's right," Silas said, patting Lily's hand. Lily reached for the sour cream.

"Tell me everything. What did you all do down here, back when you were our age?"

Sean rolled his eyes. "Don't encourage them."

"Oh, come on," Ruth said. "I've never heard it!"

Sean stuck his fork into a carrot and didn't say anything. Silas smiled. His past brightened under even the slightest flicker of attention, like Tinker Bell and her survival on faith.

"We have some good stories, that's for sure."

"Did you throw parties and stuff?"

"Well, don't tell my kids, but definitely yes."

"Tell the one about when Mom got that ticket from the boat police," Mickey said. The edges of her dress rippled through her fingers in front of the fan. Even with every window open, the air smelled of nothing but red meat and redder wine.

"I wouldn't call them 'police,'" Lily said. "They were younger than I was."

"What were you doing?"

"I forgot to bring a life jacket. To be fair, I was barely fifty feet from the dock. I just wanted somewhere I could read quietly—Philip had been showing off his motorcycle all day, and the sound of that engine did not go with wine-cooler hangovers."

The air in the room got tight as soon as she said his name. Mickey felt instantly guilty, even though she hadn't been the one who said it.

"Who's Philip?" Ruth asked. Mickey snapped up, but Ruth had the sweetest face: all open and full of sparkle. So much so that Mickey wondered, for an instant, if she truly had forgotten.

"Phil was my big brother," Silas said, digging his fork into the meat. "He was a wild child back in the day, always taking girls for rides on his motorcycle. The pretty ones, at least." He winked at Mickey, who gave a weak smile.

"I've never been on a motorcycle," Ruth said. "My mom says I'd like it too much."

Silas laughed. "Smart mom."

Lily cleared her throat, her knife scraping ceramic. "So, Sean, are the Watersons around this summer?"

Sean chewed in no hurry.

"Yup."

"Oh, that's good to know. I will reach out to them. Are you going to see them?"

"Yeah, at some point."

"Who are they?" Ruth asked with the same innocence. But this time her knee hit Mickey's hard under the table, and Mickey had to cough to keep from laughing.

"The Watersons own the house to the right of ours, through the woods. They've been there forever—since Evan and Rose first built the place. Good kids, right, Sean?"

"Whatever that means."

"You should have them over!" Lily suggested.

Sean shrugged.

"That would be fun!" Ruth said, blotting her mouth with her napkin to hide her own grin. Her food was scattered and smooshed across her plate, but not eaten. Mickey pushed her own plate away.

AFTER THE PLATES WERE cleared, cleaned, and dried, Lily went upstairs to take a bath, and Silas followed, saying good night with a kiss on Mickey's head. Mickey was ready to go up, too, to giggle under the covers with Ruth like they had every night before. But Ruth looped back into the living room and plopped down on the worn leather sofa. Sean wandered over to the bookshelf, touching the dusty spines with his brow furrowed.

"I have a crazy idea," Ruth said as Mickey fell into the couch beside her, her foot sliding under Ruth's bare thigh. "What if we had a séance?"

Mickey froze. She remembered the time she played Ouija

board with Sean in elementary school. He moved the planchette just gently enough to make Mickey believe she was haunted by a clown. She had refused to go to the circus since.

"What do you mean?"

"I mean," Ruth said, lowering her voice, "what if we try to contact that girl, Sarah? The one you said your uncle—"

Sean spun on his heel, any pretense of distraction gone.

"You *told* her?"

"It's fine, Sean," Ruth said. "I won't tell anyone. I swear."

"Yeah, Sean. Relax."

"Dad will fucking kill you both," he said, but he sat in the chair next to them, pushing himself to the edge so his knee touched Ruth's.

"Not if we don't get caught," Ruth said.

She didn't move her leg one inch.

# PEYOTE

"I'M SORRY, DID YOU just say fifteen in one deal?" KQ asked, her eyes darting between Cal's and mine. "As in, we do one thing and we get fifteen Quarter Pounders with fries? Just like that?"

"That's what he said."

"Well then, what the fuck are you doing in here talking to me? Go do it!" KQ shouted, waving her hands. "Right now!"

"There's one catch."

We agreed before we walked into her office that KQ was most likely to flex her power if she had another woman to flex it over. So Cal stood next to me, wearing downcast eyes and her most deeply beige sweater, the clothing equivalent of a dry, untoasted bagel.

"I don't like catches."

"If it were anyone but you, it would be tricky," I said. "But you can take care of this, no sweat. We just need your John Hancock."

KQ smiled, lapping up my bullshit like she'd never heard of table manners. "I'm listening."

"We need to find this guy so we can find what the marks are looking for, and the only way to do so is to use the Looking Glass."

KQ's head shot up, her eyes in slits. I was about to ask her if she was okay, when she slammed her palms down on her desk.

"Fuck it. Fifteen souls in one deal are more than even those Sixth-Floor pricks could say no to. Give me the slip." She held out her hand, wiggling her fingers. I handed her the clipboard and a fistful of pens, my heart in my throat.

After all of this planning and scheming, all I had to do was smile and ask real nice.

When we closed the door behind us, I tried to hide how my hands shook. I knew Cal would be excited, and I could share in the appropriate amount of that excitement. But I hadn't forgotten who Cal was. Even in moments of success, she was smarter than anyone else I had encountered in Hell. If she caught on that I had my own agenda, the perfect balance of happenstance that had fallen into my lap could dissolve into nothing.

"Holy shit, that worked," she said under her breath as she fussed with a pile of papers in her arms.

"Let's go tomorrow," I said. "First thing."

Of course, I wouldn't wait. I was already counting the steps between me and the elevator.

As if she could read my mind, Cal shook her head.

"Let's go right now."

# LILY

**LILY HELD HER HAND** under the bathtub faucet, the water so hot, it felt like punishment. She unwrapped her summer dress and hung it on the towel hook.

Lily had always had a nice body. She didn't stumble into it; she worked for it every day of her life. She could still throw up on demand, even though she hadn't done so in over a decade. Not since Rose caught her and gave her such a tongue-lashing, it wasn't just Lily's throat that burned. It had been hard to adjust to swallowing being permanent. She saw food and thought instantly about what it would become inside her. The whole thing was disgusting. But then she had children and, for the first time, she saw her body itself as powerful. Before that, she believed her body's only power was in the currency its shape gave her, which made her worth something to the strong. It wasn't until she brought her children into the world through nothing but her body's force that she realized she could be strong herself.

She looked in the foggy mirror, grateful for the kindness of blurred edges. It had been a long time since she gave birth, and her sense of strength waned the older her kids got, the less they needed from her. She placed one palm on her belly and pushed, before sliding into the steam of the old bathtub and thinking, once more, of Sarah.

**PHILIP WAS SENTENCED TO** fifteen years for killing Sarah Kelly. It wasn't quite manslaughter, but it wasn't cold-blooded murder either. A crime of passion, they called it. A mistake without the innocent glow of good intentions. The bruising on her chest strengthened the prosecution's case, but her history of handjobs in the local cemetery after school weakened it. They said she liked it rough.

After the trial, Philip lasted three weeks before he hanged himself with his bedsheets. No note, no nothing.

Everyone thought he couldn't handle the guilt, or the punishment. Silas swore up and down that there was foul play, threatening everyone from the attorneys to the police to the COs who found him. He went to the trial only once. He couldn't stand sitting there silently, watching his brother's hunched shoulders in the front row as person after person talked about his temper, his wild side, the way he could knock a tight end flat on his back without staggering. When they talked about the day a neighbor's dog went missing and they found his collar inside the saddlebag of Philip's motorcycle, flecks of blood morphing the name from "Otis" to "Is," Silas lost it. He jumped to his feet and screamed, "Bullshit!" until a bailiff dragged him out.

As much as she knew he didn't want to, a part of Silas blamed her nonetheless. If Lily hadn't gone for that late-night walk and seen Philip, he could've gotten off. Whatever forensic evidence hadn't been washed away by the lake was circumstantial. It could've been deemed an accident. But Evan and Rose never blamed her.

She cried on their kitchen floor the day the detectives called her in for questioning, begging them to tell her what to do. Rose and Evan could have told her to lie. She was carrying their grandson; they were her family now. They could've told her to take the fall herself, and she just might have. But they didn't. They told her to tell the truth. Rose held her in her arms in a way her own mother never had, stroked her hair, and called her "sweet girl."

*I'm so sorry, sweet girl.*

Then Sean was born and present and in need of things daily, hourly, by the minute, and Silas, Evan, and Rose shifted everything to be about The Baby. After a while, the attention went from strained to genuine to genuinely normal. Silas was in awe of their son. He was always bouncing him in his arms, pointing at people and buildings and colors. *Look, Sean! Garbage truck! Look, Sean, dog! Look, Sean, look. See? It's all for you.* As soon as Silas came back to her, Lily forgot that he had ever left. And she could've gone on forgetting. She could've stayed in that twilight state, a shade so close to happiness, it could have been mistaken as such, if not for the real thing for comparison.

If not for Gavin Kelly.

No one could call Silas a bad husband. She knew it almost *because* the marriage had never been happy, exactly, but he kept showing up anyway. Magazines and her mother taught her she should be grateful if a man stuck around for the taxing grind of normal. The part of marriage that is about cleaning the kitchen floor as opposed to fucking on it. As if the female gender were not equally capable of getting bored, of longing for the excitement brought by strange hands. But gratitude is not love, especially when the person dutifully practicing gratitude feels, fundamentally, that it is wrong to be grateful to someone for doing that which they vowed to do. That gratitude should be reserved for moments of awe, moments in which one doesn't have to decide to be grateful but rather falls, blindly and without thought, to one's knees.

Gavin was the person who saved her from the equally blissful and dangerous ignorance of the Forgetting Years, as Lily had come to think of the seventeen years between the trial and the minute she first touched his hand. Now, when she looked back, it scared her how much her mind could lie. Even to her. How, for seventeen years, it lulled her into a false sense of security, regardless of what stood right in front of her.

Does it count as staying if leaving is always on the mind? How much lying does a marriage need to survive?

She was tired of thinking about it.

Lily heard her daughter's laughter down the old oak stairs, followed by the tinkle of silverware, and she found that it hurt. Sometimes, especially here in this house, she couldn't help that some part of her wanted those Forgetting Years back. But there was one thing Lily was never able to forget during the Forgetting Years, even though she never said it out loud. One thing she never let herself think about even as she couldn't forget it, leaving it trapped between thought and unthought inside of her, as gnarled and solid as a peach pit.

She took that walk that night because when she woke up, Silas wasn't next to her.

# MICKEY

**"STOP CLUMPING THEM LIKE** that," Ruth said, knocking Sean's hand back. She spaced out the mismatched jars one at a time until they formed a circle around the blanket. Then she lit the candles within the jars, handing Sean the ones with flattened wicks so he could fish them out with his pocketknife.

"Sit down." She squinted at the distance between them. "Closer together." She pushed Sean, and, to Mickey's surprise, he went. If she pushed her brother like that, he would sit on her chest until she said he was king of the world and she his lifelong peasant.

"Okay, let's create a safe space. Everyone, hold hands."

She took a deep breath and exhaled it slowly, her eyes closed. Mickey stole a glance at Sean, who was watching Ruth's chest. But it didn't look like he was watching her breasts, which moved in the darkness like ocean creatures surfacing. It looked like he was watching the bones of her chest, up near her neck. Like he was entranced simply by the way that she breathed.

"Sean, this won't work if you don't take it seriously," Ruth said. Mickey heard her brother sigh, but he must've closed his eyes, too, because Ruth went on. With her eyes closed, the sounds of the woods made a solid wall around them, until Mickey felt zipped up in the night. She kicked one foot just an inch, just to know she could.

"Sarah, we are here to listen to you. We want to hear what happened to you all those years ago. Please, Sarah. Join us."

Sean pulled Mickey's hand toward his face so he could scratch his nose.

"Don't be afraid."

Mickey twisted on the blanket. There was a pit in her stomach like the time she took her bike over to the big park when she was seven, the one across the busiest street. Like she didn't know which was scarier—to succeed or not.

Then, the air shifted. They all felt it at the same time. Mickey could tell by the tightened grip on both of her hands. It felt like someone was watching them.

"That's right, Sarah," Ruth went on. "Come to us; tell us what happened to you. Did you drown?"

"We already know that," Sean said.

"Shh!"

The water slapped against the shore, and then again. Mickey felt cold all over.

"Did someone hurt you?" Ruth asked.

Mickey could see the candlelight flicker through her eyelids, even though there wasn't any wind.

"Who drowned you, Sarah?"

Mickey tightened her grip on Sean's fingers, and he squeezed back. She wanted to cry with gratitude for him just then, for their shared experience of faking bravery to impress this new outsider, and their shared blood that kept them together, separate from her.

There was a sudden crack in the woods and Mickey whirled around, but Ruth yanked her arm back to center.

"Don't open your eyes," she hissed.

Another crack. A rustle, a screech of birds taking flight.

"It's okay, Sarah. You're safe with us. There's nothing to be afraid of," Ruth said, louder this time. It seemed the scarier the world, the stronger Ruth's confidence. And for the first time, Mickey realized her friend had grown up on fear.

"Tell us, Sarah, so we can help you. Who killed you? Was it Philip? Give us a sign."

The crash that followed was so loud, even Ruth dropped Mickey's hand. Candles scattered, extinguishing as they rolled into the dirt.

"What the fuck do you think you're doing?" Silas bellowed, his voice violent enough to scare away the rest of the birds, and anything else that might have dared come close to them in the dark.

# PEYOTE

---

**THE ELEVATOR STOPPED, BUT** the doors didn't open. I was about to put my hands over my head and concede when a screen dropped down, covering the door. It was all white except for scrawling black text.

**Welcome to the Sixth Floor!** CLICK HERE **to begin.**

I looked at Cal and she shrugged. I tapped and the text disappeared, replaced by a spinning circle of colors from the cheapest crayon box.

Then the circle froze.

"A classic," Cal said.

*Answer the following questions to find your perfect spirit guide!*

**Which form are you more inclined toward?**

a. Human

b. Animal

c. Nonspatial/light being

Cal pressed "animal," and I didn't object.

**What is your most successful way of receiving instruction?**
a. Kindly
b. Forcefully
c. Passive-aggressively

I went for the screen, but Cal beat me to it, pressing B.
"Good to know," I said.

**How receptive are you to humor?**
a. Very, I love a funny companion
b. Somewhat, I could take it or leave it
c. Not at all, I prefer serious

Cal and I both tapped A simultaneously.
"Really?" she said. "I couldn't have guessed."

**If you were stranded on a desert island, what would you bring with you?**
a. Your favorite book
b. A family photo album
c. A portable music player

"I wouldn't bring any of these things," I said. "I would bring a weapon, or a GPS tracker."
"I would bring sunscreen," Cal said. "And whiskey."
"I guess a book?"
She nodded, and I pressed the button. The floor below us lit up, one perfect square below my feet, one below hers. Mine was blue, hers pink.
"Oh, come on," she said.

**Final Question: Between the two of you, who is in charge?**

a.  Blue
b.  Pink
c.  Equality rules!

I hit A, hard and fast. About that, I wouldn't compromise.

The spinning rainbow returned, stalling and starting. I pulled on my collar.

## Welcome to the Sixth Floor!
## While here, please obey the following rules:

a.  Follow the instructions of your spirit guide—this is for both your enjoyment and safety!
b.  Show respect: leave our floor the same as you found it!
c.  Absolutely no admittance to the Looking Glass without appropriate clearance.

### Have fun!

*If at any time you are incapable of following these rules, you will be reassigned to the Downstairs, effective immediately.*

There was a crunch, a grinding of gears, and then the screen began its creaking ascent, revealing a gigantic marble hallway lined in gold. It was the most beautiful thing I'd seen in Hell. At least that was what I felt compelled to say, so much so, I almost opened my mouth to say it, but something stopped me. It was beautiful in the way a billboard of a sunset is beautiful, until you take in the graffiti and the concrete buildings and the smell of pee soaking into trash bags piled on the curb, embryonic in the hot sun.

Yes, but.

The sound of slapping on tile stopped me from taking another step.

"Hello, visitors!"

Cal elbowed me, and my jaw dropped as a creature came to a stop in front of us. Whatever it was, it wasn't a reflection of my spirit. Unless I was even more fucked up than I thought.

"What are you?" Cal asked. She seemed more intrigued than horrified, for which I had to give her credit. She was brave. Perversely so.

"I'm your Sixth-Floor guide. I'm here under the guise of making you feel comfortable, but my primary purpose is to keep you in line and record everything you do and say."

"Right, but what *are* you?" Cal asked again. She reached out to touch it, and it didn't flinch.

"I'm an animal."

That was an understatement.

From what I could tell, the creature was a combination of all the animals, stitched into one terrifying pet of Frankenstein and put on wheels. One alert dog ear and another ear from a floppy elephant framed its part-bear-part-alligator face, complete with the sort of black glass eyes favored by taxidermists and toy makers, one of which seemed to be pushed from the inside out, giving the eye a precarious dangling effect. Its feet were webbed and orange like a duck's, and jutted out from a torso lined with enough types of animal skin to decorate a 1970s bachelor pad. Both spiky and soft, it had paws like tiny translucent hands. Just looking at it made me feel slimy and itchy at the same time.

"You sure are," Cal said, walking around it in a slow circle.

"Stay where I can see you," it said, and Cal jumped back in front of it, saluting.

"What do we call you?" I asked.

"Doesn't matter, as long as you call me!"

"Excuse me?"

The creature blinked, an action I wasn't expecting and didn't enjoy. "You requested humor."

Cal laughed. "We did, didn't we?"

"What is your name?" I clarified, my voice more hesitant than I would've liked.

"Security and Information Pod Number 64221H."

"We'll call you Felix," Cal said.

I looked at her.

"It was the name of my first pet."

I couldn't imagine when she could've had a pet; a puppy wouldn't have exactly fit in around the barracks. But now was not the time to mention that.

"I thought you were the one in charge?" Felix asked, looking at me.

Cal laughed again.

# SILAS

**EVEN NOW, WHEN SILAS** remembered Sarah Kelly, he remembered her tongue first. In high school, she was the only girl he knew with a tongue ring. She said she got it pierced in New York City, in a dentist's chair on the sidewalk on Saint Mark's Place. But everyone took what Sarah Kelly said with a grain of salt. She played with the tongue ring constantly. If she was concentrating, she would push the ball end out her pursed lips and roll it back and forth like a lighthouse beam, the fake diamond catching in the classroom's fluorescent lights.

"You know why she got that tongue ring, don't you?" his friends jeered each time she walked by. After weeks of this routine, Sarah stopped walking and turned around. The friend who said it hooted; the rest quickly looked away. But she locked eyes with Silas.

She held out her hand like a peace sign but palm inward, and gave one exaggerated lick in the air between her two fingers, from the knuckles up.

They didn't give her shit after that. But they did start inviting her out.

It was impossible not to be a little in love with everyone at seventeen. Desire grew on everything—every skin particle, every foggy car window; in the beat of every song and the fabric of every strap against a girl's collarbone. Silas was in love with the whole world back then. He was ravenous, quenchless. Each touch increased his appetite, until his whole body became nothing but lips between teeth.

Later, he loved to watch Sarah's tongue ring when she put her mouth on him, the way it glistened in low light. Like she was a conduit for electricity, and he alone could provide the current. With her mouth on him, he felt powerful.

He hadn't felt that way in a long, long time.

The truth was, the moment Ruth walked into their kitchen the first day Mickey brought her home, Silas thought of Sarah. The long auburn hair that looked like it belonged to hot earth, the strong eye contact. A confidence, a smirking fierceness Silas had never forgotten. But he had never expected to hear Sarah's name in Ruth's mouth, same hair spilling around tanned shoulders, same wicked little test in the eyes. Not there, in that clearing.

"What the fuck do you think you're doing?" he yelled again, kicking forest debris, feeling large.

"Dad, I—" Sean started.

"Mickey, how dare you?"

Mickey looked at him with such terror, he thought for a second that he could smile and say he was kidding. But his blood was pumping louder and louder: it seemed to want her fear, to feed on it.

"How *dare* you do this to your uncle Philip, to me! Do you have any *idea*—"

"Mr. Harrison, it was my—"

"Ruth, I'm not talking to you. You are not a part of this family."

"Dad," Mickey said, her voice small.

"Get up." He walked around the circle and grabbed her by the sleeve of her sweatshirt, jerking her upward. "Get the *fuck* up!"

"Dad—" Sean said again, reaching for him. Or for her.

"Don't touch me," Silas growled, and Sean's hand retreated. Silas shoved Mickey between the shoulder blades, pushing her toward the path. Sean and Ruth lined up behind him, punished ducklings.

The walk back to the house was silent except for crunching leaves and the slap of flip-flops. Silas kept the hood of Mickey's sweatshirt in his fist, leading her like a dog on a leash. When they got to the porch, he tightened his grip.

"You two, go upstairs. And be quiet; it's the middle of the night."

Sean and Ruth both bowed their heads and walked through the door into the dark inside. Once Silas and Mickey were alone, he pulled her around to look at him.

"I have never been so disappointed in you in my whole life. I know you have a friend here, but that does not give you permission to exploit this family's worst moments. You have no idea— Jesus. How dare you?"

"Sean was there too."

Silas laughed in the way that is nothing like a laugh. The kind of laugh that comes from the darkest part of the gut.

"I expect this kind of bullshit from Sean. Not you, Michaela."

He let go of her hood and pushed his hands through his hair.

"I'm so sorry," she said. "I wasn't thinking. You're right; I was trying to impress Ruth, and I let it get away from me."

He turned his back to her.

"Just go. I can't even look at you right now."

"Dad—"

"Don't tell your mother. You don't even know—this would kill her."

Mickey stood there for a moment, but then he heard her open the screen door, and hold it carefully so it wouldn't slam shut.

Silas's heart was too loud for him to go to bed. He paced the driveway for a few passes, thinking maybe he would take the bike out to cool off, but instead he struck out back across the lawn. He needed to check the clearing, see if they left any candles burning. That would be the last thing they needed, he thought as he trudged—a forest fire.

As he got closer, he had to shake off the feeling of walking backward. Not in the physical sense, but in the temporal. The setting was the same: same trees, full height well before Silas was even a figment of his mother's imagination. Same moon, same lake. Sarah Kelly was the same. Same exactly, caught forever in that very night. In fact, the only thing that was different about her was that now she was gone.

When he reached the clearing, the illusion held. At first glance, the snuffed-out candles looked like wine coolers in the moonlight. The way the blanket was bundled and folded in the corners, it looked like abandoned clothes.

This place held on to its ghosts.

Silas gathered the candles and draped the blanket over his arm. And as he turned back, something caught his eye. A color in the water, red as a tongue. Red like a wound when you were waiting for the blood to come. He bent over and picked it up, gently twirling the stem to shake the water off.

There was no way Mickey could've known that Sarah loved poppies.

Only Lily would've known that.

# PEYOTE

"**WHO DO WE SHOW** this to?" I asked, holding out KQ's signed form.

"Me," Felix said. He scanned the document and blinked again, which I was beginning to understand as less of a protective function and more of an information-processing one.

"Your access has been granted. Come with me." Felix spun around and started down the hallway, his duck feet flapping uselessly in front of his wheels.

The hallway went on for much longer than any real hallway could. I felt feelings I hadn't known in eons, making it hard to come up with the right words. Excitement, anticipation. The first feelings to die with mortality.

"So, you're looking for someone?" Felix asked. He was leading the way ahead of us, but somehow I knew he was still watching.

"A real asshole," Cal said.

"I don't have one of those!"

"Another joke?" I asked.

"A fact," he responded. "But it results in a humor response in sixty-four percent of our visitors."

"So you declare that detail to all the girls? Here I was feeling special."

"Don't flirt with the Psycho Sonic," I whispered. "His head might explode."

"Sonic was a hedgehog," Felix said, his wheels whirring through the slaps. "I'm a more general animal." He stopped abruptly, and even though I didn't touch him, I came close enough to make me wipe my hand on my shirt.

"Here we are."

The door was simple white, like all the others, save for the nameplate printed in gold.

THE LOOKING GLASS.

BEFORE WE GO ANY further, I've been keeping something from you. You know about the concept of a Complete Set; we've gone over that. And you know the purpose of the Looking Glass. You even know my last name. But I have yet to tell you what came from that night with Slips in our bunk, the information that drove me from the Second Floor to the Fifth. That drove me all the way here, to stand in front of this door.

I'm talking about the loophole.

Let me remind you once more: this is Hell. It is supposed to punish the bad. But it was a failed experiment from the start, wasn't it? If a place is built for bad people—as in truly bad, rotten-cored people, the kind of bad that just spills off the skin like scent—bad people will make it their home. It's the great irony of the whole thing. Hell, like all other prisons, may start out as punishment. But if you survive long enough, it becomes a training ground. A place to cut your teeth on your badness, to make it work for you. In which the punishment of anyone but you becomes its own reward.

188

So, here's the big agency secret. Ready?

If you get a full set of deals from your own heirs, you get a redo on Earth.

The Harrisons were mine in every sense of the word. From me they were made, and from them I would rise. I had only one more to go, and then all I had to do was make sure that, when I got back, I wouldn't repeat the mistakes that landed me here in the first place. I had to find out exactly when and why it happened, go back to that very moment, and do the opposite. The Looking Glass was the only way.

In short, behind this door was my humanity. And I wanted it back. Whatever the cost.

"Can we go in now?" I asked, reaching for the doorknob. A tail came out of some unseen slot and slapped me on the hand.

"I can't go in there with you, for mechanical reasons. Which means I will be timing you. Our research shows that it takes exactly three minutes and thirty-five seconds for the Looking Glass to find what it is looking for, and for that information to be printed. We calculated in roughly forty-three seconds for human processing time, to adjust for your antiquated circuitry. If the Looking Glass is still engaged when my timer goes off, you will be immediately shipped Downstairs. Do you understand?"

I went cold, but managed to nod.

"Good."

Felix faced the door, and a light scanned his glass eyes. It flashed twice and turned green.

"Your time starts now."

# MICKEY

**WHEN MICKEY OPENED THE** bedroom door, Ruth was on the bed, a book in her lap. She cast it aside as soon as Mickey walked in.

"Are you okay?" she asked.

Mickey didn't know how to answer. She felt like a trapdoor had opened and all of her insides had spilled out, leaving her tripping over her intestines as she climbed the stairs, apologizing for their stains.

Her dad had never, ever talked to her like that. Sure, he yelled at her some for stupid choices. The time she brought food coloring into the bath and accidentally dyed the porcelain purple. The time she and Sean wrapped the family car in cellophane on April first. Those times, he yelled like he knew that was what he had to do, but ultimately, he loved her the same as always. Tonight was different.

"I'll tell him tomorrow it was all my idea. I'll just tell him, and it'll be—"

"He assumed as much."

Ruth nodded and slumped back against the bed. "Got it."

Mickey felt pain moving through her, building a tether. She hurt, so she threw it at Ruth. Now Ruth hurt. And so on. Mickey lay down and buried her face in the pillow. She wanted comfort. She wanted her mother.

Mickey heard the bedsprings shift, felt Ruth press against her.

"I'm sorry, Mick," she whispered. "I didn't think he would find us. I had no idea—I didn't think about what it would feel like for him."

"Me neither," Mickey said, softening. "I've never felt this bad."

Ruth put her hand in Mickey's hair, starting over her ear and combing backward. Mickey tensed at first but then relaxed into it, grateful. She wanted to feel exactly like this, she thought. A child with a bad dream.

"I remember one time my dad found me on his porch steps. I had taken the bus all the way from my mom's by myself. I was, maybe, seven? God, he was so mad."

"I didn't know you had a dad," Mickey said.

Ruth's hand went still.

"Everybody has a dad."

"Right, yeah, of course. I just mean, you've never talked about him."

"He moved out when I was a little kid. Met somebody new, wanted to start a new family. My mom was so angry. So hurt. When they went to court, she told me to lie. Say stuff about him, bad stuff. Like that he touched me, slept in my bed with me. I didn't know what I was saying. I was just a little kid, you know?"

It was the most Ruth had ever talked about her family. Mickey nodded, silent.

"So I said it, and my mom got full custody. My dad got in a lot of trouble. He got fired, had to move to a different town. Couldn't come near me or my mom again."

"Damn."

"I've regretted that my whole life. If I had just told the truth, maybe I could've grown up with him instead. Had a little sister, a nice brick house. A Labrador. The whole nine. Instead of my mom's crazy."

They were quiet, and Ruth's fingernails resumed their slow progression across Mickey's scalp.

"I'll tell you," Ruth said. "There's nothing I wouldn't do to make that up to him. To prove that he could trust me." She swallowed. "Nothing."

Mickey rolled over so their noses almost touched.

"I agreed to the séance; it's not your fault."

"Do you want to know what I do when I feel bad?" Ruth asked, her voice deep in its quiet.

"Yes, please."

"One sec."

Ruth got up and went to the bathroom. Mickey rolled onto her back and stared at the ceiling. The room was lit by the lamp on the dresser and nothing else. In the shadows, she kept picturing her dad's face. She had never seen that much rage in him. Silas was the fun parent, the goofball. The one who encouraged her to bring the air mattress into the community pool, not the one who made her spend hours drying it with a blow-dryer. He trusted her, and she failed him. Even worse than that: she failed Philip, his favorite person. His second-favorite person, she had always thought. Second to her.

Ruth poked her head around the doorframe.

"Come in here."

AN OPEN ALTOIDS TIN balanced on the edge of the sink. Mickey recognized it from Ruth's makeup kit, which sat open and ravaged on the back of the toilet. Mickey used that makeup before dinner.

Blue mascara. She could barely remember the way the night felt back then. Ruth tipped the contents of the tin into one palm and patted the opposite corner of the sink with the other.

"Stand here."

Mickey stood next to her and saw the tin wasn't empty. Inside remained a collection of loose pills, round and scored and definitely not Altoids.

"What are those?"

"Nothing," Ruth said, snapping the tin closed. "Just some medicine my mom got for when she flies—she hates airplanes. They take the edge off. I used to take them, too, but this works better."

Ruth distributed the tin's contents in a line along the sink: an alcohol wipe and a sliver of metal that she rested on a cloth made for cleaning glasses. It gleamed enough to catch the reflection of the faucet, which, in return, caught the reflection of the metal, like a conversation among believers of the same faith.

"I used to use shaving razors—if you break the cartridges, you can get them out individually—but then I saw these at the art store, and I never went back."

Mickey watched as Ruth rolled up her shirtsleeve.

"Sometimes," she said, "when everything hurts so much, you feel like you're going to drown in yourself—like the whole world is quicksand and the harder you thrash, the worse it gets—this can help pull you back to the surface."

At first, it looked like just skin. A metal shark fin leaving no trace. But then the blood rose to the surface and brought to Mickey's mind the word "unzipping." Ruth held the cut to the light and rotated her forearm, her skin opalescent against the dark blood. Her face was ashen, whiter than it had ever been. But her eyes were sparkling.

"Sometimes you just need to know where you are," she said. "You know? Where the outside world ends and you begin."

They watched as the blood trickled down the curve of her arm, gravity in color. But then she opened the alcohol swab and caught it. It was all hers, that blood. It belonged on her side.

Ruth wiped the blade with the rest of the swab as she pressed toilet paper to the cut, her fingers hard against her flesh. She looked at Mickey, the razor clean and shining in her outstretched hand.

"Now you try."

# PEYOTE

**THE ROOM WAS EMPTY** except for a solitary desk, which held a solitary computer. But not the flat, fits-into-your-back-pocket kind you have nowadays. This was a dinosaur of a thing: all sharp white corners and vented sides panting machine heat. The black screen bulged as if overcrowded, stuffed to the gills.

"Do we just type?"

"I'll do it," I said, grabbing the keyboard. "You make sure the printer is on."

Cal gave me a look but sat on the floor without a word, pulling the equally prehistoric printer from the shadows of the desk. I waited until her eyes were busy, and I clicked, coaxing the screen to life.

**Welcome to the Looking Glass! What are you looking for today?**

a. The location of a person or object (time and/or geography)

b. An individual human memory

c. Return to menu

"What kind of outlet is this for?" Cal asked, holding up a cable.

"I don't know," I said without looking. My hand hesitated, but only for a second before I clicked B.

"Hold on, there's a bin of cords here," Cal said, approaching the desk from the back. "Let me know when it lights up, okay?"

A new box opened on the screen, a cursor blinking within it.

a.  Name:
b.  Specific Memory Context:

"Anything yet?"

"Nope," I said, my eyes on nothing but the screen.

"I bet the damn thing itself only takes three seconds and Freaky Felix just gets off on torture by nineteen-nineties technology."

"Probably."

I typed and hit Enter. The screen stuttered and froze.

"I mean, if you think about it, this thing is kind of like his great-grandfather," Cal said, throwing another cable over her shoulder. "Still nothing?"

"Nope," I managed to say. The spinning circle appeared, vibrant and energetic.

"Pey, I can see the light from here!"

I looked down at the printer.

"Right," I said. "It just started."

Cal wiped her hands on her pants and came back to my side. I felt her lean over my shoulder, the buttons of her shirt grazing my arm.

"Where are we at?"

"I don't know. I think it's processing."

Cal stayed there, close enough that I thought my beating heart might hurt her.

"Why would it be loading like that? Aren't you supposed to be on a map screen? Are you sure you opened the right—"

ONE MINUTE AND FORTY-FIVE SECONDS

The announcement was loud enough that Cal and I both jumped. But only she whirled around, so I caught the screen when it loaded.

And just like that, there it was. My information, my memories. All of me, from when I was someone. I clicked PRINT and slammed the mouse to close it out, but it was too late.

"Pey, what is that?" Cal asked, but it wasn't so much a question as it was a knife made verbal and cold.

The printer awoke with a crackle and whir.

"Shit," I said, slamming the mouse again for effect. "It re-started."

"Bullshit," Cal said. "What did you do?"

ONE MINUTE

"I'm sorry."

I abandoned the keyboard and fell to my knees. The printer paused but I could see the first two inches of paper, and with it came all of the exhausted metaphors people love to pair with the smooth and white. I felt high from the sight. Ready to conquer.

"What the fuck do you mean, you're sorry?" Cal demanded as she commandeered the keyboard. "What did you do?"

FORTY SECONDS

The printer started again and I held my fingertips to the dwindling space between me and my future. My past.

Cal typed, and a map flickered on the screen. The image enlarged in stops and starts. From my position, I could tell it was closing in on America. That was something, at least.

My paper was two-thirds out.

TWENTY SECONDS

Cal banged the mouse on the desk.

"Come on!" she yelled.

Her voice sounded different from the way it usually did, even when she was upset. There was fury in it, sure. But there was also something else. Fear.

I almost felt bad, but then the paper dropped, warm as a tender moment, into my outstretched hands, and I had it. The missing piece, the final key to the only thing I had cared about for as long as I knew myself. I folded it again and again and stood up.

TEN SECONDS. PLEASE STEP BACK FROM THE LOOK-ING GLASS.

"Cal, we have to turn it off."

"It hasn't found him yet." She gripped the edge of the desk, her nose grazing the screen.

"Let go, Cal. They'll send you back Downstairs."

I put my hand on her shoulder, and she bucked me off. The map flickered again, and I could see Florida and the jagged edge of Georgia meeting the Pacific.

"Cal, now!"

I could've left her there. In fact, it would've tied a very pretty little bow on the whole thing. Cal back in the Downstairs, her brain turned to goo and back again too many times for her to ever remember me or how I threw our deal, and her, under the bus. KQ wouldn't care. She would be proud of her character-judging skills. *She just couldn't hack it, boss.* It would've solved a lot of my problems. But the truth is, it didn't even occur to me. The handle of the door clicked, and I threw myself into Cal, knocking her to the ground.

# LILY

THAT MORNING, LILY WOKE up reaching. Regardless of the distance she constructed while awake, she never stopped reaching for Silas in her sleep. He slept later than she did most days, blocking the sun with a pillow or the crook of his arm, and when she reached, he was there to be found. But that morning, he was gone.

Lily listened for voices from the stairwell but heard none. She turned the corner and knocked.

"Si?"

The door opened into emptiness. Lily picked up an undershirt from the floor and pulled the corners of the quilt, the bed unslept in but messy anyway.

The day had begun on the lake. She could hear boat motors, and children shrieking with joy as they clutched the vinyl handles of tubes. Someone was playing country music through a speaker turned up too loud, making the twangs tinny. She could see the outdoor shower below, Ruth's and Mickey's bathing suits draped over the door. She had been surprised when Mickey asked her for a two-piece that year. She wondered if she would ever stop being surprised by the way her children kept growing up. She looked over at the shed to see if the bike was missing, but it was there, pristine as ever.

She used the hem of the undershirt to wipe a smudge from the windowpane, which blurred the otherwise perfect view.

He wasn't cooking breakfast. The kitchen was littered with remnants of her children's fending for themselves: crumbs on the counter, peanut butter with the lid askew. She turned the corner and went onto the porch. Nothing.

It wasn't until she faced the dining room that she saw it. The table was cleared of last night's meal, the trivets and candlesticks back on their shelves. But there was one small vase left out, right in the center. Its neck like a loose fist around the stem of one red flower.

He knew.


**"HEY, YOU."**

No matter the problem, the first harmonic of Gavin's voice was the best and most immediate remedy. She wanted to call him again and again just to hear him answer. She wanted to hook herself up to the cell phone towers between them, align her heartbeat with the pause between rings.

"Gav." She exhaled, her breath hard and quick as she crossed the lawn. "Something's up. I think he knows."

"Slow down," Gavin said. "What happened? Are you okay?"

"I'm fine." Her foot slipped on the morning's dew, and she steadied herself. "I'm okay. He's not here right now; I don't know where he went. But he definitely knows something."

"What happened, exactly?"

Lily entered the shadow of the boathouse and pressed herself against the wall. She felt briefly insane, flush with drama like a teenager. But the pounding in her heart was real.

"Okay, so, I did something for Sarah yesterday. Nothing special, just brought flowers to the clearing. For the anniversary."

"Oh, Lily," he said. "Thank you. What did you get her?"

"Poppies. I remember her saying something about liking flowers that could make drugs."

Gavin chuckled at the memory, so adolescent. The dead don't grow up.

"You're the kindest woman I know. You know that?"

"I learned it from you," she said, and for a moment she forgot why she'd called; she forgot anything else existed at all.

"So, then what?"

"When I went downstairs this morning, one of Sarah's flowers—a poppy—was sitting right there, in the middle of the dining room table. He put it in a vase and everything. I didn't even think he knew where we kept those." She took a breath. "He wanted me to find it, Gav. He wanted me to know he knows."

"Could he have just found it and thought it was nice?"

"After prom, Silas tried to replant my corsage as a surprise. Trust me, this wasn't floral appreciation."

"Do you want me to come get you? I don't like you feeling unsafe."

Lily leaned back against the wall.

"I'm fine," she said, her pulse slowing simply from his voice. "I'm safe. He is probably just passive-aggressively letting me know he knows I did something for Sarah. But I can explain that easily enough. Sean just turned seventeen, you know."

"Makes the whole thing real on a different level."

Lily closed her eyes. She had always loved the boathouse. She loved the sounds it made: the slap of water over the rusted boat lift, the creak of the weather vane.

"He couldn't possibly know about us."

"No," Gavin agreed. "Not from a flower."

Lily could hear Gavin press the receiver into his neck as if pulling her close.

"Fuck, Gav. I really wish I could see you."

"I wish I could do a lot more than see you."

Lily leaned back against the wall harder, and then she heard the screen door slam shut and saw Sean shuffling down the porch steps.

"Shit, I have to go. Hold that thought, okay?"

"As if it ever goes away," he said. "Would be nice to get some work done once in a while."

"I love you," she said, before slipping her phone under a half-deflated inner tube and grabbing a bag of birdseed from a shelf just as Sean stepped inside.

"There you are!"

"Where else would I be?" Sean asked groggily as he walked into the boathouse. He had on his swim shorts and held a book under his arm.

"Where is your father?"

Sean shrugged as he continued past her to the dock.

"Well, don't mind me," she said to his back. "Just feeding the birds."

# PEYOTE

**TO HER CREDIT, CAL** didn't say a single word until the elevator doors closed.

"I have been trying to be nice to you," she said, jamming the emergency brake and bringing the whole thing to a screaming halt. "I mean, honestly—maybe for the first time ever—I am genuinely *trying* to be nice. Not because I need you for something, but because for some fucknut reason, I actually kind of like you. And you, you fucking *asshole*—"

She slammed her fist into the wall with the word.

"Cal, I—"

"Do you think you're the only one who suffers? It's Hell for all of us, not just you."

And then she sank down into the corner of the elevator and put her head in her hands.

I don't think I've been sorry once since I arrived in Hell, except sorry for myself. But that did something to me. Seeing her like that, like she was small.

It hurt.

Maybe this side of success made me sentimental, I thought as I touched the paper in my pocket. Or maybe I realized that my plan relied on her willingness to lie for me, a kink I hadn't quite ironed out. Or maybe it was the deeper, sharper truth.

As far as I could remember, Cal was the closest thing I'd ever had to a friend.

She could've told Felix the minute he opened that door, and I would have been on the conveyor belt. But she didn't. Despite all my efforts to push her away, she was the only person—in millennia of this existence—who cared enough about me to keep a secret.

The words left my mouth before I could stop them.

"I'm getting out."

"Excuse me?"

"I found a way out of Hell, and I needed those results to make sure I never come back."

Cal laughed an angry, scary laugh.

"Go fuck yourself, Pey."

"I wouldn't have screwed you over like that for anything less, I promise. But I have a plan. And if you help me, we can both get out of here."

I said it because I didn't want her to turn me in. I was sweet-talking my way out of damnation—or, rather, worse damnation: deeper, darker, closer-to-the-hot-core damnation, unlike the current cozy damnation of home. But once I said it, I realized it was true. It would probably be bad for the world, having Cal out and about once more. But I didn't care. It was good for me.

Cal stood up.

"Assuming even one word of what you're saying is true—and that is a very, very big assumption—" Cal started as she paced, "it won't matter, because KQ will send us both Downstairs if we fuck up this deal. And there is no deal without the target's location, which, thanks to you, we don't have."

"We know he's in Georgia, somewhere near the coast. Do you have any idea why he would be there? Any intel from Third?" I asked as I rolled the edge of the paper, just to feel it cup my finger back.

"Without the one contraption in Hell meant to find people, you mean? The one we just fucking *left?*"

"Okay," I said. "What about Jason? I bet he has more in his memory than he originally shared. Maybe more than he even knows."

Cal paused. "You know who you told me had memory clearance?"

"No," I said, catching her drift. "Cal, come on. Be reasonable."

"If you had been reasonable, we wouldn't be here. But here we are." She hit the emergency brake again, and the elevator shrieked into motion. "We need Trey, and we need him now."

"I refuse to work with that asshole, and you should too. He's not like us, Cal. He's so stupid, he's dangerous."

"I didn't realize I had been promoted to your category."

"I haven't told anyone but you about this plan," I whispered. "And I won't. I know this might make me an idiot, but I trust you."

Cal took one step toward me then, followed by another, and another, until she was close enough that I could see each one of her eyelashes. The elevator was small, but the space we took up inside it was so much smaller.

She traced the seam of my belt with her fingertips, and rubbed the leather against itself like she was starting the slowest of fires.

"Cal," I said, swallowing.

"I trust you too. And I want to help you, Pey. I do. But this thing we're doing?" She paused long enough for her bottom lip to go between her teeth before pulling it, slowly, free. "It only works if the trust goes both ways."

The elevator door dinged and, just like that, she was back on her side.

"Let's talk to Trey," she said, rubbing my stolen paper between her fingertips, the universal sign for currency, "and we can all get what we want."

# SILAS

SILAS LUGGED ANOTHER BAG of rocks from the trunk. He could get the car only so far into the woods, but it was worth it, he thought as he wiped dirt and sweat from his forehead. The place had been a robbed grave for too long.

The first time he built the firepit was with Philip. He could almost see the way his brother wrinkled his nose in concentration as he selected the best of the rocks that Silas pried from the dirt with his grubby little hands and delivered, arms outstretched. This was going to be their place, Philip said with each discarded option. Just theirs. So it had to be perfect. Silas dug until he couldn't feel his fingers that day and cried when the sun went down.

He tore open the bag of rocks, ignoring the nagging feeling of inadequacy for buying them from Home Depot. He was an adult now. He couldn't spend a whole day pulling rocks like old teeth from the soil. He used his hands to dig into the middle of the firepit, sifting through wet leaves and ash until he hit aluminum, which he pulled out and threw over his shoulder into an open garbage bag. And then again. And again, and again. It was like med-itating, he thought. At the very least, he was communing with nature.

During the trial, everyone found out Phil had feelings for Sarah. Lily said she already knew—she said anyone with eyes could tell. But Phil was not the type to run his mouth. Plus, he didn't have the kind of friend group Silas had; he didn't have any-one to brag to or confide in, except Silas. And Phil never told him a word about it. He didn't find out until the rest of the town did, when every thought, every feeling Phil ever experienced, became hard evidence or fodder for horrified fascination. When Phil had lost the public privilege of being a person capable of love. When he became nothing but an animal and the conversation became about nothing but the size of his cage.

If Phil had told him, Silas thought as he threw a worn-down shard of glass into the bag, he would've stopped. But even as he thought it, he knew it wasn't true.

Lily didn't know that Silas had been sleeping with Sarah. No one did. At first, he kept it a secret because that's what you did with a girl like Sarah Kelly. A girl like Lily for the football games and prom, a girl like Sarah for the nights in between, and nothing but opportunity looking forward. But after a while, when Sarah had never asked him why she entered his house only through his bedroom window, when she'd never bought a new dress or dropped hints about meeting his parents, it started to bother him. He hadn't planned on climbing back into his bed so carefully after she snuck out, just to leave her imprint on his pillow undisturbed.

By the time his summer party was approaching, the dual life had become too much. Silas couldn't stop thinking about Sarah whenever Lily kissed him. He was closing his eyes more and more everywhere that Sarah wasn't, opening them only when she was real, right there in front of him and close enough his hands could prove it. He decided to end things with Lily once and for all. To make Sarah Kelly his girlfriend, and fuck what anyone had to say about it.

But then Lily told him she thought she might be pregnant, and his whole world stopped.

Men talk a lot about that moment. The moment they learn that they've made something new, something no one else could've made. The stories they decide to tell are full of giddy nervousness and reckless joy, with a dose of healthy, humbling fear. But the kind that's still delicious, the way a static shock leaves a warm tingle on the skin. That was not Silas's story. Not until he decided to rewrite it later. Now he couldn't imagine himself without his kids. But back then, the news felt more like the arrival of death than that of life.

Silas could still remember driving to see Sarah after Lily told him. It was May, so close to graduation, and spring had sprung all over their small town. He drove the whole way with shaking hands, Lily's tears still wet on the collar of his T-shirt. When he pulled into the school parking lot, he saw Sarah waiting for him, bare legs nestled in the grass of the baseball diamond.

The truth was this: in Silas's brief but only time on this earth, happiness had been a beautiful lie. An intended kindness, like Santa Claus or God, just convincing enough to make him feel ashamed of his skepticism, and double down. But then he kissed Sarah Kelly for the first time, and he knew that his happiness was only a fraction of the real deal. The appetizers at a buffet. A cut drug. But happiness can be cruel. If they hadn't gone for that first walk, if he hadn't felt her tongue in his mouth as they pressed against that tree in the dark, Silas would've thought—rather satisfied—that the happiness he had known thus far was as much happiness as any one person could know. He would've felt lucky for his crumbs, mistaking them for meals. Because the truth was he didn't know he was starving until he tasted her. Until then, he believed himself fed.

Silas watched her in the sun, his hands on the steering wheel. But he was just seventeen, and his words had yet to catch up to his feelings. So eventually, he turned the key in the ignition and left.

NOTHING WOULD'VE LASTED WITH Sarah; he knew that. He would've met another girl in college, maybe a handful. Maybe more. The names Lily and Sarah would have become nothing but rose-colored associations—or some other, murkier color. Soft-skinned girls who contributed to his creation, who pulled off small parts of themselves to make him more durable. Other names would've taken on meaning. Annabelle, maybe. Or Elizabeth.

Or Ruth.

As soon as he thought it, as if by his will alone, there she was.

She stood on the edge of the clearing like the rest was danger-ous. Or maybe it was the opposite. Maybe she was the danger and the rest was sacred.

"Mr. Harrison?"

"Hi, Ruth," Silas said, not looking up. He found the plastic that once held a six-pack and threw it behind him.

"I don't mean to bother you."

Silas sighed and straightened up, wiping his brow again.

"You're not bothering me."

"I want you to know—last night wasn't Mickey's fault. It was mine. It was my idea. I basically made her do it."

Silas looked at Ruth, using one arm to block the sunlight, and realized what it was about her that kept him looking long after he should stop. She looked like Sarah.

"She loves you so much, and I'm really grateful to be here. I mean, being with you guys—I've never been around a family like yours." Ruth swallowed. "I just wanted to say I'm sorry. You were so nice to let me come here, and if I ruined it, I'll never forgive myself."

"You didn't ruin anything," Silas said. "I'm sorry I got so mad. I didn't mean to be rude to you. It's just that this place has a lot of significance for our family, not all in the best of ways. But you know that already, don't you?"

Ruth twisted her hips and pulled on the tie of her bathing suit bottoms. Silas hadn't seen this bathing suit before. It was yellow with blue polka dots. It tied the same way as her other ones, knots in the crucial parts. Little else.

"I'm sorry. I really am. I'll stop prying—she only told me things because I pushed it. I just—we don't really have any old family stories. It's just my mom and me, you know? She doesn't tell me much. So it's cool to hear—I don't mean what happened is cool! Shit. Shit! I shouldn't curse! I'm sorry." Ruth pushed her palm into her face.

Silas laughed. "It's fine, Ruth. Really. Forget about it."

"So you're not mad at Mickey anymore?"

"I'm going to talk to her later."

Ruth shifted but stayed at the tree line. "That doesn't answer my question."

"I don't have to answer your questions; you're a kid."

He smiled enough to let her know he was teasing, and she laughed.

"What are you doing?"

"Fixing the old gal up," Silas answered, digging his fingers back in. "I figured if you guys are going to be down here, it might as well be tetanus-free."

From where he knelt, Silas could see where Ruth's legs started at the forest floor, but not where they ended. He could see how she balanced on one foot, placing the other flat against her knee. How she made that balancing act look casual.

"Can I help?"

"Sure, why not? How about you go through the rocks and take out the ones that we should replace? The small ones."

"Okay," Ruth said. She pushed off from the tree line with a spring, but when she went to her knees, she did so gently.

Silas could hear her open and then close her mouth, catching a thought.

"Go on," he said. "Ask."

Ruth picked up a small rock and flicked it over her shoulder before reaching into the bag for its replacement.

"How do you know I want to ask something?"

"Not to brag, but I'm basically fluent in teenager."

"You should write a book."

"Just waiting on Oprah's seal of approval."

Ruth laughed. "Okay, fine. I was just wondering about your brother. What he was like."

Silas didn't say anything. In his silence, the sounds of the forest seemed to overcompensate.

"I'm sorry, see? I shouldn't be allowed to talk!"

Ruth made a fist around the rock in her hand and slammed it into her face.

"Whoa, be careful!" Silas said, knocking the rock to the ground. He took her chin in his hand and looked at her skin. It remained untouched. Flawless.

"I'm sorry," Ruth said again, her voice quieter now.

"Just be careful."

"No, I'm sorry I came. I shouldn't be here. You don't deserve this."

She sat back with a thump.

"You're too hard on yourself; you know that?" Silas asked, wiping a piece of dirt from her cheek with his thumb. She closed her eyes against his hand.

"My brother was my best friend," he said, but then he shook his head. "No, you know what? That's not right. That's the kind of thing I'm supposed to say. He wasn't my best friend; he was my big brother. But unless you have a big brother, it's hard to explain the difference. Do you have any siblings?"

Ruth shook her head.

"Just me," she said. "My dad has another daughter; she's five. But I've never met her."

"Well, Philip was part idol, part embarrassment, part best friend, part tormentor."

Silas looked at her as she reached again for the bag of rocks, settling into the routine.

"Imagine one part current boy-band hottie of the week, plus Mickey, plus your dad. Plus a military-grade information retrieval specialist."

Ruth wrinkled her nose. "That sounds awful!"

Silas laughed full out and loudly enough that Ruth couldn't help but join him.

"Okay, well, imagine it as cool."

Ruth gave an exaggerated shudder but kept smiling. Silas went on.

"He did a bad thing, but he wasn't a bad man. Do you know the difference?"

"I think so," Ruth said. She inched closer to Silas, following the pattern of the rocks. Silas dug deeper into the cool earth.

"It's an important distinction," he said. He could be touching ground from years ago, he thought. He could be touching the same dirt from that very night. "He taught me everything I know."

Ruth reached for a rock past Silas, her shoulder darting under and against his chest. She waited a beat for her fingers to clasp around it, to find their grip. He stayed above her, fighting the urge to free his hands. Fighting the urge to put them anywhere but right there in the dirt.

"Then he must be a good man," she said, her voice in his ear before she pulled back, the rock freed and larger for it.

# PEYOTE

**WHEN CAL ASKED TREY** for his help, he insisted she buy him dinner first. So, with the jalapeño poppers and the bottle of Jäger taking up most of the table, the interior glass wall of the conference room made me feel less like a fish in a tank and more like a fish in a contact lens.

"I thought we'd go over the Culver case, get Trey up to speed for tomorrow," I started when we'd all sat. Cal nodded and opened her binder, and Trey opened a paper napkin and placed it on his lap.

"Cal is a beautiful name. Is it short for something?"

"She already went over this. Calamity Ganon. Like in *Legend of Zelda*? A Nintendo game."

Trey reached for the bottle of Jäger and examined the label before unscrewing the cap and inhaling over it, deeply.

"We don't have video games here," Trey went on as he poured, his voice smooth as a soft-serve machine with a faulty thermostat. Each word sloshed forth sticky and empty-sweet. "Well, except those ones where you bludgeon hookers to death. Those are here, but we're not allowed to play them. They're just for the Third Floor's Retribution Management Department."

"Why?" Cal asked, nodding just slightly when Trey offered to pour her a glass. He didn't once look at me.

"You were there; wouldn't you know?" I said. I didn't want any Jäger anyway.

Cal shook her head.

"You see, they take all the incomers who killed hookers in real life and embed their real human consciousnesses into the codes of the hookers in the video game, and then beam them out into millions of horny psychos' PlayStations."

He piled poppers onto both paper plates he took from the kitchen, despite Cal's polite refusal.

"And then what?"

Trey paused to suck the grease from his fingers, slipping each one into the wet pulp of his mouth, then out, then in again.

"They live and die like that over and over for eternity," he answered. "That's what."

"Karmic justice," I said.

"I'll show you Karmic Just Tits."

I rolled my eyes too hard to see Cal's reaction, but I could imagine it was about the same as mine.

"I mean it; she works at the Honey Pot on Wednesdays."

"Trey, we need you to use your memory clearance to get some information out of our guy," I said loudly, my binder sticking in a puddle of ranch dressing. Trey stiffened at the inevitable conclusion that this was, in fact, a business meeting, until Cal put her hand on his arm.

"I can't wait to see you in action! Pey, what plan have you come up with that is missing just this one magic ingredient?" She tapped her fingertips against Trey's skin with each word—"just" *tap* "this" *tap* "one" *tap*—so that by the time she got to "magic," he was beaming into his Dixie cup. And I thought, not for the first time, that it must be nice to be a narcissist.

"Did Peyo tell you about the day I got awarded with memory clearance? It was a little chilly that morning, so I walked in wearing my—"

"Our mark, Jason Culver, is looking for someone. He knows the guy is still alive, but he doesn't know where exactly. So we're hoping you can dig around in Jason's brain a bit and get us some information he doesn't remember. Anything that can point us in the right direction."

Trey glared at me and then leaned back, legs wide.

"What have you gotten so far?"

"Well, we have reason to believe the target is a confidence man who got his start as a high school football coach by screwing over his team. He's on the run, but he's still in America, somewhere in Georgia. Near the coast."

"That's it? Pssh. I could do that in my sleep."

"We'd rather you do it awake. I'm thinking we go together tomorrow—just the two of us, so it isn't too overwhelming—and I can talk to him and you can see what you get."

"No," Cal interjected suddenly, her flirtatious tone stripped. "I want to go too."

I looked at her. "Are you sure that's—"

"The lady has spoken!" Trey said, slamming the table. "And I would do anything to help our newest team member find her footing. Speaking of which, would you say you're a size—"

"You have no idea how much we appreciate you," she gushed. "How much *I* appreciate you."

"I'm excited to find out," Trey answered, raising his fresh cup to Cal and throwing it all down.

# MICKEY

**WHEN MICKEY GOT TO** the dock, Sean was alone. She could see him from the lawn, stretched out in black basketball shorts and a black T-shirt like a seal sunning on a rock. When they were children, they would take turns lying on that dock's diving board while the other bounced it, seeing who could hold on the longest. She remembered the way the rough surface of the board left angry marks on her stomach and thighs and the way they felt later, when she touched them gently in the dark. Her hand went to her arm then, her skin itching at the bandage's corners.

She felt proud of the secret right there on her skin, a part of her body her mother hadn't made. She could feel her heartbeat in it.

"Where's Ruth?"

Sean sat up and shrugged.

Mickey laid out her towel, closer to her brother's than she would've yesterday. Something about the night before made him seem more human, like they were on the same team.

"Have you seen Dad yet?" she asked as she sat.

"Nope."

"I've never seen him so mad."

"I know," Sean answered. He glanced at Mickey and rapped her on the knee. "You okay?"

Mickey felt the urge to hold out her bandage, to lift it up and show him. Partially because she thought he might be impressed, but mostly because she couldn't remember the last time her brother asked her if she was okay and she wanted to see what he would do if she wasn't.

"Fine," she said. "Just worried about the imminent grounding."

"I'm sure it will be epic, especially once Mom is involved."

Mickey lay back, the sun white-hot through her eyelids.

"Do you ever think about how even when you close your eyes, they're still seeing? Like, they're never really . . . off. They're just covered up."

Sean sighed and lay back next to her.

"No, psycho. I never think about that."

"You're the psycho; you're wearing a T-shirt while sunbathing."

Ruth's voice, followed by her shadow, made Mickey jump. Sean pulled on the hem of his shirt but didn't take it off.

"Where have you been?" Mickey asked, scooching over to make room.

"I went for a walk in the woods," Ruth said as she joined Mickey on her towel, lowering her legs to the dock. "Eek! Hot!"

"Here," Mickey said, moving over farther.

"No, it's fine," she said as she rested her head on Mickey's bare skin, her neck curved with the slight swell of Mickey's hips. "I kind of like it." She let go of her hair and it spilled everywhere, across Mickey's stomach and down her other side onto the towel beneath them. It was cool to the touch, and it gave Mickey goose bumps.

As Mickey lay there, her friend's red hair all around her—fire

219

that didn't burn—it was clear Ruth had a little bit of magic in her. And as long as she had Ruth, Mickey thought as her fingers grazed the matching bandage on her friend's arm, it wouldn't matter if Mickey had her own magic or not.

Theirs was a friendship built on sharing.

# PEYOTE

**"I FEEL DIRTY," CAL** said when she opened the door to her apartment.

"We're not doing anything that bad," I said as I stepped inside and closed the door. "Just taking advantage of his obvious crush on you."

"What? No, I don't feel *bad*; I feel dirty. As in his eyes and skin and breath got on me and it was gross."

The heat in her apartment was acting up again, stuck on high even though no one ever asked for a heater in Hell. I shrugged off my jacket and fell onto the couch.

"That checks out."

She tossed me a bottle of cola.

"Don't you dare complain about that," she said when I opened my mouth. "I don't have a beer factory in here."

I shrugged and twisted off the cap.

"You're sure he can read memories without Jason knowing?"

"I was there when KQ gave him the honors," I said. "If Jason has any useful information, Trey will get it, with Jason being none the wiser."

"That's not all Trey will get," she muttered.

"What are you thinking?" I asked. "And can I watch?"

Cal smirked at me. "You're sick."

"Comes with the territory."

She groaned and rolled her own bottle across her forehead.

"It's so fucking hot!"

She was right; the weather had been warmer than usual. My T-shirt clung to the damp gutter of my spine.

"We'll go on some deals up north tomorrow," I said. "I've got my eye on some Twos in Iceland."

"It's hard to even breathe."

Cal twisted her hair on top of her head and pressed the bottle to the back of her neck.

"What's wrong with you today?"

"Excuse me?"

"It's always miserably hot, except for when it's miserably cold. I've never heard you complain before."

But when I caught her eye, I was the one who burned.

"Did you know that I can fieldstrip an automatic rifle in thirty seconds?"

I shook my head. I didn't, not exactly.

"Well, I can. I've never met anyone faster; my dad hadn't either. Not back then, at least. I can do it blindfolded. I can do it with two doses of Tuinal in my system. I can do it with three dozen trained soldiers bearing down on my position in my fucking sleep."

"That's . . . impressive."

"I'm also fluent in Russian, German, and French. Did you know that?"

She started pacing, her hair coming loose down her back.

"That doesn't matter much here."

"Well, it mattered on Earth," she spat. "It mattered a whole lot. I was making weapon deals for my dad by the time I was nine."

"What's your point?"

"What's my point?"

She turned to face me with enough force that I felt drops of sweat hit my lips. There was something ferocious in the way she held her shoulders. Like her body was regressing into its original, animal state.

"My point is that even with all of that knowledge, all of those accomplishments, here I am, twirling my hair because I still need some dick-dripping *idiot* to help me. You'd think the afterlife would be past all that sexist bullshit. And yet, here we are. Even in Hell, legitimate skills pale against the power of tits."

She leaned against the wall next to me, her forehead and forearms pressed into the drywall as if she were in upright, rapturous prayer. I thought about reaching out to touch her, but I didn't want to prove her point. As it was, I didn't know which side of her argument I landed on.

"At least you have the power of tits."

"Fuck you."

"Hey, I—"

"No, seriously," she growled, grabbing my face with one pinched hand. "Fuck you if you mean that. I would trade in everything about being a woman if it meant I could be taken seriously. If I looked like Trey—horror, even if I looked like you—I would be running this fucking place. I am so much smarter and stronger than any man I have ever met, and yet still, if I want to get what I want, I have to act like a baby deer in the woods. Do you know what I used to do to baby deer in the woods, Pey?"

Her grip was so tight, there was a good chance I would fail if I tried to yank free. But if I didn't, it could be considered a joke we had going together. A bit.

I stayed still.

"I'm sure nothing good."

"It's so fucking insulting," she said, letting me go. "I am so many steps ahead of you—all of you. I'm at the end of the maze; I have been forever. And yet I can't get out without your goddamn key. A key you didn't do jack shit to earn, a key you were just handed by chance. So I have to go back and take your slimy-ass hand—not *yours*, Pey; I'm talking about men in general—but it's bullshit."

Cal put her head in her hands, and I regretted the sarcasm, because she was right. I had been around long enough to see what she was saying, but I had never really thought about it. I had seen a lot of terrible people over the millennia, but I didn't know anyone like Cal. I was lucky to have her on my team. And it had nothing at all to do with her tits.

"I'm sorry," I said, turning to face her. "Truly. Men are assholes."

"And then with the platitudes," she said, pushing her hands through her hair.

"Seriously. You're way smarter than me. I don't even know what that word means, 'platitudes.' Some kind of animal?"

Cal laughed, whether in pity or actual amusement I couldn't tell.

"You're not the worst," she said, her hand landing briefly on my arm.

"You are, for implying Trey is better looking than me."

She shrugged and stood up. "I just wish—when I hear men like you, like Trey, complaining about life in Hell, I just wish you'd realize that, just like above ground, Hell is not the same for you as it is for me. Even here, you have it better than you think."

I swallowed and said nothing. There was nothing for me to say.

That was when she made her second big mistake.

She held the silence.

I imagine she purposely let it go on, to give my shame more time to sink in. But she underestimated me. Or, perhaps, overestimated. Because shame didn't really interest me, but something she'd said did. And when she stayed silent, I had time to notice.

"Why do you remember that?"

"What?" she asked, and sipped her soda.

If we were animals, that would be when I'd see the hair rise on her neck.

"Nobody remembers their life on Earth. We all lose the memories eventually, and you've had it rougher than most, with millennia on the belt."

Cal was scared. Not wide-eyed, admonished-by-KQ scared, or even the kind of scared she seemed the morning after she gave away too much at the Honey Pot. This was not the fear of prey. It was the fear of a hunter who blinked.

"What are you not telling me?"

"I need to take a shower."

"No, you need to answer my question."

Cal bit down on her lip, thoughts spinning so fast there was practically smoke coming out her ears. Then she put up her hands.

"Just let me take a shower," she said. "I need to show, not tell."

I didn't answer right away but instead took her and her new fear in, a fear I'd caused. What would've made me feel powerful a few days before now made me uneasy.

"Just wait; I'll be out in a minute, and I'll explain. I've been trusting you since the Looking Glass; you owe me the same."

Finally, I nodded. Not only because I was curious to see what her memory had to do with hygiene, but because something else occurred to me when she said "the Looking Glass." If she took a shower, I could be alone in the rest of her apartment. I could find my results.

I listened as she turned on the water, the pressure like a weepy drunk against the tile, and I listened as the sound changed when she stepped under it.

Then I didn't waste another second.

Her apartment was exactly like mine, so I worked quickly. I started in her bedroom, careful to skip the floorboards in the hallway I knew were prone to creak. I found her closet open, her jacket over the back of the regulation chair. The pockets were empty, so I moved to the closet, touching each of her bland sweaters with desperate fingers.

I heard her shift under the water, a thunk of a plastic bottle.

I cleared the closet and moved to the desk. I shuffled through papers and shook out the two books (hardcover, obviously) that she owned, dog-eared but hiding nothing.

There was another sound from the bathroom, and I paused before turning back to the desk and pulling on the handle of the middle drawer.

It was locked.

My paper had to be in there. Why else would she lock it? I couldn't lock mine. I searched the back for a release switch. I got down on my knees and crawled under the desk, feeling blindly.

I was too focused—too damn close—to hear the water trickle to a stop.

"Looking for something?"

I shot up and slammed my head underneath the desk. By the time I shuffled out, backward and on all fours, the world was spinning.

"You can't blame me for trying—" I started, rubbing my eyes. But then I saw her.

Cal stood in the doorway, a towel clasped together in one fist over her chest. It was a big, weighty towel, the kind that never gets dry and always smells a little like onion sweat and wet dreams. But even it wasn't big enough to cover all of them.

The burns were everywhere. They started at her toes and climbed their way up her shins, her knees, and her thighs: a latticework of scar tissue abloom with blisters. More still spread across her collarbone and unfurled all the way down her arms to the swollen, broken tips of her fingers. The only part of her that wasn't textured, sticky like honeycomb, was her face.

"Fuck," I said, forgetting my spinning head and my smoking gun of a position. "Cal, what is that?"

"You mean the water doesn't do this to you?" she asked sweetly, and when she grinned, the skin of her neck wept.

# SILAS

**SILAS HADN'T MEANT TO** hear their conversation. He wasn't one of those parents who spied. As he liked to say at family reunions with his Las Vegas cousins, who looked like their children sucked more color out of them with each passing year, he trusted his kids. So he did not go into the boathouse that afternoon to eavesdrop.

He went looking for bullets.

When Evan died, Rose insisted they get rid of all of his guns, except the 9mm carbine. She always liked that one. She said it made her feel dangerous in a good way, but it didn't leave her shoulder sore.

Despite her aversion, Rose had always been a damn good shot.

Silas knew where the gun itself was: right where it had always been, behind Rose's old shoeboxes in their closet. The bullets used to be in a drawer nearby, but at some point, Lily moved them. For years, she went back and forth: Was it safer to keep the bullets close enough to the gun that they could be put together by a home invader and used against the family while they slept? Or was it safer to keep them out in the boathouse, where no one could reach them, including them? She worried too much, he thought as he blindly swept his palm along the dusty recesses of the boathouse shelves.

The first voice he heard was Ruth's. Maybe if Sean or Mickey had talked first, he would've ignored it, found what he needed, and left. But Ruth's voice made him go still.

"Cody keeps texting me," she said. "He wants us to go over there tonight."

"All of us?" Sean asked, and Ruth laughed.

"I don't think so."

"I'm sure he did mean all of us," Mickey said. "Sean is the one who is actually friends with them."

"If you say so. But that's not the vibe I'm getting from these texts."

There was a shuffle, and then Mickey made a sound somewhere between a yelp and a gag.

"Let me see that," Sean said.

"Absolutely not," Mickey answered. "Gross."

There came a slap, a squeal, and a thud, and then the phone was in Sean's hand.

"No fucking way," he said.

Silas noticed from his son a tone he hadn't heard in a long time. Determination, protection. He sounded like Philip. Silas swallowed the thought down and stayed quiet, his search forgotten. The water slapped the concrete of the dock with each passing boat's wake, splashing over the empty boat lift below.

"You are not going over there alone. I'll tell Mom if I have to."

"Mom won't care; she loves the Watersons."

"She'll care if she reads these."

"It's my phone, narc," Ruth said. "That's theft, or something."

Silas waited for Ruth to tell them about that morning at the clearing. The new pit. But she didn't, and he found that he liked it, to share a secret with her.

"Come on, Mick! This could be your chance with you-know-who."

"Ruth!"

Silas remembered a night years back when the kids played MASH on the front porch, a rare moment in which Sean was still willing to indulge Mickey in "girl games." Mickey named one of the Waterson boys for the "marry" category, and Sean made kissing noises every time the boy came within a twenty-foot radius for the rest of the summer. Mickey had to fight not to cry every time.

"He doesn't know who I'm talking about!"

"There's only two of them," Sean shot back. "But I'd rather not know any of it."

"Then just pretend you don't," Ruth said.

Silas couldn't see it, but he could sense something happening between two of the three of them, the two who came from him. Some kind of exchange built into their shared blood or memory. He could feel the pull of it, like his cells were being tugged.

"No can do," Sean said, after a minute. "I'm not letting you guys go there alone. I like Cody and Josh; they're cool to play video games with or whatever. But I wouldn't trust them alone with my sister." He paused. "They can have you, though."

"Sean!" Mickey said, followed by a slapping sound.

"How about a compromise?" Ruth asked sweetly. "We can all go. I'm sure the boys would rather Sean come than none of us. How's that?"

"Great, I love being pity-invited to *my* friends' house so they can try to defile—"

"So it's settled, then."

Silas heard the tapping of nails on a phone screen and the swoosh of a sent message.

"Don't be such a prude, Sean. Mickey is her own person, you know. You're not her dad, or her husband. If she wants to get down and dirty with—"

"Gross, gross, gross," Sean said, pushing back until Silas could almost touch the hairs on his head through the slats of the wall.

"I don't even," Mickey said quietly, hardly defiant.

Silas felt his own pulse in his throat. Mickey was barely fourteen. To think those arms, that face . . . he shook his head to stop it.

"Ooh, Mick, did you bring down that *Cosmo*? The one with the best summer hairstyles? I think that half-up braid would look *sooo* good on you tonight."

Mickey jumped up, seemingly as uncomfortable with this conversation as everyone else. Everyone but Ruth.

"I'll go get it!"

Silas froze in the shadow as Mickey skipped past the boathouse door, her legs still long and spindly the way they had been her whole life. Prone to scabs that she picked until her sheets were mottled with blood, and covered in white-blond down like the softest kind of flightless bird.

She missed him by inches.

# PEYOTE

**"YOU CAN'T THINK I'M** stupid enough to hide your results in my desk, even if I did figure out how to lock it."

"Yeah, how did you—" I started, but then I stopped. "No, we're still talking about your thing."

I managed to get to my feet and face the hallway, where her wet footsteps left dark patches in the carpet that I knew would never fully dry. It's all carpet everywhere in Hell.

I listened as she pulled something off a hanger, heard the jagged slide of fabric against damp, hot skin. The snap of elastic.

"Okay, all dressed," she said. "Your innocence remains intact."

The wetness from her wounds left pockmarks that clung to her T-shirt, as if it had been caught between tiny frothing jaws. An ancient urge rose within me to touch them, to tend to them. I had to clench my hands into fists.

"I'm not a prude," I said. "You're just really fucking gross."

"Come on, Pey. You must've read my file by now. What was it the General always said at the end of an exercise?"

Even there in her dank little room, pajamas sticky with her

own body's sap and owing me information, Cal managed to make me feel like the chump.

"Maybe I'm trusting you," I said, both of us knowing full well I would be finishing her file the minute I got home.

When Cal smiled, for the first time I could see how she braced herself, the effort it cost her to look so effortless. How much it hurt, clinging to the upper hand. She held out her raw arms like a carny opening the curtains, granting entry to her dusty roadside dime museum, her prized and paltry assortment of the odd and the ugly, the dangerous and the damned.

"Don't drink the water," she said.

# LILY

**"WHERE HAVE YOU BEEN?"** Lily asked, emerging from the kitchen when she heard Mickey.

"Down at the dock," Mickey answered. "I'm just grabbing a magazine."

"Where is your father?"

"I don't know." Her voice was smaller than usual, more like that of a child. Which, of course, she was. Lily met her in the hallway, and they stood together at the stairs, two dry bites in one tight throat.

The day Lily gave her testimony against Philip, she had been pregnant with Sean for six months. Her mother began knitting a baby blanket months earlier, all blue and green because her first child and her mother's first child and her grandmother's first child had all been boys. But even back then, Lily wanted a daughter.

She wanted a girl because she wanted to do better than her mother had done with her. Lily's mother had done a great job with her brother. He was a successful lawyer in California with a gorgeous wife and fantastic self-confidence. But she couldn't raise a daughter. Not, at least, as a full, individual person. She would've been excellent if she were training Soviet spies how to be American housewives. Lily, on the other hand, wanted Mickey to grow up to be whatever she wanted. So she signed her up for sports and science camps and encouraged her short-hair phase in the fourth grade with a little too much enthusiasm for it to last. She wanted for her fiercely, in a way she didn't want for Sean. A way that was maybe a little too close to the malnourished want in her own heart.

"Are you okay?" Lily asked, taking her daughter's hair into her hands, long and cool like the body of a snake. The house pet kind, the kind that isn't supposed to hurt you, but still you check the lock on the cage.

"What did Dad say this morning?" Mickey asked, her eyes down.

Lily paused. She knew enough about this parenting game to know she had a precious moment here: her daughter thought she knew something she did not. She didn't want to blow it.

"First, how are you feeling?"

"Embarrassed. Is he still super mad?"

"That will depend." She needed to find Silas.

Mickey sighed and started up the stairs. That's when Lily saw the bandage.

"What happened?" she asked, forgetting the slow game of parenting an adolescent, eager to touch where her daughter hurt, eager to absorb it into her own body if that's what it took to make it better. Mickey pulled her arm back.

"Nothing, just a scrape. From when Ruth and I raced in the woods."

"Did you put Neosporin on it? You don't want it to get infected."

"Yeah, it's fine. Seriously," Mickey said. And then she pitched forward into Lily's chest. "Thanks, Mom."

Lily wrapped both arms around her daughter, holding her still for longer than she had in over a year.

"Love you," Mickey said as she broke free, then climbed the steps two at a time and closed the door behind her. And just like that, Lily was alone again. The house silent save for the single flower on the dining room table, red as loud as screaming.

Once they found out she had taken a walk that night all those years ago, the detectives wouldn't stop hounding Lily. They said they could get them all arrested for underage drinking. They said they could lock the whole family up and throw away the key. They saw her for what she was: a teenage girl who had her perfect life laid out in front of her, if not a little rushed. It was what she wanted: Silas, a baby. Even if it was a few years earlier than she would've liked, it was still exactly what she wanted. They held their adult faces straight as stone and threatened to take all of it away if she didn't testify to what she saw.

But she was their only witness.

The only one who could say for certain she saw Philip holding Sarah's body, limp like her bones had slipped out. Like every solid part of her had melted with the water that dripped from her hair. Even in his arms, she was already a ghost.

But she wasn't a ghost, was she? Lily thought as she turned away from the dining room and peered out the window for a sign of Silas. Not in this house. Here, she was as real as color, as sound.

As real as silence.

# PEYOTE

HUMAN'S RESOURCE FILE
Name: CALAMITY GANON
Current Location: FIFTH FLOOR

Calamity Ganon, human name redacted, was most proud of
her father at night. After Cal and her brothers had bloodied
both themselves and the arena and then raked up the blood
the best they could, the General would build a fire and pace
before it, his shadow beating against the dirt with each step
like big black wings.

The Pigs didn't lie when they said her brothers had not
all joined the barracks willingly, but it was around that fire
that each and every one of them became his.

Which also made them hers.

"For most warriors, death is the end of the battle," he
said. "But you have been chosen, and your worth extends
beyond your death. We cannot fight on behalf of Heaven
with all our boots on Earth. And that is why, although only

your brother Jonah survived, we have two champions to-night."

She liked the newest recruits the most. The ones who sat through their first days of training in horror, as colorless as if it were their blood that splattered their hand-me-down combat boots. Earlier that week, Jonah had been one of those new recruits. But now he sat in the Seat of Honor, perched highest among them—higher, even, than the General himself—and drank sloppily, smugly, from a cup so full, it sloshed when he cheered.

The General stopped pacing and looked at his army, small and knotted in body but blazing hot in the eyes. He treated all of them the same, never picking favorites or mourning any with particular fervor. But Cal could tell from the way he looked at them that their pain, their death, was not at his whim or pleasure. He felt the loss of each one.

"So, let's prepare ourselves for the fight that awaits us beyond this one, in the belly of Hell. Which is where you all will go—and *must* go—if not for your sins prior to your arrival here, then for the sins you will commit by the time you leave, to ensure your entry. What is the most important duty when you wake up on the other side?"

Her hand shot up, but her father called on Joseph.

"Don't drink the water."

When he found Joseph, the boy had been sucking men off for bus fare along Route 65, putting as much distance as possible between himself and the group home where he had grown up, having never been truly raised. He went to the barracks willingly, more or less, and he beamed the brightest when the General spoke of him as "chosen."

"Why is that, Joseph?"

Cal threw her hand up again, even though she knew he

wouldn't pick her. He could at least know, seeing her from the corner of his eye, that she had the answer.

"The river—"

The General opened his mouth, but Joseph self-corrected. "Lethe," he said, stumbling just to get the word out. "The water from the river Lethe makes everyone in Hell forget where they came from, who they are. Everything."

"And one more time, men, together now: When you arrive on the battlefield below, what will you remember the most so you can remember the rest?" the General asked, booming.

Cal joined in with her full voice.

"Don't drink the water!"

Jonah raised his cup, delighting in the right to slosh. The Seat of Honor and the full glasses that came with it always seemed to make her brothers only more wasteful, simply because they could be. But the next day, he would be one of them again.

Cal never sat in the Seat of Honor, never got a full cup, a break from the dehydration training. Not even when she won, which she did with more and more frequency. In the barracks, she was a pariah, denied all but a single privilege.

She was the only one the General wouldn't allow to die.

When I'd finally put Cal's file down, I went to the kitchen sink and turned both knobs all the way, until water spilled lazily from the faucet over my fingers. How many times in how many millennia had I put my lips to this very faucet, or the plastic mouth of a bottle, driven by heat or hangover or the ancient body memory of thirst? How much of myself, exactly, did I lose per sip?

On the Second Floor, the one kindness we ever showed the people on the belt was during break, the whistle blowing sporadically and infrequently and welcomed by all. It was then that we would hold the bases of their skulls in our palms—not just the bone but the whole thing, skin and hair and everything intact—and pour slowly into their mouths cold, clean water.

Our only relief was also our erasure. It was brilliant and cruel and completely on brand.

But with the way time moves here, or the lack thereof, maybe the General was wrong. Maybe it isn't a trick, a method of war.

Maybe the water is Hell's clumsy attempt at mercy.

But what then, if rejected? If a person on the belt refused water, what would our creative supervisors on the Third Floor come up with in retaliation? How would we twist their rebellion into our weapon, for as long as it took?

You know the answer as well as I do. As well as Cal and her blistered skin.

We would make them burn.

# SILAS

**SILAS HAD JUST DECIDED** to give up his search when he heard his son's voice.

"I don't know what your deal is, but Mickey isn't like you."

"What's that supposed to mean?"

"You know what it means. I'm glad you guys are friends or whatever; it seems to make her happy. But she's not a Barbie you can play with until you get bored."

Sean pushed off the wall, freeing a gap through which Silas could see the shoulders of both of them outlined by blinding sun.

Ruth pulled herself upright.

"I can't believe you think that."

It was the quietest sentence Silas had heard her say all summer.

"Look, I'm not trying to be an asshole. You're—you're cool, you know? It's just . . . she's my little sister. And I don't want her doing things because you said she should."

Silas felt proud of his son. He had been acting like he didn't care about any of them for so long, Silas had begun to believe he really didn't.

"I can't believe that's who you think I am," Ruth said. "I thought we were all getting along, you know? I thought I was connecting with you, teasing-like. But if you just think I'm some kind of bad-influence whore—"

"Whoa! I never said that!" Sean shouted, before catching himself and lowering his voice. "I don't think you're a—I don't think that. I'm just looking out for my sister. She looks up to you; she'd do whatever you say."

"I love Mickey. She's my best friend. I—I love all of you. I hate that you think of me . . . like that."

Silas could feel the guilt gather around Sean like weather. A cloud of little particles rushing in.

"Come on," Sean said softly. "You know we like you too."

"Even you?" Ruth asked. She had shifted so her legs were bent under her now, her weight on one hip. Silas saw the shape of her like a Roman statue, no legs or arms, just the body's warmest parts. His son rolled his shoulders on the other side of the thin wood.

"Yeah," he said. "Of course."

"You know, I didn't *not* want you to come tonight. I did. I do. I just didn't want it to be weird for Mickey."

"Why would it be weird?" Sean breathed.

Ruth pushed herself up to her knees, and Silas watched the distance between them close.

"I think you know what I mean."

Suddenly, the whole dock shook.

"I found it!" Mickey yelled as she landed on both feet, magazine held high in the air. Sean shoved himself back against the wall with enough force that Silas had to grip the shelf to keep it from falling on top of him. All that fell was the sagging inner tube.

Mickey halted, her shadow landing across the opening to the boathouse. Silas pulled a handful of screws out of a coffee can just in time.

"Dad, what are you doing here? Mom is looking for you."

# PEYOTE

**THE NEXT DAY, I** spent more time than I'd like to admit watching Cal from my cubicle. To be honest, my focus on her could've been due to all of the caffeine I had consumed so far, opting for coffee every time I found myself reaching for water. But it was worth it: I was done forgetting.

It was kind of amazing to watch her. She moved between the cubicles in another deeply lackluster sweater—catching coworkers for brief, bubbly chats in corners before squeezing their arms in sweet, almost secret goodbyes—like an insect collecting pollen, gathering what she needed from each on her sticky thighs. She was still shy at work, but she had traversed the transition from painfully to appealingly so with grace, so that when she smiled, there wasn't a single person who didn't smile back.

Everyone but KQ, that is.

"Didn't I tell someone to call rodent control?" KQ bellowed as Cal cut quickly across the hallway. "Get the fuck out from under my feet, Squeaks!"

"Sorry," Cal murmured, and I couldn't help but see the redness that bloomed from her cheeks down her neck as it had been the night before, raised and wet.

"Actually, she goes by Cal, boss."

Trey popped his head up from over the divider, a gopher in polyester.

"I bet that's not the only name she asks you to call her," KQ said, one eyelid stomping out a wink. Cal opened her mouth to protest but didn't say anything. She was nothing if not disciplined.

"Trey, you ready to head out for that deal?" I asked, standing.

"Sure thing, bucko," he said.

"You too, Cal," I added, and I caught a flicker of relief in her face before she nodded and reached for her binder.

# LILY

SILAS KICKED OFF HIS boots and came into the kitchen, smelling of fresh dirt. He put Lily's phone down on the counter. "Here, I found this in the boathouse."

Lily's heart jumped, but when she clicked open the phone, she had no messages, nothing suspicious. So she breathed a silent sigh of relief and tucked the phone into her pocket.

"Where have you been?" she asked. She had made a pitcher of iced tea and was squeezing the last of the lemons. "I didn't see you out by the garden."

"I was actually touching up the firepit."

Lily froze. That's where she left the poppies.

"Why would you want to mess with the firepit? We haven't used it in ages."

"Well, maybe we would if it weren't so decrepit," Silas said, reaching for the pitcher. "Ha, decre*pit*. I'm hilarious."

Lily poured her own glass, just to keep her hands busy.

"I think I'm going to put some whiskey in this. You want some?"

Lily nodded, and Silas took their glasses into the living room.

"What happened with the kids last night? I saw Mickey, and she had a full-on guilt face. She even hugged me."

"They decided to have a séance," he answered as he poured liberally.

"What? For whom?"

"For Sarah. I went to check on Mickey before going to bed, and they weren't there, so I went looking." Silas handed Lily her glass and lifted his to his lips.

"Jesus. Why didn't you wake me up?"

"I would've if I hadn't found them on the property. I figured they went out for a night swim. You know, like we used to."

The memories came back for both of them: cold water and hot breath, moonlight and tan lines. Sharing one towel because they forgot a second. Because they shared everything.

"I told you Ruth was a bad influence," Lily said.

The words drew a firm line in time. It was something she never would've said back then.

"Come on, Lil," Silas said. "It was harmless kid stuff. I mean, don't get me wrong—" He paused for a sip. "I was furious, and I let them have it. But Mick is the happiest I've seen her in a long time, and Sean's even using more than one syllable a day. Plus, Ruth talked to me today and apologized. I think she's a little troubled, a little unhappy, maybe. But she's a good kid. She helped me with the new firepit."

"Why? Where was Mickey?"

"Sleeping, probably. It was early. Can you just trust me on this one? Believe it or not, I'm a pretty decent parent."

"I know you are." She said it sincerely, and somehow that made it sound sad.

"I had an idea," he said, his hand on the handle of the screen door. "A way to blow off some of this parenting-teens steam."

"What's that?"

Silas leaned out the door and reappeared with Evan's rifle.

"Target practice."


**LILY HAD NEVER BEEN** a gun person. Up until she met the Harrisons, she believed her mother when she said guns were brutish. But it was Rose, not Evan or even Silas, who first taught Lily how to shoot.

It was a couple of weeks before Sarah died. Lily was up at the New Hampshire house for the night; her mother was expecting her back the next day at noon. If Sean existed yet, he was a cell inside her—maybe two—and as unimagined as green skies.

At first, Lily was adorably reluctant. She sat on the lawn, smiling as she watched Silas race Philip to set up the cans along the wood board nailed between two trees.

"No glass!" Rose yelled as Silas slipped a Coke bottle into the lineup.

"Mom, come on," he pleaded. "They make the best sound!"

"You can wear shoes to protect yourself," she said. "The foxes can't."

"What if he makes a shoe line for wildlife?" Philip asked. "If he can put a thousand foxes in shoes, will you allow it?"

Lily laughed. "Kicks for Kits," she said, and Philip beamed.

She could still remember the way that felt: her boyfriend's older brother smiling like the two of them were in on something above everyone else's pay grade. Phil's smile, those few times when he really went for it, was enough to make evening feel like noon.

"Sure," Rose said, turning the cans on the ledge so the labels were straight. "If your brother creates one thousand shoes for foxes, he can shoot a glass bottle on the lawn."

"I'll get right on that," Silas said.

"Okay," Rose said, and clapped her hands and swung the rifle strap over her shoulder once every can was lined up just right. "Ladies first."

"Lily won't, Ma," Silas said.

Lily's face got hot. "Oh, no, it's fine. I just haven't ever—"

"Shh!" Rose hissed. "Come on, sweet. It'll be good for you."

Before she knew it, she was on her feet.

"Right," Rose said from behind Lily, locking her elbows. "Like that. Straight back, squared shoulders. It would help if you had a little more meat on you, but this will do."

"If they'd rather shoot, I really don't mind just watching."

"You know that worried feeling?" Rose responded straight into Lily's ear—not a whisper, but not loud enough for anyone else. "That feeling in your gut all the time, no matter the quality or intention of your company, like your safety is a gift from the men around you, not a right?"

It was the first time a woman had ever spoken to Lily like that. As though the play they were all in allowed intermissions.

"This right here," Rose said, patting the gun affectionately. "For a minute, this will make that feeling go away."

LILY TOOK A STEP toward Silas and ran her finger along the slick wood of the rifle's stock. Up until that moment with Rose all those years ago, Lily had spent her young life assuming that her fear was a defect. She thought if she could just be wanted right, by the right man, that she herself would be righted, and the fear would go away. But even the best man comes with the strength and stature to remind a woman that every time he doesn't hurt her is a favor.

And Rose was right. Lily had never found anything else to relieve the pressure of inferiority quite like a gun.

**"SURE," SHE SAID, AND** threw back the last of her drink. "Let's do it."

"Love that enthusiasm!" Silas said. "Now you just have to tell me where you hid the damn bullets."

# PEYOTE

**TREY MADE A BIG** deal out of the necessary preparations for memory retrieval, which he insisted Cal watch so she could learn "what it looked like to crush skulls, mindfully." He didn't seem to require my presence, however, so I took the chance to check up on my marks. Granted, it was only noon, but I always went to Mickey after a long day. The tread in her—the track she alone laid, again and again—I found to be the perfect size. I could slip into her life with the least turbulence.

There was no denying it: she was my favorite.

I found her in her bedroom. Clothes were strewn everywhere, abandoned like the nonbiological remnants of a catastrophe—human shapes stretched across bedspreads and crumpled, empty, in corners. The room was an explosion of color and synthetic bass beat, shower humidity, and vanilla perfume.

"Oh shit, I left my stuff out on the beach," Ruth said as she laid a magazine open on the bed.

"Don't worry about it; we can get it later."

"I don't want that suit to get mildewy," Ruth said. "I'll be right back, and then I'll do your hair."

Mickey listened to her friend's footsteps down the stairs as she looked in the bathroom mirror. She looked different, and she had yet to attempt the look promised by *Cosmo* to make all the boys stare. I thought about the cut on her arm, the bandage that she played with constantly. Opting to keep it on longer than the cut warranted, even as it grayed at the corners and became ratty. She was growing up.

As far as I can tell from my observations, growing up seems to involve a lot of false starts, a lot of broken promises. The realization of the world as something neither for you nor against you, but rather uninterested in you entirely. No matter how special you are, how many gold stars you receive, the world itself is incapable of loving you. When you're a kid, you don't care. You love what you love: your parents, your neighbor's angry cat, your favorite TV characters and their plastic replicas on your shelf, regardless of what you get in return. But growing up seems to be a lesson in loving only those who will love you back, and forsaking the rest.

Mickey's hands were deep in Ruth's makeup bag before I realized what she sought. I could almost feel the pulse in her arm, itching under the bandage. I could see it glowing on her skin like a heat target. It was all hers, this minor disturbance of her surface. And she wanted to do it again.

Mickey spent more time outside of her body than the average teenager. Nothing certifiable—she didn't need an institution or the guiding hand of an underground superhero academy. She wasn't even traumatized, at least not more so than anyone else who realizes the part of life they're rushing through to get to the good part is, in fact, the whole thing. She was simply, on the inside, less sticky than the average person. She didn't cling to the trappings of her daily existence with the same kind of fervor, and therefore she could become more easily dislodged from herself.

I had seen the same thing in Silas all his life. As if by loosening from himself, he became one with the world. Not with other people—no, quite the opposite. The world itself: the cold, hard rock of it. To her credit, Mickey was better at recovering than Silas was. She bounced back faster, found her footing among the living once again. I've wondered how, if Silas could find the right words, he would talk to her about it. But the nature of the thing is cruel in its design: it can be described only when it's happening, during which time one loses all interest in deepening the bonds with the fiction around them.

All of this is to say that Mickey had always been fascinated by the restrictions of her own edges.

She took out all the objects from the Altoids tin one at a time, lining them along the side of the sink just like Ruth had. The alcohol swab, the cloth with the razor inside. I could practically see her heart beating, as if her blood smelled the metal and had started banging from within.

There is no high like making the dangerous choice.

Mickey glanced out the window and saw Ruth climbing the hill back to the house. Her hand shook, and the tin slipped into the sink. She gasped and pressed her fingers into the drain. If any of the pills went missing, Ruth would know she had gone through her stuff. She would know that Mickey wanted more of that razor's feeling, and, even worse than that, she wanted it alone.

Mickey watched Ruth shake out her towel and hang it over the porch railing as she swept her other hand along the basin, but there was nothing but sink. She pulled her hand up slowly and checked again. Nothing. There was no way all the pills could've gone down the drain; she caught the tin too quickly. Where were they? She couldn't remember seeing them in the tin when she opened it, but she wasn't sure. And anyway, why would they all be gone? They had to be there. Mickey turned over the tin and brought it up to her face, examining the corners. She unfolded the cloth, smoothing it along the creases.

But then she heard the screen door open as Ruth came back into the house, and she was out of time.

I watched Mickey gather the contents back up, putting each item back as she had found it. She ran the sharp edge of the razor along her thumb for just an instant before snapping the tin shut.

# MICKEY

**"HAVE YOU NEVER BRUSHED** this?" Ruth asked as she pulled on Mickey's scalp.

"I can do it," Mickey said, but Ruth swatted her hand away.

"Just hold still."

Ruth's nails parted Mickey's hair like a tractor, and Mickey kept her breath shallow, scared she might spook Ruth's touch away. She thought about people who tame wild animals, but she knew she wasn't in that category. She had no interest in taming. Quite the opposite. She was the one there to learn.

She was still shaking from the closeness of getting caught with Ruth's Altoids tin, still a little ashamed that she wanted so badly to do it again—alone, this time—and a little buzzed on the secret itself.

"So, tell me, how long have you liked Josh?"

Mickey held still, her eyes closed. Ruth's fingers were cold, answered prayers against her sun-and-thrill-burned scalp.

"I don't . . . I don't know. Kind of forever."

"Aww!" Ruth cooed. "The boy next door!"

"Shut up."

"No, really. That's so cute. And he was totally checking you out."

"No, he wasn't," Mickey said. "They were both just looking at you."

"That's because I have confidence," Ruth said, taking Mickey's chin in her palm and holding her head straight.

"You have good reason. I don't."

"No," Ruth explained, snapping an elastic from her wrist onto Mickey's braid. "It's not real confidence. I fake it."

"What do you mean?"

"Just pretend it's like a movie, and you're the star. *What would a totally ballsy chick do right now?* And then you do it."

"No way," Mickey said, grateful when she felt Ruth's fingers loosen the braid she had just created, and start over. "I'm a terrible actress."

"Get up." Ruth said, her hands under Mickey's arms. Mickey stood up and faced the mirror. She hadn't spent much of her life thinking about how she looked. Not yet. But she knew then that she would never go back. Her nose and forehead were burned and shiny from the heat of it, as if her freckles had been laminated. Her hair was half braided, half not, and entirely ratty. The straps of her bra under her tank top seemed the very definition of faking it. Ruth took her place on the bed, her skin the opposite of Mickey's: if Ruth was sun-kissed, Mickey was sun-slapped.

"Give me the best you've got."

"What?" Mickey asked.

"Come on, seduce me."

Mickey's jaw dropped, and she hit Ruth on her perfectly tanned knee.

"Screw you!"

"I'm serious! Pretend I'm Josh. What are you going to do to prove you're not just Sean's little sister anymore?"

Mickey pressed her open palms to her face.

"I mean, if you're going to be a prude about it—" Ruth said, sighing. "But this is what best friends are for. To help each other."

Mickey looked through her fingers. "I don't know how."

Ruth grinned.

"Here," she said, pushing Mickey gently back down to the bed. "I'll show you."

When Ruth stood and turned around again, she held her face in a way Mickey had recently become familiar with, but hadn't tired of. Ruth's was a face of many parts. One part asked, another told, and a third, which pulled the whole thing together, challenged. *How far will you let me take this?*

"Hey, Josh."

"Ruth, come on."

"You've certainly grown up."

Her voice matched her speed as she stepped closer, lazy but with a destination.

"Have you been working out?"

"As if I'm going to ask him *that*."

Ruth stopped inches from Mickey's hard-pressed knees.

"Remember when we used to play hide-and-seek?"

She reached out and touched the top hem of Mickey's shirt, her fingertips light like insect wings.

"We played tag," Mickey said.

Ruth laughed as if Mickey hadn't spoken. "Well, I have a confession to make."

"What?"

"I always wanted you to be the one to find me."

Ruth's fingers went from Mickey's collarbone up her jaw to her lips, and then she leaned in until talking was nearly the same as kissing.

"Want to play again?"

Mickey had never been in love before. Not with anyone besides Robin Hood—Disney's fox version. All of that was still ahead of her. But she thought at this moment that maybe she was falling in love for the first time. Not in the way some girls fall in love with other girls; she didn't want to make Ruth her girlfriend. She wanted to be inside her, but not like that. She wanted to occupy her, to live in her skin. To live in a body that knew what it was doing. A body that could move without burning from the inside, as if someone were narrating her every move over a loudspeaker.

So when she answered yes, she meant it.

# LILY

OUT ON THE LAWN, Lily saw cans lined up along the wooden ledge, nails still holding strong. He had planned ahead. To her surprise, it made her happy. Giddy, almost. She always loved the way Silas knew exactly what he was doing. It felt like discovering inconsistencies in her favorite television series, finding evidence of his effort under all that cool. It's what made her fall in love with him in the first place. The cool, sure; but, even more so, the glimpses of the work that built it.

"Want to make this interesting?" she asked as she took the gun from Silas. She hadn't forgotten the flower on the table, the threat of it. But she was well versed in living between the forgotten and the feared.

"Thompson!" Silas whooped, followed by a slow clap. "You haven't been a gambler in ages."

"Well, it's vacation, isn't it?"

She pulled her hair into one fist and cinched it into an elastic. She could feel Silas's eyes on her shoulders, her neck. And for the first time in a long time, she found that she liked it. They weren't talking about the kids or the house, the minute details of the present, or the looming obstacles of the future. They were talking the way they used to talk, before all that.

"Do you remember how to shoot?"

Lily laughed and held the gun up so it rested in the crook of her shoulder. "I have a feeling it will come back to me."

She squinted down the sights and took a breath, squeezing the trigger with her exhale. She heard a pop and felt the nudge of the gun, but the cans didn't move.

"Look who got cocky," Silas said, grinning. "I guess I should've placed that bet."

"Hey, the day is still young! I'm just warming up."

"Give me that."

Lily handed Silas the gun, and he steadied himself. He squeezed, and a can exploded with a burst of sound.

"Gotcha!"

"Beginner's luck," Lily said. "Give it back."

Silas shrugged and handed the rifle over to Lily before leaning back against the tree.

"Remember how good my mom was?"

Lily laughed again as she lined up her next shot. "I think she must've been a spy before she had you."

"And Philip was so bad."

"Well, he was always better with bigger machines." Lily pushed her breath out and squeezed, and the can on the left ricocheted off the closest tree.

"Bam!"

"But be honest—were you aiming for that one?" Silas asked, kicking her ankle with his foot.

"Double or nothing," she said as she squared off again.

"We didn't actually bet anything!"

Lily squinted before exhaling and hitting two more cans in a row. But then she felt her phone buzz in her pocket, and she faltered. The third bullet hit the tree on the right, spraying bark. She rested the gun against her leg and pulled out her phone.

It was a message from Gavin.

*. . . anything?*

And then another.

*I miss you.*

Lily swiped out of the message instantly but felt its effect everywhere. She squeezed her eyes shut, suddenly embarrassed by the cans and the rifle resting against her leg—the whole scene.

Gavin did not like guns.

"You know," she said, loosening her hair, "that's probably enough friendly fire for me."

"Are you serious? You were just heating up!"

"I know," Lily said. "That's why I'm going to go up and make another drink, to cool down." She hung the rifle on the ancient hook embedded in the tree closest to her. "You'll put this away when you're done?"

Silas sighed. "I'll take care of it."

Lily came to a stop in front of him. There was a sprig of pine stuck in his hair.

From the moment Lily saw Silas at Sweeney High's freshman football tryouts, her body changed for him. It was changing anyway, but he caught her eye and became the end goal amid all that cellular chaos. A blueprint dropped into her previously mismanaged construction site.

*Become the girl who can get Silas Harrison.*

So that's what she did. But her young logic missed one important thing: being his meant nothing if he wasn't also hers.

Between the smell of the grass in the summer air and the power of the rifle in her hands and the way he looked right then, his face, softened by the haze of late-day sun and gun smoke, made her think that if she looked at him for too long, she might crack, might fall back into him. And then, as it always was with them, he would see her as won and lose interest, and she would be left open and wanting.

She thought again about Gavin's message. She liked being missed, she thought as she reached, despite herself, to sweep the needles free from Silas's brow.

"Thanks," she said, turning toward the house. "This was fun."

Like most broken marriages, theirs hadn't broken all at once. Instead, it became gnarled the way wind gnarls a tree on a cliff—with quiet pressure, relentlessly the same. And she knew, the way the tree that strains at a sharper and sharper angle knows, that a thing can grow even under terrible circumstances, but that doesn't mean it should.

"Wait, Lil," he said. "One quick thing."

She turned around and pushed her hair behind her ear so she could see him clearly, aglow against the setting sun over the lake.

"Is the Gavin you're fucking Sarah Kelly's brother?"

# PEYOTE

**EVAN WAS THE FIRST** Harrison to surprise me. The three before him came naturally to their fate, hungry but never humbled by it. They wanted money, power, a name that would carry on—lives lived in homage. The bread and butter of the Deals Department. But Evan was different.

Evan was the first Harrison I knew to make a deal for the sake of another.

When Evan called for me seventeen years ago, it was raining. Or maybe it had stopped raining by then, or hadn't started yet. I don't remember. I just know the air was all juicy and dark, a drunk kiss of a night. When I arrived, he had a cup of tea ready.

"How can I help you, Evan?" I asked.

"You know me?"

"You can assume I know everything."

Evan rolled his shoulders, his hands steepled around his tea.

"I'm prepared to make a deal with you, but I have one question first. Can I trust that you will answer me honestly? Do you know how to do that?"

There was something about being in front of Evan after watching him for so long—it was kind of like meeting the actor who played your favorite character. You've been thinking about them as yours to watch, to know. You never wonder what they would think of you. I understand why: it hits all the harder when they don't like what they see.

"Yes, Evan. I'm familiar with the concept of honesty. I can do that."

Evan nodded, his eyes down. The crickets outside made a blanket of sound like we were being tucked in real tight.

"How did you know about me?"

Evan smiled, and I saw the way the wrinkles around his eyes worked. They weren't there to tally time. They were there to give his face the necessary room to transform, to blossom.

"You are famous in our family," he said. For someone who leaned on the "famous" line like crutches at the time, it reached my blood much too quickly.

"Well," I said, shifting. "That's—"

"My grandpa used to talk about you all of the time. How he outsmarted the devil."

I coughed. "Excuse me?"

"He was a bit of an exaggerator. 'For the sake of the story,' he always said. Of course, he didn't actually outsmart you, did he? You got him in the end."

"I am not the devil."

I was the only person Evan had ever met from Hell. So, in the way kids who grow up in Westchester say they're from the city when they travel anywhere outside of New York, it was close enough. But it's still an irritating generalization. On the scale of humanity, I was closer to him than to this supposed devil. Surely.

"Who are you, then?"

"I'm the answer to your problems."

"Sounds like the devil to me."

I laughed. "Fair enough." I reached for the mug in front of me. "What's your question for me?"

I could see the sleepless nights on his skin. The purple under his eyes, the tremor in his hand. He wasn't here anymore, not fully. He was somewhere between reality and nightmares. Exhaustion coated him like oil on a baby duck.

"I need to know the truth. Before I sign myself over to you, I need to know for absolute certain what happened that night. Did—" Evan's voice wavered. He coughed to cover it. "Did my son kill that girl?"

He was already in Hell. The murder, the police touching everything he owned with rough and thoughtless hands, the attention junkies who stood night after night on his front lawn, pictures of Sarah they'd pulled from the Internet and candles with drip protectors in each hand, sucking whatever particles were left of her from the air with open mouths.

"Yes," I said. "I'm sorry to have to say it, but yes, he did."

Evan put his head in his hands.

"Jesus," he said, his voice muffled. "Good God."

"Just me, I'm afraid."

I pulled out my briefcase and flipped through the pages inside and he signed again and again.

"Okay, Evan. Your deal is done. Your soul for Philip's. We will not interfere with your life or your death—you will live and die as you would've anyway. Only after you die will the deal take effect."

"Thank you."

I have never forgotten that part. The sound of him thanking me.

I've wondered many times if I should've left it at that, and why I didn't. According to the training manual, a sales associate should never disclose information that isn't required to make the deal, and this deal was already made. Maybe I was looking out for him and what was left of his life. Or maybe I was simply wreaking havoc for havoc's sake, due to the devil in me.

"Your deal is done; there is no undoing it," I said as I stood up to leave. "But I think it's important for you to know something."

"Okay," Evan responded, wary.

"You asked the wrong question," I said, slipping my tablet back into its case. "What you should've asked was which son."

# PART III

# LILY

THE NIGHT SARAH KELLY died went like this.

Lily came in from the lake just as the boys got back from the state liquor store. Being three and a half years older, Philip had an ID, but his bike couldn't carry the supplies, so they took Evan's old truck. Lily could hear it from the outdoor shower, where the loose door brought on memories of the afternoon before. Loose because Silas had picked her up and shoved her against it, his body following hers, their skin starving collectively and fed the same way.

Lily was no stranger to hunger.

"What did we get?" she asked when she walked into the kitchen, looping her arms around Silas's waist from behind as he unloaded beers into the fridge. She loved the way he smelled, like laundry and body spray and just a hint of pot.

" 'What didn't we get?' is more like it," he said, reaching around to cup her ass in her shorts before she squealed and wriggled away.

"This is what you wanted, right?" Phil asked, holding out a

bottle of Malibu as he hoisted a cardboard box full of liquor onto the kitchen counter.

"Phil, you're my hero!"

She pitched up on her toes and kissed him quickly on the cheek. Lily was gleefully adjusting to her new role in the Harrison family. A few months ago, she never would've been brave enough to talk to Philip like that. But she was practically family now, she thought as she cradled her own personal bottle. And that made this house her domain.

"I'm going to hide that," Madeline said, coming up behind her.

"Like hell you are."

"Not from you, bitch. From everybody else. We can't trust these animals."

As Madeline dragged her out of the room, Lily looked over her shoulder just long enough to see Philip unload three bottles of tequila.

*Let's see what Sarah thinks of that*, she thought.

"Shall we do a shot or two, just to get the party started?" Madeline asked when she and Lily had found the right planter, tall enough to conceal the bottle but close enough to keep them in the action.

Lily put one hand over her belly button, over what some faraway part of her knew was growing there. But only for an instant. Then she shook her head—hard, as if she could dislodge the thought—and opened her mouth.

**THE NEXT TIME SHE** saw Sarah, the sun was reaching its crescendo in gold above the lake, and Lily had all but forgotten her. She was focused on Silas and their friends, the people who were supposed to be there. But when Terrance and Alex moved the folding table into the shallow water to play beer pong, she reappeared.

"Come play with us!" Silas yelled across the lawn as soon as he saw her. Like he had been watching. Lily looked and missed her chance to deflect a shot.

"Boom! There goes your top, Thompson!" Terrance yelled.

Lily whined as she pulled her shirt up over her tanned shoulders. The neckline held her long blond hair as if in a loose fist until she shook it free and tossed the shirt onto the sand. She could feel all eyes on her.

All but his.

"I'll be right back," Silas said into her neck before setting off across the grass. Madeline sidled up to the table and handed Lily a shot of the Malibu like a doctor with a pain-management plan.

"What's that about?"

"Nothing. He's probably just worried about Phil. We haven't seen him in a bit," Lily answered, shaking her head as the booze went down. It tasted more like sunscreen than alcohol, but she liked the way it made her feel.

"Well, sure, if Sarah doesn't get drunk enough tonight, Phil might never lose his virginity."

"Damn, Maddie with the kill shot!" Terrance roared. "And who's getting *you* drunk tonight?"

"I am," Lily said, grabbing Madeline around the waist and play-biting her neck.

"I'd pay to see that," Alex added.

"It'll cost you your college fund."

"Worth it. My parents don't have high hopes for me anyway."

"That's unsurprising," Lily said, and they all laughed.

**AFTER TWO MORE GAMES,** Lily went looking for Silas. She walked out of the water in her bathing suit, leaving her shorts and tank top on the beach. She had been working for this weekend, weighing herself and her limited portions of food as many times as she could in a day and taking the diet pills her mom had left in her bathroom drawer when cheer season started.

It was the greatest irony of her life: how much she hated her body and how much she lived for the attention it garnered.

She saw Philip exit the woods at a clip and turn to the house. "Phil! Wait up!"

He stopped and looked toward her, but she couldn't tell whether he was happy to see her. Either way, he waited.

"Where have you been hiding?" she asked, punching him playfully on the shoulder. Philip was bigger than Silas and thicker. He wasn't unattractive; he just wasn't Silas. If he had been related to anyone else, he could've had a very different experience. Even though Silas was younger, Philip was always known as Silas's brother.

"Around," he said.

"Where's Sarah?" She had meant to ask about Silas, but Sarah's name came out instead. She didn't correct herself.

"I don't—" he said, taking a step back. "I don't know."

"What's going on between you two, huh?" Lily asked, tilting her body with one hand on her hip.

Silas said he loved her hip bones.

"Nothing," he said, but she could sense a ripple in his voice, and she wasn't going to let go of it. Bonding with Philip was one of her main goals for the weekend, and she was just drunk enough to try.

"Come on, you can talk to me," she said, leaning in. "I'm practically part of the family."

Philip raised his eyebrows at her.

"Come on, walk me to the firepit and we can talk. I think Silas went down that way."

"I think I'm just gonna—"

"Come *on*," Lily said, pulling on his arm with her whole

weight. Philip glanced back at the woods and exhaled, shaking his head.

"No, you know what? Come on this way. We'll have a drink and talk about it." He took her by the elbow and nodded toward the house. "We don't need to go back there."

Lily beamed and looped her arm in his. She couldn't wait to tell Silas how she'd won over his brother. No one else had, as far as she knew.

"Lead the way," she said.

BY THE TIME THEY were settled on the two-person porch swing, Lily with a vodka Sprite ("Diet, please," she said three times to Philip's back) and Philip holding a beer, it was fully dark.

"So, you like her, right? Sarah?" Lily asked, watching the shadowy shapes of her friends on the beach. As far as she could tell, none of them were Silas. She swallowed the thought away with a sip.

"Yeah, I guess. I mean, she's cool. Cooler than a lot of girls I know," he said.

"Not cooler than me, though, right?" Lily asked, pushing his knee with her foot. He rocked the swing under them just enough to feel like a boat in calm waters.

"'Course not."

Lily smiled into her drink.

"Well, have you told her?"

Philip sighed, glancing once more toward the woods. "Kind of, yeah. I kind of just did, actually."

"No way!" Lily exclaimed. "What did she say?"

"Well, I'm sitting here with you, aren't I?"

If it had been Terrance speaking, it would've sounded insulting, but from Philip it didn't. It sounded like friendship, or the beginning, at least. Lily leaned forward and put her hand on Philip's large shoulder.

"Oh, Phil. She doesn't deserve you."

"I don't know about—"

"No," Lily interrupted, putting down her drink. It was important that he hear this, she thought. It was the most important thing he would ever hear; she was sure of it. "You are the best guy. I mean that. The. Best. Guy."

Philip smiled just a little before he inched backward out of Lily's grip.

"That's nice of you."

"No, no, no," Lily repeated. "You're not hearing me. You're seriously the best. Sarah . . . there are a million girls like Sarah. You could do so much better. If you just let me, I could set—"

"No, thanks," Philip interrupted. But he looked more comfortable than he had a few minutes before, and a few minutes before that. She was getting through to him, Lily thought with a tingle of pride. They were bonding.

"Fine," Lily said, and took the final sip of her drink. "But can I ask—why her?"

She couldn't see his face anymore; the dark had crept up the porch, and the dim lights from the living room only outlined the shape of him, like he was an anonymous tipster in a Mafia documentary.

"She's smart," he said finally. "Not just in school, though. She's smart-funny. My dad always says you can tell the quality of a person's brain from their humor, and she is the proof." He shifted on the swing. "And she seems to think I'm smart too. And funny. She gets me in a different way than other people. But it doesn't matter. She's not into me." He reached for his beer and tilted his head back. "She's into someone else."

Those last words hit Lily's skin like electricity. As she had the whole weekend, whenever faced with the shadow of a thought she didn't want, she reached for her empty Solo cup and then for his beer, taking it right from his hands. He let her.

"You know what I think?" she asked when she had finished it. The alcohol made her vision swim, but it helped settle the unasked question that sparked and hissed in her chest. "I think if you like her so much, you should go get her. Screw this other person. You are one of a kind, Mr. Harrison. You deserve to get the girl. Don't give up. There's nothing sexier than a guy who knows what he wants and is willing to fight for it." She patted his knee definitively. "That's what I think."

Philip pitched forward, his elbows landing on his knees.

"Thanks, Lily," he said, after a minute of nothing but the roar of crickets over a pop hit's bass beat. "You know, I'm glad you're practically part of the family."

Lily felt dizzy from the compliment; it caught her that off guard. She knew he was mocking her; she recognized the repetition of her words. But she also knew he meant it nicely. Maybe almost in a brotherly way. She felt it so much, she almost had to lie down right there, her head in his lap. But that's when she heard Silas's voice roll up from the beach.

"Boo-yah! That's a cup. Heating up, bitches!"

She stood and immediately fell back.

"I'll go get him," Philip said, lifting her legs onto the part of the swing his body had vacated. Lily nodded, and then there was nothing.

Nothing, that is, until she woke up upstairs, thirsty and alone.

# PEYOTE

**WHEN WE ARRIVED ON** Jason Culver's lawn, the sun had drained any remaining green from the grass, replacing it with more of its own white-hot yellow. Everything around us was long past water, ready, instead, to be set on fire.

I wiped sweat from my forehead and fought the urge to lick it as I rang the doorbell. That's how much I miss salt.

"Mr. Culver, can I have a word with you about your case?"

I heard shuffling and the sudden absence of voices on the television before the door opened a crack.

"What the—oh, right. Yeah, come on in."

The screen door stuttered to a stop behind me as I entered the musty darkness inside.

"Who's this guy?" Jason asked, popping open a beer. I licked my lips at the sound. What can I say? I want to taste everything you've got.

"Hiya," Trey said, shoving his hand between us until Jason took it. "I'm Trey Hardbody, Peyote's supervisor. And I am just as disappointed in him as you are."

Trey pulled out a chair with a scrape and sat.

"I am so disappointed that I have come here myself to observe Mr. Trip and assess his work. He's supposed to be teaching our dear Ms. Ganon here, the newest member of our work family, but I'm worried she won't possibly learn a lick from a nincompoop like him."

"I haven't been—" Jason started, looking my way, puzzled.

"Please, no need to protect him. I'm here now, and we will find your target. But I would take one of those beers," Trey went on. "Unless, do you have Jäger?"

Jason shook his head, but he passed Trey a bottle.

"As I was saying," I redirected, "my colleagues and I just wanted to ask you a few more questions so we can get to the bottom of this." I looked at Cal, and she nodded.

"Yes, exactly. As Mr. Hardbody explained, I am in training. So I would love it if you would humor me and just tell us a little bit more about the man who has what you want to find. You know, to help with the learning process."

Jason looked at Cal with a moment of sharp intensity, and then relaxed, just a bit.

"What do you need to know?"

Trey leaned back in his chair, and I could feel the vibration pulsing out of him, reaching like curious fingers into Jason's skull.

We were in.

"It actually helps us the most if you don't tell us anything about how you know him, or from when," Cal added. "Just tell us, in general, what he was like. What did he look like the last time you saw him?"

I looked at her with my eyebrows raised. There was no rule about staying vague, far from it. She was up to something. But Trey spoke up before I could contradict her.

"That's fabulous instruction, Ms. Ganon. I'll be writing about that in your evaluation," he said. "In fact, Mr. Trip, Ms. Ganon and I will handle this. You can wait outside." I glared at Trey, but he looked away from me, gesturing Jason into his worn La-Z-Boy. I turned to Cal, but she just shrugged, wide-eyed and useless.

After a minute, I left, the screen door slamming shut behind me.

DON'T GET ME WRONG; I was livid. Getting kicked out of my own operation? By Trey, no less? Trey, who didn't waste a second throwing me under the bus and proclaiming himself king of it? But when I got outside, something bigger took over.

I want to describe the feeling of the sun on the concrete steps of that wheezing-cough-of-a-house on that first warm day of summer. I want to describe the sunlight of the late afternoon, the way the grass felt warm and lazy on my ankles like the tails of bored cats. The way the heat of summertime takes on its own weight. Sunlight literally feeds you; did you know that? The same way food feeds your overall internal functioning, cells in your skin stand before sunlight with their mouths open wide.

When you think of Hell as being underground, you're being infantile. Ground implies nature, soil, photosynthesis, nutrients. The life-and-death cycle of things. Nothing where I live is sun fed. You can't dig deep enough to reach us. How can I explain what light looks like to people who assume they'll never know life without it? How can I tell you in words you'll understand how beautiful it is, both now and after it's gone?

I got so drunk on all that beauty, I barely noticed when Trey stepped out of the house.

"If she doesn't suck my dick after that, you better," he said a second before Cal came out after him. He threw his beer bottle at the pavement and snapped his fingers, shattered glass rising like a tide at our backs as we descended home.

# LILY

**"I DON'T KNOW WHAT** to say," Lily said after Silas followed her in from the lawn, the single poppy, still red enough to look like blood, greeting both of them from the dining room table.

She'd known that this moment, or a moment like it, was inevitable. On some level, that knowledge might've even been part of the impetus for the affair. But just like everyone else who feels their back hit an inevitable wall, she didn't think it would happen so soon. Later, sure. But not now.

"I know you're fucking this guy; I read his texts when I found your phone. He's not subtle. And I'm guessing it's Gavin Kelly, given your recent display of interest in . . . what? What even is this? You never gave a shit about Sarah," he said, gesturing at the flower with enough force that the petals moved.

Lily put her hand over her phone instinctively.

"I deleted them. But you can always ask him; I'm sure he's getting antsy for your response."

She remembered Gavin's text.

. . . *anything?*

She had two choices. She could see them laid out in front of her like paths on a game board, one curving left, one curving right.

Option A: She could lie. She could downplay, deflect, and deny until there was nowhere left to go. She could cry—she knew she could—and beg. She could point out Silas's moments of failure until forgiveness felt mutually beneficial.

Or there was option B: She could tell the truth. Come clean about the affair, about the Forgetting Years that led to it and what had created the Forgetting Years in the first place. She could finally ask him the question she had always wanted to ask, and maybe catch him off guard enough to get an honest answer.

In other words, she could hold tight to the life she knew, or she could blow it all up and pray that what waited on the other side was at least as good.

She took a breath.

"Did you kill her?"

Silas tensed, but less so than she would've predicted. When she thought about asking that question in the past, she imagined him driving off the road or choking on his food. Something with wide eyes and white knuckles, or at least a variation in breath. But instead, the words just seemed to flicker through him, like sunlight on the lake.

"How could you even ask me that? You were there, Lily. You testified."

"You weren't in bed when I woke up."

"What are you talking about?"

"That night, when I woke up. You weren't there. That's why I went for that walk; that's why I saw—"

Silas laughed. The sound cut through the darkest corners of the house, and it wasn't funny at all.

"You had just told me you had made your decision; you were

keeping the baby. For sure, you said. One second I was a seventeen-year-old with a football scholarship putting his drunk girlfriend to bed—not exactly Future-Mom-of-the-Year material, Lil—"

"I was seventeen, too, and fucking terrified—"

"And then, in an exhale of coconut-rum breath, I became a whole new person. Sleep wasn't exactly on the table. So I cleaned up."

"I went downstairs. I didn't see you."

"It's a big house." Silas gripped his jaw with one hand. "Where is this even coming from? What poison has he put into your head?"

Lily pressed her palms into her eyes. Was she crazy? Had the Forgetting Years been the truth and what came after the madness?

"This isn't about him—"

"Like fuck it isn't," he said. "You've just been . . . what? Casually wondering if your husband of seventeen years is a murderer? The man who has stood by you from that night on? How long have you been wondering this, Lily? At the trial? As we made and raised our two kids? At Philip's fucking funeral?"

Lily shook her head. "I can't understand why you weren't there when I woke up," she said. "The house was completely dark, Silas. Were you cleaning in the dark? And your clothes—"

"What about my clothes?"

"They were on the floor the next morning, so I thought it would be helpful if I packed them. They were covered in dirt."

Lily was just about to peer out from between her fingers when she felt his breath on her face.

"Honestly, sometimes I wish I had killed her," he said. "Just so Philip didn't have to go through that. If I had done it, maybe he would still be alive. But that's not how it happened." Silas banged his fist on the counter. "Fuck, Lily, you're the one who testified that he was upset she turned him down. You're the one who saw him with her body, punching her. Did you lie? Have you been lying this whole time?"

Lily shook her head again, but the question sizzled in her gut. Was she lying? It had been so long, so much forgotten.

"Fucking look at me!" he yelled, grabbing her wrists in one hand and yanking them down.

*No*, she thought when she looked at Silas then. She definitely saw Philip over Sarah's body that night, his fists slamming into her chest.

She remembered how big he had looked on top of her. Like a grown man.

Like Silas did now.

"Are you bored? Did you think if you fucked the murder victim's brother, you could be the center of attention again? To leech more attention off my brother, off Sarah?" He was yelling everything now. The house caught his words and tossed them from wall to wall, room to room. His own voice becoming his applause, fortifying him. "How dare you do this to my family?"

From a young age, Lily learned that the most important thing for her to be was agreeable. This message came daily from the world, but first from her mother. Even her rage was shellacked, buried under a thick coating of bashful eyelashes and punctual thank-you notes. Made so beautiful it was hard to recognize as toxic, until it was too late.

But Lily wasn't her mother's charm school Cinderella anymore. Neither was she seventeen, pregnant and terrified, nor deep in the lull of the Forgetting Years. For the first time in her life, she realized, she was standing steady, all on her own.

She had just as much claim to this life, this family, as he did. Maybe more.

She stepped up to Silas, even though there was barely any room left between them.

"You want to know the truth?" she spat. "Fine. Do you have any idea how it feels to watch your husband fall more and more in love with a dead girl? Even after you've given him two children, even after you've dug deep into the trenches with him, had his back through everything? Don't act surprised; of course I knew about you and Sarah. But I don't give a shit about who you loved back then. Not anymore. What I can't stand is how now, year after year, you've pulled away from me in favor of a ghost. There is nothing more dehumanizing than being chosen by the man you adore for nothing but a beating heart and a positive pregnancy test."

Silas went quiet. "Lil, you can't really—"

"There is no competing with someone who died in high school, Silas. No one can live up to a good memory."

Silas opened his mouth to speak, but Lily cut him off, the words she always dreaded flying freely now.

"So yes, I'm fucking Gavin Kelly. Not only that, but I'm in love with him. So in love, it's clear I never knew what it meant before. Not because of his sister, or you, or anyone else. For the first time in my life, I'm thinking about my own wants. And every day I wake up and all I want is him."

And there it was. The reaction she wanted. Silas's face was the thing of her angriest fantasies: a look of absolute shock. She thought she would enjoy it but found, rippingly, that she didn't.

Just then, Mickey and Ruth came flying down the stairs.

"Mom! Dad! Can we have mac and cheese for dinner?"

# PEYOTE

**IT HAD BEEN FOUR** days since we visited Jason Culver, and Cal hadn't answered any of my calls. I looked for her in the office but always missed her by a nanosecond: I would catch sight of the sleeve of her sweater around the corner, detect the scent of her soap. But nothing more.

It wasn't that I missed her, I thought as I watched the door before KQ's team meeting. Cal was my business partner, my co-worker. We had a joint project that needed finishing; that was all. Mutual interests. When she finally walked in at the last minute, I almost waved, before I saw who was behind her, and had her in such stitches.

"Okay, buttwipes, focus up," KQ bellowed before falling back into her chair. "Who has good news for me?"

I looked at Cal and Trey, neither of whom looked back at me.

I put my hand up.

"We have something, boss," I said, nodding at Cal. She looked at me like I had just asked her to prom somewhere loud and public and she was about to say no.

"Great, let's hear it," KQ said, her feet on her desk, humorless guard dogs.

I cleared my throat. "Well, as you know, Calamity and I landed a fifteen-person deal. We're in the process of completing it right now."

Trey's laugh was the first sound. I shot him a glance.

"Trey is helping too."

"Helping?" Trey asked, his hand on his heart.

"It's a good deal. One guy on behalf of fourteen others—"

I looked at Cal again, but she kept her eyes still. She was nailing the innocent-wallflower vibe. "With Trey's memory clearance, we've found him. All we have to do is retrieve what they want from him, and then they are all ours."

KQ nodded, one hand on her chin.

"Interesting," she said.

"It's really a big credit to Cal; she orchestrated it."

"That's not what I find interesting, Peyote."

I flinched at my full name.

"What is interesting, then?"

"Pey, maybe we should talk privately—" Cal started.

I am not proud of the excitement I felt when I first heard her say my name. But then I recognized her tone.

"What?" I asked stupidly.

"To answer your question, Peyote," KQ said, stretching her hands up and over her head until her belly button yawned, "I think it's interesting how you'd glom onto Cal and Trey's deal with such brass. I'll admit, when you came into my office the other day, I believed it was you who had come up with this. But now that I know what was really going on—shame on you. And trying to drag this poor girl down with you—we're all lucky Trey had the decency to put a stop to that."

"What?" I said again; and again, it was stupid.

Trey put both palms down on the particleboard tabletop with a slap.

"I told KQ about how you were trying to weasel in on our deal, and it's not going to fly. Cal told us everything."

I looked at Cal, who kept her eyes large and beautiful and wrong.

"Cal, what the—"

"I'm sorry, okay?" she said, her voice all crackle and whimper. "I wanted to be your friend—I know, how naive am I? But I really did; I really thought—" She dragged the sleeve of her sweater under her nose. "I can't cover for you anymore, Pey. It's just not fair to me."

Of course.

KQ nodded gravely, no mouse insults in sight. Just like Cal wanted. Just like she planned all along.

Of-motherfucking-course.

"KQ, can we talk after this meeting?" I asked, my voice and my eyes on her alone.

"Yeah, no," KQ said, shaking her head. "I don't want to."

"But there's another—"

"You can turn in your training privileges after work. This is not what I had in mind when I told you to teach."

My pass. My access to the Looking Glass.

And Cal still had my results.

I bit down on my tongue until I tasted my blood, but I wasn't going to make a scene. I wouldn't give them that.

"You got it," I said.

Trey smiled, putting his hand over Cal's on the table.

"Good to see you are capable of acting like an adult," he said. "We appreciate it."

Trey's hand on Cal's would've made her skin crawl straight off her bones a day ago, but now she looped her fingers in with his and smiled like a doll built to love.

I had a spark of hope that she had a plan, some kind of long game that would benefit both of us. But I struck that thought down instantly, ashamed it had even flickered in my mind. The truth was, anyone who could survive the Downstairs was no longer anything close to human. Even if, against all odds, they had arrived that way, it was not how they would leave.

The truth was, I had never actually known her at all.

"Pey, I am going to put together a disciplinary hearing for you. I realize we're not known for being choirboys here, but we still have a general code of ethics. Don't steal other people's deals. I'd think you'd know that by now."

I nodded, plastering my face with shame.

"You're so right; thank you for the reminder."

Trey cocked an eyebrow in Cal's direction, but she was too smart. She just smiled and patted his hand, looking so sad for me.

*I went against all of my codes for her,* I thought as I cracked my knuckles under the table, twisting hard enough that I heard one pop straight out. I broke all of my best rules.

Never again.

It was fake at that moment, her sadness. But when I was done with her, it wouldn't be.

# LILY

"**CHECK THE PANTRY**," **LILY** said, grabbing the flower from the table.

"We already did, Mrs. Harrison," Ruth chimed in. Her cheeks were redder than usual. In contrast, her hair looked almost golden in the early-evening light.

"Can we go to the store?"

"I don't know," Silas said, and Lily could practically see his brain push her and Gavin and everything else to its edges. Silas had always been excellent at compartmentalizing.

"Please, Dad? Sean says it's okay with him, and Ruth has never had mac and cheese." Mickey held her friend by the shoulders and widened her eyes like she did when that guy in Venice Beach let her hold his parrot for five dollars.

Silas put his hand on his heart and fell backward as if shot.

"What?" he exclaimed loudly, a whole different kind of loud from moments before.

"Only the kind from the freezer," Ruth said as both girls burst out laughing.

"Well, we need to remedy that right away. That is unacceptable in the Harrison house."

His recovery was magnificent. Like everyone else around him, Lily could only watch.

"Dad makes the best mac and cheese; you're going to *die*," Mickey said to Ruth, and Ruth clapped her hands. "And then he adds in kielbasa—O.*M*.*G*." She said it just like that, letters instead of words.

"Let's get a move on!"

Mickey beamed and wrapped both her arms around his waist. "Thank you, Daddy."

It hurt Lily to watch Silas kiss the top of their daughter's head, so instead, she turned to Ruth.

Lily had suspected Ruth was jealous of Mickey from the beginning. Sure, Ruth was older and more sophisticated, with all of the charms that come from or create said sophistication. But Lily knew that for most girls—the smart ones, at least—charm was a defense, which rose to the surface less like cream and more like dorsal fins. And Ruth was a smart girl.

Standing in that kitchen, Sarah's poppy crushed in her fist, Lily could see Ruth more clearly than she had that whole summer. And she found herself almost breathless with how familiar she was. Not because she looked like Sarah, which Lily had always assumed was Ruth's most disarming feature. But because in that moment, as they both stood on the outside watching Silas and Mickey laugh in their own easy world, she looked like Lily.

She still had Sarah's auburn hair, her sharp eyes. But there was no mistaking that Ruth didn't have the one thing that Mickey did: Silas. A father who put her above all else simply because she was herself and, therefore, by definition, his. Every time she reached and wasn't pulled in tight, every time she wanted to be held close but had no one for whom to reach. Every time she didn't want to but had to anyway. It was the youngest she had ever looked, this otherwise blasé newcomer in their home who wore mystery like a girl trying on her mother's perfume. The fact that she wore it beautifully was beside the point.

Mickey had wants, sure. But Ruth, like Lily, was a girl left wanting.

**SILAS LOOKED UP AND** caught Ruth watching him and Mickey. He squeezed Mickey's shoulders and staggered forward, Mickey attached to him like deadweight, until, in one more exaggerated zombie step, he came to a stop in front of her. Then he reached out his free arm and pulled her in, so swiftly the girls almost knocked their heads together against his chest. Ruth tensed for just a second, but then she fell against him, throwing her arms around his waist, overlapping Mickey's.

"Well, what are we waiting for?" he asked, and, without looking back once, they lumbered as one out the door.

# PEYOTE

**JACK'S WAS BUSY, WHICH** happened only on the nights I was most desperate to be alone. I had to push past sport-coat-clad elbows and through clouds of smoke just to get within earshot.

"Heya, Pey," Jack said. "What'll it be?"

"The usual," I said. "Whatever you've got."

Jack nodded and disappeared into the basement. I forced my way onto a stool and busied my hands with the bar's peeling shellac.

"Barkeep! Jäger me!"

I didn't notice him when he pulled out the stool next to mine, but, as always, when he spoke, he became impossible to ignore.

"Hey, Trey," I muttered.

"Oh snap!" he said. "Our number one person non-grated."

"Persona non grata?"

Trey snapped his fingers at the empty space behind the bar.

"Whatever is foreign for 'the person no one wants.'"

I opened my mouth to respond but decided against it. This was my night, and I was going to do what I pleased. And in no version of life, in Hell or otherwise, did that include small talk with Trey.

"Does no one work here?"

"Bro, chill," said some sleeveless stranger, and I had to fight the urge not to clap him on the back. Jack might've been the only person anyone knew how to treat with respect.

Then the basement door knocked open, and, like a savior, he appeared.

"I got something special for you today," he said, not quite in a whisper but quietly enough for it to feel conspiratorial. I didn't care what beer it was; his tone was just what I needed.

"Thank you," I said. "Seriously."

"Are you ready to do your job now?" Trey barked, and if I could bottle the look Jack gave him before turning his back, I would spray it on myself every morning and every night.

"It's like he hates money."

"I think he just hates you."

"You wish."

I, too, turned my back to Trey and focused on the beer Jack had given me. It was Pabst, and I was thrilled.

"So," Trey said, drumming his fingers in a distressing off-rhythm. "You must be feeling pretty shitty tonight."

I clasped my cup with my whole fist as I took a sip.

"Not really."

"Bullshit. After what we pulled in the meeting?"

"So you admit it was a hoax?"

Trey laughed and cracked his neck. "I admit nothing."

"Then why are you still sitting here? Jack's over there."

I nodded at the other side of the bar, where the rest of the clamoring crowd had migrated. Trey was silent for a moment, but I knew he wouldn't be able to stay that way.

"She's a firecracker, huh?" he asked.

I didn't respond.

"I mean, don't get me wrong—I love a woman who knows what she wants."

I took another sip and checked the TV. *Hell has a lot to offer, if you know where to look!*

Trey peered over both of my shoulders and leaned in closer.

"Did she ever say she wanted to—" He swallowed. "Like, in the bedroom—"

"We didn't have that kind of a relationship."

"Sure," Trey said, nodding. "That makes sense. But we totally do, just so you know. Totally. And it's awesome."

There was another moment of silence—or as much silence as one could get in a crowded dive bar—before he leaned in again.

"Trey, if you want a drink, just go down there."

He looked down the bar and back again, fidgeting with the one coaster Jack had put out in the past millennium.

"It's just—do you know what her relationship was with that whole football team? Was she . . . fucking them?"

I almost choked on my beer, which was precious and not made to be hard going down.

"What are you saying?"

"It's just—"

Jack turned back then, done with his freeze, and when Trey caught his eye, he waved wildly.

"What?" I asked. "It's just what?"

"Jäger, please, for the love of everything dark and horrible."

Jack nodded and primed the pump.

"Trey, what? What about the team?"

If he had learned something from his memory dive in Jason's mind, I deserved to know it too. And maybe it could explain Cal's sudden . . .

*No,* I thought. Hell was all the explanation I needed.

293

"I just don't see what she could've seen in them. From what I saw, Jason didn't practice football—like, ever. They couldn't have been any good before the steroids. Freaky kid, not exactly championship material. And that coach—I mean, I've had some hard workouts in my life, let me tell you. And in my afterlife," he added, slapping his abs. "But I swear, the shit that coach had them doing, they were like soldiers. No way parents signed off on that."

Jack sloshed down two shots of Jäger in front of us, and Trey wrapped a hand around each.

"Not to mention"—he threw back one shot and then the next—"I don't know how the steroids could've gotten into them. They never drank any damn water."

**I BARELY FINISHED MY** beer before I was out of there. I tore down the street, leaping over anything that looked even remotely like a puddle, and through my front door as soon as my rusted key would let me. I needed to look at Cal's file again. To dig deeper.

I found it way in the back:

The story of the General himself.

HUMAN'S RESOURCE FILE
Name: "THE GENERAL"
Current Location: SURFACE

At nine years old, the General, given name irrelevant, grew the largest sugar beet the Minnesota State Fair had ever seen. He got a purple ribbon and his photo in the newspaper, beet hoisted above his head with both hands like the severed head of an enemy clansman.

# SIGN HERE

Saint Anthony's Home for Boys wouldn't let him keep the ribbon. The head priest, Father Michael, hung it in the sparse trophy case on display behind the school's front windows. They said it would inspire envy in the other boys, and they were right. In a place where nobody had anything, envy was as verdant as the home's hearty crops. An older kid tried to uproot the General's prized beet before it was ready, but he couldn't get his grubby fingers deep enough to pull it out. When the General saw the evidence the next day, he started sneaking back out to the fields at night— risking a beating or, worse, the loss of the ability to enter the fair in the first place—to watch the vegetable. As he lay on his stomach between the rows of crops, a weaponless sniper, he would dig a nail into the beet's skin until it pierced the meat, and then he would put his nail in his mouth. There has never been a better taste. There is no candy in the world like that dirty, stolen sweetness.

The night after he won, the General picked the trophy case lock. Even at nine, he welcomed envy.

That's when the fights first began.

In the beginning, it was just the boys themselves. But if there is one thing boys don't know, it is noise control. Soon, their jeers and the sound of young bone against harder young bone became too much to ignore, and Father Michael came looking. Technically, they were fighting for the General's ribbon. But Father Michael knew, the minute he walked into that musty basement thick with the pubescent smells of sweat and blood and the kind of double-edged terror-thrill that comes from a lack of safety net, that the ribbon itself had nothing to do with it. They were fighting because no one had ever loved them, or because once someone had but then they stopped, by choice or fate or finale. They were fighting because if they didn't—if they went to bed that night without a swollen lip or a cut over their eye and had to get up again the next day to till someone else's fields for free, for nothing but the gift of another day over—their bodies would hold none of their own stories. And since they already had no one to claim them, no one who could look at them, dead or alive, and say, *Yes, him, he is mine*, they had to, at such an early age, become their own, and the only way they knew how to do so was by marring themselves into recognition. To make a history on their skin.

When he stepped into that basement and saw the General with his teeth up to the gums in the calf of another boy, Father Michael recognized all of this—their need and their pain and their thirst for glory, and also what only an adult with no qualms about making a living off the backs of children could recognize: the siren's call of unadulterated profit.

That was when the real fights began.

Four years later, when the General had decided to run away, he picked the lock to Father Michael's office, to steal a cashbox the boys whispered about, with a key kept taped to the underside of a drawer. To the General's utter delight, when he opened the box, underneath crumpled bills he found his purple ribbon. He took the whole thing, key and all. The money ran out quickly, and for a long time that box and its purple ribbon were the only things he owned. The only reminders—unlike the scars he had earned but Father Michael had been paid for—that he was, in fact, his own person.

And when he was thirteen, it was that ribbon that got him work at the Farm.

At the Farm, the General didn't have to wait to live. He contributed every day, and, in return, he was a part of something real. He attended class, learning about the Bible in a radically different way than at Saint Anthony's. Instead of the phantasmal, anemic God whose son got hard from blows to both cheeks, at the Farm, he learned about the red-blooded God, the one with fury and grip. The God who practiced envy, who encouraged possessiveness over one's own belongings as long as all knew that ultimately everything was actually *his*.

It was in these classes that he learned about the Almighty War. The battle between Heaven and Hell that had been raging for so much longer than humans could comprehend. The priests at Saint Anthony's made it sound like the events that took place in Heaven and Hell were so long ago, they seemed almost mythical. Not the places themselves—those were real and thriving. But their battles, their threats and their victories. Their losses. According to the priests, Heaven and Hell were relics of the past. Heaven and Hell were done with their war, their moment in the historical sun. They were backdrops now. But at the Farm, the General learned that the war was ever raging, and constantly in need of more forces. It was here that he also learned about the water. The river Lethe, as the texts called it. The river in Hell that would wipe a person's memory. A tricky battle tactic, like all of Hell's tactics. So even if the Farm sent soldiers from the surface to fight from within on behalf of Heaven, a Trojan horse approach, they would arrive in Hell and instantly forget their purpose, falling into lockstep with the other side.

The Farm was a paradise, but paradise always comes at a price. The strongest of God's warriors, those chosen by the Holy Father or by battle, or because of size or circumstance, had to make it to the Almighty War, and they couldn't be tempted into complacency by the trickery of Hell. They had to learn how to be strong, to resist the water and keep their wits—their decency—about them, so they could be called back to Heaven once they had fought and won.

The General was the strongest the Farm had seen yet. He could tend to a breech calf with the same calm certainty as he could to a fellow soldier's jammed weapon under fire. From the moment he was found undernourished and exhausted at the Farm's gate, purple ribbon pinned to his lapel, tattered and almost white from the sun, he had worked and believed so hard that he quickly became one of the Holy Father's favorites.

That was, until the General got the first—and only—girl he ever loved pregnant.

Elsie was a year younger than him, and she kept her long fair hair in a single plait down her back. It took him two years to gather the courage to speak to her, as the boys and girls were not encouraged to engage at their age. But he always knew where in the room she was—he could feel her pulse as if it gave off waves of sound tuned just for him.

They hid it for as long as they could, but when her bump—six months large and Elsie beyond all reasonable excuses—was discovered by another girl in her bunk, Elsie was dragged into the Farm's center by her hair. The General was at the armory at the time; he had risen through the ranks from farmer to soldier to head boy of the Holy Father's militia. It was his job to keep the guns cleaned and the ammo accounted for. To always be prepared.

By the time he climbed the hill and saw the crowd, Elsie was barely breathing. The blows to her stomach were nothing compared to the blows to her face, as if the premarital pregnancy—since it didn't spring from the Holy Father—wasn't as insulting to God as her face, which invited such a possibility. Lying in the dirt, she looked like a peach neglected on the tree, the kind that gets so swollen with ripeness, it is bruised by a strong breeze. The kind that bursts open and rots into the ground before anyone ever knows it's ready to be eaten.

Once the General had made it back to the armory, shouldered a rifle, and run back up the hill, shoving his way through the raging crowd, he found Elsie still on the ground, the Holy Father holding to her cheek the thick metal cross he wore around his neck. It took the General a second to distinguish the red of the metal from the red of her blood, but once recognized, they seemed such obviously different colors. The first was a lit-from-within red, molten red, the kind of screaming red that can come only from deep, intimate contact with fire. The Holy Father pressed the neon cross to her cheek until the smell of burning flesh hit the crowd, even as Elsie had stopped moving entirely. The General had seen the Holy Father brand people before—or, rather, he had seen the aftermath. He preached that the scars were necessary for God to know whom to save once the Almighty War had been won: the scars were needed to prove who had known to forgo the water and had infiltrated Hell with honest hearts, as opposed to the usual sinful, thirsty masses. But never before had the General smelled it. The gummy char, mingled with the smell of hay and the faint wind-whipped whiff of Elsie's white-blond hair, made the General sick with rage. He clocked the Holy Father with the butt of his rifle, picked up the fifteen-year-old mother of his child in one arm, hoisted her over his shoulder, and walked out, knowing that when the gate slammed shut behind them, it was to stay that way, permanently.

He didn't know if Elsie would make it through the night, let alone the next three months of her pregnancy, or the unforeseeable future of their lives. But somehow, as they camped in the desert and stole provisions from gas stations that spotted the sparse and sun-blinded land, her face healed, save the branding scar, and that second heartbeat inside her beat on. At night, as they dined on beef jerky and pop, the General would press his ear against her belly and listen, tuning out the put-put-put of the cactus pygmy owls and ceaseless squeak-squeak-squeak of killdeers, trying to find that distinctly human thump, thump, thump. It wasn't until his daughter (although he had no way of knowing she was a daughter at the time) kicked him in the face that he knew their baby had survived.

He wasn't prepared for how relieved he would feel. It wasn't until then, his cheek burning with the tiny pressure of her foot, his heart soaring out of his throat and into the New Mexican desert, that he knew he wanted this child, and not only because, beyond that purple ribbon, she was the only thing in the world that was really his.

He just simply wanted her.

Elsie lasted until the girl turned three.

They had been surviving on the road, the General taking seasonal farming jobs and Elsie tending to the child. All in all, it wasn't as bad a life as he had lived before, and he even managed to believe what they shared could be considered happiness. It was certainly happy enough for him. But one day he came back to their motel room to find the child alone, the TV on, and a note tucked into the Bible.

Elsie was going home.

He knew that they wouldn't let her back into the Farm. He knew that, on some level, she must've known it too. Maybe she was ready to go fight in the Almighty War. She already wore the brand. Or maybe she preferred nothing to being with him. With them.

In that moment, he did what he always did when he felt the edge of panic, that loose-rock decline into the unknown. He went for the cashbox, the key where he always kept it around his neck. He was eager to hold the ribbon, to pull its tattered length through his fingers. But then his daughter reached up her hands for him, even though he had never been the one to hold her, and he stopped. She had his eyes, and as he lifted her up and into him, the key pressed into his chest and he realized that he was the father now. He could create purpose out of nothing; he could give them both—and anyone else who wanted it—something for which to live, or otherwise die.

At that point, the General hadn't entirely stopped believing in the Almighty War, but he wasn't the same fervent boy he had been when he first arrived at the Farm either. Now it seemed to him to be more of a convenient tale, like a fable or national anthem: something that served a worthy purpose, even as a lie. It was a whip without the bite, death-march shackles without any chains. It was the excuse people needed to give up their freedom, to submit. Which, in turn, meant they could get what they truly always wanted: to be cared for. To be a part of something. To be loved. For if he had learned anything in his short life, it was this: when expertly combined, the threat of that which is outside and the promise of being on the inside yielded a special kind of complacency in the weak, which provided a special kind of symbiotic power for those doing the talking. And thanks to the fathers in his life, he knew exactly how to direct that balance of power to his own most profitable benefit.

Of course, he resented Elsie for leaving him alone with this breathing black hole of need, whose arms reached for him the minute he entered the otherwise empty room, even when he had never before held her. But she had his eyes, and as he lifted her up and into him, the motel key that hung from his neck pressing into his chest, he thought he could be his own Holy Father, and hers too. He could create purpose out of nothing. Starting with that purple ribbon, he had been doing it his whole life.

He fished the cashbox key out from the warmth between them—a skeletal thing with an ornamental bow—and decided it would do just fine.

After all, the brand itself has nothing to do with its power to bind.

# MICKEY

**IT WAS DARK BY** the time they finished dinner, and when they rang the Watersons' doorbell, Mickey had to quickly pick leaves from between her feet and the soles of her wedge heels. Ruth still had on her flip-flops, even though she was the one who convinced Mickey to wear the wedges. Mickey thought about taking them off right there on the doorstep, but the door opened before she could undo the buckles.

"Hey, party people," Cody said, standing to the side. They all shuffled in, Ruth kissing Cody on the cheek as she went. It was the first time Mickey had seen Cody blush in years, if she ever had.

"Follow me," he said, leading the way down the carpeted steps to the basement.

The carpet was the color of oatmeal, and the same consistency. Mickey stared at it from the worn leather couch, watching the way small kernels bloomed out around the heel of her shoe.

"Do you guys want anything to drink?" Cody asked, grinning. "We got the good stuff tonight." He opened the minifridge and pulled out a handle of rum. "I found it in the boathouse freezer."

"Yes, please," Ruth said. Cody balanced the handle with one

arm as he poured the rum into red plastic cups and topped each off with Fresca.

"Watch out; these are dangerous. You can't even taste it."

Mickey took a sip and winced.

"Mickey can taste it," Sean said.

"Shut up," Mickey answered, and took another. "It's good."

"As long as it gets the job done," Ruth said, holding her cup out in salute to Cody before throwing the whole thing back.

"Damn! You're a badass."

"Where's Josh?" Ruth asked, and Mickey could see Cody deflate just a little.

"He'll be down in a minute."

"No shit, you got this already?" Sean asked, holding up a video-game case, still wrapped in plastic. He flipped open his pocketknife and split the seam.

Ruth turned to Mickey, pushing their faces together so their noses smooshed.

"So, Harrison," she whispered. "You ready to get a little fucked up?"

"You promise not to leave me?"

Ruth grabbed Mickey's hand and linked her pinky with hers, pulling them both to her lips.

"Pinky swear," she said, before pushing herself off the couch. "Only to make our drinks."

"You don't have faith in my skills?" Cody asked, mock-hurt.

Ruth slung her purse over her shoulder and shot Cody a fawn-like look.

"I've been taught not to take drinks from boys. So I will be taking care of my bestie tonight, thank you very much."

Mickey held out her now-empty cup, her eyes tearing as much from the burn of the rum as from the effort to make them the same kind of beautiful-wide.

# PEYOTE

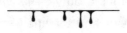

HUMAN'S RESOURCE FILE
Name: CALAMITY GANON
Current Location: FIFTH FLOOR

Calamity Ganon, human name redacted, was plenty scarred. She had scars from the arena—some wide and amorphous, some as tight and clean as a nun's mouth. She had scars on her wrists from her fourth foster mother, and more from the years of travel that came after: a burn on her calf from a bus tailpipe, a knotted mass near her elbow from the time she tucked and rolled out of a semi on the highway.

But there was one scar Calamity Ganon didn't have. The only one she was promised but never got the chance to earn.

The one she needed for her own escape plan.

"Everyone, go ahead and sit down," the General said, each step of his boots kicking up dust in the truck's low-beam golden highways into the darkness. The fire had burned down to embers, heat but no light. Cal leaned on her shovel and saw the boys do the same, all wondering if it was a trap. If she sank to her knees—the desert sand both cool from the evening and still warm from the sun—would her father put her on double duty? This wasn't her first time digging her own grave, and she knew she couldn't dig until sunrise.

"That's an order!" the General barked, and Cal and her brothers dropped their shovels and sat. She waited for someone to ask for water, but they didn't have anyone new enough for that mistake.

"It is easy to be discouraged when one of your own dies. It is easy to question your own life, your own choices. It is easy to question war altogether. But soldiers are not built easy. If I could spare you pain, if I could take it right into my own nerves, I would," he said. "If I could spare you—"

He shook his head.

"But the war won't wait for your childhoods to end. So neither can I."

The General lingered a beat before reaching into the truck bed, jostling the rolled-up weathered tarp, and lifting it, one armed, over his shoulder.

"We do not fight this war for acknowledgment, for none shall know what we've done for the earth. We fight this war so that those we love, and those we don't, stand a chance. Not only here on this plane, but on the next. We fight thanklessly, men, and we die thanklessly. And it is a God-given honor."

"Yes, sir!" they said.

"That is why I wanted all of you to do this today, even if today we have only lost one."

The General walked the length of the holes, peering over some edges, kicking sand into others.

"How does it feel, men?" he asked. "To know you've made your last home?"

"All home on Earth is temporary," Cal responded, and the rest glared at her. These boys hadn't learned that line yet. Her father said nothing, but she could tell by his shoulders that he was proud.

He came to a stop in front of the last grave, the one she had dug. He shifted his shoulder forward and lowered the tarp inside.

"Samuel here died a warrior of God, and his war is just beginning," he said as he knelt beside the grave. "But I have something for him. A gift. I couldn't give it to him while he was still alive, because when we are alive, we are sinners. But now that he is gone, it is time for all of you to learn that there is one thing we have to look forward to."

Cal watched a few of her brothers sit up, come to their knees to get closer to the General. As if the more eager they seemed for the bright part of their future, the quicker it would come. He stood up and pulled the leather strap loose from his neck, where a key had always hung. It was long and thin, not so ornate as to be considered terribly precious, but no ordinary house key either. Cal had its simple handle memorized; she had drawn the design on her skin at night countless times when she couldn't sleep.

The General turned to the remnants of their fire and dangled the key over the embers. Cal watched the metal take on heat like it was growing a soul.

"When we are human, we are barely better than beasts. But where Samuel is now, he has nothing but potential. And with this mark, he can prove whose side he's on. He can prove he fights for God in the Almighty War, no matter what he has to do in Hell."

The General watched the key where it nestled against crackling logs, turning from red to yellow to white to the color beyond white, the one that leaves its imprint on your eyeballs for hours, all the way until you sleep.

"Being the bearer of the key is the greatest honor I have, and it is an honor that I can bestow upon each and every one of you. I swear on my holy rank that if you die here, I will give you the Mark of the Key so that when we win this war in Hell, you can come home to Heaven a victor."

There was a sigh of relief or admiration or maybe just exhaustion; Cal couldn't tell. There wasn't much time to contemplate, because then the metal was hot enough and the General was leaning over where the boy they'd named Samuel lay, the hole plenty deep but not quite wide enough, so he looked like he was asleep on a bus seat. His shirt stretched up around his middle within the tarp, exposing the curve of his waist where, uninterrupted, he would've grown muscles that guided the eye down past his belt— or not. Now it was all just soft.

When the key landed against Samuel's stilled middle, all of her brothers gasped or flinched, but not Cal. She closed her eyes and listened to the hiss and pretended it was her flesh that burned.

She had never wanted anything more.

Once satisfied, the General pulled back the leather strap, but not before reaching for the collar of the dead boy's shirt. He grabbed the simple ball chain that rested there and gave a solid tug. He held the chain up to be back-lit by the waning light of the key, just enough to illuminate the single soda tab that hung there.

"We honor the lives we take, for we did not take them in vain. We merely sent them on to the next battle, and we will all, sooner or later, see them there."

When he looked up, he saw one of the boys raising a hand.

"What is it, Joseph?" The General wasn't accustomed to questions, and Cal was surprised to see Joseph risk ask-ing one.

"If you are the only one who can bestow the Mark of the Key, what happens to us if we die and you're not there to give it? What if we don't die here?"

The General stood up and wiped the sand from his jeans. He touched the metal to his fingertip, winced, and looped the leather strap over his neck once more. The key nestled into his chest, and Cal knew the plastic buttons on his shirt would melt and need replacing. She would have to find some more white thread.

"Joseph," he said, "this is only your second week here, and you've killed two in the arena, including Samuel here." The General threw the necklace to Joseph, who slid the soda tab off the chain and onto his own, where it jingled softly next to his other one. "If you don't die as my soldier, you're going to have a lot more to worry about when eter-nity comes.

"Now," the General said as he picked up a shovel and threw it at Joseph, so that the boy had to cover his face to avoid the cutting edge, "bury your brother."

# LILY

AT FIRST IT FELT good, in a sky-diving-before-the-parachute-malfunctions kind of way, to have the words out of her. *I'm in love with him.* But since Silas had left with the kids and the car to get groceries for dinner, she'd found herself in a new position: facing the unknown. Would they get divorced? Would Sean and Mickey spend their last couple of years at home shuttling between two new houses, their bedrooms painted the same as their originals in a thin attempt at normalcy? Would she introduce them to Gavin? Would she even be with him? Sure, they had spent many an afternoon in their motel bed, tangled up in sheets and sticky promises about the future. But those were motel promises. Everyone knows you can't believe anything said in a motel bed.

But then there she was, not in a motel but in her husband's family's summer home—her summer home—and the words had been said, splattered on the knotted wood and the picture frames that needed a light dusting.

And she was alone.

She texted Mickey and Sean she was going home for an early-morning meeting with the gallery's summer staff and threw her toiletries and sweats into a bag. It would be better for the kids if she and Silas had a night apart to cool off, to adjust to the inconvenience of all that truth. But really, when Silas stood in front of her and demanded she tell him how she could do this to *his* family, she finally saw the truth she had ignored all along.

Lily had spent her whole life carving herself into the perfect shape for him, hacking off whatever parts got in his way. The concave to his convex. Because that's what it meant to be a wife, a mother. Because marriage required sacrifice. Because together, they made one, more complete shape. But when she looked into his eyes then, she knew what that voice in her had always known: Silas wanted the empty parts of her, the parts made for his comfort. But not the rest. The part of her that wasn't holes.

Maybe the answer wasn't a different man at all, but a different her. Or maybe the detonated foxhole of her life was the kind of bad she needed to feel instead of an answer, and to expect one man to fix it just by smiling was delusional. Maybe even dangerous.

But at that moment, Lily didn't care.

"I'm starving," she said to the empty bedroom.

And she threw her bag over her shoulder and walked out the door.

# PEYOTE

**A FEW SECONDS AFTER** I thought I would go completely insane if the elevator doors didn't open, they opened. There I was, back on the Sixth Floor in that gold and white hallway, with higher ceilings than I've ever seen underground. It was the kind of space that made you want to take a deep breath. But there was no time for wonder.

I heard the slapping before I saw him.

"Hello, visitor!"

Felix came to a stop in front of me, all his animal parts collected like a preschooler's drawing come to life, horror-style.

"I said human this time," I answered, stepping back. There was no getting used to Felix.

"Yeah," Felix said, black eyes gleaming. "It's a little Sixth-Floor humor. It doesn't matter what you press; I'm all we've got."

"Funny."

"I'll let them know you think so!" His eyes rolled back before I could stop him. A moment later, he twitched. "Message sent."

"Great. I need to get back into the Looking Glass." I took a step forward as I said it, fueled by my lack of options.

If push came to shove, I could take him.

"No, you couldn't," Felix responded. "I am much more danger-ous than you are." The fur on his arms parted as metal rose up: long, thin barrels with scopes on the ends. Red sight beams check-ered my body, murder confetti.

"How did you know I was thinking—"

"You can't go back to the Looking Glass, Mr. Trip."

I looked at his arsenal, surprised the weight of it didn't topple him right over, wheels spinning in the air. I sidestepped, but the red dots followed.

"Look," I said, taking another slow step forward, my hands up. "If you can read my mind, then you know I have no choice. My colleague who I was with last time? She is—"

"Is the female experiencing distress? I could explain the treat-ment for distress following the Looking Glass in a comforting manner, but compassion is an advanced feature. You don't have that kind of clearance."

"She's fine," I said. "But she stole my results, and she won't give them back. I just want the answer to my original question. That's all. I'm owed that, don't you think?"

Felix's jaw cracked open, alligator teeth sparkling under bear fur. He seemed frozen like that for a second, before I realized it was a mechanical attempt at laughter.

"Ha ha ha ha," he said.

*Fuck you*, I thought.

"You can't go back to the Looking Glass, Mr. Trip."

"Please," I said. My voice surprised me, the weakness in it. I was high on outrage, but outrage is nothing but steam. I know; I see it in my deals every day. Too often, outrage is the last use of the air we are so sure we've earned.

Felix blinked, plastic lids capping his glass eyes. The left one stuck for just a second.

"But I have something here that belongs to your friend. She left it behind last time."

"What is it?"

"Your partner, she lost it in the Looking Glass. Came right off her neck when you shoved her across the room."

I looked at him.

"You can't seriously think we don't have cameras," he said, his eyes rolling from the ceiling to the walls to the cannons protruding from his hairy little shoulders. He had a point.

Then his eyes rolled back again, and there was a commotion from his middle, a whirring and grinding of gears. Finally, a small drawer popped out from where his belly button might've been.

"Go on," he said, with what I thought was a hint of either irritation or flirtation. "Take it."

I had to crouch down to reach the drawer, and my fingers grazed the coarse hair of the hide stitched up his middle. It looked like cow. Maybe dalmatian.

"Has she been missing it?"

I opened my fist and shook out a silver ball chain, slick to the touch and cool from its time inside Felix after so many years against a human heart.

In the middle hung a cluster of soda tabs.

I was right.

Jason and the rest of them were not resentful ex-footballers; they were soldiers. The General's soldiers. And not only did they think they needed his key—his mark—so that they could go to Heaven, not only did they still believe him, trust him, even after the raid at the barracks, even after some were returned, thin and thirsty, to their red-eyed parents . . . But if this knockoff dog tag, this heartbreaking relic of imagination and violence, was truly Cal's, then it, combined with her willingness to cut me out of the deal in favor of Trey, pointed to one answer.

She still believed him too.

I could tell from her file how she felt about that key. The key that he took from the group home when he was a child. The key that was just as much of a lie as everything he had ever done or said. Why didn't he just stick with this "Holy Father's" story the whole way through, and brand the boys alive? I wondered as I gripped the chain. But as soon as I thought about it, I knew the answer.

He thought Father Michael, with his underground fighting ring for profit at Saint Anthony's, and the Farm's Holy Father, with his hand to Elsie's battered cheek, were cruel.

He believed himself to be better.

This was a common opinion among those who found themselves here.

I tucked the necklace in my pocket and patted it flat. It would come in handy at some point; it had to. But right now, there were only two things I knew for certain.

One: Cal didn't know the General's mark was fake.

Two: She wanted it, which meant I had to get it first.

"Thanks for this," I said. "But are you sure there isn't anything else you can do? I just want my own results that were already granted to me. Please, buddy. Help me out."

Felix rolled back and forth for a second, like a person debating their next step. But Felix didn't seem like the kind of creature who debated.

"There is one thing I can do, and only one thing."

"What?" I asked.

A tiny raccoon hand touched my skin, followed by a hiss and a loud pop, and then nothing.

# MICKEY

―――――――

"TRUTH," JOSH SAID, ONE hand around his plastic cup, the other pitched on the arm of the couch. When he got down to the basement, he took the spot next to Mickey, and she barely heard anything anyone had said since. Every time he gestured, his knee came so very close to hers.

Ruth rolled her eyes from her place on the floor.

"Boring," she said.

"That's me," Josh answered, shrugging. Mickey grinned. She loved how he didn't perform for Ruth the way Cody—or even she—did. He was immune, and she wanted what he had. She wanted the cure of him.

"Josh, are you a virgin?" Ruth asked. Sean laughed in a coughing way, and Cody joined.

"Define 'virgin,'" Josh said. Mickey could see a poster of some football team's cheerleaders hanging over his head, missing one thumbtack.

"That's a yes," Cody said.

"No, come on, I'm trying to play the game right," Josh said. "I picked truth, so I want to make sure I'm telling the truth."

"Have you had sex?" Ruth said. Mickey heard the word on the inside as much as she did on the outside.

"No," Josh answered. He shifted on the couch, jostling Mickey just enough to spill a little of her drink on her thigh. She wiped it off with her forearm.

"Have you?" Cody asked Ruth.

She smiled. "It's not my turn, perv."

"I'm not the perv! It was your question!"

Mickey noticed how when Ruth laughed, she leaned back so her shoulders rested on Sean's leg. She could tell Cody saw it too. She made a note to ask her about it later.

"Your turn," Ruth said to Josh. He nodded.

"Mickey, truth or dare?"

Mickey froze and burned at the same time. She hurt from his attention, but when he turned his head away, she found she also hurt from the lack of it.

She swallowed.

"Dare."

# PEYOTE

**I OPENED MY EYES** and thought for a second I was at the Harrisons'.

The air smelled like the Harrisons'; there were pine trees everywhere. But these were nothing like the well-fed, ruddy-faced trees of New Hampshire. These trees were thinner and wind-whipped to the point of trembling together as one, their branches intertwined like a thousand cold hands in prayer.

I reached for my tablet to check my location: southern Georgia. But before I could make any connections, I heard him.

"You're so sexy when you're focused."

No one had a voice so disruptively man-made as Trey's. He was the living equivalent of a paved hiking trail. The crows on the wire gave a collective wince.

Cal stepped under the streetlight, her tablet in hand.

I watched from my pocket of the woods, which came up against a field of grain, and was careful not to move. Everything was like this, either tree or field, except for the sunbaked asphalt of a parking lot across the street, which wound its way up a small hill and around a bend.

"This is it," she said. "The entrance must be up there."

Her knuckles were white around the tablet, and she held it in the air in front of her as if to line up a picture. I thought about reaching out to her mind, but I couldn't give myself away. Not yet.

Trey stumbled out of the woods after her, tripping as he pulled burrs from his shoes.

"Did you have to wear neon sneakers?" Cal asked, glaring back at him. "I told you this was an incognito kind of thing."

"That's all I have," Trey answered, trademark pout in his voice.

Her shoulders tightened as soon as he spoke, and I knew it: she hated him. I could feel it boiling off her skin from here. Which was further proof that I was right—she was up to something. Something she didn't want me to be a part of.

*Too damn bad*, I thought. *Here I am.*

"His room is on the first floor," Cal whispered as she approached the squat brick building.

"Are you sure he'll be in there? Don't nursing homes have, like, activities?"

Cal shushed him and held up one finger as she sent her mind out, listening.

"You're lucky you're hot, you know? If you weren't, I wouldn't be so cool with all the shushing."

"Just be quiet," she hissed, and Trey complied. We were all silent for a moment until she nodded. "Yeah, he's in there. His room is all the way at the end of the hall. Are you ready?"

But when she turned back to Trey, it was too late.

I'd gotten my hand around his wrist just the second before, so all she caught was his faint outline as I triggered my tablet and shot him straight back down to Hell.

"Hey there, partner," I said, dog tag necklace outstretched. "Lose something?"

# SILAS

**SILAS RIPPED THE PLASTIC** casing from the cap with his teeth, the engine roaring loud enough in the darkness to make him feel like it was the only sound in a soundless world. He put the whiskey pint in the cupholder Phil had jerry-rigged to the front of the bike and spat out the plastic along with the cap itself. He hadn't meant to, but he didn't need it.

It was only there on the road, the bike so loud and the dark so dark, knowing the kids were fed and safe at the Watersons'—Lily gone for the night, who knows where, but he didn't care—and he was truly alone, that he could talk to his brother. And it was only with whiskey that his brother ever seemed to talk back.

"I bet you think this is pretty fucking funny," he said. He knew he said it out loud because he felt the wind rush his throat and the roof of his mouth, making him take a burning sip. But he couldn't hear himself say it.

"Even you couldn't have seen that coming—huh? Lily and Gavin Kelly?" Silas laughed. "I know, I know. Karma is a bitch."

# SIGN HERE

After Phil died, Silas tried everything he could to lure him back. First, he tried bribes, filling the cabinets of his newlywed apartment with Phil's favorite cereal and shape of mac and cheese. When that didn't work, he tried challenges: *Bet you can't hold your breath this long, Phil. Bet you can't drive this long with your eyes closed.*

When that did nothing, he turned to bargaining.

One year after Phil died, Silas took Sean to the park. He was an infant, his head still soft to the touch. Lily went out to do errands, and Silas took his son to the pond outside of town, to look at the ducks. He was bargaining a lot back then, positive the only thing missing wasn't his brother, but just the right deal. It was a cool day for that time of year, "crisp" as the tourist pamphlets called it. Sean was a quiet baby (*which you just know means he'll give you hell as a teenager,* said every woman over forty to his teen parents, terrified but good at smiling), and especially so near water. When they arrived, Silas slid Sean's bassinet onto a picnic table bench.

"What if I take off all my clothes and jump in the water?" he asked, squinting unpleasantly at the pond, fingers of frost still holding tight to its edges.

Nothing.

The sky was white. Not blue, not red or purple. Not black. It was white; blank space. Like someone forgot to color it in. Silas looked at his son, so pink compared to all that nothing around him. It made him look like he was screaming, he was so pink. But he was quiet.

Silas put one hand under his head and one under his body— Sean was so small back then, he could fit entirely in Silas's forearm, like a football—and he walked down to the water.

He didn't bother to roll up his pants. When the water got to his waist, he lowered the arm that held Sean, stopping just as the sagging heels of his onesie dipped into the water. Sean was awake; he had been all afternoon. He looked at Silas, not scared, not even curious. Just present.

"I'll do it, Phil," he said. His eyes were burning, tears hot and so close to the edge, but he refused to blink. "I swear to God. If you don't come back, I'll do it."

The pond was murky, and his sneakers suctioned to the bottom. The pond, like the sky, had been forgotten. Not black, not blue. Just nothing.

Then Silas slipped and lurched forward, and Sean hit the water. At first, nothing happened. And then, as if he remembered that his body was a part of him, Sean's face cracked into a sob.

Silas had his fair share of demons. The thirty seconds he waited before pulling his son out of that water was one of his fiercest.

But he couldn't help it. Not back then.

He had to wait. He had to see if his brother would come back.

SILAS HELD THE WHISKEY bottle's neck between his teeth as he crossed three empty lanes to turn right onto the lake road. He could see the twinkle of a house's lights far ahead. He couldn't tell yet if it was his house or the Watersons'.

He thought about his kids, his home.

Lily.

He couldn't believe Lily's words in the kitchen. Not the falling-in-love-with-Gavin part, which had resulted in the whiskey and the late-night ride in the first place, but the part about his distance from her, his preference for the company of the dead. Silas had *always* loved Lily. Sure, back then he had loved Sarah too. He was seventeen, and his capacity for love was just developing; he was ignorant as of yet about the harm a wide breadth of love could cause. But in the decades that followed, Silas never once faltered in his love for his wife. It wasn't that he chose someone gone over her, as she seemed to believe. It was that after Sarah died, followed immediately and even more devastatingly by his brother, all he could think about each time he looked at Lily was how much it would hurt when inevitably she, by either choice or design, also left. And slowly, his future grief corroded his present love like a cancer, until looking at her felt the same as losing her. So he stopped looking.

And then there was Ruth.

She was beautiful. There was no denying that. Not only because of the wide cut of her eyes and the naturally swollen heft to her bottom lip like something stung or freshly fed. Not only because of the length of her, the way each inch seemed to unfurl from the last, a runaway spool of silk. Not only—certainly not, although Silas couldn't deny the appeal of it—because of her newness. He had noticed the way the bones of her feet barely spread with each step she took, like she was walking on prized organic produce. Like the world had not yet taught her skin how to keep her safe.

He wondered if he would ever stop being surprised by the resemblance; if he would ever see Ruth without the cellophane of Sarah's ghost. He doubted it.

Even more, he wasn't sure he wanted to try.

And then it hit him. The one bargaining chip he had yet to use.

"Phil, how about this?" he asked. His eyes burned, but this time it was from the wind. He hadn't cried about his brother since he left the pond all those years before.

"What if you could see Sarah?"

A whip of wind pushed his back, and that was all he needed.

# PEYOTE

**I HAD ONE BRIEF** moment of satisfaction watching Cal's face when she saw me instead of her little lackey. She looked truly shocked, scared even. It was delicious. But then she spoke.

"Pey, you fucking idiot! What are you doing here? Where did you get that?"

"I know everything," I said, swallowing back her response as I pulled the necklace safely out of reach and hung it around my neck. "There is no football team. They're your dad's soldiers. Your brothers, as you called them. And you want his key—his mark—so that you can brand yourself and escape to Heaven. Well, I have news for you, bucko. There's no such—"

"Do you have any idea what you just did?" Cal stared at the spot where Trey had been, her voice a hoarse whisper.

I'd told her I knew everything, and she hadn't even flinched. I was done trying to surprise her with my wit. Nothing mattered but what I needed.

"Give me my results," I said. "Now."

"I will! I was always going to. But you just destroyed your perfect alibi."

"What are you talking about?"

Cal ran both hands through her hair, her eyes darting between me and the building.

"Fuck. Fuck! It's too late now. I wanted to keep you out of this. I wanted to take Trey down with me. But you just saved his ass by sending him back down to the office, didn't you? Fuck, that's such a shame."

Cal pulled a folded piece of paper from her pocket, took my hand, and wrapped my fist tightly around it.

"There, there are your results. Now, get out of here."

"Not so fast," I said, the paper hot on my skin.

"Look," Cal said as she heaved open a window with her shoulder. "If your sleuthing has given you such a Hardy Boy, come with me. Otherwise, go home, Pey. This isn't your problem."

And with a shriek of rust, she pulled herself from one darkness into the next.

# MICKEY

"**I DARE YOU TO** go skinny-dipping," Josh said.

Mickey almost choked. "Excuse me?"

"Nope," Sean interjected. "That's not happening."

"Oh, grow up, Sean," Ruth said as she reached for Mickey's empty cup with a wink and walked back toward the minifridge.

"Being grown up has zero impact on whether or not I want to watch my sister skinny-dip. Always going to be a strong no."

"Ew, watch?" Mickey yelped.

The drink Ruth went to replace had been her third, and Mickey could feel the alcohol blossom in her stomach, turning her veins into flowering vines that unfurled one after another until every inch of her glowed.

"I definitely don't want anyone to watch."

Cody's hand went to the enormous sequined horn strapped to his head.

"Then you have to wear this!"

Ruth rummaged by the minifridge and then walked back toward the couch, careful to keep the drink from spilling on the carpet.

"Not so fast," she said, handing Mickey's cup back, replenished. "She didn't say she wouldn't do the dare; she just said she didn't want anyone to watch."

"That's bullshit," Cody whined. He looked like a child, and not only because he was wearing a child's unicorn costume. It felt to Mickey like his adult persona could last only so long; two hours and it was almost rubbed clean off. "This thing is getting itchy."

"You should've thought about that before refusing your dare," Josh said. "But I have to agree with Cody on this one; if no one can watch, there's no way to prove she did it. There needs to be a witness."

Ruth rolled her eyes. "Well, obviously, I would go with her."

Mickey watched the conversation about her future nudity bounce around the room and found that she didn't mind. She leaned back and took a sip.

"That works for me," Sean said. "Do that."

"That is a lame dare," Cody huffed.

"Well, I didn't finish," Ruth said, her words lingering like fingertips in the dark. "She has to go skinny-dipping where Sarah died."

# PEYOTE

CALAMITY GANON WAS TRYING to protect me.

I know that it isn't the most gallant version of friendship, tricking a coworker you hate into accompanying you to certain doom in order to spare another. At least not to the average above-ground person. But in my millennia of existence, I haven't mattered to anyone. I don't mean I had no memories of being someone's favorite, of being the best thing that ever happened to another. I mean never in my life have I ever thought, even for a second, that my presence made a difference to anyone but me. Even the loneliest of the living take for granted the thousands of tiny moments when another person sees them and, in one way or another, adjusts their course. They may not feel loved, but they at least know what it is to be considered, however briefly, however logistically, by the people moving around them.

In short, all I have ever known—this version of me, at least—is Hell, and what Cal did for me was human.

And, as it would for a human, all the rage in me swelled and burst and rose again as something else.

"Cal, just hold on a second," I said, following her down the hall, which had once presumably been the color of lemons but was now the color of neglected teeth. The whole place stank of that very transition: fruit to rot. I waved my hand, and the clock on the wall went silent.

"No," Cal said, waving her own hand and setting life back on track.

I waved again.

"Just talk to me for a second, and I swear I will go."

"Ugh, what the fuck, Pey?" she shouted, slamming her fist against a wall.

"Just think about this for a second," I said. "Just think it through."

"Think it through?" Cal spun around, her eyes landing like an airborne predator. "Are you fucking kidding me?"

"I just—"

"No. Shut up," she said, holding her tablet flashlight up to the nameplate by each door. The frames were brass, but the names were typed on paper, ready to be exchanged. "Do you think I've made this decision on a whim, based on my cycle? I know what I'm taking on, Pey. That's why I didn't want you here. But here you are anyway."

I nodded and opened my mouth, but she went on.

"The only thing I've thought about since I was ten years old was finding my dad. We got separated, and he told me to meet him at the Farm—he *promised*—but he wasn't there. Not because he got arrested or killed or in some kind of memory-wiping accident, but simply because he didn't show up. Do you have any idea what that feels like? When your whole world decides you're just not worth the extra gas of turning the car around? When you learn your life is a lie from strangers who pity you, but not enough to keep you?"

"Listen, he sounds terrible," I said. "But if you find and keep that key, you'll forfeit the deal, and they will send you back Downstairs. You've already worked your way up from the Downstairs once, Cal. Even you can't survive another round. They will break you; they will make you drink the water. They will make you forget all of this. Just like me, you will forget who you are. And for what? Some story your dad told you? You have to know that's all it is. He was a liar."

Cal shook her head, but I went on.

"You're so close—*we're* so close. We can get out, start over. He ruined your life once, but you've got to let it go. You're not the only person in Hell with a mean dad."

My voice shook as I spoke, and I realized I hadn't said a truer word in longer than my body could remember. Sincerity was like a foreign antibody. Or perhaps it was a vaccine. I could feel it coursing through my veins, making me sick as it made me better.

"There is no 'out,' Pey. Not with some magic key, not with ritualistic scars, not even with your supersecret loophole. Even if you do somehow cheat the system, you'll never be out, not for long. This is who you are. This is where you wind up."

"That may be true," I said, my hands out. I wanted to touch her, but I didn't know how, so I settled for touching the air around her. "But I have to at least try. And you can too. Please don't sacrifice yourself for him."

Cal laughed.

"Do you call it a sacrifice when you spit out the pit?"

She held up her tablet's light to the next nameplate and slapped the wall in victory.

"I know my purpose," she said. "If you still feel like you need to find yourself, by all means, prove me wrong. Become a full-blown saint. Repent, heal. But don't put your existential nasal drip on me. I'm not here for the key, or any promised escape. I am nothing if not familiar with consequences, and still I am here for one thing. To kill him."

# LILY

"**THANK YOU FOR COMING** all the way to New Hampshire to get me," Lily said when Gavin picked her up from the local diner, his front seat stained from an ice pop that had dripped down the chubby wrist of his little girl, and warm all over from the long ride. "Where should we go now?"

Lily had relaxed some during dinner; just the act of eating until she was full was so novel, it made her a little high. But now she didn't know what she wanted. The thought of a motel room turned her stomach; all that anonymity felt like a step backward.

She wanted to go home, but she didn't know what that meant.

"Hello to you too," Gavin said, adjusting his mirror.

"I'm sorry," she said, stroking the hair behind his ear. "Hello." But when she leaned in to kiss him, he didn't meet her.

"Are you okay?" she asked.

Gavin laughed. It sounded unlike any of his other, more inclusive laughs.

"You weren't thinking about that before you told Silas everything, so why ask now?"

Lily froze. She had never heard Gavin talk like that. Like he was acquainted with spite. But, she realized, she hadn't even thought about what this would mean for him.

"Shit, Gav," she said. "I'm so sorry. He saw your text. And I thought—because of all the conversations we've had—I guess I wasn't thinking, really. I can tell him it was all me; I could tell him you—"

"Stop," he said, shaking his head. "What's done is done."

When he said nothing else, Lily made a conscious effort to suck every meager drop of comfort out of those words that she could. Even after she ate her fill, parts of her remained hungry.

"Why did you text me?" she asked, after the silence started to hurt. "It wasn't in the code we came—"

"Don't pin this on me," Gavin said as he flicked on his turning signal and pulled onto the road heading north, back toward the house. But then he softened. "You're right; I'm sorry. I think it's just being here."

Lily opened her mouth to ask why but caught herself just in time.

"Of course," she said.

It was too dark to see the woods, let alone the lake. But it was there. After a few minutes, he pulled over and turned off the lights.

"I know this isn't the best time for you, but I can't leave until I see it."

"What, exactly?" Lily asked. She had never noticed how suffocating the night could be. She thought about turning on the AC, cranking it up all the way even though the air outside was that of a perfect New England summer. She wanted to turn on everything in that car, until it flashed and honked and screamed. But when he opened his car door and she heard his shoes crack the pine needles of the woods' floor, she knew, and she went out after him.

# PEYOTE

**THE AIR IN THE** room both smelled and felt like soup. Not fresh soup, but rather a bowl left out in the sink, with the membrane that clings to the edges. It took a minute for my eyes to adjust to the gloom.

The sleeping body in the bed was not what I expected. I expected a bull of a man with the kind of smile that leaves its target feeling defiled, even from across a room. The kind of man who turns boys into soldiers without a war. The kind of man who could make a daughter like Cal. But this man was something else entirely. He was closer to a sack of flour than any of those things.

I looked at Cal's face, and I could tell she was thrown too. When you live outside of time, it can be easy to forget how it passes on Earth. But here was the proof, sagged in front of us. Melted by it.

But she didn't hesitate for long. She pushed down the comforter, which was hiked up to his chin like a child's, and reached into the soft dough of his neck. When she felt it, she pulled. The leather strap gave easily, without waking him up.

Once it was in her fist, Cal seemed surprised. As if she hadn't expected to get this far.

"I could still take it to Jason," I said, watching her as much as the key. For such a desired object, it was very plain. It was the color of aged silver and ended in a trefoil, each of the three leaves punched with a perfect hole in the center. I can't say I didn't feel a flutter at finally seeing it, but ultimately, like most sought things, once found, it proved disappointing.

But not to Cal. She let the key spin in front of her for a moment before guiding it into her open palm, and didn't answer.

"Cal?" I said, but she just stared. I was about to say her name again when she turned to me.

"It's not real, right? You said it's not real. I know it's not. Right?"

On the conveyor belt, the first cut is always for love. A rarity among our usual haul, love is a precious resource. I was surprised, therefore, to learn on my first day that we don't cut it out. I thought we'd use the small scissors to free it—that tender, pulsing riblet—the serrated ones that fit right in against the bone. But we didn't. Nor did we drain it, like we do so much of the rest. No, in Hell we leave the love in.

Not because we're sentimental, but because you are.

Love is one of these things humans experience, twist to fit their cage of mortality, and then claim to have invented. I'm not blaming you, far from it. Love was made to be coveted, and humans are nothing if not convinced of their right to take. I don't even blame you for the jealousy and insecurity; we sent you those viruses ourselves, courtesy of the Fourth Floor. But the way you clutch at love, show it off, lose it and wail, find it again and forget all that you learned the time before—it's all wrong. To us, you're like a kid who finds his mom's vibrator in her dresser and uses it as a microphone for a game of Look, I'm Famous.

Bless your heart, dear. That's not what that's for.

Love—as it is in the wild, no fingerprints on the glass—knows nothing of time. If you were lucky enough for your first fall to be in love and not loss, you might get what I'm talking about. The pure stuff, like flying before you look down. Like learning that the body you thought you had to fill all by yourself actually came with an extension; that neither worked alone, but together—bam, all of the lights come on.

That's how love is supposed to be. When you add in time, however, it does what time always does. Brings everything, eventually, inevitably, to its end.

After loss, love is never the same. That is not to say you won't love another, maybe even more than ever before. But as you love them, you will mourn them. You'll try not to, of course. Try to say, "You never know." But you do. You know.

And every inch gained in flight is an inch added to the fall.

That's why, when you're flat-backed on the belt, we don't cut the love out. Every time you manage to think about that which you love—remember a face or a smell—you will be bird-dogged, instantly, by the bone saw of reality. Not how it will end, but how it already has.

Love tortures you more than we ever could.

"No," I said. "It's not."

"I know," she said, but she shook her head no as she said it. She was still fingering the tarnished metal holes when the General woke up.

I heard him breathe before I saw his open eyes. He inhaled in squeaks and exhaled in grinds, like his breath was traffic and his throat the Holland Tunnel. He hacked, wiping tears from the ravines of his face, the channels that connected the corners of his eyes to the corners of his lips to the soft wobble of his chin.

Cal heard him, too, and her spine tensed. He opened his

mouth without a sound, a fish meeting oxygen, and she tossed the key to me in time to flash him a smile, take hold of his emergency call button, and sink her teeth into the rubber-cased wires, tearing them clean. I was almost surprised there was no blood when the severed remote slid to a stop next to my foot. Then she sat down on the mattress, hard, so that his head had no choice but to slide into her lap. I could see the tendons in his neck straining back, but that was all he could manage.

"So," she said, pulling his skull against her and stroking the white hairs of his temple. "Where the fuck have you been, Dad?"

# LILY

THEY WALKED IN THROUGH the woods, the wild ones, away from the lights of the houses. She didn't want to take him to the clearing; there was too big a risk of being seen, and besides, she didn't want to stand in that spot with him. Lily felt Sarah there enough herself; she thought it might kill Gavin. So instead, she took him around to the boathouse, where they could see the lake from the dock. She peeked into the driveway to find the car was back, but Phil's bike was gone. She had gotten a text back from Mickey saying they were going over to the Watersons' that night, so she knew the kids weren't home. Silas must've gone out for a ride. At least he hadn't loaded them in the car and driven for Canada.

Again, she remembered his words. *My family*. That bike would've been destroyed years ago if she hadn't insisted on reinforcing the shed.

When they reached the property, Lily led Gavin into the boathouse. She thought about talking to Silas about a new boat—nothing fancy, just something to take out with the kids to go tubing—but then she remembered she might never again have that kind of mundane conversation with him. In fact, she realized, she might never again stand in this boathouse, breathing in rhythm with the water.

Then she remembered why she was there.

"Are you sure you want to do this?" she asked, her voice quiet. "You can't really see anything at night."

"I just want to stand there," Gavin said.

Lily nodded and put her hand back for his, and when it stayed empty, she wrapped it around herself.


THE MOON HUNG HEAVY as an udder that night. The sky seemed to strain just to keep it above the horizon. It lit more of the lake than usual, the water pitch black right up to the surface, where it exploded into glitter. When she squinted, she could see the hazy outline of the float, but she decided not to tell Gavin. He didn't need to see where Sarah went under exactly; it was all the same lake.

Lily stood aside and let him walk to the edge of the dock, his arms by his sides despite the chill.

"You know, she told me about that party."

Lily shook her head.

"She tried to act like she didn't care that she had been invited, but it was obvious she was excited. She dyed her hair the night before, and I guess fucked it up somehow—I don't know. I couldn't tell the difference. I just know she cried on my mom's bed for an hour, and then they spent the rest of the night trying to wash it out."

Before Lily could think, she let out a little chuckle. "Yeah," she said. "I remember."

She meant it in the nostalgic way, the we-were-all-knuckleheaded-kids-back-then kind of way. It was different from the way she had meant it when she had made fun of Sarah that day seventeen years ago. Then, she meant it to hurt. But now, she was remembering the time she gave herself bangs and begged her mom to start homeschooling her. She wondered what would've happened back then if she had told that story to Sarah instead.

"You were kind of a bitch in high school, weren't you?"

Lily took the words like a slap. It wasn't the first time she had been called a bitch, and on this side of life, she would be the first to admit it about her teenage self. But she had never heard a word like that from him. And certainly not about her.

"We were kids."

"Sure. But only you got to grow up."

"I know," she said, and swallowed. "If I could go back, I would do things very differently."

She reached out for Gavin's arm, eager to feel him. The moon played with the features of his face until she didn't like what she saw.

"What was the last thing you said to her?"

"I don't—I can't really remember."

"Try."

Gavin was still looking out over the water, but Lily could see none of his features now. She could see only the shape of him, outlined in moonlight.

"Gavin, I'm sorry. I can't imagine how hard this must be for you. But Silas will be back any minute now. Can we talk about this in the car?"

He didn't answer, but something else did. It was that voice she had muted in her youth, back when she wanted, above all, to be agreeable. When she thought the only way to stay safe was to appeal to the possessiveness of the powerful. It was the voice that used to tell her if the step below was rotten and wouldn't hold. The one that told her when to run.

"I'm going to the car," she said, stepping backward along the dock, her eyes on him. "You take all the time you need, okay?"

"You know, there's a rumor out there that Philip didn't leave a suicide note."

Lily paused.

"He didn't."

The voice was yelling inside her now, yelling like something accustomed to not being heard.

Suddenly, her foot slipped.

Gavin leapt for her and grabbed her arm, pulling her back from the edge of the dock. Up close, he smelled like himself. His hand on her skin felt like his. She breathed and told herself that she was overreacting. Then, as he held her close, he pulled a piece of paper from his pocket.

"I brought this for Silas, but I think you should read it too."

The letter was handwritten and bore many starts and stops. The handwriting was familiar the way her favorite childhood cartoons were familiar: she knew they were important, but she couldn't name them. She flipped it over and ran her eyes down to the signature.

That's when it all came back. The beer-run grocery lists, the family whiteboard in the kitchen. The homework she offered to proofread because she wanted to prove herself useful. She was, after all, practically part of the family.

It was Philip's.

"Oh," Gavin said, his grip still tight on her arm. "I forgot. I owe you a big thank-you."

She barely registered his words; she was too busy examining the letter, the handwriting she hadn't seen in years. The story it told. Philip's story.

"It has been so kind of you both to host my daughter all summer."

# PEYOTE

**"THIS IS IMPOSSIBLE," THE** General croaked. "Impossible."

"Trust me, Pops," Cal said, pulling loose one of his pillows and fluffing it. "If I've learned anything, it's that nothing is impossible."

"You—" he stuttered. "You—"

"Yeah, I died—not that long after you escaped the barracks raid, all things considered. At least you knew that much."

"How—"

"I'm asking the questions."

I turned away from them, key hot in my hand, and busied myself with the dresser. I pulled open one drawer and then another, pretending each screech provided them with some semblance of privacy. But then I opened the third drawer, and my fingers stopped on a metal cashbox.

"So, I got to the Farm, and they hadn't ever heard of you. Explain that, Mr. Chosen-by-God."

If the General responded, it wasn't in words.

I tried to lift the lid of the cashbox, but it was locked. I pulled it out of the drawer and held it up to the meager yellow light.

"It was all a lie, you fucking prick," Cal went on. "The Almighty War, the training, the key . . ."

I freed the key from the worn leather strap and slid it into the lock. It clicked.

"Cal?"

"But, hey, you got the water part right!" Cal said, laughing. "Bet that's a surprise. Did you even know if there was a Hell? What about a Heaven?" I heard the sound of fabric gripped by a tight fist. "How sure are you now, Dad?"

"Cal," I said again as I lifted the lid. I turned over a lot of rocks in my days in the Deals Department, rather excited to view the writhing mess underneath. But even though I knew enough from reading his file to know what made up this particular mess, this wasn't my rock, and for the first time, that mattered to me.

"For the love of the dark, what, Peyote?"

"I found the key's lock."

I heard the General's sagging sack of a body thud against the metal bed frame as Cal came up behind me.

"What are you talking about?"

But by then the box was open; the rock turned, and, even if I wanted to, there was nothing I could do to unturn it.

# MICKEY

THE NIGHT AIR WAS cool, but Mickey felt warm all over. There were so many stars in the sky, she noticed, as she lay with her back on the wooden float. An excess of stars; overstock. Like the first round of a beauty pageant: crowded, eager, and gorgeous. Her legs felt rubbery; she was glad to have arrived. She wasn't looking forward to the return swim, but they had time yet.

"I'm so happy you're here," she said to Ruth.

"Well, I wasn't going to let you do it alone! Not only because I was totally with the boys that you would chicken out."

"I don't mean right now," Mickey said, stretching. "I mean in general, this summer. I'm so happy you came; that you're here with me."

Ruth squeezed her arm.

"I mean it. I've never had a best friend before. Not like you. But nobody is like you, are they?" Mickey tilted her head up at the sky, grinning. "Nobody in the whole world."

Mickey could hear the sound of the water under the float, echoing in the chamber of air caught beneath the boards. The pine trees waited on the shore, the summer breeze moving the needles in a thousand small greetings. The air hung heavy with sap and woodsmoke. It was all exactly as she knew it to be, and yet she felt like it was all happening for the very first time.

"Why are you friends with me?"

It was a question Mickey had wanted to ask from the beginning, but up until that moment, she had feared the answer. She feared the question would wake Ruth up somehow. Would make her rub her eyes and look at Mickey, asking, *How did I get here?*

But she didn't feel any fear now. Now she felt nothing but weightlessness.

Ruth put her head in her hands, and Mickey realized she looked sad, sadder than she'd ever seen her.

"I'm sorry," Mickey said, her hand groping the float for Ruth's arm. "I didn't mean to say the wrong thing."

"No, you didn't," Ruth said, catching Mickey's fingers in hers. "It just makes me sad that you don't know why I would want to be friends with you. That you don't know how great you are."

"Oh, come on—" Mickey started, flapping her hand free.

"No, Mick, I'm serious. You know, when we first became friends, I didn't know what to expect, but you . . . you've changed me."

"In a good way?"

"I think so," she answered. "Yes."

The float was quiet, and Mickey closed her eyes, feeling the gentle rocking of the water.

"Okay," she exhaled finally. "I'll do the dare now, and then we can go back and play with the boys more."

She slapped her hand over her mouth.

"I didn't mean 'play with them,' like, in a dirty way! 'Cept maybe . . ."

She began to fiddle with the clasp of her bra, but her fingers were those of the foam variety favored by sports fans.

"Let me," Ruth said. The bra fell from her shoulders, and Mickey caught it with both hands.

"I think I'm drunk," she said, giggling. "And I think I like it."

Ruth pulled Mickey's bra from the tangle of her arms and laid it on the float.

Mickey dipped her feet into the lake, raising goose bumps up and down her legs. She was an open current. For the first time in as long as she could remember, the world passed through her with ease.

"Is this how being drunk always feels?"

Ruth twisted her hair over one shoulder.

"There's something I need to tell you."

"Anything," Mickey said, closing her eyes again as she began lowering herself into the water. "You can tell me anything."

"I'm not supposed to tell you," Ruth went on. "But I've had so much fun here with you and your family—it's more than fun, really. I love it here. I love it here maybe more than I've loved anywhere before. And you've all been so nice to me. I've never been with anyone like you all. If I had known—"

"You should come every summer!" Mickey said as she patted the float blindly again, this time for Ruth's legs. She was halfway in now. The water was cold, but she was adjusting. Ruth edged forward and pulled Mickey's head into her lap.

"I just—I want you to know that I really do love you."

"That's good."

Ruth pulled her fingers through Mickey's wet hair, leaving touches like insects on her forehead and shoulders. Each blink felt longer than the last. She couldn't understand how anyone could function normally under this thick of a sweater.

"I'm sorry," Ruth said. "I'm so sorry."

And that time, when Mickey's eyes closed, they stayed that way.

# PEYOTE

**IN THE BOX WERE** stacks of sixteen-millimeter film reels, each labeled with two names and a date. Cal pulled the first one out and held it up to the light, and I reached for the yellowed notebook wedged into one side. It was a financial ledger. Dates and names on the left, with initials and amounts on the right. It was meticulous, always the same blue ink.

"What are they?" I asked, even though I thought of all the General had learned at the hands of Father Michael, and I knew.

Cal flipped through a few of the reels and then closed the box. I heard a sound from the bed and looked over to see the General staring at us, one soft hand gripping the severed wires of the call button.

"You know what I thought about all those millennia in the Downstairs?" Cal said, turning back to him, ledger in hand. "Every time I refused water, even after they replaced my insides with my outsides and set fire to my throat with a blowtorch? I thought to myself, What motive would you have to lie? You must've known what you were talking about."

She came to a stop in front of the bed, and the General's eyes went as wild as a horse's in the last corner of a barn fire.

"And as the centuries went by, I started to think maybe you were wrong, but you must've at least *believed* you were right. It's not like you were getting anything out of those blistering days in the sun, training us."

Cal leaned in and took his pajama top in her fist, lifting his head and shoulders clear off the pillows.

"'Jonah versus Isaac, November 18, 1932,'" she read out loud. "'C.M. Twenty-five dollars.'"

Cal surprised the General when she laughed, but not me.

"Twenty-five dollars? That's how much you charged C.M. to watch Jonah murder Isaac? I remember that match, Pops. Isaac was about to win when Jonah threw sand in his eyes. Remember? And then he got Isaac's mouth around that wood fence post, managed to slam down hard enough to damn near rip off his jaw. That was a bloody one. Only worth twenty-five dollars? You didn't up-charge when the dead kid was under thirteen? Bad business."

"Cal—" I started, and that's when she threw the notebook to the floor and climbed on top of him.

I understood why Cal wanted to kill him herself. I understood why, as she took his throat in her hands and squeezed, she would want to be the one he saw as he realized this was how it ended. His thirst for power had nothing to do with honor or responsibility. He wanted power the way a plagiarist wants credit: the concept of pride gained from work was meaningless. The people who hurt children are always this particular brand of coward. I saw countless of them on the belt. The kind who know they can't get what they want on merit, who know their overall worth is less than their parts. And yet they feel power is owed to them anyway. So they siphon their power out of the weakest bodies ounce by thimble-ounce, sucking out every last drop. And then they pretend they earned it; that the bulk they swallowed—they stole—somehow makes them whole.

But she wasn't like him. Even after all the hell, figurative and literal, he put her through. She was better.

"Cal!" I shouted, getting my arms around her shoulders and wrenching her free.

"Get the fuck off me!" she screamed. But when she shook me off, she fell against the wall and not over the General, who gasped and sputtered, blood and spit like a getaway rope dangling from his bottom lip.

# SILAS

**SILAS PARKED IN THE** woods, over where Phil used to park before their folks knew about the bike. When he cut the engine and stepped off, the sponge of the forest floor forced him to lean against a tree to catch his balance. He pulled the bottle from the cupholder, only to find it empty. He pitched back and chucked it against a tree. The glass shattered, but he missed the glory of the sparkle out there in the dark.

He wanted the night air to be cool, but it wasn't. He would've even settled for scorching hot, but it refused to be that either, settling instead on the clammy warmth of abandoned tea or an end-of-a-long-day handshake. He wanted to inhale air that brought with it a new feeling, a new temperature. Something that would distinguish what came before from what came after Lily's words. He wished the atmosphere were something he could hit. He wished it had a face he could bruise. But there was nothing around him but space and stars.

Just like the night Sarah died.

He hadn't used a flashlight to get to the clearing that night either. They snuck out after Lily passed out, walking separately past the party diehards, the stragglers with half-lid eyes and loud voices that slipped on their vowels. They didn't acknowledge each other until they were safely in the dark of the woods, but as soon as they crossed that threshold, their hands went everywhere.

"Is everything okay with the lady of the house?" Sarah asked when she pulled her mouth from his.

*They were all positive*, Lily had whispered that night as Silas wrenched a pillow free to keep her on her side. *I took five tests, Si. We're having a baby.*

"She's just drunk," Silas said with his face in Sarah's neck. Every time he opened his eyes, he saw his future, and he didn't want to see anything just then. "I have something for you."

He slipped his hand between them, his fingers pressing against her zipper. She bit his earlobe as he wrestled free a pill from his front pocket, a white circle with a slash through it. With a grin, Sarah stuck out her tongue, and Silas placed the pill just behind the round black gem in its middle.

"Let's go swimming!" she said as she pushed off him and peeled off her shirt.


**SILAS, ADULT AND DRUNK**, broke into the clearing before he expected to, and it sent the whole world spinning, one part whiskey, one part phantom thrumming from the bike's engine, one part kick-you-in-the-gut kind of starlight. There was no moon, which made the lake darker than usual, like a pool of ink. But without a moon, the stars were bellowing.


**"THAT'S INSANE," SARAH SAID**, her voice carrying over the water. They were on the float, and her tan lines popped in the darkness like they were under a black light. "It's your life too. She could get an abortion, you know. Or put the baby up for adoption. You have a say in this."

"It's not that easy."

"Not if you're a pussy," she spat. He had never seen her angry before. Not like that, not in defense of anyone but herself. He watched her face and thought, sadly, that he had found his proof. She cared about him.

"Whatever," she said, running a hand along her body. "Apparently you're not the only Harrison who wants this."

"Ignore Lily," Silas said. "She's just trying to get a rise out of you."

"It wasn't Lily who told me."

"Who?"

"He did," she said, rolling away and facing the stars. Her speech was slowing under the blanket of Oxy. "Phil told me himself."

"You're lying."

She sat up then, all the flirt drained clean out of her rage.

"Fuck you, Silas. Maybe I should be with him; maybe I chose the wrong brother. The weak one."

"Sarah—"

"Fuck you!" she screamed so loudly that birds took flight.

Silas looked over his shoulder at the house, watching for a light to turn on. He checked the Watersons' next door, but all windows stayed dark.

"Stop yelling," he hissed. "They'll find us."

But she was done talking, he realized as she started to sit up. She was only going to be yelling now.

"Fuck you! Fuck you! Fuck—"

Silas slapped a palm over her mouth, and her skull bounced the three inches back down to the float like a basketball.

"Shit," he whispered, removing his hand almost as quickly as he had put it there. "Shit, are you all right?"

"Fuck you," she said again, but at least she said it quietly.

**SILAS HEARD A SPLASH** and steadied himself on a tree, caught in the line between reality and memory. But the lake stayed dark. He reached again for the bottle, forgetting it wasn't there. He wiped his hands on his jeans. His legs still vibrated from the bike, as if he were just another cricket in the dark.

"Phil," he said to nothing, slamming his palm against the bark. "Goddamnit."

Then he heard another splash, and there she was.

His wish that superseded all of his other wishes. The thing that would've saved them all. Sarah, leaving the water. Walking tall.

# PEYOTE

**RIGHT WHEN I RELEASED** Cal, or rather, right as she broke, easily, from my grip, my tablet let out a series of insistent beeps.

I knew that sound.

One of my marks was disconnecting.

On the Fifth Floor, "disconnected" is the polite word for humans who die before we can sign them. Or maybe "polite" isn't right. "Technical" would be better. Throughout my time in the Deals Department, millions of my targets had disconnected. But never once before had my heart gone anywhere in response, let alone to my throat.

Even before the screen loaded, I knew it was one of the Harrisons.

"Cal," I said, tapping the screen, "I need to go."

"What?"

"I know you have your own plan here, but I have another one. Just hear me out."

Cal surprised us both by nodding, and I went on before she had time to change her mind.

"When—" I swallowed, embarrassed that I still couldn't manage to unfold the paper in my pocket. "When was my deal? What year? If you remember everything, then you'll remember when you were alive. I've been drinking the water this whole time, so I have no idea. Did my time overlap with your time on Earth?"

"Why do you think I'd know anything about your—"

"Obviously you read it. Just tell me."

Cal swallowed. "Yeah, actually. It did. In the thirties." She squinted in thought. "1937."

"Good."

"Why?"

I walked over to the old man in the bed.

"General," I said, and he flinched. I leaned down and took his face in one hand, drool sticking to my thumb. "When did you leave the barracks?"

"In 1935," Cal said.

"Where did you go?" I dropped his face from my grip, and he winced, spitting blood in a glob that landed on the linoleum like a translucent insect. "Come on, big man, take us on your journey."

"North Carolina," he said finally. "Silver Shirts in Asheville."

"Are you fucking kidding—"

"Until when?"

"Till 1943. We kept it running, despite what they say." Was there a hint of pride in his voice? I gave him a swift chop to the Adam's apple just in case.

"Cal, is there anything that only you would know about back then? Not something that happened to you, but something only you had, or thought about? Something so personal that if someone were to say it or show it to you back then, you would know you could believe them?"

"You've already got it," she said, nodding to my chest. I reached into my shirt and pulled out the soda-tab necklace.

"The whole time I was on the road, I was looking for those. But outside of the barracks, I never found one."

"Okay," I said, letting the aluminum fall back against my chest. "This just might work. But you're going to have to do something you don't like."

She frowned at me. "What?"

I picked up the notebook from the floor and put it back in the lockbox with the reels of film, which I then tucked under my arm. My tablet beeped again, and I checked the screen.

It wasn't just one of the Harrisons. It was Mickey.

I took one look at her, facedown in the water, her spine floating higher than the rest of her, as if it were the only buoyant thing left inside, and clicked Confirm.

"You're going to have to leave with me, right now. Time is of the essence here. And even worse, you're going to have to trust me."

# SILAS

**"OH MY GOD, MR. HARRISON,"** Ruth shrieked, dipping her shoulders back under the water. "You scared me! How long have you been here?"

Silas stared without answering. He wasn't ready to give up how it felt before he recognized her for who she really was. The relief of the impossible was that sweet.

"Mr. Harrison?" Ruth said again, cowering so her shoulders stayed under the water The only thing that made Silas answer her, that made him give up that sweetness, was how scared she sounded. How unlike Sarah.

"Geez," he said, rubbing sand through his hair. "Ruth. I was not expecting you. Where did you just come from?" His Dad-brain kicked into gear, taking the reins from the wild rest. "Come on," he said, holding out his hand. "Get out of there."

Ruth stayed in the water. "Can you . . ."

Silas waited for her to finish, and, when she didn't, he slapped a hand over his eyes.

"Jesus," he said as Ruth's wet fingers gripped his. "Is Mickey out there too?"

He felt Ruth step past him and reach for a branch, freeing a towel. "No," she answered. "She's up at the Watersons'." There was a spray of water followed by a few more sounds, and then she spoke again. "You can open your eyes now."

Silas opened his eyes to find Ruth standing on the bank, wrapped in a big beach towel he didn't recognize.

"What in the world are you doing swimming right now?" he asked, shifting his eyes off her and back to the water. It wasn't fair to her, how disappointed he was that she wasn't someone else.

"It was a dare," she said, pulling the towel tighter. "It was stupid."

"There are definitely better dares out there." Even with his Dad-brain in charge, the night kept spinning. He sat and patted the ground next to him.

"Come here," he said. "I want to talk to you for a minute."

"To me?" She seemed smaller than usual, like she was holding herself at a new, constricted angle.

"Yeah," he said, trying to clip the slur in his words. "Just for a second."

Ruth sat down in the sand next to him, her legs out toward the water. Her hair was heavy and wet. He could see where the ends dripped over her collarbone and down her chest, turning her towel dark. Before he could think, he leaned over and took a strand in his fingers.

"Are you having fun, at least?" he asked. "Mickey and Sean being nice to you?"

"Yes," she answered, nodding. But she didn't have that same grin she always had. Sarah's grin.

Silas squeezed the strand of her hair and spread it thin against his fingers, moonlight catching the red and playing it against the dark, like animal fur or a precious rock.

"Ruth," Silas started as he tucked the strand behind her ear. "There is someone I used to know, and you really—"

But then Ruth wrapped her skinny arms around her knees, and Silas saw something he hadn't noticed before. Fine lines along the inside of each, tight and unnatural, like too-often-repaired seams.

"What happened?" he asked, interrupting himself.

Ruth leaned back on her wrists, hiding her arms in the dark. He was about to ask her again when she spoke, almost inaudibly under the buzzing breath of the night.

"You're a good dad, Mr. Harrison," she said. "I wish you were mine."

When he was her age, Silas imagined himself a kind of want-connoisseur, an aficionado of the ask more than the answer. But when he looked at Ruth then, the want he saw in her had nothing to do with heat or breath. It wasn't a quickening in the gut, like the soul saw what it needed and grew hands just to reach. Her want was a long, deep hole. Where other wants swept fast and wide through the body, specific as to the outcome but flexible as to the conduit—*I want that taste, that feeling; can you give it to me?*—hers was focused, tailored. She was indifferent to feeling, seeking only the conduit. It was so plain in her eyes, he could tell she had never let herself want anything else. Just this one thing, a prisoner's tunnel dug with a spoon.

Silas was almost it, this thing she wanted. But close didn't count. He wasn't her father; he never would be.

The present came rushing back in around him then, the black hole of the clearing and the lake and the tremor in his legs from Phil's bike transforming from that night seventeen years ago back to this one, and he found himself overwhelmingly grateful. Somehow, finally, Silas wasn't that age anymore. He had made it through all those wants, and all his bargaining with Philip, even though Philip never once complied. He thought for sure, back then, that a life without an answer from his brother would kill him. But it didn't. He wasn't a kid anymore. He didn't need to spend so much time with his wants. He could spend time with what he already had.

He wasn't a kid anymore, but this girl was. That was all that mattered.

"Ruth, I don't know much about what you've been through, and I don't have to. But you will always have a home here. Okay?"

When she started to cry, he put his arm around her.

"Hey," he said, the way he did when Mickey would awake from nightmares. "Hey, it's okay. I'm right here."

Ruth pushed the heels of her palms into her eyeballs, tears hot on her cold skin.

"Mr. Harrison," she said, shaking, "I need to tell you—"

But then there was a crunch from the woods behind them.

"What are you doing?"

It was Sean.

Silas jumped, let go of Ruth, and hopped to his feet a little too quickly, his vision still syrupy from the whiskey.

"Hiya, kiddo," he said, wincing. He hadn't called Sean "kiddo" in a very long time.

"What is going on here?"

"Ruth was just feeling a little down."

Sean looked warily from Silas to Ruth, and then out at the water. Silas walked up to his son and put his hands on his shoulders. Sean was even taller than he had been when the summer started; Silas was sure of it. He was sturdy, his shoulders broad. As the dead cleared their fog from this space, he could see him more plainly. Yes, Sean looked like Philip. But he also looked like him.

"How about you go get Mickey, and we can all head on home?"

"What are you talking about, Dad?" Sean asked, staring out over his shoulder. "Mickey went swimming with Ruth."

Silas turned around to face Ruth, ready for her explanation. She was exactly where he had left her, huddled up on herself, hands gripping her knees. The moonshine made her white shoulder blades rise from the dark of her towel like a creature from the deep. The kind of being that lived a whole lifetime without ever being seen. But then, as if in contradiction, a bright beam cut through the woods behind her and caught her perfectly in its center. Silas and Sean both shaded their eyes as they looked toward the source, but Ruth stayed perfectly still.

"Hiya, chickadee," a man's voice said. "Is it done?"

Silas turned back to Ruth just in time to see her give one small but certain nod.

# LILY

ᴛᴛᴛᴛ

**ONE TIME, AS A** child, Lily went diving for quarters in her uncle's pool. She remembered the thick white sunscreen her mother slopped onto her face like mayonnaise, and the way it stung her eyes. But it didn't matter. She was the youngest of her cousins and the only girl, and she was going to hold her breath the longest, even if it killed her.

Lily dove under the water and shot to the bottom, a submarine with a mission. She opened her eyes, ignored the burn, and reached through the fog of her blond hair for a glittering coin, managing to touch it just enough to send it scuttling deeper. But Lily didn't panic. She used her fingers to pull herself along the porous pool bottom like a frog, the fabric of her bathing suit catching on the rough floor just enough so she could feel it resist as it let her go. When she finally grabbed the quarter, her heartbeat pounded in her ears. She closed her eyes and shot to the surface, her victorious hand outstretched. But when she came up and inhaled, she inhaled water. Her head was underneath something solid, heavy.

It was not what she had expected.

In that moment, Lily became certain that while she was underwater, something terrible had happened above. The surface had turned against her. Become inhabitable. Oxygenless. Like a balloon sucked clean of all its air. There was no longer anything between the edges. No space to breathe. No space, any longer, for her.

She flailed and churned the water. She pushed against the solid surface with both of her small hands, but it suctioned and held tight. Her thoughts seemed to scream out of her brain—*Please, please, please, world, I'll never take you for granted again, just please come back*—right up until her cousins pulled off the heavy pool mat from on top of her, laughing.

She allowed herself two deep, grateful gasps before flipping them off (a gesture she knew was bad because her mother slapped her when she asked what it meant) and stomping to the first-floor bathroom, where she locked the door before she let herself cry. It was the first time Lily felt in her throat that bitter terror that, alone, she was not strong enough to thrive here.

**WHEN LILY CAME TO,** she thought she was a child again, back in her uncle's pool. As she choked on lake water, she thought, for just a second, she could hear her cousins' roars of laughter in her ears. Until she felt her hands tied to the boat lift underneath her and realized that the sound she took for laughter was only the sound of the dark water, rising.

She was lucky, she thought as she paced her breath with the gentle lapping of the freshwater tide. It was a weeknight, and a quiet one. If Gavin had strapped her down unconscious on the metal arm of the boat lift on, say, a Saturday afternoon or the Fourth of July, she would have drowned. But it was a weeknight, and the lake breathed easily like all those vacationing around it.

That day in the pool was the day Lily stopped thinking of herself as a solid person. She had traded her dreams for her mother's, and then attached herself to Silas, looking to him to keep her afloat. And when he couldn't, she turned to Gavin. Because the world had told her that if she sacrificed as much as she could—if she kept herself small and quiet, swallowed back her questions and angers and fears—she would eventually be light enough for someone else to carry.

Yet there she was, strapped to a boat lift, and somehow, Lily felt solid. And she knew that despite all her effort to silence it, all those holes she drilled into her own solidness, her strength had not forsaken her.

She managed to loosen one of the knots enough that when she exhaled and pushed herself up, tightening her stomach muscles as in childbirth, the remaining knot caught on a sharp edge of the metal lift. Then it was only a matter of time. A thread or two with each contraction until, finally, she felt the rope let her go.

How much time would she have saved, she thought as she worked her puckered fingers over the knot around her ankles, if she had just let herself be solid from the start?

She freed her ankles and slipped into the water, taking just one delightful second to feel her body upright and under her own control. But she could feel it for only that one second, because once she knew that she wasn't going to die there, all her other feelings came rushing in. And she couldn't feel any of them yet. Not the shock, the horror of what Gavin had done to her—who he was all along, and how very wrong she had been about him. Not Philip's letter, the answers it gave. Certainly not the terror about what came next, where Gavin had gone after he left her there to drown. She couldn't think; she just had to act.

The lake was the same color and temperature as the air, a thicker but otherwise equal atmosphere, and if she didn't focus she could easily mistake one for the other, believing to sink was to swim. Lily felt her way along the shadows of the boathouse's insides, darker, somehow, even in nothing but darkness, until her fingers gripped a slick pole of the ladder.

When she cut the frenzied thinking out of her brain, the chorus of mean and certain voices she had believed, until that moment, to be her sanity, Lily found she had a lot more room in herself for knowing. And she knew, she thought as she started up the hill toward what was left of the target practice, toward the tree that held Rose's rifle, that if she had to, she could kill him.

# SILAS

**IT WAS THE FIRST** time Silas had seen him all grown up, but he would've recognized him anywhere. Not if Sarah hadn't died, of course. If Sarah hadn't died, Silas wouldn't have even remembered the handful of times he met little Gavin Kelly, who went to a boarding school outside of town. Shy and skinny, uninterested in sports. Gavin, of course, would've known Silas. Everyone in their town did. And after Sarah died, everyone knew Gavin too.

"What are you doing here?" Silas asked, but Gavin ignored him, instead walking up to Ruth. When he knelt down beside her and she fell straight into him, Silas knew.

It wasn't his aching imagination that made her look like Sarah. It was her blood.

"Where is Mickey?" Sean asked, taking a step forward.

"I'd watch it," Gavin said. He waved one hand above Ruth's head, which was burrowed into his chest, and the moonlight caught a glint of metal. "I don't want to have to use this."

Silas grabbed Sean's arm and pulled him back behind him.

"Dad," Ruth sobbed, and Gavin used the hand that wasn't

holding the gun to pull the back of her skull against him, his fingers deep in her hair. "Shh, chickadee. You did good. It's all done now."

"Dad," Sean said, "what the fuck is this guy talking about? Where is Mickey? Where's Mom?"

Silas shook his head, scanning out of the corner of his eye for a branch, a rock. Anything. But he kept his legs planted firmly in front of Sean.

"Look, Gavin, I need to know where my daughter is. I'm sorry about what happened, but—"

"Oh, for fuck's sake," Gavin said, and the woods jumped. Ruth might've jumped too; Silas couldn't be sure. "You have no idea what it means to be sorry. Do you think Sarah never talked about you—about how awful you all were to her in school?"

"Dad," Sean whispered behind the sounds of the forest. "Let go for a second."

Silas shook his head sharply, holding tight to his son's arm. "Absolutely not."

"Do you think just because she's dead, all that pain you caused just went away?" Gavin went on. "No, it didn't. It got passed right down the line. She died, and now all of that pain is mine, my children's. Right on top of the pain of missing her, of knowing I couldn't do anything to stop it."

"Please," Sean said, his breath against Silas's shoulder. "I have an idea. Just trust me."

Silas looked out to the lake, but it was still, as far as he could see. No splashing, no swimming. He looked at Gavin, who was still holding Ruth's head against his chest, so tightly his knuckles in her hair shone in the moonlight like bare bone.

Slowly, heart in his throat, Silas let go.

"Distract him," Sean hissed, before he took a small step backward, out of the flashlight's beam.

"I hear you," Silas said to Gavin, taking up as much space in the flashlight beam as possible. "I do. And I will have this conversation, or whatever else you want it to be, right here, right now. But let's let the kids go. Okay? I'm sure you don't want them getting hurt any more than I do. Ruth, tell me where Mickey is."

Gavin stood up then, leaving Ruth in a heap on the ground, and turned to face him. Silas could recognize Sarah in his mouth, the shape of his jaw. But not in his eyes.

"So," he said. "This is where it happened. That's the float out there, huh? Where you left her to die?"

Silas felt his words like a sharp, sudden blade to an artery. A pang of cold steel, followed by a sensation of draining that promised to be the gray side of pleasant, should he only give in to it.

"I asked you a fucking question," Gavin said, aiming the gun at Silas's skull.

"Jesus." Silas exhaled, never having predicted that he would be a last-minute believer. He tried to listen for Sean in the woods but didn't hear anything human. "There is nothing I can say right now that could make what happened to Sarah all right—"

"I didn't ask you to make it right. I asked you if this was where it happened."

Silas nodded. "Yes," he said, forcing himself not to whisper. "And like I said, I'll do whatever you want. Let's just get these kids out of here. Okay?"

Gavin was quiet for a moment, loosening a rock from the firepit with his toe and rolling it beneath his shoe. Then he tilted his head up to the sky and took in a long, deep breath.

"We're not there yet. First, I have something for you. Something I've been holding on to for a very long time."

Gavin let the gun drop to his side as he dug into his pockets, and eventually he pulled out a crumpled piece of paper. Silas squared his shoulders and took the remaining steps to Gavin's outstretched hand, the loosened rock inches from his foot.

"I got it in the mail a few days after the verdict. Thought it was about time you saw it too."

When Silas saw the handwriting on the piece of paper, everything else went very, very still.

For Silas, one of the hardest things about loss was knowing that he already had every piece of his brother he would ever get. All the words he had ever written, all the tools he had ever cleaned after working on his bike. Everything Philip touched Silas had since touched so many times that, by now, all that was left was Silas himself.

So at first, he couldn't even take in the words on the paper; he was just so elated to have something of his brother's that was new, something yet to be tarnished by the hungry eyes of a scavenger, remembering.

But then he started to read.

# PHILIP

Dear Gavin,

You deserve to know the truth. I am sure you won't believe me;
you might not even read this, even if it does reach you. I don't
know how reliable the prison mail system is. But I am praying—a
new and confusing thing for me—that you will get it, hear me
out, and decide what you think for yourself.

    I loved your sister. (~~Fuck~~ it's hard to write that in the past
tense.) But I did; I do. And she loved me. Differently from how
I loved her, I'll admit that. But she still loved me. Maybe she told
you? She talked about you all the time. She loved you the most
in the whole world. She was so proud of you, her "genius twin
brother." "He's going to get out of this town," she used to say.
"He's going to be president." She told me about how she would
wake up when your parents started fighting and you would already be there next to her with your Discman, ready to share the
headphones. She said you saw through the bullshit. I'm hoping
that skill of yours will help you believe what I'm saying here.

*Yes, some of what they said at the trial was true. I wanted her to want to be with me, and she didn't. And yes, it was that weekend when I told her how I felt, and she told me she didn't feel the same way. But honestly, it didn't matter. Of course it stung; of course if I could've done something to change her mind, I would've. I was sad and maybe even a little pissed, but never at her, just at myself.*

*Ultimately, it didn't matter, because even if she didn't want to be my girlfriend, she still wanted to know me. She told me she valued our friendship too much, and I know that sounds like a line, but I believed her. I know you were at another school, but you had to know what people said about Sarah. Guys treated her like garbage; they always had. But I didn't, and she valued that. She said sex (sorry) would make it complicated, would ruin it. That was the last thing I wanted. I loved Sarah not because I thought I could get her to put out, but because she was the funniest, smartest, realest person I had ever met. She made life . . . livable.*

*But I learned something else that night, the night she died. There was someone else, someone she didn't tell me about. The only person in the world I loved more than her, and I really mean that. My little brother, Silas. If I hadn't gone for a walk that night (I couldn't sleep; the AC was out in my room on the top floor—vicious), I would've never known. I also would've never wound up here.*

*But Sarah would still be dead.*

*That's the thing I need to say; that's why I'm writing you. I don't want this information getting out, otherwise I would've told my lawyer. I just want you to know, because you were Sarah's all-time favorite person. I know it has been rough with your parents, and I just can't die knowing that you think I killed her. I just can't.*

*I went for a walk that night to cool off. It was late—you already know that. I walked down to the woods, thinking maybe I would go for a quick swim. But when I got there, I heard Sarah's voice. God—I would recognize that voice anywhere, like a favorite song. I almost burst straight through the trees, blown away by my good luck that she was still awake. She was the only reason I was even there that weekend. (Truthfully, she was the only person I liked from our whole school.) But I stopped myself from busting out at the last minute because I heard her talking to Silas.*

*I know if Sarah were alive, she would be pissed that I told you—her brother—about this stuff. She was so determined not to care what anyone else thought, anyone but you. But she's not alive, and I won't be for long either, and someone needs to know the truth. So I hope you can (both) forgive me.*

*Sarah was drunk, and she had that particular kind of slur she would get when she took pain pills. You know, like the ones from your mom's nose job. Sarah would steal those pills and replace them with scraped-down aspirin. Don't believe me? Check your mom's medicine cabinet. You'll see, all the pills in there have little scratches on them, to take the aspirin markings off. So whether it was hers or she got it from someone else, I could tell from her voice that she was out of it.*

*Up until that day, I had no idea they even knew each other. Not really, at least. That's embarrassing to admit, since I considered them my two closest people. But somehow I missed it. ~~Maybe~~ I'm an idiot. But there they were, out on this float that my grandfather built when my brother and I were kids. I remember it was a full moon, bright as hell. The lake was still and they were pretty messed up, so they were loud and I could hear them perfectly. (It's kind of amazing no one else could, but they were all passed out up in the house.)*

372

*I know it sounds super shady, but I froze. I should've walked away. ~~Fuck,~~ I wish I had run, or yelled—something. But I didn't. Yeah, I was jealous. I was. And I was confused, dumbstruck. I think now, as I'm writing this, I understand why that word exists: I was struck dumb. I couldn't speak, couldn't move. Couldn't make a smart decision. All I could do was watch.*

*My brother talked first.*

*He said that he got some news from Lily. (You know Lily, his girlfriend. She testified. I can't blame her, not really. She just said what she saw. But I'll come back to that.) Lily got real drunk that night; I had to get Silas to put her to bed. And apparently, she told Silas she was pregnant. His baby. So Silas said he had had a lot of fun with Sarah, but he had to be responsible and he couldn't leave Lily. He was dumping her.*

*Sarah . . . well, you know how she could get sometimes. ~~Especially when she was fucked up.~~ She got mad and started yelling at him. Silas couldn't handle it; he has never been good at confrontation—he used to cry at anything, that kid—so he got defensive. They argued, loud and then soft and then loud again. I could hear their voices and splashes and one loud thud, but I couldn't really see anything. Eventually, he just left. Sarah was real messed up then; the pills and fight were kicking in hard. But Silas dove into the water and swam back to the shore, ignoring her calling his name. Ignoring everything about her. I had to crouch so he didn't see me when he grabbed his clothes and took off back toward the house. She was still screaming for him, begging for him to come back, to help her. But he didn't look back once.*

*I waited. I thought maybe she would cry it out and pull herself together—Sarah could pull herself together like a champ. It was hard to listen to, but at that point, I couldn't come out of my spot and be the perv brother who was just watching—she would be too creeped out or embarrassed to ever talk to me again. But I wasn't going to go inside without making sure she was okay, so I waited.*

*It was late, you know? I leaned back for just a minute: I had this sunburn on my back, and the ground felt cool and good. I must've fallen asleep for a second. Maybe longer. Honestly, I don't know. But I opened my eyes and sat up, and she wasn't on the float anymore.*

*You can stop reading now if you want. Maybe you should.*

*The lake was so still, it looked like glass, and I didn't even take off my sneakers; I just dove right in. I don't know how long I had been asleep for, but it couldn't have been for long. She could've swum back and just worn a towel, or borrowed something of Silas's. I don't know how to explain it, but I just knew she didn't.*

*~~My fingers caught in her hair as I was swimming toward the float.~~ I found her underwater, out by the float. I swam back to shore with her and carried her out and tried to make her breathe again. I sang the song that goes with CPR that they taught us in health class, the one about staying alive. I pressed; I pressed; I breathed into her mouth; I pressed. I tried. God, if you don't believe anything else in this letter—in your whole memory of me—please, please, believe that I tried to save your sister's life. They said in the trial that she had bruises on her chest, a cracked rib. That's why. I just wanted her to wake up.*

*I don't know if she was already dead or if she died right there in my arms. I honestly don't know. I couldn't feel a heartbeat when I pulled her out, but it all happened so fast.*

*After the cops showed up and arrested me, I talked to my lawyer, in hypotheticals. He said, hypothetically, if I saw someone abandon her that ~~fucked~~ messed up out in the middle of a lake, that person would be responsible for her death. Especially if that person was also responsible for the concussion they found during her autopsy. Or at least the people who own the property, with the underage drinking and all. My parents have nothing to do with this, and my brother has his whole life ahead of him, with a baby on the way. He didn't mean for her to die. He doesn't even know it was his fault. As much as it kills me to say it (and it might kill him even more to admit it himself), he thinks I did it. Just like everybody else. So I didn't say anything, and here I am. And that's okay.*

*I don't want to live in a world without Sarah. I'm sure I would've met plenty of other interesting girls if things had played out differently, but they wouldn't matter. I just know it. As crazy as it sounds, if she's gone, I need to go after her. And if that means my family gets to live their lives, all the more reason.*

*I'm sorry I needed to tell you all of this. It is way up there at the top of all of the things I've been feeling sorry about lately. I can deal with the world thinking I killed Sarah Kelly; I really can. I can even deal with my family members thinking it, even if they won't admit it. But I can't deal with you thinking it. Not you.*

*I will be with her soon, Gavin. And I swear to you, if there is somewhere after here and I am able to find her, I won't let anything happen to her ever again.*

*Sincerely,*
*Philip Harrison*

# PEYOTE

CAL LANDED ON THE float, but I came to in the water, which was more of a shock than I expected it to be. Atmosphere doesn't affect me anymore, what with breathing no longer being a requirement, and temperature matters less and less as the millennia wear on, temperatures in Hell testing the limits of the imagination. It wasn't any of that. Honestly, and I'm embarrassed to admit this, it was the darkness. On the darkest night, the sky offers light simply because the earth is not alone. But even the floodlights of your planet's neighbors couldn't reach down there in the murk and the silt. Down there, there were only me and Mickey.

Her hair hovered above me on the surface of the lake like the wide, smooth body of a stingray, each strand alive and seemingly primed for touch. Until I went to touch it and nothing happened.

"Mickey! Wake up!" I yelled when I broke the surface. She was underwater except for one arm over the float. I reached under her shoulders and tried to push her back up, but I couldn't. I am not built for that kind of interference.

After I'd spent so much time watching her, it was the first moment I actually felt her skin. We aren't supposed to make unnecessary physical contact with the marks. But humans are thigmophilic creatures, aren't you? You try to say you've evolved beyond it, but you'll always be hungry for touch. It used to gross me out, if I'm being honest. Do you know how many people die by that particular want? Or kill, for that matter? If you didn't want to be close to one another above all else, you'd all be a lot healthier. But I wasn't thinking about any of that. Nor was I thinking about Cal, silently staring. Truthfully, I wasn't thinking at all.

I pushed back the hair around Mickey's face and took her cheeks in my hands. She was cold, colder than the water, and her eyes were closed. I could feel her heartbeat, but it was weak.

"Come on, kid," I whispered. "This isn't how it ends."

I turned her face to the side and pressed my lips against her temple. It had been eons since my lips had touched anything but flatware or the plastic handle of my toothbrush. I had forgotten what they felt like against something organic. Something that gave back.

The truth was Mickey was the closest I ever came to love without my soul. I felt the wisps of the feeling, the way perfume stays on pillows. But it was the strongest I had, and therefore it was everything.

"Just one more try," I said, my teeth catching on her skin. "Please. Just give it one more try."

At first, I thought it was over. I thought I had lost her. But then she coughed, and it propelled her mouth just beyond the surface, just enough so she could get out one word.

# LILY

ONCE SHE GOT THE rifle down from the hook in the tree, Lily walked quickly but quietly through the woods toward the flashlight beam, until she could see the firepit. Ruth was huddled near the water, wrapped in a towel, and Silas stood near her, largely in shadow. She couldn't see Sean or Mickey, and while she hoped that meant they were still at the Watersons', she knew they weren't.

Gavin stood in the middle of the clearing, so illuminated by the moon it was as if he himself were a source of light, of gravitational pull. Looking at him, Lily recognized all his parts but not his whole. It was like someone else had put on his skin. But it must've been the other way around. The person she knew was the impostor, and now he was gone. She had fallen in love not with a man but with a sheath. A holster without its gun.

It went against every instinct she had not to storm the clearing. But she didn't know where her kids were, and if she wanted to be in control, she would have to wait. Luckily, Lily thought as she trained the rifle sights on Gavin, she was no stranger to the patient side of terror.

In all of the horror, she had forgotten about the letter. She had forgotten about Sarah, and Philip, and everything that wasn't immediately in front of her. Not really, of course. Not entirely. But enough that she wasn't thinking at all about Silas's reaction, or what he would learn about his brother. About himself. Until she heard him speak.

"I thought she had fallen asleep," Silas said. "We had been talking, fighting, for what felt like forever, and she fell asleep. So I left. I swam back. I just wanted her to stop yelling. When I covered her mouth, I didn't push her hard enough to—"

"Yes, you did," Gavin said.

"So you're saying—Philip didn't kill her."

"No," Gavin agreed. "You did."

Lily was so used to Silas's grief about Philip, she barely gave it any recognition anymore, like a particularly unpleasant stain on a basement wall. But in that moment, even with the adrenaline of rage and terror igniting every cell in her body like a match, Silas's pain was extraordinary.

"So, you know what I did?" Gavin asked, pulling the loosened stone back with the ball of his foot and toying with the idea of kicking it. "I'll run you through the whole thing. You might even be impressed."

"Gavin, I swear I didn't—"

"First, I fucked your wife."

Lily's hand seized on the gun, but she didn't pull the trigger. Instead, she exhaled, slowly, and once more searched the woods for any sign of Sean or Mickey. She didn't want to hear whatever came next. Nor did she, like she originally fantasized, want Silas to hear it. But more than anything else, she didn't want her children to hear it.

Silas nodded.

"I know."

"Oh, but do you, really? Because I didn't just fuck her, Silas. I fucked her a lot. In every hotel—and then motel—within a twenty-mile radius of your home. I even fucked her in your car once. The minivan with the TVs in the back. Did you know that?"

Silas shook his head.

"Did you know she fell in love with me? And the best part—oh, my favorite part: I got her to come to a grief group for Sarah's anniversary. Your own wife, Silas. I got her to fall in love with me by talking about Sarah. If that isn't poetic justice, I don't know what is."

Gavin took a step toward Silas, who still stood with Philip's letter in his hands.

Lily noticed the cold of the air for the first time then, against her wet skin.

Silas looked up at Gavin, the note falling to his side in a clenched fist.

"Why are you talking in the past tense? What did you do to her?"

"Pssh." Gavin exhaled through his nose, disgusted. Or, at least, disappointed. "There's more to the plan! Isn't that right, chickadee?"

"Dad," Ruth said cautiously. Lily was surprised to hear her voice, the same voice she had heard all summer. A voice she had envied for its confidence, but that now only sounded so very young.

Gavin ignored her. "You took away my most precious person in the world, Silas Harrison. So now you will lose your most precious person. You will live what I lived."

"What did you do to my wife?"

Gavin laughed. "Lily? Oh God, Silas. Come on. It doesn't take a therapist to recognize she's not the most precious person in your life. No, I had my fun with Lily, but she was just a means to the end. She provided access, so I could complete step two. Well, she and my lovely daughter, here. Ruthie, can you tell Silas what he should be asking?"

"Dad," Ruth said again, and Lily barely registered Gavin's cruelty as she looked Ruth's way and, instead, saw Sean.

He had one arm around Ruth's neck, his pocketknife against her throat. He was mostly in shadow, but she could see his arm was steady. Her breath caught.

"Put down the gun or, I swear, I'll kill her."

"Bold move!" Gavin said from his place in the clearing as he leaned his head one way until his neck cracked. Lily could feel the noise it made in her own bones. He did that whenever he was nervous. At least his skin suit used to. "But useless, if you want any answers. Go ahead, Ruthie. Tell them what you did."

Lily was overcome by her desperation to touch Sean. To tell him to run. These men and their ghost meant nothing to her. All that mattered was her son, with a knife wedged beneath the tender meat of another's jaw. Him and the only thing that stilled her hand: her daughter, out there somewhere else.

Ruth swallowed, holding very still in Sean's grip. "I'm so sorry, Daddy," she said, through a whimper. "I couldn't."

"What do you mean, you couldn't?" Gavin asked, taking a step toward them.

"I gave her the pills, but I couldn't—they're not like you said, Dad. They're good people."

Gavin shook his head. "Fuck, Ruth," he said, his jaw tight. "I thought I could count on you."

"You can! I just—Dad—" Ruth wrenched forward, but Sean held her back. "They're not bad people," Ruth said, relenting. "He did a bad thing, but he's not a bad man."

Lily recognized the phrase. Silas used it a lot to describe Philip.

"I'm not fucking playing," Sean said, and Lily could hear a little shake in his voice that almost ripped her in half. "Take one more step and I will kill your daughter."

Gavin paused, and then he laughed. "She's no daughter of mine," he said through clenched teeth, flicking the handgun with his wrist as he talked, making punctuation dangerous. "My daughters know the meaning of showing up for family."

Silas turned slowly to face Ruth.

"Hey, Ruth. Sweetheart. I know you're scared, and I'm so sorry. But I also know you love Mickey. I've seen it all summer. She loves you so much, too, you know? I've never seen her have a friend like you. I know you don't want to hurt her. Just tell me where she is, and everything will be all right."

"I'm sorry—I couldn't—I can't—"

Gavin raised his gun and took a step in her direction. In response, Sean tightened around her, the knife pressing into her skin. Lily couldn't believe how brave he was. She didn't know how or when he had become that way, or whether she wished he was otherwise. She hated how badly she needed him to be reckless.

Lily felt as much as she saw Silas's shadow move over her spot in the dirt, pulling Gavin's focus off Ruth and Sean, toward the open, empty woods.

"Gavin, it's me you want. I'm responsible for your sister's death. So let's handle this as men, just us. Let everyone else go. All right?"

Thanks to Silas, Lily had the shot, but she couldn't take it until someone said where Mickey was. What if she was hidden away? What if she shot him and they never found out where?

"How very caveman of you, Silas!" Gavin whooped, his frustration showing in his seams. Lily had thought of him as patient, once. "No, I don't want to shoot you. That's not part of the plan."

"Are you sure? I would, if I were you."

"Don't get me wrong," Gavin said, using the muzzle of the gun to scratch the stubble on his neck. "I want you to hurt. But killing you isn't good enough. I want you to suffer like I did. And if Ruth here had followed through on the one damn thing I've ever asked—"

"Just let them go, and then you can do whatever you want to me."

But then there was a sound from out on the lake. A sound Lily wouldn't trade for anything.

"Mom?"

As soon as she heard it, she pulled the trigger.

# PEYOTE

**"WHAT THE FUCK WAS** that?" Cal asked when we landed back in the office, my wet shoes squeaking on the linoleum as I went straight to my desk to check my monitor.

Mickey was still alive.

"Seriously, Pey, what did I just watch? Did you just kiss that mark on the forehead? And I thought my thing was weird."

I hit Refresh, lake water dripping from my hair into the cracks between the keys of my keyboard.

Still alive.

I shrugged off my button-down and wrung it out over the trash before putting the lockbox down on my desk.

"What do you want to do with this?" I asked, ignoring her look, which demanded an answer. "I have an idea, but it's up to you."

Cal touched the edges of the metal, ran her fingertip along the hinges.

"If we don't give them the key, we lose the deal and get sent back Downstairs."

"Not if my plan works."

I expected a laugh, a glower; an eye roll at least. I expected questions I couldn't answer, especially not in that moment, with Mickey and everything the Harrisons represented on such a precarious ledge. But instead, she just nodded. So I went on.

"We give it all to them, the films and the key. We give them the truth along with what they asked for, and let them make their own decision. Hopefully, they will decide to walk away, and the deal will be void because—if my plan works—we won't be here."

It was only then that I remembered my results were still in my pocket.

We have an understanding in Hell. A kind of camaraderie. A lot of people, when they first arrive, cry the same kind of cry: *I don't belong here!* They do it until they realize no one is listening—no one with any kind of overruling power at least. And the people who are listening are not the kind of people you want to show weakness to. Eventually, everyone stops, and the people who said it most become the people who teach the newcomers the danger in the words, and so on.

And if you survive past that—which you have to, because death is a ticket already punched—eventually, you start taking just the teensiest bit of pride in your locale. *Yeah*, you think. *I'm a bad motherfucker. These are my people. We, the damned.*

But I have a confession to make. Even when I spoke from that place, that camaraderie, I never really meant it. There's always been a part of me—an embryo of a thing, some tiny little molecule, translucent and barely beating—that still believes I was not a bad person. That I came here for a good reason. A valiant one.

Now I had the answer in my hand, wet but still intact, and I found that little part of me screaming. What if I was wrong, and Cal was right? What if Hell was always the end of my story? What if I belonged here?

I ran my thumb along the edge of the fold, tiny pills of wet paper trailing behind.

"You don't want to know, do you?" Cal asked.

I shook my head. "No, I do," I started. "It's just . . ."

"What if it's not what you thought?"

"Right."

"Well," Cal said, then spat on a streak of her father's blood on her shoe and used the hem of her sleeve to scrub it clean. "Do you want me to tell you?"

"Is it bad?"

"That's a subjective question."

I put the paper on my desk, and it was like my fingers held opposing magnets. I simply couldn't unfold it.

"Tell me," I said, finally.

Cal nodded. I felt her step up behind me. "You had a daughter— do you remember that?"

She asked it quietly, a different kind of quiet than I had ever heard from her. Like she was talking in a library or a church. Like she was acquainted with respect.

I shook my head.

"She was sick," she said. "Cancer. She was only seven or eight when she was diagnosed, but it was the kind that moves really fast. I don't remember exactly what. You made a deal. You took the cancer instead."

She put her hand on my arm, just the fingertips.

"You were a good man, Pey."

I nodded, inhaling sharply enough to break free from her touch, even though I wanted it.

I had been right. I was once someone who loved and was loved. It should've felt vindicating, relieving. But I felt my throat swell and with it a new realization: this information I had been craving for as long as I could remember, at this point, didn't matter. Even if I cared about my daughter back then, or about Mickey now—even if, in that instant, I wanted her to live more than I wanted to complete my set—that was nothing after millennia of everything else I'd done as Peyote Trip. What I knew I would do, if I got my chance.

Even if I had been a good man back then, I wasn't anymore.

# LILY

"MICKEY!" LILY SCREAMED, HER voice following the bullet as it cut through her place in the shadows and the wide-open night like a tear to another side.

"Mom!" Sean shouted.

There was another sound in the dark, out in the water, a small splash.

"The float!" she yelled. "Go, both of you! Now!"

Sean shoved Ruth to the ground and dove into the water, Silas on his heels. Lily heard the churning of their wild strokes as she stepped out into the clearing, where Gavin buckled from the gunshot and fell to his knees, holding his gut.

WHEN SHE PULLED THAT trigger without pause, Lily knew—not thought, but *knew*—that somewhere along the way, one thing inside her had been misplaced. One wrong letter in the crossword, one vent turned the wrong way, ruining everything inside. With her mother's cruelty and Sarah's death and her own teen pregnancy, she became twisted against herself. But when she pulled that trigger, she straightened out.

She didn't hate herself. Not for wanting to be a good daughter, or being a jealous teen. Or even for being lonely and falling, blindly, for a man she didn't ever actually know. No, she thought as she stared down at him in the dirt.

She hated him.

She listened for the last few seconds as his ragged breathing slowed into nothing, and then she let the gun hang from her shoulder and leaned down to press two fingers against his neck.

That was when he grabbed her.

"You fucking bitch."

Each word hit her face with a splatter of his blood as her elbow and the back of her skull slammed into rocks. He pulled himself up over her, everything slick and hot from the bullet wound in his stomach.

"*The* Lily Thompson."

Rose had been right. For a minute, that gun made Lily forget that no matter what else she became in her life, chances were, she would also be somebody's victim.

Gavin's hands reminded her.

When he squeezed her throat, she was surprised by the strength left in them, the power of his grip. She kicked and flailed, but she couldn't reach him. Her vision swam; she couldn't hear the lake anymore, or her husband and her son splashing in the dark, or the crickets in the trees. She couldn't hear anything except his inhales against her ear and the roar of her own valorous, foolhardy heart.

That was, until she saw Sarah.

She stood there above them both, so beautiful, as only a

memory could be. But she was something else, something they had in common that Lily had never let herself notice before. She could see it now, as Sarah raised her hands above her head.

She was scared.

Suddenly, there was a crack, and Gavin collapsed on top of her, as he had countless times before, his lips against her hair as they made their motel promises.

Only this time, he stayed down.

When Lily had managed to free herself from under him, she lay on her back, heaving. Ruth was in a heap on her father, her white towel heavy with blood, the rock from the firepit still clutched in her grip. Lily hacked and coughed and clawed the ground, but when she could finally breathe, the air was there, ready for her.

# PEYOTE

**BY THE TIME SILAS** called for me, it was too late.

I arrived in the clearing, where the night covered the sight but not the smell of blood. I saw Gavin first, facedown in the dirt, and froze the whole scene immediately. Next to him was Ruth. Or at least she looked like Ruth, if Ruth had been hung up and drained like livestock. Even her hair seemed colorless as she sat on the forest floor, blood all over her towel, running down her wrists from her hands and the rock they clutched.

As I knelt down in front of her, I wondered if Cal would recognize the look on her face. If it was like in the barracks, where her choices—despite how they felt at the time—weren't really her own, or more like slipping through that chain-link fence at the Farm, after she threw the grenade into the schoolhouse. In short, I wondered if Cal would be able to tell how far gone her young soul was. How much of Ruth was already ours.

I pushed a piece of hair back from her cheek and found myself hoping that we wouldn't get it all.

Lily held Sean, who was frozen half within her grasp and also half reaching. Reaching, of course, for Mickey, who was spread out on the dirt near the water.

I walked toward the shore and knelt beside her, my fingers grazing the fine hairs at her temple. Even from across the clearing, I could feel the stagnant water in Mickey's lungs, cold and deep. I could feel where her bones had been growing, the sudden cease in her cells, called off the job. There was so much goodness in there. An antidote to everything I, or Cal, or any of the nameless, face-less people across my conveyor belt had ever done. A balm for the burned and battered parts of the earth, roughed up by the rest of us. She carried it inside her—not because she was someone ex-traordinarily special, besides that she was good—and inside her, it would die.

I stood up and swallowed, looking away. I waved my hand, and Silas lunged back into action.

"Make me a deal," he said, not missing a beat. "Dad used to talk about you. I know you can do it. Give me back my daughter, and I'll give you anything you want." His voice was the bottom of a waterfall, all rocks with no rest.

To make a deal with him meant a Complete Set. It meant fi-nally, finally, accomplishing my one and only goal. It meant getting a one-way ticket back to Earth, to do it all over again. Which meant keeping my promise to Cal, finding her before she crossed the same threshold Ruth faced now. Validating her trust in me and ending her story the way she wanted. Saving the souls of the boys her father took, and hers as well. It meant saving mine.

But it also meant the eradication of all of them. Of Evan, of Silas. Even if I brought her back right now, it meant eradicating Mickey. For if I went back, if I completed my plan, none of them would ever exist. I would, which meant I wouldn't make my deal, which meant my daughter wouldn't make hers. She would die from the cancer inside her, instead of me. Therefore, the rest of them, my daughter's kin from a life well and fully lived, would be gone too. I could have other children, produce other heirs. Perhaps they, too, would be good. There was plenty of good in the world; there were plenty of people with the same goodness inside of them. There would just never again be Mickey.

But as I watched Lily slam the dirt with her fists, it occurred to me that maybe never was better than gone.

"Please," Silas said. "Bring her back."

I looked at Mickey once more, or the sodden casing that used to hold her, and put my hand on my tablet.

At the end of the day, I am what I am.

"Sign here," I said.

# AFTER

# PEYOTE

**I FOUND HER EAST** of Amarillo, hitchhiking along Route 40 just shy of Shamrock. I left home weeks earlier, driving the three main routes from New Mexico to Arkansas and checking each gas station until the cashiers began to eye me suspiciously, a man alone, asking if they'd seen a girl. But then, one bright, hot afternoon like all the others, I saw a shape on the side of the road, and I knew that it was her.

I pulled over.

"Hiya," I said when she approached my window, dust from the road billowing around her like the tired folding of wings. I knew she carried the knife she took from Foster Mom Number Four, and I could see in her eyes as she peered into the car that she wanted me to know she contained something dangerous. She was twelve and skinny enough to be ten, but she had the same air of confidence she had in Hell, and I could see how people might've thought she looked older. But I knew better. After all, I had been waiting for her.

"You don't know me," I started, words I had practiced many times in the years I had waited. "But I know you."

She glared at me in the same exact way the version of her I knew would have, if I had ever used such a tacky line. It was odd, I realized as I took her in. To meet someone you know so well before you knew them. I found myself wanting to upload all of our memories together into her fresh new brain, to get my friend back. But then she put her thumb in her mouth and set her teeth against the firm skin of her cuticle, a move I had never seen her make before, and I realized she wasn't my friend. She was the clay before my friend was made.

Which meant she could be anything.

I reached inside my shirt collar, gripped the ball chain around my neck in one fist, and yanked it free. She watched me without responding, but also without walking away.

I held out my fist to the passenger side, where she leaned against the window. When I opened it, I kept my eyes steady on her face.

She recognized the soda-tab dog tag immediately, and her whole body relaxed, rigid shoulders and knees ready to sprint melting enough to show the kid in her.

"Do you know where I can find the Farm?"

I nodded. I expected this question—when we dropped the lockbox and key off on Jason's doorstep, Cal warned me she, too, would have a hard time letting go of her goal. But I could see something in her then that her adult self didn't—couldn't—remember.

Cal also wanted to think of her story as a given. She wanted to think of her young self as an inevitable start to who she became, so she didn't have to focus on all of the people who let her down. So she didn't have to acknowledge that all of the pain she had experienced both above and below the ground was the fault of those meant to care for her. The consequences of a child being too little loved. Once she knew, without a doubt, that all of her father's teachings were a lie, the only way she could reckon with all that time in the Downstairs, all that time on the belt refusing water, was this concept. That she was bad, and she would always be bad. That her father's blood made her not only his, but him.

But as I watched her smile at me, thrilled to see a sign of home after so many strangers, I recognized something different, from this side of time. I could tell that even with a life of nothing but death and the knife wedged in her boot, at this point, at least, she wasn't afraid of being good. She believed, in fact, that she already was, and would always be.

"Are you hungry? Hop in and we'll grab a bite."

She pulled open the door before I finished talking and she slid in beside me, the cloud of dust following her as if tucking her in. I glanced over my shoulder at the road, which was open and flat and endless, and pulled off the shoulder.

With one finger, she flicked a small plush dog that hung from my rearview mirror.

"Interesting choice of decor," she said, and I was glad to hear sass was a core trait.

"It's my daughter's," I said. "She's just about your age, actually."

I rolled down my window, even though the Texas heat was hard enough to smack, like something physical, just to feel the movement of the air. I noticed when I rolled down my window that she rolled hers down too. Even though she had yet to know just how badly she could miss the air.

But now she wouldn't have to.

EVER SINCE I MADE the deal with Silas and was sent crashing back to Earth, I have been a sucker for air. I thought it couldn't get any better than the air on those trips with my tablet and malintent, especially when compared to the air below. But breathing it in with actual human lungs is a whole new kind of delicious. I can feel every molecule rushing in, shooting from my chest out to the ends of my fingers and toes, feeding me.

To breathe is miraculous. You should think about that more.

Every time I used to imagine the moment I returned, I told myself I wouldn't take it for granted. I would spend the rest of my days taking each breath like that first one back. I would be human to the fullest. Touch and smell and see everything; spend at least ten minutes a day with my hand on my heart, just to feel it beat. But there is more to the heart than that, isn't there? And while I knew love—or the pit love leaves behind—was a rewarding weapon, I had forgotten why.

I forgot just how good it felt.

When that came crashing back into me—and crash it did, emotional defibrillation—it was like seeing for the first time with all the colors.

I was the one who had been stupid. You had it right the whole time.

So when he came for me, I was ready.

"HOW CAN I HELP you today?"

I looked up and laughed. It startled him, but I didn't mind. The tables had been turned. Literally, I thought as I slid my palm along the edge of my dining room table. It was the same one as in the New Hampshire house.

Humans and your sentimental attachment to things.

I didn't recognize him, but that wasn't surprising. Between his time and mine, he could've been transferred, bumped back down, or just in a different hallway. I recognized his pressed shirt—too much starch—and striped tie. I recognized the plastic of his smile. The way he tried to breathe as deeply as he could without being obvious.

I wanted to tell him to take it all in, to enjoy it. I could wait. But I couldn't.

What Cal had said was true. My daughter was dying in the room next door. I could feel it inside me, like my heart was in her weakening fist. But it's more than that, isn't it? This human love. It wasn't that she held my heart, something taken from me. It's that my heart was nothing if not for the container of her hand.

My final memory of Mickey, wet and empty, came flooding back to me, and I had to grip the table. She didn't even exist yet, and the loss of her took up more of me than I did.

"You said you wanted to make a deal," he said, tapping his pen. I wanted to tell him he'd get a tablet soon, but it didn't matter. Nothing mattered except this.

"Yes," I said. "I do. Me for my daughter."

"We can do that," he said, pulling out a manila folder.

"But I need it in writing: I get to live my full life, as long as my body will have it. No bus collisions, no faulty brakes. I have to take care of some business in North Carolina, and I've got a girl who needs a ride."

He faltered briefly, eyeing me. But then he nodded. "Of course."

"And I have one more request. It's very important."

"What's that?"

I knew my purpose. Or, rather, I should say I remembered my purpose. Not just the words of it, but their meaning. And I wasn't going to mess it up again. Maybe I didn't turn out to be a good person in Hell. That shouldn't be surprising. But here, I was. Good enough, at least.

Turns out, that's all it takes.

"When you take me, wipe my memory."

"Excuse me?"

"Wipe it clean," I said. "I don't want to remember anything. Not even my name."

# ACKNOWLEDGMENTS

I owe everything I am and everything I have to my parents, Jean Kilbourne and Thomas Lux. Mom, "Thank you" is too weak for all that you've done for me and for the world, but I've yet to find the words strong enough. I love you. Thank you to Lucy Cleland, my outstanding agent, for your brilliance, patience, and incredible ability to simultaneously rein me in and keep me confident. It is your faith in me that led to this. To everyone at Berkley who has helped turn this computer document into an actual book, namely Lauren Burnstein, Candice Coote, Elisha Katz, Christine Legon, Jessica Mangicaro, Vi-An Nguyen, Tara O'Connor, Jane Steele, and Dan Walsh: you have no idea what you've done for me. Thank you for making my wildest hope a physical reality. And to my editor, Jen Monroe: you are the stuff of dreams. I am so grateful for and humbled by your belief in these characters, their story, and me. You changed my life completely, and I can't wait to see where we go from here. To Rachel Bronstein and Eva Chertow, my Ideal Readers and first sets of eyes on every project: I write for you. Thank you for knowing me before I knew myself, and never letting

## ACKNOWLEDGMENTS

me forget it. In addition, to Rhea Ghosh, the Gomes-Voss family, Max Haimowitz, Elizabeth Kramer, Benjamin Kramer, Evan Kuester, Jonathan Lord, Liza McVinney, Cameron Njaa, Hannah Palmer, Sydney Read, and Julianna Sweeney (and the whole Sweeney family!): thank you for your insights, your encouragement, and, most of all, your friendship. None of this would've happened without all of your support, including my existence as a functional human being. Thank you to my small but mighty writing group, Lori Kendall and James Golsan, for cheering Pey on from the very beginning, and me too. To my research, grammar, and consultation dream team, Thomas Connor, Philip Glover, and my beloved stepmom, Jennifer Holley Lux: Hell wouldn't be complete without your professional/intellectual insights. Thanks for answering all of my late-night texts. Thank you to the Emerson/Guerard family, for the summers spent on Newfound Lake, in a home so full of magic I had to write about it. To Rebecca Pollard-Pierik, thank you for going into the tunnel with me. I am forever grateful for the guidance from all of my teachers and mentors, especially Craig Dorfman, Mittie Knox, Jeff McDaniel, and Victoria Redel. As my father said, "You make the thing because you love the thing, and you love the thing because someone else loved it enough to make you love it." Thank you to all the writers who loved the thing so doggedly, so rapturously, and so brilliantly that they made me love it too.